· Man of the Month Club ·

MAN

· of the ·

MONTH

CLUB

jackie clune

G. P. PUTNAM'S SONS

New York

G. P. Putnam's Sons
Publishers Since 1838
Published by the Penguin Group
Penguin Group (USA) Inc., 375 Hudson Street, New York, New York 10014, USA •
Penguin Group (Canada), 90 Eglinton Avenue East, Suite 700, Toronto,
Ontario M4P 2Y3, Canada (a division of Pearson Penguin Canada Inc.) •
Penguin Books Ltd, 80 Strand, London WC2R 0RL, England • Penguin Ireland,
25 St Stephen's Green, Dublin 2, Ireland (a division of Penguin Books Ltd) •
Penguin Group (Australia), 250 Camberwell Road, Camberwell, Victoria 3124,
Australia (a division of Pearson Australia Group Pty Ltd) • Penguin Books India Pvt Ltd,
11 Community Centre, Panchsheel Park, New Delhi–110 017, India •
Penguin Group (NZ), Cnr Airborne and Rosedale Roads, Albany,
Auckland 1310, New Zealand (a division of Pearson New Zealand Ltd) •
Penguin Books (South Africa) (Pty) Ltd, 24 Sturdee Avenue, Rosebank,
Johannesburg 2196, South Africa

Penguin Books Ltd, Registered Offices:
80 Strand, London WC2R 0RL, England

Library of Congress Cataloging-in-Publication Data

Clune, Jackie, date.
Man of the month club / Jackie Clune.
p.   cm.
ISBN 0-399-15366-7
1. Single mothers—Fiction.   2. Man-woman relationships—
Fiction.   3. Chelsea (London, England)—Fiction.   I. Title.

PR6103.L86M36   2006   2006041001
823'.92—dc22

Printed in the United States of America
1   3   5   7   9   10   8   6   4   2

BOOK DESIGN BY AMANDA DEWEY

This is a work of fiction. Names, characters, places, and incidents either are the
product of the author's imagination or are used fictitiously, and any resemblance
to actual persons, living or dead, businesses, companies, events, or locales is entirely coincidental.

While the author has made every effort to provide accurate telephone numbers
and Internet addresses at the time of publication, neither the publisher nor the
author assumes any responsibility for errors, or for changes that occur after publication. Further, the publisher does not have any control over and does not assume
any responsibility for author or third-party websites or their content.

Acknowledgments

My thanks must go to Robert Caskie, Sean Lock, and Alan Davies, who made me do it, and to Capel and Land for all their support.

For Richard, Saoirse, Thady, Frank, and Orla, with all my love

First
Trimester

. 1 .

There it was again. "Ak ak ak ak ak ak ak!" Every morning this week the same grating, high-pitched staccato cackle from somewhere on the roof terrace just above Amy's head. And here it was again this morning, the dawning of her thirty-ninth year to be exact, when she was nursing a prebirthday hangover.

"Ak ak ak ak ak ak ak!"

Slowly pushing up her sequined "The Bitch Is Sleeping" eye mask (gratifying to remember she had at least one witty ex), Amy squinted at the alarm clock.

"Fuck. Fucking six fourteen. Jesus.

"Just stick your head under the pillow and block it out," she reasoned to no one in particular. "Mind over matter."

A blissful twenty seconds passed.

"Ak ak ak ak ak ak ak! Ak ak ak ak ak ak ak!"

Now it was in stereo.

Forget the noise, forget your birthday. Birthday. God, what a nightmare, thought Amy. Surely it wasn't necessary to celebrate your birthday after the age of twenty-one, was it? What was the point? Amy only ever got crap joke presents because she already had everything she needed and none of her close circle of friends could afford the sorts of things she liked to buy as treats. Who out of her requisite Five Good Friends (she'd read *Marie Claire*) could afford the vintage wine she'd just ordered, the limited-edition Fendi handbag, the hardtop accessory cover for her convertible BMW? Brendan? With his crap copywriting job for QVC's jewelry website? Gay Brendan, who did his bit for homosexual equality by spending his days thinking up different ways of describing cheap baubles made of "rolled gold." Bleeding-heart Soph, teaching her adult literacy evening classes for next to nothing while her husband, Greg, lounged about at home, claiming to be a stand-up comedian? Angela, her oldest mate from convent days, who'd banged out five kids and hadn't so much let herself go as emigrated? Or Jules, her work colleague and all-drinking, all-pulling mate who spent every last penny (and then some) on the latest plastic-surgery fad? There wasn't an inch of Jules's perfectly average body that hadn't been tucked, lifted, Botoxed, or liposuctioned into submission already.

"Ak ak ak ak ak ak ak!"

What the bloody *hell* was the noise? It seemed to cut through her skull and pierce her nerve center at exactly the right pitch to cause maximum irritation. The clattering, aggressive, insistent "aks" followed by the few seconds of sinister silence—just long enough for you to think it was over.

"Ak ak ak ak ak ak ak!"

Amy rolled over and imagined it was a haggard old witch who'd crash-landed on her Japanese roof garden, mistaking the bubbling ornamental water feature for a cauldron. No. It was only April 12— far too early for Halloween. Maybe it was her mum, miraculously morphed into an airborne banshee, come to prick her single child-free conscience once again? No. Mum would wait until Amy was there over the weekend (to receive the mandatory, tragic, trying-too-hard-but-getting-it-oh-so-very-wrong gift: American tan knee-highs, "Great under trousers for work!"; an egg poacher that could cook six eggs at a time, "Well, I thought in case you had one of your dinners . . ."). It wasn't that Amy's mum was trying to rub it in regarding her grandchildless state—it was more of a constant drip, drip, drop of sad expressions and a subtle moistening of the eye when walking past prams. A gently leaking tap.

"Ak ak ak ak ak ak ak!"

"Right, that's it, you bastard—I'm coming to get you, whatever you are!" yelled Amy, abandoning any hope of sleep.

Pulling on her dressing gown and stumbling down the mezzanine stairs from her platform bed, Amy scooted across the floor, hotly pursued by Germaine Greer. It had been such an inspired choice of name for her scruffy, wiry gray-haired terrier with the bright, alert eyes and the faint air of jaded wisdom. Germaine had been a thirtieth birthday gift from another long-gone ex who erroneously thought buying a dog would cement their relationship. In reality, Germaine had been the final fluffy nail in the coffin. Amy wrenched open the access door. Bugger. It was raining. She scooted back to the shoe rack and pulled out first a trainer, then a flip-flop. *Sod it, no one's looking.* As she struggled into her Nike, she caught a glimpse of herself in the mirror—eye mask askew, mascara circling her bloodshot eyes, the vestiges of last night's red wine staining her lips a deeply un-this-season goth purple.

"Well, hey, Miss Thing—happy birthday! You got it going on!" she Marlboro-croaked at her reflection. She'd smoked so many fags last night that her lips had virtually set in that cat's-anus wrinkly pout. She made a mental note to ask Jules about that Botox party. At one time it was Tupperware, then nylon lingerie, then "adult accessories," but now women of Amy's age gathered together in one another's lounges.

Back to the matter at hand, Amy scooted back to the door, clambered up the fire escape stairs—*thud, flip-flop, thud, flip-flop*—and arrived soaked and breathless in her ornamental rooftop paradise.

Not that she'd had much to do with it—an old flame had constructed it in happier times, and had stolen the onyx Buddha as he left. *Now, was that good karma?* Silence. No piercing cackles, no unidentifiable hawking, no strange, clattery disturbance. Just the cold, raw, seeping damp of an early-spring morning in London, Canary Wharf winking away conspiratorially at the Docklands developments it overlooked. It was still pretty dark, and by the look of the sky, today was going to be one of those London days with a gray ceiling, when you swore you could feel invisible hands from the heavens pushing you downward into the cracked pavement and potholed roads. Flicking on the security floodlight, Amy flip-flop thudded her way round to the skylight directly above her bed. Nothing.

"Ak ak ak ak ak ak!"

Amy wheeled round just in time to spot two—no, three— enormous hopping magpies descending into a monster nest that they had obviously spent the past week thieving for.

"Go on—shoo! *Scram!*"

Clearly out of shock more than indignation, the three magpies scattered into the thick sky as Amy odd-shoe shuffled her bird-scaring dance.

Did I really just say "scram"? Nobody says "scram," apart from the villain at the end of Scooby Doo, she thought.

It was at this point that the glint of metal caught her eye. Just a flash at first, but something pulled her over to the nest. Niftily woven in among the twigs, leaves, and bits of moss was a thirty-nine-year-old silver locket, blackening in the dew, the catch slightly ajar, revealing Amy, aged two weeks, sausage-wrapped in swaddling clothes. Amy had turned the flat upside down for three days, cursing and crying, thinking she'd lost for good the one thing she had left that her dad had actually bought for her. It wasn't worth a lot, but it was her one link with her useless, dead old bastard of a dad. At forty, he'd drunk himself to an early grave, pawning anything worth the price of a pint along the way. Amy had been just fourteen when the saggy armchair by the radiator had become permanently and eerily vacant one Saturday afternoon. He'd gone out to the pub at a quarter to twelve—the landlord of the depressing prefab sixties bar he propped up could set his watch by her dad—and simply never come home. It wasn't until the Monday after that Amy found out he'd died. That obstacle course of diplomacy and sensitivity had been given to Sister Kathleen to navigate—"Amy Stokes, you'll not be joining us for the Fun Day because you'll be burying your drunken father, God rest his soul." For years she had worn the locket despite the dictates of fashion (albeit often hidden beneath her Gucci and Nicole Farhi casuals).

"You thieving little shits!" she shouted as hot tears of relief sprang to her eyes. She'd heard that magpies liked to steal shiny things but had always assumed it was an old wives' tale. But apparently the much-maligned old wives were bang on the money. The magpies—or one of them at least—had flown in four days ago, nicked her necklace, and used it for a nest makeover. She wouldn't have minded so much if it had been any other piece of jewelry she owned—the black pearl earrings, the Tiffany solitaire engagement ring she'd guiltily wangled out of a no-hoper would-be fiancé, the platinum charm bracelet she'd been adding to for seven years. But the locket—the locket was a no-go area. Nobody touched the locket. It was hard to say why it held such potency for her—it wasn't as if her dad had ever even really noticed she was around. Only when she had any money— the odd fiver from relatives on a birthday or Christmas—would he turn his watery, sad eyes on her and pay her any attention. She'd always relented and handed over whatever she had, if only to see that alcoholic mask of self-pity disappear momentarily from his face. But the one thing she would not budge on, the one thing she had taken great pains to hide under floorboards, down the back of sofas, in the cistern of the toilet at one point, was the locket. Not that he would have forced it out of her hand and into the pawnshop—she'd hidden it more from herself as much as anything. She got so good at it that she herself would almost forget where she had hidden it. Almost. In some ways, Amy supposed, as she teased the locket from the thickly thatched nest, it had become a symbol of her triumph over poverty. If you've got something, if you hang on to something of value, however small, you've always got something to build on. And look at her now, on the roof of her Docklands penthouse, mistress of her own business, able to buy whatever (and whomever) she wanted.

.2.

Unlocking the door to Precious Little Darlings and punching in the alarm code, Amy reflected glumly on just how she'd come to be one of the leading designers in baby kitsch this side of the pond. At school, the smell of the art room had always been the most heady aroma to her nostrils: that mixture of paint, new paper, stale water, and dusty frustration. So different from the resigned and defeatist atmosphere of her home life. She spent most of her time there, encouraged by an incredulous Scottish art teacher named Alan who drew saucy nudes and erotic scenarios alongside her before dragging her off to the pub for lunchtime discussions about Cubism. She didn't really bother with any other subject, instead devoting her time to maudlin self-portraits and developing a unique new screenprinting process, which she sold to a local design firm. Alan had pushed her to apply for the Chelsea Art School and had sprayed her with cheap sparkling wine when, miraculously, she got in—the only pupil he'd ever had who'd gone on to college.

Chucking her keys on the counter, she wedged the door open with a Peter Rabbit draft excluder and lit up a cigarette. It still seemed like only yesterday that she had left home for college.

At Chelsea, despite fitting in as well as a one-legged woman at an ass-kicking party, her star continued to rise. She'd felt at once intimidated by and superior to the trust-fund babies who populated the corridors, their piecrust collars and velvet headbands a daily assault on her good taste. She'd felt similarly irritated by the tortured souls in black; their hollow eyes and artistic temperaments merely seemed affected and unproductive compared to Amy's pragmatic approach. She felt lucky to be there and couldn't understand the casual laziness, the studied disinterest shown by many of her classmates.

She worked hard and quickly became the unlikely star of her class. After her finals show, she had been offered various prestigious positions in several small but well-established design partnerships but, ever the maverick, had opted instead to set up her own company, hand-printing T-shirts with political slogans and selling them at her own stall on the Portobello market. One of her most successful lines had been a set of Babygros with hand-painted Enid Blyton fairies and *Magic Roundabout* characters on the front. She had meant the designs to be witty, postmodern nostalgia. She had meant them to wink a knowing, too-cool-for-school retro irony, a sort of "God, weren't our childhoods sad?" kind of vibe. Instead, they were snapped up each Saturday by well-heeled trendies who thought them "sweet" and "adorable." Within weeks, she was selling whole bundles to foreign buyers and taking orders on all sorts of soft-furnishing requests, from nursery curtains to crib frills. It became impossible to spend any time on her other lines—the anti-Thatcher oversized T-shirts, the cutting feminist slogan aprons, or the nuclear-disarmament bed linens. Her business had snowballed so fast that she'd had to employ seven staff members by the end of the first year just to meet demand. Just how she wound up owning three shops and a successful mail-order business specializing in clothes, fabrics, wallpapers, painted murals, and furniture for overprivileged infants was beyond her comprehension. Despite her initial resistance, her insistence that she was better than the soft market of children's design, it had seemed increasingly churlish to turn down the lucrative commissions and large overseas orders. Against her better judgment, Amy had become the darling of the chattering breeding classes, opening her first shop at the height of the consumerist eighties on a fashionable Chelsea backstreet. Not that she was complaining. The money was great—more than she knew what to do with most years—and she still kept some hands-on links with her team of designers. She was even known to personally paint the fairy grotto frescoes she had become famous for on the nursery walls of her rich and famous clients. She'd done a Spice Girl brat's room, for God's sake. But sometimes she regretted the lure of the success and the easy money. Sometimes she yearned to be in the adult world of chic minimalist urban-cool design. She could have done it— she could have gone into any field. She had the business head and the technical skill. To think that by now she could be entering the glittering premises of Conran's emporium or swanning about in senior creative management at the Designer's Guild—it was galling beyond measure. But somehow she'd got the biggest buzz from her first roll of children's fabric, had wanted to stroke it and wrap herself up in the long, luxurious roll of brushed cotton, with its clean promise and unsullied possibilities, and her hands had unilaterally decided they wanted to paint beautiful, fluffy chicks on stripped pine chests of drawers, or flower-capped pixies dancing around the bottom of old oak trees in trompe l'oeil extravaganzas.

Amy stabbed out her ciggy and picked up the stub. It wouldn't do to make the Chelsea ladies step over her detritus. It didn't seem fair that her own hands had cornered her into this cutesy world of unrealistic utopian childhood, especially as it was so at odds with her own rather gnarled worldview. It was a cruel joke, she thought sometimes, that someone as unmaternal, as disinterested in babies and children and fluffy things and faux olde-world sentiment as her should have made such a success of marketing such ridiculousness. Coming into one of her own shops, however, she was filled with that same sense of excitement she had always experienced at the start of a working day. She couldn't help but be thrilled by the prospect of customers with their ready cash and their easy dreams of the perfect child in the perfect nursery receiving the perfect childhood from Precious Little Darlings—Amy's firm, Amy's ideas, Amy's designs. Even though she knew deep down that these people were sad and it was a crock of shit.

Sarah would be in soon—all smiles and offers of lunchtime spritzers. Amy suspected she would do what she usually did on Fridays at lunchtime: slope off and go drinking at The Wheelbarrow with her unlikely advertising exec mates from down the road. After an estrogen-infested morning on the shop floor, she always welcomed their testosterone-fueled joshing and no-nonsense chat. Plus, they didn't know that it was her birthday, so she could avoid any of the dreadful tepid celebrations her staff was so fond of. It wasn't that she didn't like her employees—they were all perfectly nice, hardworking, and decent people. But she had absolutely nothing in common with them. Their very niceness alienated her so much that at times she wanted to run screaming around the shop, slashing at fabric and spray-painting the walls. It was as if the twee décor and the sugar-and-spice platitudes of the baby books they'd sold had entered their very souls by a process of osmosis. They made the Stepford Wives look like a bunch of rabid Valkyries. This was perfect for the business. Most of Amy's clients responded so well to the cooing and sighing of her staff that her business was constantly exceeding its annual profit predictions. It seemed most people wanted this kind of insipid service when it came to buying things for babies. Sarah was an absolute mistress of the honeyed smile and the whimsical reverie when it came to steering new parents toward what to buy for their young. She knew exactly when to push, what to match things with, and how to maximize a spending spree without ever appearing as if it was for any other motive than to make the newborn as welcome and stylish as possible. Indeed, she had mastered the art of making all new parents-to-be feel that she would be entirely justified in placing their unborn children in foster care if they refused to buy a complete matching nursery set. It was all in the soft suggestiveness of a manicured stroking of a fleece blanket. Amy and Jules—her mail-order chief and fellow cynic—survived by rolling their eyes in unison and giggling uncontrollably in the storerooms. If it wasn't for Jules—hired over the first of many champagne cocktails at the top of the Oxo Tower—Amy felt sure she would have hung herself with one of her own tinkly musical crib mobiles by now. On too many occasions she'd had to stuff her sleeve in her mouth and run spluttering to the loo as Jules expertly patronized yet another moronic customer.

And soon they would be in—the customers. Friday was always a good day for the Chelsea shop. The Ladies Who Lunch (who, it seemed to Amy, were getting younger every year—careers were so last millennium) seemed to favor Fridays for their shopping expeditions. They came in and fingered swatches dreamily, then ordered cribs and matching bed linens on a whim after feasting on pregnancy-friendly salads and spring water. So many of them substituted their cocktail habits for spending sprees during pregnancy.

From the front of the shop, Amy heard the unmistakably corny rendition of "Teddy Bears' Picnic," which Sarah had insisted should indicate the arrival of a new customer in the shop. In another life it had been the soundtrack to a horror movie in which ax-wielding teddies marched grinning into close-up. But Sarah loved it, and so did the many snotty toddlers who tripped through the door only to insist on going out and coming in again several times to re-trigger the cacophony.

"Hiya!" chirruped Sarah, neatly folding her Mac and placing it on the back of her chair. Everything she did was neat, efficient, preppy. Amy casually wondered when (or if) she ever orgasmed it would come out as a polite, brief "aah" of ecstasy followed by perfectly served tea and crumpets.

"Happy birthday! God, you look awful! Coffee?"

Without waiting for a reply, she was off into the staff room to boil a kettle and deposit whatever spongy monstrosity she was concealing in that baker's bag at the back of the fridge. No doubt it would be covered in some gooey pink icing and would carry the wobbly inscription "Happy Birthday Amy." The lady who iced the cakes was eighty-four and had once iced what looked like "Happy Binday," which was pretty apt really, as her cakes were so inedible they usually ended up in the bin. Amy would smile and eat anyway, pretending to enjoy the fuss of her employees.

"Isn't it good that you're here today? Hasn't it worked out well? You could have been at the store in Islington or even Bath! And we all know that we're your absolute favorite team!"

"Yes, isn't it fortunate," said Amy, absentmindedly sorting through a few letters she'd picked up from the mat. Two bills, a birthday card from a favored customer, and a reminder that her pap smear was three months overdue. Happy birthday. Just what you wanted to be reminded of on your birthday—imminent invasion by a brutal metal duck with an ice-cold bill and a nasty habit of cranking you up like a car in a pit stop. She'd told her doctor's receptionist a million times to send all mail to her home address, but the fact that the surgery was just around the corner (near Harrods, so convenient for that post-appointment picnic lunch) had foxed the poor girl into thinking Amy *lived* at the shop in Chelsea. God forbid. I mean, did she look like she lived in Chelsea? Despite the business being rooted there, despite her college days in the area, Amy felt much more at home in the sleek new urbanism of Docklands. It was an antidote to all the old-money casual wealth that cloyed away at her every time she visited the shop.

"Teddy Bears' Picnic" juddered to life, and Amy swung round to welcome the first customer of the day. It was only five past ten. Must be someone keen to buy. It was.

"Hello, Mrs. Cummings! How's things?"

Amy couldn't stop her eyes from darting downward to the smart woman's belly. *Nope.* Still no sign of an impending infant.

"Yes, well, you know the fertility treatment's getting me down a bit, but onwards and upwards, that's the way!"

"Sorry to hear that. How many times have you—"

"Oh, this is the seventh. One of the embryos is bound to take sooner or later. Never say die. And we've got the money, so why not?" said Mrs. Cummings, sweet and brittle as an overcooked meringue. Amy felt that if she were to tap the surface lightly, the whole lot would shatter into a powdery mess.

"Well, yes, these things can be quite mysterious, can't they? Nothing for ages, then whoosh! Three at once! Like buses, I suppose . . ." Amy said lamely. These conversations always made her uncomfortable.

"Yes . . ." Mrs. Cummings, who had never so much as been on a bus, let alone waited for three, said unsurely.

Amy left Mrs. C to get on with her weekly ritual. She couldn't help but feel sorry for the poor woman. For five years now she'd been in nearly every week, pawing at fabrics and measuring high chairs. She'd notate each decision carefully in a beautiful pink leatherbound notebook. She'd stay for perhaps an hour, then leave, throwing a shy smile backward as the teddy bears announced her departure. But this was nothing compared to the yearly ritual. Over the past five years, Mrs. Cummings had redecorated an entire empty nursery six times, from top to bottom. She'd started with the London theme Amy had designed seven years ago (big red buses, Buzzby-wearing guards outside

Buckingham Palace, Big Ben with a smiley face). With no baby in sight, she'd decided to feng shui the room by totally stripping it back and opting for the more minimalist pandas chinoiserie style (long-lashed pandas chewing amiably on beautiful bamboo stalks, hand-painted on Chinese silk). Still no baby joy. Next, it had been the turn of the circus to drum up the much-wanted baby's enthusiasm for arrival. Curtains, wall coverings, and crib had been festooned with clowns, lions, and seals balancing colorful, stripy balls on their shiny noses. Amy had run riot with that one, designing an optional big-top crib surround, which fell in luxurious red and gold folds around the cot. Despite the comical ringmaster's captioned invitation, nothing had "rolled up" for Mrs. Cummings. Next she'd gone for the magic faraway tree nostalgic design—Enid Blyton's moonface and spinning treetops leading to fantastical lands painted in vivid frescoes. Nope. A brief excursion into the contemporary children's TV market had seen Amy slumming it with the Teletubbies. Mrs. Cummings had even gone for that, perhaps thinking her exclusive tastes were prejudicing her chances of conception. At present, as far as Amy was aware, the ghostly nursery in Beauchamp Mews was covered in the ever-popular fairy design, which still took up an entire wall of the shop. Each time the redecoration was ordered, the staff kept their eyes lowered, their voices kindly, and their respect to the fore, despite the sighing and shaking of heads that went on behind their most regular customer's back. No one could quite understand the level of this woman's pathological addiction to all things baby-related, least of all Amy. Still, if she was desperate enough to count her chickens before they were even conceived, then more fool her. At least she kept the business rolling in; more and more of Mrs. Cummings's IVF support group—In Vitro Veritas—were coming to Precious Little Darlings determined that the best, and only the best, was suitable for their hard-won bundles of puking joy. Mrs. Cummings had sat by and endured dozens of success stories while she remained resolutely childless. And here she was today, a flesh-and-blood reminder to Amy that at least she had made it to her thirty-ninth birthday without succumbing to the hideous shackle of baby-and-chain.

So far.

.3.

H appy birthday!" cooed Soph as she pulled open the door to her
bike-cluttered hallway.

"Sorry about the mess—I had the Kurds this afternoon and one of
them needed help with his dole-form thingy, so I didn't get the
chance to, you know . . ."

"Like you ever tidy up anyway, you sad old hippie," said Amy with
a wink. She squeezed her way past three mountain bikes rammed up
against the woodchip wallpaper, dodged the cat twisting its way
through her legs in a bid for front-door freedom, and sidestepped the
overflowing cat litter tray. The familiar waft of Sophie's dinner party
specialty filled her nostrils.

Christ, not lentil lasagna again, thought Amy. *What is it with these
unreconstructed eighties activists that makes them so morbidly addicted to
legumes?*

Oh, well, Amy was tired of nouvelle cuisine anyway. And after all,
didn't she read somewhere that home cooking is the new dining out?
Although presumably not the way Soph did it.

Squeezing open the kitchen door, Amy came face-to-face with Greg's baggy, tighty-whitied backside.

"Greg, Amy's here!" shouted Sophie, too late.

"Dressing to the left for dinner, Greg?" asked Amy, catching an eyeful of Greg's dangly bits as he tried to retrieve his knackered old jeans from the dryer.

"Oh, shit—sorry, Amy. You must stop creeping up on me like this, Soph's starting to notice and, frankly, you're only embarrassing yourself. Now just turn around while I make myself decent, you lucky, lucky bitch!" Greg mock-chided as he slid his skinny legs into the jeans, breathing in to fasten them over his ever-expanding belly. Men like Greg never got fat all over, they just sort of swelled around the middle like a sparrow at Christmas.

"Happy birthday, doll. Don't say I never give you anything!" He winked, slapping Amy's ass for good measure.

"Oh, don't—I've had enough of it already," said Amy, already looking for the corkscrew. "And hasn't anyone told you there's a new by-law prohibiting men over forty from wearing jeans?"

"Bad day in baby heaven? No one willing to spend four grand on a mink-lined diaper pail?" asked Greg, tugging on an old anti–poll tax T-shirt.

"No, just the usual wet cake and even wetter women getting tiddly on paper cups of sparkling wine. They didn't even get proper champagne! I mean, come on!"

"My heart bleeds, you poor thing—get any nice pressies?"

Sore point. Amy flinched.

"A gold pen. With my name on it."

"That *is* nice!"

"I mean, who has fancy pens anymore? I hardly ever write longhand anyway—except to sign a credit-card slip," said Amy, aware that she was sounding petulant but not really caring. Greg and Soph liked it when she did the old "having expensive things is pointless and overrated" routine. She imagined it made them feel better about their paltry income and their pathological aversion to accruing wealth.

"Oh, dear," sighed Soph, as she handed over a hastily wrapped rec-tangular box.

"Oh, you shouldn't have!" cried Amy, already trying to fix her face into a grateful smile.

"No, we really shouldn't have," spluttered Greg as Amy ripped open the package and snapped open the plastic case to reveal . . . a gold-plated ballpoint pen bearing the inscription "Amy, love G&S."

"Sorry! But, hey, ours is OK 'cause you said it was pointless to have a *fancy* pen, and as you can see, this one is really crap. I got it from one of those booths in the shopping precinct. Five ninety-nine. Enjoy!"

Amy laughed, despite the slight sting she felt at getting two we-didn't-know-what-to-get-you businessman's pens in one day. It wasn't the gift itself, it was more what it said about how others saw her. Was she turning into one of those old maids that other people don't know what to buy for, one of those sad old bitches who got anony-mous, impersonal "professional" presents, even from close friends and family? What next—monogrammed hankies? A silver business-card holder? Amy pulled the cork on her vintage burgundy and sloshed it generously into three glasses, careful to release the heady chocolate of the wine.

"Cheers. Down the hatch," she ordered as she threw the first of what she hoped would be many down her throat.

"Cheers—and sorry about the pen, Amy. It's just that we never know what to get you."

Soph smiled as she sipped at her wine.

"Oh, don't worry; I'll keep one in the car and one at work. Quite handy, really," she lied, her awkwardness being cut short by the un-mistakable jaunty rat-tat-tat of Brendan at the front door. "I'll get it," said Amy, relishing the chance to escape the whole lentil hothouse experience.

"Darling! Happy birthday, you shriveled old hag!" Brendan threw his arms around Amy's neck and shoved his groin deep into hers. For a gay man, he liked nothing better than to flirt outrageously with women, especially Amy. For a time they thought about having a fling; they had often indulged in harmless drunken snogging, and once, when Brendan had turned up at nine a.m. one Sunday morning E'ed off his ass, he'd climbed into bed with her and started fiddling about in her pants. She hadn't stopped him; she'd found the oddness of it strangely alluring, but he'd freaked at the last minute, saying he just didn't like the "squelchiness" of it. They'd called it quits right then and there, and gone off for a delicious brunch at one of the ye olde traditional pubs by the Thames—so much more civilized than shagging. Brendan had ordered sausage, as if to prove a point.

"Thirty-nine today, darling—that was never in the plan, was it?" he goaded, pushing her backward up the hallway, still hugging her tight. "The big four-oh next! Who'd have thought that Amy Stokes, onetime youthful radical feminist socialist whale-saver turned hardworking, hard-drinking, professional woman-about-town would ever be thirty-nine!"

"Thanks, Brendan—you sure know how to bring a girl down."

"Any time, my angel. Any time. Hello, you git—wow! Say no to poll tax! Very topical—about as topical as one of your gags, Greg."

"Hello, good evening, and fuck off," snarled Greg, only moderately exaggerating his distaste for this loud, offensive queen Amy had never managed to get rid of since college. It wasn't his gayness, it was his wankerdom Greg took against. Greg was the first to support equal opportunities—just not for Brendan.

"Glass of wine, Brendan?" asked Soph, always there with a bucket of water to extinguish any hint of conflict.

"Why not—got to toast the old slapper, haven't we? Let's have a look at you, then—hmmm, those wrinkly eyes are looking more and more like chewed-up toffee every day."

"They're not wrinkles—they're laughter lines!" cued Amy.

"Nothing's that funny," chorused the kitchen.

"The old ones are the best," said Greg.

"And you'd know," lashed Brendan, draining his glass in one go.

It was difficult to remember in that moment exactly why Amy hung on to this fat, depressive, alcoholic fairy who had been such a shining star in the National Union of Students. They had become firm allies. Hardly any other art students bothered with politics—too busy slagging off the world to try and change it. They had marched side by side, literally, on dozens of occasions—for the students against student loans, for the right to choose against the pro-lifers—they had even been arrested together after getting caught up in the middle of a police charge on horseback.

What had happened to that sparkling, fearless optimist? The boy who'd regularly endured with great wit and humor the homophobic taunting of the jocks on campus during his Boy George phase? The boy who'd come out at a packed student union meeting, shaking like a frightened dog as he read his speech against the divisive government bill to ban the promotion (whatever that meant) of homosexuality in schools? He was still there, somewhere, she felt sure of it. Despite all his studied cynicism and caustic barbs, he was still Amy's closest ally.

"Right, just Jules and Angela now," said Soph, testing the vegan cheddar crust of her bubbling lasagna.

Bang on cue, there came a tentative rat-tat-tat on the door.

"That'll be Angela," said Soph, as she shoved the gurgling gloop back into the blackened chasm of the oven. It looked like it had served as an emergency crematorium for the vegetable world; pieces of charred carrot and cindered parsnip cracked in the gaps between oven and door each time it was opened, and there was always a faint echo of disappointment as the door slammed shut, as if the oven knew what culinary death it was party to. Amy smiled fondly at the familiarity of it all. She felt herself beginning to relax as the wine and the good company took hold. Maybe this wasn't such a bad birthday after all.

"Hello, all!" shouted Angela as she squeezed her overflowing bosom through the cluttered hallway. Unashamedly fat and forty, mother of five children, and Amy's oldest friend, Ang's substantial presence always grounded Amy in a crisis. Ang's big diner-lady arms had enveloped her on more than one critical occasion, and although she didn't have much in common with Amy's more middle-class friends, she was an essential and enthusiastic guest at Amy's table.

"Look who I bumped into on the path!"

"Hi," muttered Jules, slinking straight to the back door and parking herself on the rickety deck chair, silently lighting up the first of forty cigarettes.

"Would you open the back door, Jules, please? It's just that Greg and me don't really allow smoke in the house," said Soph, visibly flinching in preparation for the backlash.

"Yes, yes, yes—it's OK, I don't mind if you eat while I smoke, it doesn't put me off," replied Jules, hauling herself up to wrench open the rotten back door.

"Oh, happy birthday, Amy," she remembered, tossing a plastic bag at the birthday girl. It was a bit unimaginative, but she'd not felt much like shopping after the latest boob-job consultation. Another four grand for one measly cup size. That was two grand per extra handful. If only she hadn't listened to Amy's advice the first time round and gone for the double-D right off.

"Thanks, Jules!" said Amy, unwrapping the small, hard, flat package.

"It's . . . it's . . ."

"What is it?" shrieked Angela, clapping her hands together delightedly, so grateful to be out of the house for a rare night of adult company that she had already regressed to the age of six.

"It's a silver business-card holder," replied Amy, pretending to examine it minutely so as not to have to show the horror on her face. *Great.* Just the monogrammed hankies now and she could ritualistically impale herself up both nostrils with the gold and gold-look pens.

"Thanks. I really like it." She was getting good at this—no one seemed to even notice.

"My turn! My turn!" skipped Angela, pulling a hastily wrapped bundle from her large, saggy handbag.

"Oh, Angela—you shouldn't have," said Amy, taking the gift guiltily. OK, so they weren't the best gifts in the world, but they were from her friends, and Angela more than anyone could ill afford to throw money away on gifts.

"Oh, it's not much—but you've got to have something to unwrap on your birthday," gushed Angela, grabbing a tumbler and filling it with wine.

With a sense of impending prophetic closure, Amy peeled back the hair-covered sticky tape on the Barbie paper to reveal a small expanse of crisp, white cotton. Folding back the last corner of paper, her heart preparing for a deep-sea dive to the floor, Amy finally revealed two curly-swirly embroidered letters: AS. Never had two simple letters seemed to portend so much to Amy. AS. The machine-stitched monogramming seemed to be signaling something. AS: All Spent? Alcoholic Spinster?

It was all too depressing.

"Thanks, Ang—they're really . . . perfect. They're perfect," said Amy, leaning over to plant a kiss on her friend's cheek.

If only I had a novelty paperweight, too . . . I could glue it to the wall and run head-first at it, she thought.

Finally, Sophie announced that the gloop was ready to be disembowelled, typically, just at the point at which the wine had run out.

Shrugging on her new leather jacket, Amy struggled past the mountain bikes and cat shit and back into the drizzly night. Her birthday celebration had become a ritual, an annual milestone for the whole group. In the absence of any real family life it was all Amy had, and although this thought made her feel queasy—she hated any Waltons sepia glow or *Friends* "Hey, you guys" bonhomie—it was true. She loved it and hated it in equal measure, just like a family Christmas or wedding. The fact that she could moan and detract her way through the evening gave her a warm and familiar feeling of bittersweet inclusion. These people didn't expect her to be full of birthday joy. They expected the sour hors d'oeuvres of Amy's arrival and the looser-tongued main course of her conversation, followed shortly by the wine-soaked opining and general bullishness of her tone. Dessert was always a mess of tears, tantrums, and taxis. Happy bloody birthday. But the presents! The presents were always bad and always just so plain wrong. Any feeling of being known, of being accepted and loved for who she was, had always been viciously wiped out by the extraordinary sense of existential loneliness she felt upon opening the gifts. It had always been this way. Her parents had never really honored the usual traditions of gift-giving on special occasions. Her dad soaked every spare bit of cash there ever was, and her mum was perpetually too anxious and preoccupied to even remember. Once, on her ninth birthday, her mum had absentmindedly handed her a badly wrapped bar of carbolic laundry soap, obviously thinking it was better than nothing. It wasn't.

Oh, well, fuck it, she thought as she picked out six overpriced bottles of red, and in the time-tested tradition of all borderline avoidant alcoholics, she resolved to get heartily pissed.

By the time Amy had chinked and clunked her way back up the street, Brendan had already made three catty remarks about Angela's size, Jules had started on Sophie's ancient bottle of ill-advised, holiday-purchased grappa, and Sophie had lit three noxious, "mood-enhancing" candles (presumably a double-whammy attempt to hide the vile sight of the food and mask the stench of the cat litter trays). Business as usual, then. Greg grabbed the first of the bottles and uncorked it with attention-seeking adeptness while Angela raised a nearly empty glass in a typically ill-timed toast.

"To Amy!" she bellowed. "Happy birthday!"

"Happy birthday," mumbled the rest of the table, who were busy fending off large portions of gloop and procuring full tumblers of wine.

"Cheers," said Amy, as amiably as she could allow.

"But it's not just Amy's birthday we're here to celebrate . . ." Angela twinkled naughtily.

"Don't tell me, you got that gig as Heidi Klum's body double!" deadpanned Brendan, dribbling a trail of vegan gravy across the Amnesty International tablecloth.

"No, it's not that. . . . I've got an announcement to make."

"You're up for the next series of *Baywatch*?"

"No, not that, either. . . ."

"You're the new—"

"Oh, for Christ's sake, shut up, Brendan," said Jules, picking over her steaming portion suspiciously.

"I'm going to have a baby!" Angela beamed with all the excitement and enthusiasm of a first-timer.

"Jesus! Not another one!" said Greg before he could stop himself, and before anyone else did.

"But you only had Bernie seven months ago!" said Sophie, who had stopped in her serving tracks to take in the full shock of the news. "I mean, that's fantastic! I don't know how you do it!"

"Well, the man lies on top of the lady and bounces up and down and then some fishes swim out of him into her belly button and that makes a baby," said Brendan in his best annoying four-year-old voice.

Amy took this exchange in with some horror. Angela seemed to be on a one-woman mission to populate the entire planet. This was her sixth child, and Amy could not help but feel that this was becoming an addiction. Whether it was the attention Angela got, the seats offered on the tube, the small kindnesses from strangers, or the fact that she could wear tents all year through, year after year, while stuffing her face, Amy did not know. But it seemed as though Angela had given up any ambition she ever had and in its place had opted to be permanently up the duff. Indeed, because of the weight she piled on during the first pregnancy (weight she could ill afford, due to her already generous proportions), it had become difficult month by month to tell if she had just dropped one or was eight months gone. For fourteen years now, since her meringue-dress wedding to Dave the Plasterer, Angela had been a blob in a frock, her swollen ankles squeezed into old lady's bunion shoes, her hair a dull frizz. To have one baby might be considered carelessness . . . but to have six? Did anyone still do this anymore?

And then there was the Sophie-and-Greg issue. For three years now, Soph had been battling with her own fertility. Determined to save the planet before adding to it, she and Greg had left it until they were thirty-eight before finally trying for a baby. One year down the line they had gone the IVF route, only to be told they had just a year's worth of free treatment on the national health plan before each jelly baby-in-waiting would cost a cool three thousand to implant. After a year (and three failed attempts), they were still childless. By this point, they were desperate and had scrimped and saved their way through three privately funded failures. It seemed to Amy that what had started out as a simple desire had become an all-consuming, self-defeating obsession. Mrs. Cummings, but without the cash. From her standpoint, it was difficult to see what all the fuss was about. During her twenties, Amy had watched in lip-curled distaste as more and more of her contemporaries grew fat and estrogen-stupid, each new bump signifying another tomb to a dead friendship. It had started out being just those girls from school whose only capability seemed to be their biological function: the ones who wore lipgloss at thirteen, who endured school with dreamy indifference, and who were always to be found in submissive embraces with hot-groined boys at cider-fueled teenage parties. To these girls, getting pregnant was not creating a new life but creating their own. As their bellies swelled, so did their own quiet sense of self. "I am fertile, therefore I am." They bore the stretch marks, the sickness, the weight gain, and the sagging breasts with the resigned grace of the virgin herself as they limped to and from their shop jobs. Although Amy felt no misplaced sadness at their lost potential—if everyone was interesting and successful, who would scan her groceries and iron her G-strings?—she couldn't help the rising anger she felt at these girls.

Amy had since surrounded herself with seemingly like-minded women whose careers and inner lives mirrored her own.

But suddenly, about two years ago, several of her friends had started going all gooey over prams in the park. In one full-moon, crazy-making week, one friend had got married "in order to start a family" and another had ditched her high-flying job to be more attractive to a potential husband and future father to her children. Amy had felt shocked, betrayed, and queasy. As she reached her late thirties, she had begun to feel increasingly isolated—the only sane one left in a sea of ticking biological clocks and ovulation kits. She had numbed this isolation with great gulps of cynicism, washed down with post-work cocktails in exclusively male company.

"Well, congratulations!" said Jules, before downing a full glass of red in one gulp. "What does Dave say?"

"Well, you know Dave. He didn't say much, but I can tell he's pleased." Ang blushed, aware that reactions were mixed but unsure why.

"Did he jump up and hug you and take you out for a double cheese-burger to celebrate?" asked Brendan.

"No, he just sort of rolled his eyes and said he'd take the crib ad out of the classifieds then. . . ."

"Blimey, Ang, that'll be six!" said Amy, with as little judgment in her voice as she could manage. She added a tinny laugh for good measure.

"I know—we'll be able to do the von Trapps soon!" laughed Ang, clearly delighted at the idea. Amy mentally pushed away the image of acres and acres of flowery curtain fabric wrapped around the porky family.

"It's incredible, isn't it?" started Soph lightly. "Here I am, trying desperately to get one of my green old eggs to hard-boil, and you just churn them out like a battery hen!"

Greg reached around and squeezed her waist protectively in a gesture so spontaneous and so secret that it brought surprise tears to Amy's eyes.

"I'm sorry, that sounded terrible. I didn't mean to say you . . . oh, God, it's just so hard to hear about other people. I'm happy for you, I really am," said Soph, as she tried in vain to choke back a well of tears. No chance. Collapsing onto Greg's shoulder, she sobbed openly.

"Oh, Christ," muttered Brendan.

"Oh, I'm so sorry, Sophie," said Ang, rising and enveloping both Soph and Greg in her huge bosom. "I shouldn't have brought it up. I just wanted to tell everyone together. . . . I'm so sorry." She too started to gulp and shake before joining in with the discrete version of wailing now going on.

Lurching drunkenly and uncertainly to her feet, Jules piled onto the grief mountain and added her own woes.

"I'm getting so old, and I don't even know if I've *got* any eggs!" she wailed absurdly. "And even if I have, who's going to want to fertilize them? Justin's buggered off with some twenty-year-old dental nurse, and I can't even look depressed about it because of all the Botox!" she cried, her face maintaining the neutral, frown-free mask of a privileged adolescent.

"Well, happy birthday to you, Amy," said Brendan, slyly grabbing his coat from the back of his chair and tipping Amy the wink. In one clean move, they were out of the kitchen and at the front door.

"Bye!" Amy shouted cheerily as the heaving mass of misery continued its snotfest.

"Magpie?" asked Brendan, raising a mock quizzical eyebrow. It was always The Magpie on nights like these.

"Oh, yes," said Amy, zipping up her new jacket to remind herself it was her birthday more than to shield herself from the Stoke Newington drizzle.

. 4 .

They walked in silence to the pub. There was no need for words between them. Brendan knew what was rattling Amy so much tonight, and it had nothing to do with aging. *What was the matter with everyone all of a sudden?* Try as she might, Amy just could not get her head round the idea that a woman can function as a rational and self-determining individual for the best part of thirty years but will ultimately be slain by internal biochemical forces beyond her control, even beyond her conscious will. That this archaic and frankly insulting idea was peddled as a sad but beautiful truth—on TV discussion shows, in newspapers and women's magazines, even by intelligent friends of hers who needed some get-out clause for their sellout pregnancies—angered Amy even more than the idea itself. Traditionally, the "women are ovens waiting to be filled with buns" mantra had prevailed, even among a lot of thinking people. Even the great philosophers of history had been totally unreconstructed on the issue, going all misty-eyed on the existential purpose of womankind as creators of life. It frustrated her beyond measure that women she loved and respected, women with whom she'd marched to preserve abortion rights, with whom she'd agonized, and whom she'd supported through the trials of male-dominated working life, were now starting to bleat this rubbish about feeling "unfulfilled" and "incomplete." Fine to have those feelings—even Amy sometimes (annoyingly, usually right after a hard-won achievement) felt that sinking surge of "Is that all there is?" malaise. But why then deduce that the hole, the gap, the crater between desire and fulfillment needs to be crammed full of baby? Learn a language! Do something for charity! Be nice to a stranger! Don't immediately jump to the conclusion that your life will suddenly assume some grander purpose, some cleaner, more precisely defined function, by banging out a few squawking, shitting infants. These days, Amy felt her army of supporters dwindling. Gone were the days when she would sit joking with friends about ramming any car with a Baby on Board sticker, when they would scribble their own Baby on Roof signs and attach them to their cars' rear windows just to worry people.

Inside the pub, as Brendan ordered two pints of bitter and a couple bags of nuts, Amy felt momentarily guilty for slipping out of her own birthday dinner. But sod it, it was her birthday and she was damned if she was going to let it be hijacked. *They wouldn't mind,* she told herself. In fact, they'd relish the opportunity to share and support one another without the sneering, disapproving presence of a poof and a pathological baby-dodger. She'd known about Jules's latest relationship trauma already, and besides, Justin had gone off so many times in the past year it was difficult to keep regurgitating the same "you deserve better" spiel every time. She could catch up with Ang next week, which would give her a few days to muster some new-baby enthusiasm. Soph she would call in the morning. She dimly remembered offering to drive both Greg and Soph to the hospital for the final batch of implantation on the following Tuesday. Well, it was an afternoon out.

"There you go!" said Brendan, plonking a frothy pint down in front of Amy with the genuine cheer of the heavy drinker newly arrived at a pub.

"Thanks," said Amy, casting an eye over the rest of the clientele. A few Stokey types in distressed denim affectedly sucking on limp roll-ups and a couple of therapists from the natural-health center complaining about the smoke. Despite the inauspicious surroundings, it felt good to be out of the party. As she got older, Amy experienced contradictory feelings toward her friends. It was so hard to maintain proper friendships, old-fashioned friendships where you know about each other's lives in detail, know what each week's triumphs and disappointments are. Yet despite their failings, these were the old friends she clung to. It was so hard as you got older to put the energy into an unpredictable stranger, to fill them in on your childhood, your relationship history and how that explains your current single cynicism, your phobias, and your joys. If there were a computer chip that she could just insert into a new potential friend and download her CV, transcripts of her dreams, and video clips of formative moments, Amy might more readily entertain the idea of finding new friends. But as things stood the idea was just too exhausting. Better to stick with the crew of depressive no-hopers she'd known for years than risk branching out and putting her stock behind a time-consuming and unsure investment.

"Christ, what a nightmare!" sighed Brendan as he gulped down half a pint. "'Ooh, I want a baby, I want a baby!' 'No, I want one more than you!' 'Ooh, boo, hoo, hoo!' It's pathetic. Honestly—this obsession with kids. Now I know why I spend the majority of my leisure time with homosexuals and barren, sour old dykes. Cheers."

"Cheers," said Amy, supping the bitter, tepid liquid without wincing. "They can't help it, I suppose. But it gets to the point where it's the most important thing. Bugger the fact that it's my birthday, I've already been born! Hello, I'm here already!"

Brendan eyed his friend with characteristic peskiness.

"So . . . thirty-nine . . . Doesn't it ever occur to you that you might like to have a kid?" he asked, all measured innocence.

"Yeah, right! Shh . . . What's that sound I hear? There—can you hear it?"

"What—that loud ticking noise? No, I can't hear a thing."

"Exactly. My biological clock doesn't fucking work," said Amy.

"So you've always said," persisted Brendan. "But I was just thinking . . . you know, that it's the age thing really that turns the most adamant antibaby thirty-nine-year-old into a gibbering, baby-obsessed wreck. Once you get to the age where it's now or never, isn't it frightening? Don't you ever wake in the night and ask yourself if you're really sure? Don't you picture yourself in twenty years' time going on vacation with no one to send a postcard to? No one to guilt-trip and no one to cook for at Christmas?" Brendan held her gaze, knowing he was pushing at all the wrong buttons.

"No, I don't, Brendan," Amy replied coolly. "I generally wake in the night wondering where I should take my next long weekend, or whether I should get that new Armani navy skirt suit or splash out on bespoke."

"Yes, because that's what Amy Stokes does, isn't it? She doesn't have any real feelings or needs, does she? She sails above us mere mortals with all our flesh-and-blood concerns, and she doesn't need anything or anyone, does she? That's what you'd have us all believe, isn't it?" he pushed. He always liked to do this when he'd had a few. The tiresome devil's advocate drunk.

"All right, Brendan. You win. Yes, you're right, the lady doth protest too much; underneath this grim, self-serving spinster exterior there beats the heart of a woman aching to bear fruit, a woman whose womb churns and strains each time she passes a virile young male. A woman who yearns to become a milky, sleepless balloon with only a puking, wriggling bundle of raw need for company. I've got to hand it to you, Brendan, you've seen right through me."

"But people like you should have children—you owe it to the

planet! You're attractive, intelligent, you're a nice person—you should be adding those qualities to another human being and passing them on! If people like you don't have children, it'll just be morons out there! I really worry about that, I really do. All the nice people who could actually improve the next generation are too busy leading full lives to procreate. Where would we be now if Mrs. Einstein had thought, *Actually, I don't think I'm the mothering kind. I won't bother with having children?* You're being selfish! You've got something special, and it is your responsibility—no, your duty—to pass it on!" said Brendan, warming to his theme. Amy knew it was the alcohol, but at times like these, with all the talk of babies and motherhood and parenting, Brendan always got strangely animated. She wondered if secretly, like a lot of gay men she knew, he harbored hopes of fatherhood at some point in his life. His tack was clever. Of all the arguments for having a child, this, it seemed to Amy right now, was the most seductive. She had always had a sneaking suspicion that she was something to write home about, a cut above the rest. Her mother had often slapped her down for the way she sauntered up the aisle to Holy Communion as if she were on par with the Almighty Himself. At school she had been bullied for not looking nervous when she had to read at Assembly—she had slouched casually, used her clear, loud voice unashamedly, and looked over the page a lot at the cross-legged captives in front of her, and this was not the done thing for a working-class kid.

Was such high self-esteem the middle-class reason to have kids? Did she possess Nobel Prize–winning eggs? The idea of having a baby had always been so abstract, so impersonal somehow. She hated the way new mums claimed such ownership of their babies: "My baby, *my* children." The one thing that always struck her about even the tiniest of babies was just how *themselves* they were, how frighteningly *them* they seemed to be. Any influence one could have on them was purely cosmetic, totally after the fact of their personalities. Far from divesting her of the fear of responsibility, this awareness of the *indi-*

viduality of babies made Amy feel panicky. *What if you didn't like your child? What if it turned out to be stupid? Ugly? What if it became a murderer or a rapist? What must mothers of those children feel?* Amy did not want to end up feeling as though her own womb had betrayed her and played host to a future crack-addict mugger.

She became aware that Brendan was staring at her in triumph. He had gotten to her. As far as he was concerned, he had gotten her thinking about it and that was a huge triumph. Little matter that he'd probably be absolutely horrified if she ever did U-turn and try for a baby.

"'Nother pint?" chirped Brendan, maintaining the know-it-all look he reserved for occasions when he couldn't think of how to seal his victory right away.

"Yes, as long as you don't think it will deplete my folic acid reserves," said Amy, draining the last of the dishwater from her glass.

"Well, you're drinking for two now," said Brendan as he skipped off to the bar. Outside, the rain pelted down on a young couple pushing a pram along Church Street, presumably trying to get a young baby to sleep. They wore the look of resigned slaves, their tiny emperor dictating their every move, day or night, rain or shine. Amy shuddered and did something her mother was always telling her to do. She counted her blessings.

.5.

Still foggy from the cheap wine and warm beer, Amy slung on her shades and headed out east to Essex. Her birthday fell on a weekend this year, which meant one thing—she would have to make the requisite mum visit and suffer the minimum contracted two hours of sighing, overfeeding, and non sequiturs. The birds had woken her again that morning with their angry guffawing, but now that she knew what the noise was, she could more or less ignore it. Three magpies. What was that bloody rhyme? One for sorrow, two for joy, three for an almighty hangover. Her usual dawn breakfast in bed of a couple aspirin and a pint of Robinson's barley water settled her back down to another three hours of sleep before she had to get up and at it, throwing a disgruntled Germaine into the only other seat of the car.

"Come on, stinky, we're off to see Grandma—you know, the old lady who stuffs you full of choccy drops when she thinks I'm not looking."

Germaine perked up at the mention of choccy drops and adopted the "Let's go!" position: chin resting on the dashboard, ears aloft, paws perched on the edge of the seat. Amy thought for the first time in ages what a great consolation a dog is. She didn't *need* Germaine like some sad, lonely bastards needed their dogs—partner, baby, and life substitute all rolled into one—but nevertheless, it was nice to have someone to talk at in the morning, someone to displace all of the anxiety of a parental visit. In their nine years together, Amy reckoned Germaine must have seen her in just about every mood, every situation, and every phase, and she had always just sat impassively, nonjudgmental and ever-patient, her only concern that the dog walker arrived on time. She was a witness to Amy's life, proof that Amy existed. If a woman cries in the middle of a Docklands development and there is no dog there to see it, has she really cried?

Although the day was gray and drizzly, she threw down the cover of her BMW and sped out of the underground car park, almost knocking over a young girl pushing a baby stroller.

"Oi!" shouted the pram-faced teen mum. "Watch where you're going!"

"Sorry, but you shouldn't stick the front wheels into the road and think it'll make the traffic stop," said Amy, putting her foot back down on the accelerator. In her rearview mirror, she registered the girl's obscene gestures as the trailing wind carried her shouts of "Fuck you!" along the deserted Saturday street.

Heading out of town was always such a pleasure on a Saturday morning. Amy only ever felt like a real Londoner when she was leaving it behind. As the empty northbound lanes of the M11 snaked out ahead of her, Amy felt a smug sense of superiority as she glanced at the tailback of gauche day-trippers streaming into London. She didn't have to queue to visit London; she lived there and was therefore able to treat it with easy contempt, as if it were her longtime wife, whose body and company held no further surprises. She stroked the leather of her passenger seat and felt a guilty shiver of pleasure. *Everyone wants what I've got,* she thought, before her latent inner Marxist had time to suppress the idea.

Slamming on the radio, she tuned with one hand while expertly steering with the other. Snatches of crappy love songs crackled in and out of focus as she twizzled the dial, looking for some stirring classical music.

"Bye bye baby, baby good-bye" . . . *zzzz wwwrrr* . . . "Baby you can drive my car!" . . . "And you can say baby, baby, can I hold you to-night?" . . . *ggggrrrr eeeee* . . . "Baby baby baby, where did our love go?"

What was this pop obsession with the word "baby"? It had always made Amy shudder when anyone had used the word as a term of endearment toward her. She couldn't help thinking of cheap American porn actors or Barry White. To her, the word meant one thing only: money. Finally settling on classic FM, she pushed back in her seat and put her foot down just as "O Mio Babbino Caro" blasted out. It felt good to be cold and windswept.

The vestiges of last night's failed celebration still clung to her, as did the rancid cigarette smoke she'd once again given in to. Just this trip to her mum's, and then the whole sorry birthday affair could be put away for another year. And this was going to be a good year. After seventeen consecutive years at work, Amy was taking a six-month sabbatical, and the thought of all that free time was intoxicating. She hadn't yet decided what she was going to do with her time: get fit (naturally), travel (well, go on holiday—she had never really got the whole uncomfortable expeditions-to-unspoiled-wildernesses thing), lounge around moaning about being bored, then going out and spending stupid amounts of money on unnecessary distractions. Whatever she decided to do, she was looking forward to it. She hadn't had a long break since her school days; not for her the long summer of relaxing in Europe looking at Giotto frescoes or Gaudi cathedrals. It had always been three months of temping, operating industrial dish-washers, and being patronized by middle-management losers. This was going to be *her* time, the time she would use to decide what she wanted to do with the rest of her life.

It wasn't that Amy was unhappy with her career—far from it.

She'd never bothered with that "Oh my God, what is my life about?" bullshit that so many of her friends seemed to go in for. If you followed that line of thought, reasoned Amy, then everything on this Earth becomes both as meaningless and meaningful as you wish to make it. But if we provide our own structure, our own moral code, and our own criteria for leading a good and fulfilling life, then surely true happiness is more attainable? The black dog of depression had never so much as sniffed at Amy's lamppost, let alone cocked its leg at her life.

The speedometer hit 100 mph as she fell in love with her life anew. It would be good to have six months off. Time to relax, research a few new design possibilities, and source a few more Asian suppliers. Besides, she was suffering from baby overdose. She needed a break from nappy talk and cuddly toys and doe-eyed bloody women with fashionably neat bumps.

Well, the dead arose and appeared to many! Hello there, Amy, come in, come in, you're very welcome," fussed her mum as she pulled open the door.

"And little Germaine—go on through, the back door is open," she added, ignoring the fact that the dog had already bolted through the house toward the cat-infested garden.

"Hi, Mammy, how are you?"

"Are you hungry? Did you have any breakfast? You don't eat enough. Have you had breakfast? Would you like a bacon sandwich? Cereal? Or shall I do you an omelet?"

Amy ignored all of the questions. She had learned early that having an Irish mother meant all food-related inquiries were purely rhetorical. No matter if you'd just come from a Roman banquet of seventy courses that required four emetics and an enema, Amy's mum would still force you to accept a plateful of buttery sandwiches and a few slices of Guinness cake, washed down with as much strong tea— "tea you could trot a horse on"—as you could swallow.

Amy headed ritualistically for the kitchen and performed the universal action of all adult children returning home. She opened the fridge and stood gazing into it, hoping for inspiration.

"Did you have a good journey? That M-eleven is very busy Father Don was saying at Mass that the new slip road for Stansted is the culprit did you get stuck in traffic? I have a cake in the oven there's ham there, nice ham with bits on the one that you like or there's yogurts if you're watching your weight although I don't see why you should there's not a pick on you." It was always like this. The stream of a lonely consciousness emptying itself on the first available pair of ears. She'd calm down in a minute and remember to be disapproving.

"No, I'm fine, Mum. Honestly, I had breakfast only an hour ago," she lied, wincing at the old-lady contents of the fridge. "How are you, Mum?"

"Oh, not too bad now, but remember that Martin McFinnegan you were friends with at school? The boy with the blond hair and the harelip? Hugh's son? He was in your class. Oh go on you must remember him—he was a good friend of yours."

"We were in the same class, Mum, he wasn't a friend of mine. He was terminally dull."

"Well, he's terminally ill now, Amy, God help him. Leukemia. They say he's only a few months to live. I've put in for a Mass for him. Or there's corned beef in the cupboard or a bit of pink salmon. It's boneless."

"Poor Martin," said Amy, trying to remember his face.

"Three children under five. God help his poor wife. You could put a bit of pickle on it."

"Oh, dear. That's awful," said Amy, wondering all over again at her mother's morbid fascination with the misfortune of others. It must be part of the Irish DNA.

"And remember Maura at the crossroads back home her with the chickens you used to feed? And the whiskers? She used to ride down the lane muttering about the price of butter? Well Auntie Annie stopped in to have a look at her last Friday morning and wasn't she stone-cold dead in the bed? Annie was very upset about it. I could do you a bit of chicken if you like. I've got salad dressing."

"Oh, dear," repeated Amy, knowing this was all that was required for old Maura. She'd never liked the old bag anyway.

"God rest her soul, she was awfully mean. Remember that day you spent all afternoon polishing her silver, she had a lot of stuff stashed away from somewhere or other, and what did she give you? Only fifty pence and there we were, hoping for a fiver!"

"There was Dad hoping for a fiver, more like."

"Now, Amy, you mustn't speak ill of the dead. God rest his soul, he wasn't a bad man, just misguided, and he loved the bones of you. So, are you courting yet?"

"Erm, courting, no. I'm too busy at work. Did I tell you I got that Tweenies bed linen contract? Worth an absolute fortune. I was one of seven up for it and I got it."

"Well, time marches on and I still haven't got a grandchild. Seventy-two and no little one to rest on my knee, and there's Mona Brennan with seventeen."

Here we go, thought Amy. *She's read the parish death announcements, now it's time to launch her assault on my ovaries and completely ignore my work success, even though she brags about it when I'm not around.*

"Lord knows if I could've had more than one baby, if God had seen fit in His infinite wisdom to smile down upon us and send me another child, I might be a grandmother now . . . but there you have it—it was not to be . . ."

"Mum, I haven't even got a boyfriend, let alone a potential father to your grandchild. And I keep telling you, I don't even want children."

"Don't say such things, Amy, because you never know when you might change your mind and God might be listening and turn your womb to stone."

"It already is stone, so he's welcome to it."

"I see you with a couple of children, Amy, no matter what you say. You can't fight fate, and I've long had a nose for such things, so you'd better get started. Oh, happy birthday by the way, Amy, I forgot to send the card but I've got a little something for you . . . wait now 'til I see . . ."

And with that, she scurried off to the sideboard and rummaged around for what seemed like an age.

Amy uttered a silent prayer.

"God give me the strength to accept those gifts which I cannot change, the courage to change those gifts with receipts, and the wisdom to not point out the difference. At least it can't be any worse than the pens and the hankies."

"Now!" exclaimed Amy's mammy, this being her favorite punctuation.

With a gallows grin, Amy unraveled the Merry X-mas wrapping to reveal a glass orb that encased a plastic Virgin Mary holding a tiny Baby Jesus. The underside was flat and covered with badly glued-on green felt. It bore the inscription "A Souvenir from Fatima." There was no mistaking it. It was a novelty religious paperweight. The full set. It was too funny to be painful anymore.

"Thanks, Mum, it's just what I've always wanted."

Amy's mum rushed off into the kitchen ostensibly to turn off the kettle but actually to avoid the terrible awkwardness she always felt at giving gifts. She'd never really understood what they were for, never having received one from her own mother.

"I got it at the church bazaar last Christmas, but I forgot to give it to you, what with all the excitement."

"No worries. I've lived without it," she mumbled as Germaine strolled in and commenced her beard-wiping ceremony on the rug covering the new cream carpet Amy had insisted on paying for six months ago. Tired of seeing her mum's shame at the state of the house whenever a visitor dropped by, Amy had refurbished and refitted the whole of the downstairs in tasteful neutral shades, desperate to haul her mum into the minimalist twenty-first century. Thrilled with how "clean" it looked, Amy's mum had proceeded to accessorize with every dusty old knickknack and grannyish antimacassar she could find, covering the lush carpet with rags and frayed offcuts in order to "keep it nice." There was just no helping some people.

Three cups of tea and a doorstep of ham sandwich later, Amy checked her watch and tried to work out if she could slip away yet. Her mum always spotted this gesture, even when her back was turned. It wasn't that they didn't love each other—her mammy always brimmed up with irritating sentimentality every time Amy left—but that they had never formed a relationship beyond their early years together. Try as she might, despite the dreadful communication exercises she'd had to endure on her way up the corporate ladder, she had never managed to bridge the gap and "interface effectively" with her mum. Something about the long-suffering Virgin Mary routine, the thin set of her hard-done-by mouth, the Catholicism of her sloping shoulders, the fatalistic sighing, and the whispered rosaries (completed at alarming speed and seemingly without the aid of oxygen) had always antagonized Amy, from as far back as she could remember. She looked at her mum now and felt a sudden pang of—what, guilt? Anger? Resentment? Mostly just sadness. Was this the great gift of motherhood? To end up old and confused about where you went wrong, unable to understand your offspring, feeling just as alone as when you first entered the world but without the milky breast of your own mother for comfort? It seemed too sad all of a sudden to be in this familiar lounge, staring at this intimate stranger, conscious of nothing but the desire to leave, hearing nothing but the beating of her own heart as it clattered away in her rib cage, desperate for escape. How was it possible to be so distant from someone whose body had given you existence, whose flesh-and-blood interior had been your whole world for nine months? The fact that her mum sensed this unease didn't help. Rather than do what nice middle-class parents did and pretend either that it didn't exist or that it didn't matter, Amy's mum would spend hours just gazing longingly at her daughter, not even sure herself what she was looking for.

Amy bristled under her mother's gaze. She felt at once invaded and afraid that whatever it was her mum was hoping to find simply was not there.

"Better get going, Mum," she sighed, as if the wrench was as deeply felt on both sides. "Traffic, you know . . . "

"Yes, yes, no doubt you'll be getting ready to go out tonight to some party or other or maybe to a wine bar, but you will remember to eat, won't you? I hate the thought of you and an empty stomach. I'll bring Germaine out to the car."

Having announced her departure, the clattering inside her ribs subsided immediately, so much so that she was able to genuinely smile as she watched her mum wrestle a crotchety Germaine off the back lawn and to the front door, chiding her all the way. The dog loved all the fuss of a visit to Grandma's (her mum's sickening term for these duty calls). She loved the attention, the choccy drop treats produced in abundance for the simplest of paw-raising tricks, the tolerance of her muddy undercarriage on any chair she chose to perch on. Germaine knew the leaving signs only too well and protested violently at the early exit.

Impatient to get away, Amy jumped into her car and waited for the dog to be dropped onto the passenger seat.

"Come on now, Germaine, your mammy's in a hurry to get home, so don't be like this. Sure you'll have forgotten all about me in a minute. I know, I'm not stupid, now stop that licking! Stop it! Ha, ha! You silly thing, you. Come on, let's put you in the car and we'll not say another word about it." With that, Germaine landed with an unceremonious *plonk* onto the easy-wipe leather seat, throwing a "How dare you?" scowl in Amy's direction. This was why Amy loved her—she didn't need Amy, and she took every available opportunity to remind her that she was far better treated elsewhere.

"Come on, let's get you home," she said, ruffling the dog's shaggy beard as she pulled the gear stick into reverse with her free hand.

"Bye, Mum—I'll call soon," she shouted as she released the hand-brake and pushed down fast, boy-racer-like, on the accelerator. Classic FM burst out of all four speakers. A quick glance in the rearview mirror and she released all 1.9L of power onto the empty street. With a satisfying roar the car shot backward as she turned to wave her good-bye at last. But something was wrong—her mum was shouting, pointing, running down the path. A moment and a stomach-lurchingly soft thud later, her hand shot to the brake and she pulled the car to a sudden halt, only to see the empty seat beside her. *Germaine*. Where was Germaine?

"Oh, God, no. Oh, no, oh, Jesus, Mary, and Joseph, God bless and save us, no," chanted Amy's mum flatly as she ran to the back of the car. And then there came a noise that Amy had not heard for a quarter of a century, not since they lowered her father's coffin into the ground. Amy's mother let out an anguished, banshee cry and covered her face with her hands.

.6.

Three hours later, still thick with snot and numb with shock, Amy found herself on Ang's doorstep.

"Hello! Where did you get to last night, you—oh, God, Amy, what's wrong?" said Ang as she opened the door. "You look awful."

"Have you got any whiskey?"

"I'll get some. Come in, come in. Dave? Dave! Can you go down to the liquor store quick? It's an emergency—scotch!" ordered Ang to an invisible Dave, who was somewhere in the house. She ushered her friend into the chaos of the living room, shooing the three older kids upstairs.

"And when you get back, take the kids to the park," she yelled, sensing a genuine crisis.

"Now, what's happened?"

"I went to visit Mum today—"

"Oh, dear," Ang said knowingly.

"No, no, that's not it. The dog's dead."

"What? What do you mean? How?"

"I killed it."

"Killed it? Why?" said Ang, confusion clouding her soft, chubby face.

"Not deliberately, obviously. I feel like shit. I was backing out of the street and I didn't notice she'd jumped out of the car—she likes my mum. *Liked* my mum."

"But . . . how did she get out of the car? I don't understand. . . . "

"I had the roof down. She hopped out."

"The roof down? Today? Oh . . ." said Ang, casting a doubtful glance out of the window at the dark sky.

"Oh, God, Amy, that's terrible—so, you ran over her?"

"Yes. I ran over her. She's dead."

"Cool! Did she burst all over the road?" came a disembodied voice from behind the sofa.

"Jason! Get upstairs *now!*" screamed Ang, mortified at her fourteen-year-old's insensitivity.

Amy allowed herself a small smile as the boy thundered up the stairs.

"Sorry, Auntie Amy—didn't mean it!" shouted Jason, trying to re-pair the damage but mostly trying to avoid a lecture on eavesdropping.

"Oh, you poor thing!" cried Ang, her bosom approaching Amy's face at maximum speed.

And at once, enveloped in her oldest friend's maternal embrace, Amy let rip with an avalanche of tears, the ice over her heart melting and sliding, crashing in chunks to the nylon carpet.

"What am I going to do? She's in a garbage bag in the trunk. We took her to the vet, but she was already dead. I can't bury her on the roof terrace! I've got these magpies up there, they'll eat her, and there's no earth to stick her in, just bamboo tubs. Oh, Ang, what have I done?"

"Sssh," soothed her friend, rocking her gently with mum expertise. "Ssshh. Don't upset yourself—it was an accident, happens all the time, she was a daft little doggie, wasn't she? Fancy jumping out of a moving car like that! It wasn't your fault."

"But I'm such a bad person! I'm always in such a rush, always trying to get away fast, I can't look after anything. I'm sorry, you don't need this in your condition," Amy sniveled, suddenly remembering the new baby.

"That's not true! You do look after things! You keep that flat lovely!"

"That's not me—that's Joan the cleaner. It is true. I'm useless. Remember Cyclops?"

Despite herself, an amused grin spread across Ang's face. She remembered Cyclops, the one-eyed hamster Amy had begged to take home for the school holidays. She'd played with it for an hour, then got bored and let it roam the house. Within forty-eight hours, it had gone missing. Amy had at first accused her dad of selling it, but a day later, her mum had noticed a funny smell in the kitchen. It seemed to emanate from the toaster. Peering inside, Amy had discovered the charred remains of a small furry thing. It looked like a relic from Pompeii, its sharp little teeth visible through the blackened fur of its death mask. Ang had contributed 25p toward buying an identical hamster before the start of the next term, and had quietly taken it to her own home for the duration of the holidays.

"That was different! You were only a kid. You couldn't cope with the responsibility."

"*You* could!" sobbed Amy, mindless of the large wet patch appearing on Ang's blouse. "It's just me. It's just who I am. I'm no good at looking after things. I shouldn't be allowed to go near living things. I just kill them."

"Oh, come on, Amy," cooed Ang as Dave arrived back with a half-bottle of Bells. Pouring Amy a large glass, she shooed him upstairs to get the kids out and see to the baby.

"Drink this."

"Yeah, this'll make it all all right, won't it? This is what I always do—if in doubt, get pissed," Amy said bitterly as she downed the lot in one gulp.

The scotch helped. After a few stiff ones, she was feeling much perkier. The kids poured in the door, nosily peering round the door to see what a dog murderer looked like.

They gaped, unabashed.

"Ang, can I ask you a favor?"

"Yes, darlin', what can I do for you?"

"Can I bury Germaine in your garden?"

"Oh, please, Mum, can we? Can we, Mum? Oh, go on, pleeeeaaassse!" chorused the kids, desperate for a bit of morbid excitement.

"Yes. Of course. You can put her next to Lucky." Lucky had been the inaptly named black cat Jason owned, who had been found spread thinly across a hot, newly tarmaced road last summer. Jason had said it looked like a cartoon accident.

Staggering slightly, Amy went to the car to collect the poor corpse as the kids crashed around inside, fighting over the possession of the shovel.

"Let me have it! I want to dig the first bit!"

"No, it was my idea to get the shovel, let me have it!"

Ang watched from the front door until she saw Amy hesitate as the corner of the black bin bag flapped open in the breeze. A small, bloody paw flopped out as if its owner were reclining in a hammock. Rushing over to where her friend stood shaking, Ang scooped up the sack and marched toward the back garden, where the children had already assembled and were trying to generate the solemnity required for the occasion. The funeral party. They had seen it on TV, and had witnessed it firsthand at their Nana's graveside only three months ago. If dogs had souls, over the next twenty minutes, Germaine's would have hovered above the assembled mourners long enough to witness a touching display of naïve grief. She would have seen Jason dig the hole deftly and deeply enough to cheat the local foxes; she would have cocked her head to one side as Kelly played a halting, breathy but heartfelt "Amazing Grace" on her recorder and Ang lowered her earthly body into the ground. She would have even wagged her tail with pride as Sammy spoke a few spontaneous words by way of a eulogy, something along the lines of: "Dear Germaine, we didn't know you that well, but you are with Baby Jesus now and he liked dogs, so there'll be lots of biscuits and cats to chase in doggy heaven. Amen." Above all, Germaine would have marveled at the gut-churning sobs that wracked her owner-cum-assassin as she stood by the graveside.

"It's all right," she would have said. "I know it was an accident . . . but I didn't know you cared that much . . ."

.7.

It had been a difficult week. The flat seemed empty without the small, loud dog. Without realizing it, Germaine had provided a pulse, a vital sign to the cold, urban chic of the "authentic industrial architecture." The air was still thick with that wet-dog smell, a smell that Amy had tried for years to eradicate with little success. Plug-in room deodorizers, neutralizing sprays, and expensive perfumes could only vaguely mask the pong of mud, fur, and dead leaves that follows every dog like a shadow. Now Amy clung to it. In a fit of madness, she'd even dampened an old towel of Germaine's in order to resummon the odor. She couldn't yet bring herself to throw away the Burberry bed in the corner, and a few of Germaine's old toys still lay about the place, waiting to be shaken and killed all over again. On the Monday after her death, the dog walker had arrived as usual, only to find the flat dogless and Amy slumped in the corner, watching daytime TV, still in her dressing gown. The explanation had prompted a renewed bout of crying, and the dog walker had backed out of the door explaining that she was very sorry but she had a carload of rest-less canines to attend to. On Tuesday, she'd accompanied Soph and Greg to the hospital fertility unit, and had found it oppressively hopeful. The sight of all those desperate, childless couples eagerly awaiting their chance to create life had only served to remind her how she'd recently snuffed one out. The implantation complete, Soph had looked so full of joy at the prospect of what might be about to burrow itself into her that Amy had to look away. Not that she didn't want it to work—she'd even offered to pay for this, the final attempt—but she felt cut off from life in a way that totally surprised her. She felt melodramatic, childish, and kept trying to tell herself to snap out of it, that it was only a dog, and that in a way it was better that Germaine went suddenly than via a lingering old-age illness. Nothing worked. Even alcohol, her old standby in times of trouble, failed to numb the curious listlessness she felt toward her life. She'd given herself official notice that this was her last week of work before the big sabbatical she'd been looking forward to. How could she let such a small thing as the dog dampen her enthusiasm for her new-found freedom? But the moment of Germaine's death haunted her still. She recognized the grief signs—it felt as if it were the only thing that had ever happened. Wednesday, Thursday, and Friday she re-turned to her design HQ just down the road from the Chelsea shop in order to tidy up a few last-minute handover details. She'd poached the best new textile designer on the block from her biggest rivals just last week. Saskia was a perky twenty-four-year-old who'd shown just the right mixture of respect and resentment at her interview—cocky but eager in equal measure, just like Amy had been all those years ago. She'd be able to keep things ticking over, and perhaps even come up with a few new lines. Amy balked at the idea of training a new member of staff. The precise ins and outs of her quirky business felt personal, and she didn't relish the exposure. Saskia asked a lot of questions—how should she deal with Mr. So-and-so, what was the best way to approach Ms. Whoever on a late deadline. It was all Amy could do to stop herself from screaming, "I don't care! It's not important! None of this matters!" People's mouths moved, but it was as if she was hearing them from underwater, with a few seconds' delay. Her head felt full of damp cotton wool, and her heart felt tight and heavy, as if a giant, invisible anvil had been dropped from a great height and landed on her sternum. All this because of the dog. And yet . . . and yet . . . if she was honest with herself, she mused during her Friday afternoon smoke break, this feeling had been resident in her body for some months. Her work was great, her flat was state-of-the-art, her friends all loved her, and yet . . . there was something, something she felt she lacked. Was it from without? Was it something she could buy? A trip somewhere hot and exotic? She'd always wanted to go to Marrakech . . . or perhaps she should really think about upsizing and moving to the country . . . London was great, but maybe a slower pace would ease her soul? Clearing her desk and emptying the ashtray on her drawing board, she was struck by how easy it would be to wipe out any trace of her existence. She'd never gone in for toys, photos, or personal novelty items. Her desk was a model of sleek professional chic. She watched with a wry smile as Saskia staggered in with a crateful of knickknacks, grinning framed relatives and wacky desktop gadgets in citrus colors. Turning for one last look at her workstation, she was struck by just how empty, how anonymous it looked. As Saskia started excitedly taking up residence, she noticed how claimed the desk looked now, how lived-in and lively it appeared. A hollow chasm opened up in the pit of her stomach as the stark realization came that she was utterly singular, totally self-contained and alone—a discrete unit you could pick up and put down elsewhere in a moment, no strings attached, no roots pulled, no props needed. Usually this state of being was a comfort to Amy when she felt low—it was reassuring to know that she had only herself to account to, only herself to rely on. Alongside her constant, quiet sense of superiority, she had also always nursed a faint sensation that other people were more con-nected with the world than she was. There was something about see-ing groups of friends laughing in an easy way with each other in the windows of smart, glass-fronted bars, or watching in awe at the checkout as couples unloaded all manner of future feasts from their supermarket trolleys and wondering how they thought of all those things to buy (occasionally, Amy succumbed to the food police and stocked up on exotic cheeses and strange-sounding fruit, only to find it all festering in the bottom of the fridge three weeks later). As she watched the backs of her colleagues—Jules; Sam, the accountant; and Dee, the carpenter—retreating down the stairs ahead of her, she felt this sense of unbelonging, of a life lived in the ironic margins all too keenly.

"Bye, Amy!" shouted Dee, almost as an afterthought. "Though I expect we'll see you before long!" Jules was off to the doctor's up the road. Something about a hormone test. Dee would be rushing home to her two-year-old, and Sam would no doubt be flicking through yet more bridal brochures with Tim.

"Bye," Amy shouted after them, doing her best impression of some-one who was happy to be left alone.

They waved good-bye and shouted their best wishes, knowing full well that Amy would be back and forth, checking up on them over the next few months. Their end-of-the-week laughter cut into her tired heart. They couldn't have known how much she needed to be picked up and rescued right now. She was doing what she always did—pretending that everything was OK even as the ground began to crumble beneath her feet.

"Steady," she said out loud. Was this the crisis point so many of her friends had reached over the past couple of years? She knew the signs—a sudden sad event precipitating a reassessment of everything, a rejection of the old life culminating in a desperate clinging on to the nearest passing raft (drugs, religion, babies). *Babies.* Yes, that was what most of them had opted for. She'd have to be extra-vigilant on this one. It was at times just like these in women's lives that they opted for the baby card, pulling it from their handbags like a football referee, sending themselves off to the sub's bench of their own lives. Better get to the pub and get stuck in. Deciding what to do with one's life could surely wait until after that.

. 8 .

Tucked into her favorite snug at The Wheelbarrow, Amy started to feel more like herself again. She liked coming here. It was a welcome change from the trendy wine bars and dreadful chain "quality" corporate pubs that were all over Kensington like a cheap suit. Soon, her oddball selection of drinking chums would be in. She ordered a pint of bitter and drank it at the bar, marveling at how comfortable she felt there. She wasn't one of those wallflower women who wouldn't dream of going into a pub on her own. Her second pint helped a great deal—despite a wobbly moment when she checked her watch to see if it was time to go home and feed Germaine. The hollow feeling was subsiding, squashed out by the fug of beer and the jollity of the Friday-evening demob-happy crowd. Then the lads arrived, bursting into the pub with that enviable lack of self-consciousness that is the male preserve. Stephen, Adam, Ned, Marky, and Josh were OK, really, though Amy thanked her stars that her acquaintance with them was purely social. She didn't fancy encountering any of them in that testosterone-fest they called the office.

Stephen had recently bought a bassinet from her after becoming a dad for the first time, and it had mellowed him immensely. Although he was still essentially a wanker, Amy could detect a softening in his bravado. Adam and Ned were puppies, really. Barely out of college, they competed on a minute-by-minute basis, each one determined to prove the other "gay" in some way. Gay, in their mouths, did not mean homosexual. It was a sort of obscurely homophobic insult meaning "ill-advised" or "sad." Bad ideas were "gay"; tastes in clothes were "gay"; and, inexplicably, fancying some girl or other was often pronounced "gay." She could tolerate this because they were funny and young and ambitious enough to flirt with her in a Mrs. Robinson sort of way. Marky and Josh were older, more her age, although the similarities stopped there. Marky was a chippy northern misogynist with a wife and four daughters and a genius for advertising feminine hygiene products. He claimed to understand women so well that he could sell them their own menses. He tolerated Amy only once he conceded that he didn't think of her as a woman. Amy knew it was a crap line but decided it would be easier to take it as a compliment. Josh was a proper old English gentleman. He liked to think of Amy as his little sister, or perhaps his preschool nanny, even though he knew how much this irked her. He tried to treat her as an equal, but he couldn't help being totally unreconstructed.

"How's life in retail?" asked Josh, trying to talk man-to-man with Amy.

"Oh, you know . . . ticking over nicely."

"Busy day at the cash register?"

"I don't actually take the money, Josh—wouldn't sully my precious designer hands. I have elves to do that for me."

"Elves, yes, very good."

"And besides, it was my birthday last week and I hadn't seen the girls in the studio, so there was a lot of fannying about with cake and drinks and stuff."

"How ghastly. How old, may one ask?"

"Thirty-nine, and you may."

"Really? Really? Hey, chaps, Amy here is thirty-nine today! Good lord! You don't look a day over thirty!"

"It was last week! But bless you," she managed, mortified at her sudden revelation. Why had she told him that? Was she that needy?

The lads obliged Josh's request for an impromptu rendition of "Happy birthday to you, squashed tomatoes and stew," etc., as Amy squirmed in the corner. By the time they'd gotten to "Bread and butter in the gutter," the whole pub had joined in.

"Well, well, well. Aren't you taking a break from work soon?"

"Yes, in fact from next week. I'll pop in now and again, you know, just to make sure there's no slacking."

"Absolutely. Can't let the serfs gain control. What are you going to do with yourself, then? Find a nice chap and settle down?"

Why was everyone so obsessed with this all of a sudden? It was as if up to the age of thirty-nine, you were allowed to be the mistress of your own universe, but come the dawning of your next decade, you had to suddenly conform and settle down. How she hated that expression. *Settle down.* Like self-determination and joie de vivre were overexcited children who had to be calmed before bedtime.

"Well, actually no, Josh, I was going to use the time to investigate the potential in the teenage market—you know, travel a bit, do a bit of research . . ."

Even as she spoke these words, she was aware of the hollow feeling returning. Her stomach felt as though she'd just descended seven floors at high speed. Josh seemed to have picked up on her lack of conviction. He'd glazed over.

"Oh, I see, business as usual then, really."

"Well, yes, but I won't be in the shop and the studio all the time. I'm giving myself the space to . . . to . . ."

"Regroup?" offered Stephen, who'd alarmingly taken to using psychobabble.

"Erm . . . yes, I suppose so."

"Good call. My round!" said Stephen, happy with this explanation.

"*So gay!*" shouted Ned at Adam's request for crisps.

"I'll get 'em in," said Marky, pushing to the bar. "Amy looks like she could do with another drink. You look like you've seen a ghost, love."

Amy smiled weakly. She felt as though she had. Suddenly, the pub and the cheerful blokey chat seemed oppressive and irritating.

"Actually, Marky," she found herself saying, "I won't have another—I've just remembered I've got to pop back for something." It was a bad lie, but it would do. Too late. Marky was already shouting his order to the hassled barmaid. Never mind, Amy could slip out the door and make her excuses later. Someone would find a use for her pint.

.9.

Out in the cool evening air, Amy walked slowly back up the street to the shop. *For what?* The staff would be long gone. Seven forty-five, and it was dark already, the April evenings making no concession for the brighter days. Perhaps just sitting quietly among all the nursery paraphernalia would bring her back to herself. She had felt unnerved by herself lately. It had been like living with a depressive twin, and she couldn't wait for her unself-conscious better half to return, the half who knew with absolute certainty what to do and say in any given situation. Yes, she would sit in the dark and be soothed by the shadows of the soft lamb's-fleece mobiles, stroke the warm contours of the deftly turned crib legs, marvel at her own success all over again.

The street was eerily quiet for a Friday evening in Chelsea. Normally, there would be gaggles of excitable girls in expensive shoes clacking their way down the road to some bar or other. Not even an eccentric old dog walker in sight. Amy indulged her nuclear fantasy, the one where everyone else in London knew there was a strike coming and had hidden under white reflective surfaces but no one had thought to tell her and she was to be the only person to witness with terrifying clarity the end-of-everything mushroom cloud rise over the Thames. She shivered and pulled her new leather jacket tightly around her, although the gesture offered little warmth and the zipper snagged in her hair. It would be better once she was inside the shop. She could make herself a nice cup of tea and pretend it soothed her the way her mammy always told her it would.

From a distance, the shop was a comforting sight. The amber streetlamp cast a soft sepia glow over the frontage, which was tastefully decorated in creams and pale yellow—no Day-Glo neon or jolly primary colors in *this* baby shop. Precious Little Darlings was an oasis of good taste and calming neutrals from the outside, the well-appointed external lighting bathing the artfully dressed windows in a warm haze. The only thing that irked her about the whole image was the fact that someone—probably the cleaner, Lydia—had once again defied orders and left the domestic rubbish at the front of the shop rather than in the shop bins at the back. Little details but important nonetheless. It made the place look, well, sluttish. Not the right message at all to posh mothers-to-be. She sighed and wondered if this was the start of the "while the cat's away" slippage. Small lapses in standards here and there, snowballing to outright sloppiness in a matter of weeks. She would have to leave another Post-it note on the Dyson.

Arriving at the doorstep and fumbling for her keys, she was struck by a curious feeling. It hovered around her subconscious for a few seconds before trickling through to the frontal lobes, awareness creeping like a winter dawn. She was not alone. She had never felt so not alone. Was she being followed? A quick look back confirmed the oppressively empty street. Watched? Again, no one in sight, no cars parked illegally on the double yellows. Amy pushed at the feeling to go away, but it grew stronger. Perhaps someone lurked alone in the dark interior of the shop—a buggy burglar, a crib crook? Finally, she found her keys and slotted one into the first of the locks. The bunch jangled restlessly on the large ring, then silence. She listened for any sounds of a disturbance inside. Nothing. Then something stirred. She realized she had stopped breathing. A small sound, muffled and indistinct but very close by. Amy shook herself and blamed the beer for making her jumpy. But there it was again, from somewhere near her feet this time. Slowly, slowly she withdrew the keys from the lock and waited. Again, a stifled, high-pitched sound.

Amy braced herself and peered downward as if from a precipice. At her feet lay one of her own Precious Little Darlings large paper carriers, crumpled and used, the outside splashed with tea-bag stains and the interior stuffed with—what? Paper? If it was the contents of the kitchen bin and Lydia had attracted the local rats, there would be big trouble tomorrow. Balancing on one leg, Amy nudged the bag with the other foot. It felt unexpectedly heavy. She had hoped to topple it off the top step and dislodge its vermin contents onto the street, sending the unwelcome rodents scattering into the night. But the bag had resisted and moved only an inch. She stood flamingo-like for a few seconds, wondering if there would be a delayed reaction, but nothing. Cunning little monsters. They had probably frozen, hoping their stillness would fox their attacker. She would have to kick the bastards to kingdom come. Just as she retracted her raised foot to administer the fatal blow, there came an unmistakable and hearty wail from within the bag that split the night air in two and pierced her awareness once and for all. In years to come, it would seem to Amy as though this were a defining moment in her life, the moment from which all events sprang and to which all previous events led. Right now, however, she was filled with the urge to run. Defying her brain, her hands reached slowly down into the bag and pulled away the top layer. She expected paper, but the substance yielded to her shaky touch. Fabric. A rough, white towel. Gingerly pulling at the folds, Amy's heart beat full in her throat. Could this be what she thought it was? No. This sort of thing only happens on the local news. To other people. People walking through deprived areas. Not her. And definitely not in Chelsea. But in this she was wrong, for nestling under the thin layer of toweling, bathed in the soft nursery light of the shop window, lay a tiny baby girl, her bloody, blackened umbilical cord curled around its base, her fist crammed into her tiny mouth. Somewhere on a rooftop in Docklands, three magpies crowed loudly into the night. Three for a girl.

.10.

Other people, Amy felt, would know instinctively what to do. For them, this moment would be the one in which they came into their own, they proved themselves to be the useful, worldly-wise yet caring individuals they were. Amy froze. A small piece of her was telling her that this was obviously some kind of trick of the light, and that if she were to blink hard a few times and rub her eyes, like in the movies, the apparition would disappear. She did so, dimly aware of the absurdness of the gesture. She looked sharply up and down the road, checking for any candid cameras or any retreating guilty figures. Nothing. The tiny parcel began an insistent campaign of choked screams, having sensed the presence of a big person nearby. Amy reached down and clasped the string handles experimentally in one hand. Would the bag carry the weight of its bizarre contents? She lifted it a few inches from the ground. It was solid but light. Setting it down again, she hurried to unlock the door and carefully, carefully, she carried the bag into the shop—at arm's length, as though it contained an unexploded bomb that might go off at any minute. "The

Teddy Bears' Picnic" showed no such sensitivity. It had never sounded so loud and inappropriate. Nevertheless, the bomb stopped its crying and instantly fell silent inside the bag.

Once inside, she set the bag down and perched on the step by the door, wondering what the hell to do. What was it you were meant to do? Phone the police? The idea of two burly officers attaching an exhibit label and carting off the bag seemed wrong. Take it to the nearest hospital? Yes, this seemed like the right course of action. It would have to be checked out to make sure it was OK. Amy sat shivering, still in shock, and wondering about the mother who was somewhere out there, knowing that her baby had been left to fate. *How desperate would you have to be*, thought Amy, *to abandon a child on a doorstep?* Surely there were hostels, safe places of refuge you could go for help if you felt you couldn't cope? Wasn't this the responsibility of Social Services? It certainly wasn't her responsibility. Amy let herself become aware of a new emotion—irritation. Why her? She could do without this. There would be statements to make, questions to answer. Pushing the feeling away, quietly appalled by the depths of her selfishness, she resolved to transfer the baby into a basket and wrap it up nice and warm for the trip to the hospital. She could flag a cab on Walton Street. She picked out a small Moses basket, ready-made up with Peter Rabbit blankets and sheets, and placed it on the floor next to the bag. She wasn't sure how to complete the transfer—did she reach in and lift the baby out under its arms? Surely it was too small and its head would loll on its shoulders alarmingly. She decided to rip the bag down its middle and pull the baby out through the opening— a kind of cross between a C-section and repotting a plant. Incision complete, she slowly pulled the wriggling bundle of cloth out onto the carpet. The towel fell away from its little face and it opened its eyes, blinking in the glow of the streetlight outside.

Amy gasped. It was a beautiful baby. She knew that because she had seen many ugly ones declared bonny by their doting, biased parents, but she had no investment in self-deception. Its soft head was covered in tiny, tufty blond curls, its lips were a perfect pink cupid's bow, and its eyes were large and shiny. She tentatively scooped it up in her arms and began to lay it down in the basket. Should she dress it? The idea of trying to force tiny, breakable limbs into unfamiliar clothing was just too daunting, so Amy pressed a couple of fluffy blankets around the edges of the baby as she lowered her into the basket. At the last minute, she shamed herself by opting to cover the expensive linen and handwoven crib with a clean paper carrier—no point soiling shop goods for a ten-minute cab journey. The baby spread its tiny limbs out and gurgled appreciatively, rustling the paper bag beneath it with every move.

Out on the street, a couple walked arm in arm up the road. Inexplicably, they paid no attention to Amy or her basket. "Look!" she wanted to shout. "Someone's left a baby on my doorstep!" But she realized to the outside world she just looked like a mum taking her baby out to visit friends, or home to a cozy bed. From the bottom of the street, she saw the glow of a cab light heading her way, itself a minor miracle at eight o'clock on a Friday night.

"Chelsea and Westminster Hospital, please," she ordered, setting the basket down on the seat next to her.

"OK, love. How old?" asked the cabbie.

"Sorry?"

"How old is he?"

"Oh, it's a girl actually . . . erm, very small."

"Aah, congratulations love!"

Amy did her best approximation of a proud new mum smile. Later, she'd wonder why she didn't just tell the driver what had happened, tell him that the baby was not hers at all and that it had been left on the doorstep of her exclusive baby shop, probably by some desperate teenage mum who'd hidden her pregnancy from her family for nine months before giving birth in an alley and dumping the poor thing. If she were to examine her feelings honestly, she would have found that her reason was touchingly girlish; in a private, seedling part of herself, a part not yet exposed to the light of day, a part that would shrivel with shame if it were to be prematurely revealed, Amy felt foolishly happy to be, for eleven and a half minutes, the mother of the bundle beside her. It was like the time she was cast as the Virgin Mary in the school Nativity play, only better because this time she didn't have to wear a blue pillowcase on her head, and this baby was real.

. 11 .

The hospital was too bright and far too loud after the womb-like darkness of the cab. It was fairly quiet still, caught in that liminal period between the day's appointments and the late-night drunken fighters and junkies. A cleaner mopped a corridor halfheartedly, and the air was thick with thin bleach. It all seemed too calm a backdrop to her amazing drama. Amy stopped just inside the entrance to Accident and Emergency, not knowing where to go—antenatal reception? Emergency? Lost Property? She settled for Antenatal—she wasn't pregnant, but they'd know what to do.

The heavy door, however, was shut, the department having long dispatched with its duties toward its waddling clients. The wards, then. She headed for the first mother-and-baby ward, swimming against the tide of the end of visiting hours. An extremely tired-looking nurse sat alone at the nurses' station.

"I'm sorry, darling, visiting finished now," she said without looking up from her book.

"I'm not here to see anyone—is there a doctor around?" asked Amy, anxious not to have to tell her story more than once.

"No darlin', not 'til the night rounds, eleven o'clockish," said the nurse. "But you can go to the emergency room if you need to see a doctor."

"No, I don't, but this baby does."

"The doctors there will look after you, darlin'," said the nurse, finishing the conversation.

"Well I don't know if it's ill. . . ."

The nurse looked up now, clearly wondering if she should direct the well-dressed lady in front of her to the psychiatric wing. It was no use—Amy would have to spill her story here first before talking to the authorities.

"Sorry, I'm not making myself clear," Amy began, knowing that her next sentence would set in motion a chain of events that would take the entire situation out of her hands.

Back in the shop, she had wanted only that—for someone else to deal with it. But somewhere between Walton Street and Brompton Road, something inside her had altered, shifted slightly forever. Now her head suddenly flooded with the fantasy of fleeing, bundle and all. What if she were to turn now, thanking the nurse, and walk casually out of the hospital and into a cab? She could be home in forty minutes, fifty if she stopped to pick up baby formula and nappies, a sleepsuit from the all-night Tesco. *Who would know?* Surely it would be better for the baby to come back with her now than be left here in the impersonal world of Social Services, who'd wrap the baby in miles of red tape and petty bureaucracy? Even as these thoughts invaded, Amy knew she would never do such a thing. Like it or not, the baby must be deposited safely into the hands of the experts. It wasn't like finding ten pounds or a nice handbag dumped in a bin. There was every chance the mother might come forward, regretting her decision. Amy took a deep breath.

"At about half past seven this evening I found this baby on the doorstep of my shop in Walton Street."

The nurse blinked slowly, failing to adopt the amazed expression Amy had anticipated.

Amy continued.

"I don't know who the mother is—but it looks OK. It was wrapped in a towel. I put it in this basket."

Amy raised the baby shoulder-high, as if trying to prove an unlikely story. The nurse eyed the beautifully woven basket suspiciously.

"Where did you get the basket?"

"From my shop. I make them. Well, I design them and have them made. It's a baby shop."

The nurse kept one eye on Amy and came round to the front of the desk. She peered slowly into the bundle of cloth, as if expecting to find something else entirely—a brick, a pizza, a litter of puppies—and not wanting to look foolish. Her entire body changed when she spotted the little purple fist that shot out from under a fold.

"Lord, preserve us!" she exclaimed, and let out a raucous laugh. "You say you found this baby? On the doorstep?"

"Yes—it was just left there—sometime between six and half past seven. I left the shop at six, and when I came back it was just sitting there in a carrier bag." Amy felt stupidly guilty, as if at any minute she'd have to confess it was her baby after all. Uniforms made her nervous—it was a Catholic thing.

"Wait there—I'll call a doctor."

What now? thought Amy as she stood waiting awkwardly. She'd have to tell the whole story again.

Minutes passed. The baby began to stir. From somewhere behind a grubby curtain, a baby began to wail. Then another. That was the trouble with these open maternity wards—once one started, they all joined in. Amy's bundle quickly realized it was among its compadres and struck up its own piercing scream. Amy knelt beside it, rocking the basket gently. No chance. The baby revved up a gear, opening its mouth with gusto and showing the gummy tooth buds beneath the skin as if to say, "You think that's crying? I'll show you crying!" She tried talking to it, hotly aware of her inadequate baby talk. "There, there, petal, don't upset yourself . . . ssshhh."

Still the baby wailed. There was nothing else for it; she'd have to pick it up.

"Come on, you, let's get you out of there so you stop making such a fuss," she said, inexpertly shuffling baby and towel from hand to hand, trying to ditch the paper bag underneath.

She raised the baby unsteadily to one shoulder as she'd seen Angela do a thousand times. The baby continued its howling. *So small and yet so loud!* Lowering it again, she cradled it in the nook of her arm and it stopped almost immediately, shocked by the new intimacy. Amy couldn't help but smile as the baby instinctively rooted toward her breast, mouth open, fists punching the air.

"You'll get nothing from that, petal. Those are a suckle-free zone, I'm afraid."

The baby wriggled insistently for a few moments before seeming to give up the fight. Its eyelids drooped heavily. Amy found herself smiling down at the little face, every inch the adoring mother. The baby had completely relaxed. With a strange certainty, Amy knew this was the first proper cuddle this baby had ever had. She pulled her closer, feeling the importance of the moment.

"Hello," said a chocolate steel voice.

Shaken from her special moment, Amy looked up. Standing before her was a man of about forty, wearing a white shirt and black trousers. His hair was wavy and peppered with gray, but she could tell he had once been very dark. If it weren't for the stethoscope, she'd have sworn he was a leering Italian waiter about to offer her black pepper from an oversized grinder. He wore the instrument casually around his neck as they did in hospital dramas, which only added to the feeling that he was not quite real—an actor in a role, a doctor from central casting.

"Hello," said Amy, smiling gratefully. Real or not, he looked as though he'd know what to do.

"I'm Joseph Nencini; I'm the duty doctor here this evening. The nurse said you found this baby?" he asked, sounding as if he expected a stupid misunderstanding, a withdrawal of an unlikely story.

"Yes. Yes, it was just left there."

"Let's have a look," he said, taking Amy's elbow gently and guiding her to a cubicle. He pulled the curtain while Amy set the baby down on the stripped bed. She was appalled by how acutely aware she was of the proximity of the handsome doctor—at a time like this.

Joe quickly unwrapped the bundle. A greeny-yellow mess had spread across the otherwise clean towel. The smell quickly filled the cubicle.

"Yep. That's a baby all right," he said, taking his stethoscope from his neck and beginning to examine her.

"It's tiny—it must be hours old."

"No, it's about a week old, I'd say. See that black stump there on the belly button? It's about to drop off."

"Oh," said Amy, not really understanding at all. "Is that normal?"

"That happens after about a week."

A week. Was it born last Friday? Amy's birthday. For some reason, Amy found herself really hoping so.

She sat in the plastic chair while Joe carried out his basic tests. She watched as his large hands worked on the small child, checking the pulse, the reflexes, the eyes and ears. Capable hands. Goalie's hands. She noted with a small sense of deflation the simple gold band on his wedding finger. *Damn.* Still, how could she expect a good-looking professional like him to be on the market? Things like that only ever happened in the movies. The baby responded to his sure touch with a yielding floppiness. Given the circumstances, Amy felt sure she would have done the same.

"Right, let's get you a nappy and something to wear, and let's see if we can rustle up a bottle. God knows when you last had a feed," said the good doctor, whipping the curtain back and looking around for a nurse.

"No note attached to the cot?"

"Well, no, she was actually in this bag. . . ." said Amy, holding up the Precious Little Darlings carrier.

"Precious Little Darlings? Well, let's call you Precious, shall we?" said Joe, stroking the baby's head and placing a gentle kiss on her limp hand. Were they meant to do things like that? Whether or not it was strictly speaking professional, Amy warmed to the sight. Up until now, he had been pure business. But who could fail to be moved by the plight of an abandoned baby in a big paper bag? Didn't she deserve a little unconditional affection?

"Hold her, would you, while I try to find someone, Miss . . ."

"Amy. Amy Stokes," she said, accepting Precious back into her arms. Joe passed her the baby so quickly and expertly that Amy had to raise her game immediately. She was getting the hang of it, and this time did not let the baby's head droop.

She stood waiting. No doubt the questions would start again, the police would arrive, then social workers. This was probably her last moment with the baby. She pushed away the soppiness of the thought and marveled at how people could be so detached as to dump a child on a doorstep in the dark. It seemed so fundamentally unfair that couples like Soph and Greg and women like Mrs. Cummings should have to suffer the ordeal of fertility treatments, the endless disappointment and the needlessly empty crib, when babies the world over were being discarded like fast-food wrappers on streets, in toilets, and in public phone boxes.

The swinging doors flew open and Joe marched back down the corridor, followed by two young nurses.

"Amy, this is Kath and this is Sylvie—they'll take care of Precious now. If you'd like to come with me, I've called the police and I'm sure they'd like to have a chat with you, just to get the facts right. Coffee?"

And in an instant, Precious was being whisked away by the cooing nurses, who were obviously honored to be entrusted with such leading roles in the drama.

The café was long shut, so Joe fiddled around for change at the dated seventies vending machine. An apologetic approximation of cappuccino half-filled two cups, and they sat on a bench to wait. Porters and medics bustled up and down the corridor, laughing and joking.

"This is so . . . surreal," said Amy, flinching at the inadequacy of the word.

"Yes. It's not the first time, I'm afraid. A baby gets abandoned like that every day somewhere in the world. Every few hours, actually. We've had quite a few here in the last decade or so. Have to say it's a first for me, but it happens all the time," said Joe, stretching his legs out in front of him. Amy envied his ease in the environment.

"So . . . what happens now?" asked Amy, aware that she felt nervous of the response. Having been involved this far, she couldn't accept that the baby's fate was totally out of her hands.

"Well, she seems OK; she might be a bit dehydrated, but we'll soon sort that out. They're quite hardy little things, really. The police and social workers will be here soon. We might have to keep her here for a couple of days, just to keep an eye on her, then she'll be placed in emergency foster care pending inquiries."

"Inquiries?"

"Yes, I'm not quite sure of the exact statistics, but nearly all of the mothers come forward or are found sooner or later. Then they'll be assessed and everyone will decide what to do for the best. Chances are, Precious will be reunited with her mother, with heavy social worker presence, of course."

"Oh," said Amy, bleakly, feeling inexplicably disappointed.

Joe raised a quizzical eyebrow.

"And what happens now?" he countered. The question hung in the air for a few seconds as Amy tried to work out its precise meaning.

What happens now? Was he asking about what she would do when she left the hospital? Or was he trying to counsel her? Did she look upset? Did he doubt her story? Amy decided to square up to the question. She looked up from her cup and realized with a start that he was flirting with her. His eyes twinkled and one corner of his mouth was doing its best to hold back an amused smile. Typical Italian, married and using a time like this to try to make another conquest.

"Well, I'll get a taxi home and open a bottle of wine, I suppose," she said, trying to keep her voice as light as possible. She felt the sting of loneliness in the image nonetheless.

"Sounds nice," said Joe, stretching again. "Anyone at home waiting?" he threw in, all casual indifference. That old chestnut.

"Actually, no, I live on my own—I prefer it that way. I've got a lot of shoes," said Amy, rather more hotly than she had intended.

"I'm not prying, it's just that you've had a shock and you might need to talk to someone about it, that's all," said Joe levelly.

Damn these nice doctors with their caring manner, thought Amy, irritated at herself for assuming his personal interest. No doubt he'd be finishing his shift, going home, and falling into bed with his beautiful and effortlessly sexy wife, who would wake and snuggle up to him while he poured out the stories of the day before making textbook good love to her.

"Oh, I'll be all right."

"Tough chick, eh?" twinkled Joe. She felt as though he were ruffling her hair playfully.

Men always said this kind of thing to her, and it always felt more like a rebuke than a compliment. It was as if they resented her lack of need of them. They liked her well enough, but they had to diffuse her in some way—mostly by treating her as a tomboy niece. It was the most infuriating sort of exchange she ever had with men, and it was always the really attractive, capable men who reacted to her in this way.

"Oh, and they might want your picture for the local paper. Are you a local?"

"No, but I work locally. It's my shop. Precious Little Darlings."

"The baby place on Walton Street? You work there?"

"I own it."

"Wow. That's a very exclusive shop. You must be worth a few quid then," said Joe without any of the thinly veiled envy that usually accompanied the observation.

"I do all right," she said.

He again smiled his secret, amused smile and held her defiant gaze for a beat too long.

"Here they are," he said, nodding ahead to where a female police officer, her male colleague, and a couple of social workers had appeared. The PC's radio burst to life intermittently, sending its unintelligible static codes reverberating up the length of the corridor, announcing that this matter was now in the hands of the authorities. Wordlessly, Amy and Joe rose to greet them, and the handover began.

.12.

To a casual observer, the scene must have been nauseatingly Disney. They were licking ice creams covered in both chocolate and raspberry sauce. Crushed nuts and multicolored sprinkles dotted the tops, and the warm sun sent rivers of sticky goo down each of the crisp cones. He had one hand on the stroller handle and the other clasping her waist. They walked slowly, taking in the early good weather. The floral sun hat flopped over the baby's eyes as it slept blissfully in the buggy. He bent down to Amy's face and planted an ice-cream kiss on her nose. She retaliated by playfully daubing him with chocolate sauce. Laughing, he wiped his cheek and kissed her full on the lips, stopping to concentrate on the task at hand. It was a long, deep kiss. If there had been cameras, they would have swooped round a full three hundred and sixty degrees to capture the moment from all angles. If Walt were indeed responsible for the scene, cartoon bluebirds would begin serenading them in fully blossomed trees, and doe-eyed fawns would emerge from the nearby woodland to bat their eyelashes in wonder. But this was no Disney movie.

Suddenly, the baby struck up its crying, the rolling motion of the stroller having stopped. Reluctantly, they broke off from their embrace, laughing not unkindly at the bad timing. Amy found it almost impossible to tear her gaze from his adoring face. She had never felt so utterly, stupidly happy. But something was wrong now. The wind picked up, and a loud beating of wings stirred her from her trance. Turning her head from his, her smile fading, Amy looked up just in time to see three gigantic magpies swooping in a V-formation directly toward the baby. She screamed but, just like in her worst nightmares, no noise came out. He was frozen, his face still in the rictus of an absurd grin, as the magpies each effortlessly took hold of a section of the baby's summer dress and lifted her clean out of the pram, then up, up, and away into the cloudless sky. Amy stood horrified on the pathway, her mouth making a silent, black O.

"Ak ak ak ak ak!"

Nine thirty-nine. Amy pulled the mask from her eyes and sat bolt upright in bed. Her heart beat fast, and her mouth still gaped open as she took in the familiar surroundings.

"Ak ak ak ak ak!"

The magpies had interrupted her dream, perhaps sickened by the clichéd representation of domestic bliss. Funny how the outside world could act as an arbiter of good taste, censoring the unconscious. The blurry events of the previous evening came into focus now—had they too been a dream? The pub, the baby in a bag, the hospital, the police, the stunned ride home in a taxi, the large scotch? The empty tumbler next to her bed bore testimony to the realness of at least the scotch. Amy lay back in the bed and went over the extraordinary incident. It seemed as though the last week—ever since her birthday, and perhaps the baby's birthday, too—had been a series of trials. The awful dinner party, the death of Germaine, the sense of her own superfluousness at work capped by finding the child at her closed door felt like a bizarre and awful obstacle course sent from the heavens to test her. But test her for what purpose? If Amy believed in seraphim and cherubim, she would have felt the soft beating of angelic wings all week, urging her on to some personal discovery or other. As it was, she lay now and tried to work out what it all meant. Three for a girl—how dim she'd been, not clocking the old rhyme. Perhaps the magpies had known all along. Perhaps they had heralded the birth of Precious that Friday morning, and were telling her something now, prompting her to another strange supernatural occurrence. She wondered now what had made her go back to the shop, leaving a full pint and the promise of cheerful oblivion at The Wheelbarrow. Had some divine presence sent her to rescue the abandoned child? Was she the chosen one sent to deliver the foundling to a safe haven? If she was so blessed, why had the preceding events been so bloody awful? How could a chosen one be allowed to run over her own dog, to suffer the frightening hollowness that had chased her all week? Still, she had slept soundly for the first time in ages, and had woken reassuringly late.

Amy lay thinking for a few minutes. *Was that it, then?* She'd handed Precious over to the right people, and now what? Precious. The shop name had been a twee private joke. She had never dreamed it would one day, however temporarily, provide a child's name. She wondered what was happening at the hospital. There would be a change of shifts, and new nurses would be caring for Precious now, filled in on her sad story secondhand. Did tiny babies recognize people? Would Precious be alarmed by the ever-changing sea of faces looming into her blurry vision? Although she could not understand language, could Precious grasp the fact that she had been left, unwanted, on a strange doorstep wrapped in an old towel, buried at the bottom of a carrier bag? Amy shuddered as she remembered her foot raised ready to kick the bundle, assuming it to be full of nesting vermin. Did Precious sense that? She had cried out at precisely the right moment. For someone who worked in children's furnishings, it struck her now just how little she knew about children. Despite the hundreds, thousands of babies who slept surrounded and cocooned by her creative efforts every night, who had been pushed unwillingly in and out of her shops over the past fifteen years, she knew virtually nothing about them. The endless competitive chatter of the posh mums who frequented her work life had rendered her voluntarily deaf to any talk of babies and their capabilities. Besides, wasn't it all just vain speculation? How could anyone really know whether a baby thinks, or whether it feels anything other than physical need? These women spent hours pontificating on the subtle shifts of mood in their offspring, comparing notes on which baby sensed anxiety the most, or which responded most warmly to positive affirmation. She had once overheard the mother of a three-week-old infant describe how he "couldn't be around cynicism." Wasn't this all just a ridiculous attempt to commandeer the great unknown process by which we all become sentient beings, superior to our ape ancestors?

With an abrupt urgency, Amy's mobile sprung to life. She had a text message. It was from Soph.

"Hi U—where U bin? Call me ASAP x."

Would Soph know about babies? At least she'd be someone to tell the story to. Amy needed perspective.

"Hi, Soph. How are you?" said Amy, biding her time for the moment when she could unleash her amazing event.

"Amy! I've just been sick! I'm fantastic!" shrieked Soph on the other end of the line.

Was this what Amy thought it was?

"Oh my God—what's happened?"

"I've only gone and got pregnant!"

"No! It worked! How do you know—I mean, are you sure? Oh my God."

"Yes, I'm sure. We don't go to the hospital for another week, but last night I just had this weird feeling, so I used up the last of my pregnancy-testing things—you know, the early-detection ones—and the first window showed a blue line, which is just to say it's worked, and almost straight away the second one went blue, too—that's the magic window! The one that means you're pregnant! I can't believe it! And now I've just been sick!"

"But hold on, Soph, I thought it took ten days after implantation—surely you should wait 'til you see the consultant again before you get too excited?" said Amy, aware that she had just pissed on a very large fire from a great height.

There was a short silence at the end of the line. When Soph spoke, her voice was softer, calmer, winded.

"Yes, I know I shouldn't get my hopes up, but I really know it's different this time, Amy, I really feel it. I really think this is it. Please let me be excited, please?" pleaded Soph.

Amy felt horrible. She didn't want to be the evil older sister who waited 'til Christmas Eve to tell her sibling that Santa did not exist.

"OK. Sorry, Soph. Just worried about you, that's all. It's fantastic news. I can't wait. Love to Greg."

Her phone beeped intermittently. Call waiting. Jules. Early for her on a Saturday morning.

"Now go and put your feet up, Mummy. I've got to go. Call me later."

Her story could wait. She didn't want to steal any baby limelight. Jules could be the first to hear it instead, even though she'd have to play down her own emotional involvement in the night's events.

"Hi, Jules—you're up bright and early."

"Hiya. Yeah, it's been a bit of a night!" said Jules, sounding croaky. No doubt she'd been out clubbing, trying to find a twenty-year-old to take her home and make her forget her most recent relationship traumas. She'd probably just got in from some grotty boy's flat in Hoxton or somewhere. Amy felt a pang of jealousy, but the reaction was knee-jerk. In reality, she was glad she'd been where she'd been the night before, and she'd had her own frisson, even if it was just with a flirty married man.

"Big night out?" asked Amy, preparing for a blow-by-blow account.

"No, no, nothing like that. Erm, Justin came back last night," said Jules, sounding oddly nervous. Did she expect Amy to disapprove? To lecture her again on the patheticness of accepting him back time and time again? Amy was long past that.

"Well . . . that's great, isn't it? So he left the dental nurse?"

"Oh, that was just a stupid mistake."

"Of course. So what prompted his return this time?" asked Amy, trying to keep the judgment out of her voice.

"Well . . . he . . . I . . . " Jules tried to start the no doubt convoluted explanation but stopped, choking back what sounded like tears.

"Jules? What's wrong?"

"He . . . I told him I'm pregnant!"

Amy considered the many possibilities here. Had Jules sunk so low in the self-esteem stakes that she'd resorted to The Big Lie? The untruth so beloved of daytime TV victims? Or had she simply gone mad? The obvious answer, that her closest work and play buddy, fellow cynic and good-time girl, had indeed managed to conceive a child, seemed too ridiculous to entertain.

"But . . . I thought you didn't want to . . . I mean, when?" spluttered Amy.

"I didn't mean to, I didn't think I could, I mean, I really thought I was too old and clapped out, but, you know, my periods have been funny, so I thought nothing of it at first, but I'm almost six weeks pregnant. . . ."

"Is it Justin's?" Amy knew she of all people could ask that question.

"Yes, yes, I worked out the dates yesterday after I'd been to the doctors. . . . I haven't been with anyone else for three months."

"So . . . what are you going to do? I mean, if you want me to come with you again, I'll be happy to—I mean, not *happy* but . . . you know." Jules had already gone through two terminations in the past four years. It was turning into a bad habit.

"No, no. Thanks. We've been up most of the night talking, and I think we're going to have it. I mean, I know we're going to have it. That's if it sticks. It's early days yet."

"My God. And how do you feel?" asked Amy, reeling from the about-turn.

There was a deep inhalation at the end of the line.

"I feel wonderful. I'm so happy!" blurted Jules, breaking into floods of tears. Amy could hear Justin soothing her in the background.

"Anyway, I know you'll hate me and I'll probably lose you as a friend 'cause you hate sponge-brained mothers, but I just wanted you to know how happy we are."

"I won't hate you! That's a terrible thing to say!"

"I know, but you know how you are . . . so I just wanted to tell you first."

"Well, I'm honored, and if you're both happy, then I'm happy."

Amy's phone began to beep again. Call waiting.

"Listen, I'll call you later, hon—and well done!"

Amy steadied herself on the bed. The phone had become a harbinger of baby doom—the stalk's hotline.

"Hello, slapper," said Brendan.

"Don't tell me, you're pregnant," said Amy flatly.

"What?"

"Nothing. I'll explain later. Meet me at Chelsea and Westminster Hospital at twelve."

Amy screeched out of the underground garage with a surprising sense of urgency. Just in time, she spotted the young mum from the previous week's encounter about to push her pram off the curb and directly into Amy's path. She slammed on the brakes. The girl hesitated, unsure if this was some sort of cruel cat-and-mouse game. Amy smiled uneasily and gestured for the girl to cross. Teenage Mum pushed her pram gingerly in front of the car's bumper, maintaining eye contact throughout. Safely on the other side, she mouthed a baffled "Thanks." Amy nodded and sped off. She was going soft in her old age.

Why she felt such a keen need to see baby Precious again was not immediately apparent, even to her. She felt as though she needed to confirm that it had happened, that she hadn't dreamt it all. The morning's revelations had been so incredible that she had felt a strange sense of shifting ground. Taking Brendan would be a way of sharing the oddness of it all, and besides, she had a vested interest in the child's well-being, since she had delivered it to safety. It wasn't so weird, was it? On the way past the shop, she might even swing by and pick up a few bits and pieces for the baby—a cot toy, a sleepsuit or two. The hospital would have only depressing institutional emergency clothing, and baby Precious deserved a bit better than that after all she'd been through.

The Saturday girls at the shop were surprised to see her so soon after her extended vacation had begun. They hurriedly switched off the commercial radio station they had blaring out and concentrated on looking busy. They were even more surprised when she stuffed a bag full of newborn goodies, muttering something about needing samples. Amy couldn't get out of the shop quick enough, away from prying questions and the no doubt tearful scenes that would accompany her story, should she have decided to spill it there. They'd hear about it all in time. She paused briefly on the doorstep to examine the spot where Precious had been left. Nothing remarkable about it—just a concrete step. No glow, no guiding star in the sky, no manger of hay. It was just a terrestrial baby very much of, if not wanted in, this world.

Brendan stood smoking outside the hospital entrance with a look of amused indifference on his face as Amy approached.

"Who are we visiting? Or are you finally giving in and letting them lobotomize you?"

"Come on, let's go inside and I'll explain."

In the lift up to the maternity ward, she summarized the events of the last twenty-four hours. Brendan caught the newly sensitized tone in his friend's voice and for once desisted from crass jokes. Miracles would never cease, or so it seemed to Amy.

She felt a curious fluttering in her stomach—was it nerves? Why was she nervous? What did she think was going to happen? She'd see that Precious was being well cared for, leave her gifts, and then go out for a nice lunch with Brendan. Nothing to be anxious about.

The nurses' station was humming with activity. An Asian woman was trying to explain that she needed a bottle sterilizer, and a large blonde sister was bullying her into breast-feeding again. Amy and Brendan stood awkwardly, awaiting their turn for the harsh treatment.

"Yes?"

"We've come to see baby Preci—"

"I'm sorry, visiting hours don't start until three," barked the sister, returning to her paperwork.

"Well, it's a bit different, I—"

"Are you family?" the sister asked impatiently.

"Well, not exactly . . ." started Amy. "I found her abandoned last night, and I just wanted to drop a few things off for her. . . ." She tailed off now, feeling foolish under the harsh lights and the blank stare.

The sister softened her face.

"Oh, I see. Well, well done, you. If you just wait a moment, I'll get someone to see to you."

She gestured toward the plastic chairs in the corner. From a distance, Amy saw the sister speaking quietly into the phone. She smiled at Amy and Brendan in a professional approximation of warmth.

"I've never been in a baby ward," said Brendan. He smiled excitedly, glad to be part of such a great story. Amy was glad he was there, too—she hadn't realized just how much of an impact the event had had on her, and what with this morning's baby news, she felt in need of a little grounding humor. Say what you like about him, Brendan was good in a crisis, his natural sense of drama coming to the fore and his "screw them all" mentality truly liberating.

"I didn't think men were allowed in unless they were the father. All those engorged nipples lolling about. Urgh!" He shuddered, more for comic effect than any real sense of discomfort.

"Where is she?" asked a familiar voice from behind them. Amy turned to see the good doctor leaning over the nurses' station. He caught her eye and broke into a spontaneous smile.

"Hello again—can't keep you away, can we?"

"Hi," said Amy, willing her cheeks to stop flushing. He was even better looking in daylight.

"You're on again?" she asked, making it clear she was not expecting to see him, that he was not the reason for her visit.

"Haven't been home since I saw you last. We don't do nine to five like you shopgirls."

Brendan shot her a quizzical, "Who is this handsome stranger?" look.

"Brendan, this is Dr. Nencini. This is Brendan." She wanted to add "my friend" but cringed at the pointedness of the word. Married men of Joe's age needed little encouragement, and Amy reminded herself again that she was not interested in sloppy seconds. Her "bit on the side" days were well and truly over.

"This is for Precious," said Amy, awkwardly thrusting the bag at Joe. "I just thought it might be nice to bring her a few things."

"Oh, good idea, yes, I'll make sure she gets them," said Joe, picking up her awkwardness along with the bag.

"Is she OK?" asked Amy, hoping for a quick look. She wanted Brendan to see, too, to witness or something, she wasn't quite sure.

"Can we see her?" asked Brendan, pushy as ever. Despite her sense of decorum, Amy was glad of his abruptness now—she didn't know if she could have asked.

"Well, that might be difficult. . . ." said Joe. It was his turn to feel awkward.

"Oh, just for a minute. Amy just wants to see that she's all right. She's had me up half the night worrying about her, the silly old muddlehead, haven't you, darling?" Amy winced at the couple role-play Brendan was so fond of lapsing into. Still, if it had the desired effect and she got to see Precious before she was whisked off into care, so much the better.

"I'm afraid she's gone. They came for her this morning. Apparently, they've found a great emergency foster mum nearby who was able to take her in."

"But I thought you said she'd need to stay here for a few days!" said Amy, shocked at her indignation. She felt oddly cheated.

"Well, I thought we might keep her in, but she was fit as a fiddle, and it would be so much better for her to be in a home environment, don't you think?" Amy felt the pacifying tone in his voice and flushed with shame at her emotional outburst. *Damn him.* He had a way of hacking right into her Achilles heel. She hated to look vulnerable or needy in front of men. Especially gorgeous men.

"Of course. I'm glad she's OK. I just wanted to make sure; you know, I can't help but feel a sense of civic duty," she said, sounding far too pompous now.

"Of course," echoed Joe. She knew he was being kind, but still she felt stung by his echoing of her.

"Look, if I hear anything, I'll let you know. I'm sure she'll be fine. Leave your number at the desk, and I'll make sure you know if anything happens, if the mother comes forward or whatever," Joe said now, his beeper calling him to some other scene in the hospital.

"OK," said Amy, grateful of this lifeline. Though quite why she felt so at sea was yet to become clear to her.

They watched in silence as Dr. Nencini's perfect bottom receded into the distance.

"Wedding ring," Brendan intoned flatly.

"Bugger," sighed Amy.

"Pub."

"Absolutely."

. 13 .

Somewhere between the car park and the pub, Amy's life path took an unexpected turn. She couldn't say exactly which particular incident it was that prompted the extraordinary sea change she felt growing in her heart, but she had a strong, shocking, contrary awareness that she was about to undertake the most unlikely project she could have ever predicted. Caught up in her thoughts, she was barely conscious of Brendan's babbling.

"God, he was gorgeous! Like a cross between a young John Travolta and Enrique Iglesias. What's he doing wasting himself on the NHS? Now I can see why you wanted to go back—baby my ass! You just wanted to check out the doctor again. Have to hand it to you, though, great excuse. And I'm sure he's right—Dr. Handsome—she's much better off in care."

Amy winced. It seemed so sudden, so cruel, that a baby should be left out in the cold, then found and taken to safety, only to be carted off again the very next morning to some strange, probably overstretched household. Could she have done any more? She had briefly entertained the mad idea of taking Precious home herself, but she was sane enough to know that adopting or even fostering a child was the end result of a laborious screening process whereby your whole lifestyle and personality were shredded in front of your very eyes, and only then would you even be considered for adoption. Such a rigorous procedure for such desperate children. Still, she understood it had to be this way to ensure the best for the child—who had already been let down once—and the suitability of the would-be parent. She had quickly put such thoughts out of her mind, not even stopping to register her unexpectedly maternal response to a child in need. She would have to leave Precious behind and trust she would be well-looked-after. Perhaps the baby would have a happy ending and be reunited with her contrite mother, who would receive support and understanding. One thing was for sure: Beyond finding her, Amy's contribution to Precious's life was over. Little did Precious know that her contribution to Amy's life had only just begun—because a new idea had planted itself firmly in Amy's head before the first set of traffic lights. She was at once appalled and thrilled by it. If the last couple of weeks had taught her anything, it was that life conspires sometimes to push us, blindfolded, into situations we thought we would never end up in. However much we think we know what we want, however much we plan for a perfectly designed future, fate has a way of shoving the unforeseen in our faces and presenting us with a whole new set of options.

She swerved suddenly onto the shoulder, her steering wheel and her psyche seemingly no longer under her tight control. Brendan stopped mid-sentence and swore loudly as she jolted to a halt.

"Christ, what are you doing?"

"Brendan, I want you to listen carefully to what I'm about to say, and when I've finished, I want you to fully support everything that I've said. Furthermore, I don't want you to breathe a word of this to anyone, not *anyone*, until I say so. OK?"

Brendan nodded in mute agreement.

"I'm going to try for a baby. I don't know how or even why really, but it suddenly seems essential that I see if I'm meant to have a child."

"But—"

"Uh-uh! No comments, no questions, I don't want you fogging things up, and I know what you're going to say, and you're probably right, but it's just something I have to do, no matter how mad that may seem to you and me right now. Let's just say I am now aware that there have been greater forces at work on this than you or I can feasibly argue with. OK?"

"OK," said Brendan, nodding slowly as if humoring a dangerous psycho.

"OK."

.14.

For two hours, she had not spoken about it with Brendan. They had proceeded with lunch as normal, all the while knowing that a huge volcano lay bubbling under the surface of their chitchat. Secretly, Amy thought of nothing else. She didn't feel suddenly enlightened or excited by her new plan, just purposeful in a resigned kind of way. Home now, she played with the idea in the privacy of her bedroom. With an experimental thrill, Amy tested the idea out loud: "I'm going to have a baby." The words fell like awkwardly shaped pebbles from her lips. This was someone else's script, a line delivered to much oohing and aahing and delighted embracing. She tested it again, hoping that voicing the idea would implant it in her own reality.

"I'm going to have a baby. I'm pregnant." The dramatic addition made her smile at its improbability. Amy Stokes pregnant? The head of an internationally successful design business reduced to a mere biological function? Surely not! It sounded as plausible as saying, "I'm Joseph Stalin." But having opened up the possibility, she became aware now of new thoughts, new sensations beginning to flood in like grateful children from a cold playground. Yes, it was a spectacular U-turn of the highest order; yes, her friends would be horrified and overexcited by turns; and yes, irritatingly enough, it would delight her mother to no end, but despite all these pressurizing expectations and all the inevitable I told you so's from a smug Brendan, the idea still held enough sway to create a new stillness in Amy's heart. *What if? What if?* Amy tried to imagine herself heavily pregnant. With only a modicum of self-consciousness, she rolled up a cushion and stuffed it up her tight sweater, creating the immediate impression of someone about ten months gone and about to give birth to a small sofa. With a bit of artful maneuvering, she managed to reduce the bulk and mold it into a plausible shape. She turned sideways and looked in her mirror, placing one hand on her bump and practicing that beatific smile so beloved of pregnant models in baby magazines. She'd never once seen a real pregnant woman adopt this pose—mostly they huffed and complained and scowled during the last two months—but it seemed to help her connect with the idea, or at least the ideal, of pregnancy. She grinned foolishly at herself and ventured a slow, stiff-backed sit-down onto the bed. She even let out an exhausted, long-suffering sigh for good measure. It felt nice having a shelf to rest her hand on.

But now to the matter at hand. Whether it was the Catholic in her reacting to supposed divine intervention and interpreting recent events as cosmic signs, or whether, despite her past dismissal of the Great Biological Clock bullshit, she had just succumbed to the usual late-thirties tick-tocking she had so despised in her contemporaries, Amy had made the decision to put her ovaries at the disposal of fate. If it was meant to be, then so be it. She felt like Mary at the Annunciation—the handmaiden of the Lord! But not for her the neat virgin birth—she had a feeling she would have to resort to less immaculate forms of conception than Our Lady. So how? There was no man in her life at present, although she was never short of offers. She mentally scrolled through all the men she had recently dated, trying to figure out which could have been a potential father. John had wanted kids, but she'd quickly put the kibosh on that—in fact, she was pretty sure he'd listed that as one of his splitting-up grievances. Not that he'd left her—no, he'd just stayed, whining on until she couldn't take it anymore. Tom had been very cagey, citing his brother's lack of life as a young dad as a lifelong reason to bodyswerve any baby chat. It had suited her fine at the time. Nathan had been indifferent—it had just never come up. Maybe he sensed her disinterest, or maybe he'd moved on to some earth-mother type and was now the proud dad of a sandal-wearing brood in Cornwall. There was no one she felt able or inclined to call with the unlikely offer of her womb. So what were her options? In true businesswoman style, Amy sat down with a pencil and paper, cushion still intact, to weigh the situation. This would need careful planning. At thirty-nine, she couldn't hang around— fate was going to need a hand at this late stage. She drew up a list of approaches, exploring the pros and cons of each.

OLD BOYFRIENDS

Pros: ease of access; quick start; know sexual history

Cons: no one suitable, though could make do with John (for only an hour)

IVF

Pros: no third party necessary; choose sperm donor characteristics—Gene pick 'n mix!; medically monitored, so optimum chance of fertilization (check this)—worked for Soph (finally)

Cons: painful; only small chance of success; expensive; intrusive; a lot of faffing about in hospital; could take ages to get screened, etc.

SELF-INSEMINATION
Pros: no doctors poking about; control; home service!

Cons: sperm arriving in jam jars; finding right donor; health-screening sperm an uncertainty; yuk factor

TRADITIONAL
Pros: manhunt always fun; can select donor on tap; "sold as seen" rather than relying on sperm catalog; get to actually have sex; free; natural; more in the hands of fate; quicker (presuming allure still intact); less desperate-looking; more easily explainable to friends/family/colleagues

Cons: sexual health—you can't use condoms if you want to get pregnant; AIDS. Shit. Still, you can't do anything without taking a risk these days. Just have to be careful, use judgment, and hope for the best. Cavalier, un-PC, and arrogant, maybe, but used to those epithets

This exercise confirmed what she always knew—that she would have to go au naturel. If this was to be an experiment in offering one's life up to the Fates, of letting nature take over, then it made sense to go the conventional route and see if her ovaries were up for it on their own. She just couldn't face the prospect of giving over control of her body to some smarmy fertility doctor full of false promises. The endless hours she'd spent in green hospital corridors with Soph and Greg still clung to her like the smell of cabbage. No, she'd have to do it the old-fashioned way, without the aid of modern science—and fast. For lots of reasons, Amy felt that forty would have to be a cutoff point. Every experiment, however heartfelt, needed its control circumstances, and besides, all the stuff she'd read in waiting rooms was firm on the statistics for the sharp downward curve in fertility after forty—what was it, a five percent chance of conceiving? If nature had a limit, then so would she. She knew the heartache involved in hoping against all evidence to the contrary that conception might still occur after scores of failed attempts. Mrs. Cummings floated into vision and Amy shuddered. This was not to be an open-ended affair—this was a once-in-a-lifetime opportunity for her reproductive system to sparkle. She'd give it until forty, and if she wasn't pregnant by then, then the gods had spoken and she'd been right all along—she wasn't meant for motherhood after all. She could heave a huge sigh of relief and resume her life as normal.

Logistics now. This was simply a practical problem that had to be overcome. Forty. That gave her a year. Twelve months, twelve eggs. Twelve was a good number—more generous than ten, less needy than twenty. Twelve disciples, twelve days of Christmas, the twelve that was really thirteen in the baker's hot buns dozen. She'd heard somewhere that most healthy young couples take six months to a year to conceive. What chance did she have at her advanced age and with partners of unspecified sperm counts? She'd have to refine her search and target the virile-looking. She'd have to ruthlessly weed out the weedy semen, reject the straggling spermatozoa, and allow each swim team only one chance at the finals. The idea of trying month after month with the same hapless no-hoper was too wasteful. She'd read recently that one in six men had fertility problems. She'd instantly worked out that that was four men on every football pitch! Statistically, she would already be wasting two of her twelve months. She'd do her research, monitor her peak fertility window with nuclear precision, go for it mid-cycle, then wait. If her period arrived, then she'd simply have to move on—no offense, no hard feelings, but no time to waste on tardy, tired testes.

She mentally prepared a shopping list. Ovulation-testing kits, thermometers (anal and oral), temperature charts, folic acid, push-up balcony bra, multivitamins.

And man number one.

Second Trimester

. 1 .

Stephen Marchont scanned the room with discreet expertise. Slim pickings at tonight's MENSA singles mixer. Why was it that all the clever women were either dull salad-dodgers with silly knee-jerk feminist principles or thin, mean-looking academics with wispy hair and traffic-warden shoes? It was always like this, and yet every time he'd get dressed and spruced up for the evening with the same school-boyish hope, that same twist of nervous excitement in his solar plexus. Not that there were many occasions in his school days when he got the opportunity to mix freely with the opposite sex. The second division public school he'd attended was, of course, single-sex, so girls had for many years been as rare a treat as seconds of chocolate pudding. Being a boarder meant he was even denied the pleasure of a weekend trawl round some urban shopping precinct in search of totty. Visits down to the local village were few and far between, and strictly monitored. Even on such afternoons, there were precious few girls to look at in the village, if you didn't count Mrs. Gray and her three lumpy daughters at the post office, which he didn't. They'd always come out, all three of them, grinning like flabby simpletons any time a boy from St. Bede's came in to collect a parcel from home or post their weekly formal parental update. It wasn't until he'd gone up to Cambridge that he'd experienced the multiple and various joys of women in all their complex and invigorating glory. Stephen had always liked women, despite the inevitable homoerotic fumblings of the rugger scrum, and that one excruciating anal experiment in year four. His mother had been a great advert for her sex—capable, strong, always perfectly turned out, as adept at the *Telegraph* crossword as she was at baking scones for tea, warm but alluringly distant. What they would now call a Superwoman, although she never did any of these things with the self-conscious flourish and brouhaha so depressingly common these days. When she'd died, Stephen was allowed off prep for a week. He'd spent the time mooning over an old black-and-white picture of her dressed in a cashmere twinset and a double string of pearls, smiling her fifties smile, her legs crossed neatly at the ankle. He'd cried through the night when his housemaster had confiscated it, declaring that such morbid girlishness was inappropriate for a boy of ten. When he'd asked for it back at the end of term, the housemaster lectured him angrily on how it was the duty of men to be strong for the rest of the family before sending him off empty-handed. Stephen could see in his master's eyes that beyond the reproach lay the fear of being found out. He knew the picture had been lost, and for the rest of his school days, they had circled each other with unspoken mutual hatred, each despising the other's weakness, each feeling the other's critical, knowing eye. Stephen shuddered now at the memory. Why did these things spring up in his mind at such inopportune moments?

At Cambridge, the girls had been fun. Most of them came from backgrounds very similar to his and wore their upper-middle-classness with ease, unabashedly sporting blue stockings and velvet Alice bands as if unaware of the stereotype. They were generally game gals, bright enough in an art history sort of a way but not on Stephen's platonic level. Then there were the lower-middle-class ones who'd done good, the grammar-school girls with their brash veneer unsuccessfully masking chronic insecurity. Half of these girls were really looking only for a husband, preferably a chinless member of an almost extinct aristocratic family, so that they could marry up, get a nice house in Berkshire, and live a life of comfortable underachievement. But the ones Stephen liked best were the chippy working-class girls who snarled if they heard a posh accent. They dressed in androgynous combat gear, smoked roll-ups, and argued about neoconservatism. They dyed their hair absurd neon colors, shaved the sides, and went to all the lectures. These girls were usually extremely suspicious of him at first, but he always won them over with his wit. He'd adopted a highly successful talent for self-parody. He deliberately walked around with a tweed jacket and brogues, like a minor royal in mufti, and accentuated his naturally clipped home counties accent. He'd say things like "Crikey," "Hurrah," and "Do you see?" He invented a fictional comic nanny whom he deferred to out loud in moments of crisis. "What would Nanny do?" he'd ponder if there was a problem with the bill at a restaurant, or if it looked cloudy but wasn't actually raining. But it was the same pattern every time. He'd be at a party in someone's room or in some townie pub or other, and he'd find himself chatting to a spiky-looking woman in cod-military clothing, and it would be difficult at first because she'd be defensive or dismissive, but after a relentless onslaught of self-deprecating banter, she'd find herself laughing. Within an hour, they'd be getting on famously. In the next week, there'd be a flurry of notes and postcards shoved in pigeonholes (these days, it was text messaging—not nearly so romantic), and the gossip would start. Finally, they'd meet again, get drunk, and smoke some weed, and the woman would make an undignified lunge at Stephen. It would always be at this point that he'd notice something about her that he didn't like. Instinctively, he'd draw back, but later, in the quiet of his deliberately fogyish room, he'd analyze what it was . . . the set of one's jaw, the crass laugh of another. Somehow they never lived up to their initial promise. This moment of realization always came at the crunch point, and always with a sickening twist of his gut. It was as if he had been living in a state of hypnotic delusion for the previous few days, and someone had suddenly snapped invisible fingers to bring him to. He'd make his excuses and leave the spiky woman totally disarmed and dazed. This pattern had continued through most of his adult life, apart from the one relationship he had managed, which, to the amazement and joy of his many friends, lasted two whole years before it crashed and burned. But Sarah had been special—she saw through Stephen's jolly exterior and comforted him in a way no one else had been able to. After two years, though, Stephen had noticed how she had a habit of stabbing at her food with a fork, as if she was spearing fish or something. The more he noticed it, the more he tried not to. At about the same time, she started making noises about them moving in together. Stephen had pictured himself at an eternity of dinner tables obsessively watching her left hand jabbing in and out of her plate. He couldn't countenance such a life of quiet irritation, so one warm spring evening he'd finished it once and for all. Better to get these things over with quickly and out of the blue, like shooting deer. Much crueler to let them see you aim. She'd been shocked and angry, told him he had commitment problems, and, a year later, married an actor. So she was better off in the long run. There had been six months of euphoria, followed by a sudden fall into deep and lasting anxiety—how could he have let her go over something so trivial and anal? He stayed up drinking all night and tuned in to *Trisha* on ITV. He listened to ugly people with thick regional accents mouthing platitudes about "learning to accept people for who they are" and wondered if he'd ever meet anyone perfect enough. He doubted it, but he knew he'd keep on looking.

Oh, *well*, he thought, wandering over to the sad buffet table

(MENSA members had clearly been bypassed by the whole food revolution). *Might be fun, anyway.*

Just as he was idly chewing on a cold sausage roll, in walked the next love of his life. Or at least that's the way it always seemed to Stephen in that moment. Neither age nor experience had dampened his Labrador-like optimism. He watched as she teetered uncertainly on the edge of the room. This was more like it. She was about forty but had not yet succumbed to the dowdy gene so common in her contemporaries. She was wearing a satin pencil skirt that sat teasingly just on the knee, teamed with a black, almost-see-through blouse. Even at this distance, he could see the leopard print of her bra. The whole ensemble was tied together by an exquisite pair of diamanté-encrusted stilettos. In short, the look was just the wrong side of tarty to Stephen's eyes, and it was all he could do to stop staring.

He sat on the urge to run over and fall at her feet, and his patience was rewarded. She glanced quickly round the room and seemed to make as unfavorable an appraisal as Stephen had. *Good.* Already they were of the same mind. Deciding on her next vantage point, she stuck out her chin and headed straight for the buffet. Stephen noticed the slight arrogance of her posture, the way every step she took in the glittering shoes seemed to tap out a rhythmic "I'm better than you, I'm better than you." He felt himself smiling as he lost sight of her behind a portly, boorish-looking man in a car coat who was busy piling his paper plate high with miniature scotch eggs and withered cocktail sausages. He'd have to work his way round to her and strike up a conversation. She looked as though she would soon tire of the assembled company, so he would have to move fast. With studied casualness, he body-swerved the car-coat man and came to rest a few paces away from where she stood, picking at a dry chicken leg. She was taller close-up, and she smelled expensive. What was she doing at this dweeb convention? Stephen came only because despite himself it flattered his vanity to be part of an intellectual elite. He knew it was incredibly naff these days, MENSA, but he felt at home among the oddballs. But her? Why was she here? She had walked across the room with such purpose, and he thought he could detect that alluring chippiness he found so inexplicably attractive. He had to find out.

"So what's a nice place like this doing to a girl like you?" he offered, gently scooping a corn chip into a bowl of green gloop.

"What?" She turned crossly, trying to locate the person who'd delivered the line.

"Hello. I'm Stephen Marchont. IQ of one hundred sixty-seven, but don't know a single fact."

"Oh, hello, sorry, didn't see you there."

Now that he was right up next to her, it was clear she was a good three inches taller than him.

He straightened up.

"I'm Amy."

"Amying high, eh?"

Shit. What a pathetic pun. He thought he'd learned to resist those. *How to make ground?* "It's true. I can't retain factual information for longer than a week. Highly embarrassing."

"Really? I thought MENSA was for eggheads," she said, coolly looking over his shoulder.

"Yes, but is intelligence information-based, or is it not the power to think, to reason?"

"So they say. I can remember loads of stuff. All useless, mind you. Does that make me thick?"

"For example . . . ?"

"Well, for instance, did you know that all polar bears are left-handed?"

"Are they? How on earth did they find that out?"

"Don't know—heard it somewhere and it stayed with me."

"Extraordinary. More, please."

They were standing side by side now, surveying the sad little disco that was just starting up. They watched for a few moments in silence as a small woman in brown tights took to the empty dance floor and began flinging herself around like a five-year-old at a wedding.

"Well, let me see. If you took all of the water out of an average one-hundred-sixty-seven-pound man, there'd only be about sixty-five pounds of corpse left."

"Crikey. Go on."

"The Royal Goat Society was set up in 1879."

"No, you see, that's not so good, that one."

"OK, erm, did you know that there is a secret train station underneath Buckingham Palace which goes directly to Heathrow Airport in case of a revolution?"

"Now that sounds more like an urban myth to me. Wouldn't surprise me, though. Bloody Kraut yellow-bellies, the Windsors."

Amy was enjoying this now. It had seemed like such a good idea last week, but on arrival, it had looked like a deeply unpromising evening. She'd decided to go for the intellectuals first. If she was going to do this baby thing alone, she might at least have the benefit of cherry-picking from the boffin gene pool. She'd Googled the words "intelligence quota" and "baby," and her search yielded the unlikely existence of a social group for MENSA members looking for "intellectual compatibility." Despite the Aryan undertones of the idea, she hadn't been able to resist. She hadn't really anticipated that the old hackneyed cliché of clever people being dull and unattractive would prove to be so true. Honestly, hadn't these people watched TV or read a style magazine in their lives? It was almost impossible for someone as design-conscious as Amy to comprehend. How could people really not care about the way they looked—especially at a social function like this, where everyone was presumably on the make? So far, all the men she'd seen on the short walk from the car park to the hotel bar had looked like adult Harry Potter fans—the sort of nerds who cared whether the *Lord of the Rings* films accurately reflected the books. But here she was now in the company of a charming corduroy and tweed man with the twinkliest eyes she'd ever seen. He wasn't what you'd call conventionally good-looking—he was shorter than her (but then, she was wearing her "Fuck me, I'm ovulating" shoes, so she'd have to cut him some slack there), balding but shaven-headed with the sort of rounded, smooth face favored by overfed babies, but he was curiously attractive. Something about his quiet confidence, the way everything he said sounded conspiratorial, lending to their conversation an air of unearned intimacy. Amy colored slightly at the realization that if he hadn't approached her and engaged her in some chat, then she would have dismissed him along with the others.

Most attractive of all was the fact that he was clearly out of her class. Sure, she could probably outearn him, outstyle him, and probably outwit him, but there was one area in which she'd always come second—he was posh and she was not. And he was proper posh. He looked as though he'd been born into inherited family seat debt, and had toddled up ancient stately corridors with an Elizabethan antique christening rattle dangling from one sticky hand. He'd never had to earn anything, because everything was already his. She could always tell if someone was proper posh or just pretending, and despite all her working-class irritation with the unfairness of the class system, Amy had always got on with such people. It was not just a case of opposites attracting but also something about being on the outside of things. The proper posh and the working class, it seemed to Amy, were the thin wedges at each end of the social spectrum, the bourgeoisie occupying the dull middle ground.

The only thing concerning Amy about him at all was what he was doing here among all these saddos. When she'd decided to come, she'd hoped to find a room full of fascinating people with Noble Prize–winning sperm. Stephen was the only one here who'd looked even remotely interesting, and if he was a MENSA member, surely he knew how dull these functions were?

"Do you come here often?" Amy asked with a nod to the cliché.

"I've never come here. I wait 'til I get home. It's less messy."

Amy looked directly at Stephen to check if she had heard him right. He looked coolly back at her and twinkled. Yes, he was definitely flirting. Result. He had obviously decided to up the stakes right away. Not surprising for a public-school boy. She remembered that what she also liked about the aristocracy was the absolute filth of them. None of this petit bourgeois prudishness, none of your middle-class wine-and-dine—straight in there, like a stud bullock. She couldn't have asked for anyone better, considering she had come here with the express aim of finding a mate to make a baby with. Stephen was bound to be sophisticated enough to not ask for her phone number afterward—she didn't see the point of getting involved with another ultimately useless man. Just wham, bam, and thank you, sir, was all she wanted.

"Shall we get out of here before they bring the Twister mat out?"

"Now . . . what would Nanny do . . . ?" said Stephen, only half ironically.

Bang on cue, Amy burst out laughing. *Bingo*.

.2.

Surprisingly, Stephen's flat was everything she'd come to expect from your average bachelor in his early forties. Here was the hallway, littered with discarded pizza delivery menus, the woodchip wallpaper peeling and scuffed, the bare lightbulb covered in decades of dust. The interior was homely but unfussy—the kitchen a masculine blue, the units cheap and dated. But there were a few telltale signs of a winking class-consciousness—a National Trust tea towel bearing the inscription "His Lordship" was spread out to dry over the hob, a pot of good marmalade lay open on the small table, and a general sense of shabbiness hung about the place. It looked like it had never had a good clean, as if cleanliness itself were a mark of proletarian neurosis.

"Welcome to the manor! Well, Manor Park anyway," said Stephen, making a show of filling the kettle. As if coffee was really what they both had in mind.

"Tea? Or something stronger?"

"Something stronger always sounds good."

"I think I've got some dodgy sherry somewhere, and a drop of port left over from Christmas—yum!"

"Ooh, not sherry—always reminds me of funerals."

"Port then. A lovely glass of port—how cozy!"

She watched as he twittered on around the kitchen, rummaging through cupboards full of packets and tins, pouring boiling water into a chipped china teapot and breathing onto two tiny sherry schooners. The fridge, she noticed, was full of little ready meals and micro-wavable steam puddings. She pictured him sitting propped up in bed, eating custard out of the tin, guffawing at a cartoon in *Punch*. He had the air of an actor caught backstage, aware that the behind-the-scenes reality was a far cry from the front-of-curtain razzle-dazzle he put on. She liked him all the same. He yawned ostentatiously as he poured the port into the glasses. Eleven p.m. She'd have to make her move soon—he looked like he might declare it way past his bedtime any moment now.

She stood and took the chipped decanter from his hands and swigged it suggestively, maintaining eye contact all the while. It didn't have quite the effect she was hoping for. Stephen blushed and began fussing with the teapot.

Oh, dear, thought Amy. *Might have blown it by being too brazen. I always forget to let the guys do the chasing. Stupid!*

She decided to hold back now and let him make the first move. Fatal mistake in the seduction game to come on too strong to a man who liked to think of himself as a great seducer. She'd misread him, obviously. She was sure that he wanted her but she had it all wrong when she'd decided he liked to be jumped on. Of course, he was of the "men do the asking" school. It was probably as dear to him as his old school tie. She generally hated men like that—she'd encountered enough of them in the last few years to make her vow to run a mile if she ever found herself with another. The sort of man who appears to be all reconstructed—giggles when you call him for a date, lets you drive, lets you buy dinner, but the minute you put your hand on his knee during the ride home he stiffens in all the wrong places, and therein treats you like you've just taken your knickers off and run up and down the High Street yelling, "I'm a great big slut! All comers welcome!"

But Stephen wasn't like that. The beauty of him was that he obviously hadn't gone in for all that new-man stuff. He wasn't pretending to be anything other than what he was—an old-fashioned boy fumbling around in a newfangled world. It was refreshing—and even more of a challenge. Ignoring the instinctive adrenaline rush any such challenge flooded her with, Amy sat down casually, as if she swigged from strangers' decanters all the time.

"Shall we?" said Stephen, recovering himself as he carried the tray into the lounge.

A dusty but expensive-looking armchair sat right in front of the TV. Amy admired the large selection of DVDs. They covered an entire wall—comedy, classic films, drama series, all filed alphabetically. Stephen clearly spent a lot of time watching them. The room was comfortable but musty smelling.

Eau de Bloke, thought Amy.

A strange mixture of interesting inherited bits and bobs and cheap IKEA furniture filled the space—a beautiful mahogany bureau jostled with a wood-veneered CD rack. Stephen pushed his feet into a pair of grubby old slippers and patted a cushion into shape. He suddenly looked a lot older than she'd first assumed. He was probably pushing forty. His larkiness had made him seem about a decade younger in the hotel bar. Amy wondered if he was as good a candidate as he first appeared to be. All the reports she'd read had suggested that it's not just women's fertility that took a nosedive later on in life—the modern lifestyle, with all its tight underwear, bad diets, and alcohol dependence had rendered an alarming number of men almost sterile. Not that they weren't shooting—far from it. Most men of her generation could boast a dozen partners or more (about ninety-nine percent up on their fathers' score), but they were often shooting blanks. She didn't want to waste her month's egg in a duff frying pan. Too late now, though. She'd cracked open the first ovulation test kit this morning, and, after peeing all over her hands, the twin blue lines had confirmed that she was indeed ripe for fertilization. If it was going to happen this month, then it would be tonight.

And anyway, it wasn't just about age—if creepy old geezers like Michael Douglas were fathering children left, right, and center, then why not this guy? He was from good breeding stock, surely. The aristocracy always prided itself on a certain earthy ability to produce fit heirs. No choice now but to hang on in there and wait for Stephen to make his move.

Midnight. They'd had tea, Amy had polished off two glasses of port, and Stephen was still filling her in on the history of radio comedy. It was very interesting—the genesis of the sketch show, the appeal of recording in front of a live audience, the transition from radio to television and how some slipped through the net—and all peppered with some great gags and excellent impersonations, but no suggestion of any intimacy whatsoever. Plenty of innuendo, a few shy smiles, and an electric silence after he'd complimented her on her hair, but nothing else. He was obviously a slow burner. It would be fatal to make another ill-timed lunge at him now. *Patience.* He would go for it in his own time.

Two a.m. They'd finished the port. Stephen had played her his two favorite CDs of the moment—*Classical Chill Out* (he thought it "amusing") and *The Darkness* (ditto). She was beginning to wonder if she should just call a cab, but he seemed so keen. It was confusing—on the one hand here they were, single adults who'd just met at a single adults' evening in the early part of the twenty-first century, slightly the worse for wear due to rapid alcohol intake, expecting to do what single adults alone late at night in a North London bachelor flat would normally do. Yet here he was, behaving like an emotionally stunted twelve-year-old showing her his football cards. Amy began to root around in her handbag for her mobile phone. He read her thoughts.

"Don't go," he said, almost urgently. And dropping to his knees, he took her hands in his and kissed her full on the mouth.

Better, thought Amy.

It was a nice kiss. He had soft skin and he didn't shove his tongue right in the way single men who watch too much porn tend to do. She placed her arm under his jacket and felt his side—soft and doughy, girlish. Never mind—she'd never really gone for muscles and hardness. They separated and he pretended to straighten his tie in mock propriety. She laughed nervously—sophisticate though she had become, there was always the trace of the convent schoolgirl in her who found it thrillingly forbidden to be so close to a man she wasn't married to. It was nice to be kissed. She tried to work out how long it had been—two months? Three? When was that drunken night out with Jules? They'd gone to a club in Leicester Square and had fallen in with a crowd of drunken lads. She'd ended up snogging in a corner with a twenty-year-old from Birmingham, but that's tequila slammers for you. This was different. Much more her cup of tea. But as she tried to pull him to her for a second go, he stood up just as abruptly as he'd knelt and pulled a DVD from the shelf.

"Have you ever seen this?" he asked brightly, shoving the disc into the slot.

"It's brilliant. It's *Citizen Kane*. Marvelous. Although the cognoscenti all seem to support the pretentious notion that *The Magnificent Ambersons* is a superior film. Nonsense." Amy was so stunned by the sudden change of direction that she shook her head numbly and settled back on the couch to watch the film. This was bizarre. Still, at least they were on their way to a night of baby-making passion. They'd kissed. He wanted her. It was just a matter of when.

Three thirty a.m. Amy's eyes stung. Orson Welles continued to blob around on the screen. This was getting ridiculous. Amy decided she had to confront this head-on. Perhaps he just needed a gentle final shove to get him off the practice slopes. Even if it failed and he recoiled in horror, she had to do something either way. She leaned forward and touched the back of his head. He didn't move.

"That's nice," he murmured as she stroked his bristly neck. "Gosh, you're giving me goose bumps! Look at the next bit—Orson's such a bloody genius, don't you think?" he asked, leaping forward on the couch.

"What's the matter?" she asked softly.

"Nothing—why?" he responded, just a little stiffly. Amy paused. How to tackle the situation without undue heaviness? How to show her own hand without seeming needy or pushy?

"Well . . . it's just that I keep getting mixed messages from you. I'm not sure if you want this or not."

"But we're having a lovely time, aren't we?" he asked, looking directly at her for the first time in three hours. A steeliness in his eyes told her not to push any further. Not quite threatening, but nowhere near inviting. Amy couldn't let it go.

"Yes, great, but I thought you might have wanted something else to happen between us, or did I misread the situation?" offered Amy, despite the fact that she knew she had not. He couldn't have been more clear in his intentions when they stood at the buffet table all those hours ago.

"Oh, heck," sighed Stephen, switching off the TV.

"What? What's the matter?"

"The Conversation," said Stephen with mock seriousness. Amy felt inexplicably guilty, as if she'd somehow dragged him into an arena he had no intention of entering. But no, he had definitely given her clear signals. She would get a response.

"Look, it's fine, it's just that I thought you were up for it, you know, we were clearly attracted to each other, that's why we're here, isn't it? And you kissed me, so I just thought . . ."

"You just thought what? That I'd be your next *boyfriend?*" He lent the word a sneer. The sudden vehemence in his voice alarmed her.

"Erm, well, no actually, I wasn't really looking that far ahead," she stuttered, checking that she remembered the route out. His face was contorted with disgust. He no longer looked like the affable chap she'd met that evening.

"I'd better go," said Amy, gathering herself. How could she have gotten him so wrong? He was clearly a bit odd at best—at worst, a complete psycho. Suddenly, the thought of any intimacy with this lumpy, balding, autistic man was repellent.

"Look, I'm sorry, I'm sorry, that was dreadfully rude of me. Please forgive me. Please—sit down."

Detached enough now to feel simple curiosity, she sat waiting for his explanation.

This had better be good, she thought. *I've wasted a month on this freak in one evening.*

"It's not you, it's me. . . ." he started.

Here we go, thought Amy.

"I, erm, I always end up in situations like this. I suppose I must have led you to believe that some intimacy, if not some bodily fluids, would pass between us tonight. . . ."

"Yes, you did, but it doesn't matter," said Amy, ruffled at his unnecessarily sincere apology. Had she looked that desperate? Baby or not, she would never lose her dignity.

"And that from then on we would become a couple and go to dinners and so on."

"Er, well, I wouldn't go that far!" Blimey, had she looked like a mantrap?

"Don't demur, there's nothing wrong with all that, apart from the depressing normality of it. The thing is, Alice . . ."

"Amy! Christ almighty!"

"Amy, is that I can't do it."

"Do what? *It?*"

"Good heavens no, I can do that, in certain rather strictly defined circumstances. But I can't do *it*—the relationship thingy."

Amy straightened.

"How can you just assume that I—" She started, but he raised a silencing hand.

"It's all right. I'm well aware that I am in the minority here. There's no need to protest your innocence. It's what you all seem to want, and there's nothing wrong with it. But I can't do it. And from bitter experience, I just thought it fairer to head you off at the pass, as it were. I don't want to lead you a dance."

Enough. She was too tired and too long in the tooth to listen to the eternal bachelor monologue. The arrogance of it! The assumption that all women want is a man to hold on to, tie down, and drown in a sea of dull domesticity. It wasn't as if he was that much of a catch anyway, despite his obvious intelligence. And besides, what sort of man belonged to a spoddy organization like MENSA, for God's sake! True, she'd gone there looking for super-bright semen, but not at this cost. High IQ or no, being lectured at four in the morning by a pudgy man who seemed to have an overblown sense of his own desirability was too high a price.

"I don't know what sort of woman you're used to meeting," said Amy, "but I can say with all honesty that when I dressed for this evening, all I wanted was to find a man to have sex with. You know, good old-fashioned shagging. So if that's not on the agenda—"

"I'm afraid not."

"Then let's just call it quits, OK? Perhaps there's a nice Enid Blyton by your bed you're simply *dying* to finish."

Amy resisted the urge to flick out her coattails and bid him a crisp "Good day." Instead, she hobbled down the rickety stairs and tottered up the street in the direction of the main road.

"Phew," Stephen said out loud. It had been a close shave. He had almost gotten involved with a woman who sniffed too much. *Sniff sniff sniff* all night long. Hadn't modern women heard of handkerchiefs? He was never without a crisply ironed plain white hankie folded neatly in his right pocket. No, she wouldn't do at all. Better rid of her now. His only existing problem was whether to have his cocoa or go straight to bed.

"Now . . . what would Nanny do . . . ?" he asked the dank night air.

.3.

"Jules? Amy here. Reality check, OK?"

"I'm listening—oh, hang on a sec . . ."

Amy heard the by-now-familiar sounds of her friend rushing to the loo and spilling her guts, or what was left of them.

"Sorry, carry on."

"Are you sure? You've just been sick again."

"Oh that, it's nothing, just morning sickness, I can do it anywhere now. Barely interrupts a sentence. Just whoosh and on I go!"

Amy felt the bile turning in her stomach. Too much information. And too much bloody port last night.

"You meet a guy at a party—"

"Uh-oh!"

"Yes, it's one of those conversations."

"I'm all ears."

"And you don't fancy him right away, but there's something between you that builds."

"Blimey, what you looking for, a boyfriend or a greenhouse?"

"Shut up. So you go home with him, you flirt a bit, eventually he kisses you, but in the end he won't sleep with you. Verdict, please?"

"Gay."

Amy could always rely on her friends' unswerving loyalty.

"Or married."

"But I went to his flat. He's definitely a bachelor."

"How can you be so sure—ready meals for one?"

"Check."

"Pants on the radiator?"

"Check."

"Dirty bed linens?"

"We didn't get as far as the bedroom."

"Got to be gay then."

"I don't know. . . . He didn't seem to be . . ."

"Darling, they can be very discreet these days—they're not all acid queens like Brendan. Some of them even have bad hair!"

"This one had no hair."

"So let me get this straight—you met a strange bald man at a party who, it turned out, was not after a one-night stand. What's the problem here? Why are you so bothered?"

"Who said I was bothered?"

"You're ringing me for a reality check and it's eight o'clock in the morning, Amy. Oh, hang on. . . ."

Amy smarted as she listened to the distant sounds of vomiting. Jules was right. She was bothered. She'd lain awake all night, trying to work out what had happened. It was the first time she had ever offered herself so openly and been so flatly rejected. It didn't help that he wasn't even conventionally good-looking. Compared to Amy, he was a troll, so technically, according to all the magazines, he should have been worshipping at her feet. But it wasn't just wounded pride at stake here. There was also the ovulation issue. No way could she go trawling for another likely candidate tonight—that would make her feel like too much of a tramp, and anyway, her egg was now past its sell-by date. Now she'd have to get back in the saddle next month. What a wasted opportunity. And why? Hadn't she looked fantastic, despite a slight snuffly head cold? Hadn't she been charming and funny and nice?

"I'll call you later!" Amy shouted to the abandoned receiver at the other end.

Above her head, the magpies cackled.

"You can shut up, too," she shouted up at the ceiling.

She lay back on the bed and dialed Brendan.

"Hello?" said a gruff voice at the other end of the line.

"Brendan?"

"No, 'ang on, he's just 'ere," said the voice. Amy heard stifled giggles and the thud of play fighting under a duvet.

"Hi, bitch."

"How did you know it was me?"

"Because you're single and only single people phone people having sex at eight fifteen in the morning."

"You're single!"

"Ah, yes, but I'm gay. It's our default setting. Get off!" squealed Brendan to someone in the background. There was nothing Amy hated more than people parading their sexual activity over the phone.

"Look, it's obviously a bad time—I'll call later," Amy said glumly.

"No, don't you dare hang up! You've interrupted me now when I was in full swing, so you might as well say what you want. Stop it!" More wrestling.

Amy took a deep breath.

"I got turned down."

"What? What for—the police force?"

"No. A bloke. I got turned down by a bloke."

There was a short pause. Amy pictured Brendan mouthing the words to whoever was there. She heard him splutter before erupting into peals of laughter.

"That is priceless! Who, where, how, tell me everything. No, seriously, stop that now, I've got to help a dumped damsel in distress," he barked at the invisible man.

Another deep breath.

"Well, you know my little project . . . ?"

"Oh, Christ, not the pregnancy roulette."

"Brendan, you promised to take this seriously. I haven't even told anyone apart from you, so the burden of support is squarely on your shoulders here."

"Go on," he sighed, all fun gone from his voice. She knew he thought she'd lost it, but she wasn't the sort of person who needed approval for every last decision.

"Well, this was the first month, and I kind of thought it might be good to be a bit systematic about it—you know, have a target, be specific."

"Right, yes, you have to do that in your strange, straight world, do you? Can't just go out and get laid?"

"Well, I could but this is a potential child we're talking about here. I need to make sure I at least like the guy."

"OK, so where did you meet him?"

"I went to a MENSA social."

A short pause.

"MENSA?"

"Yeah, you know, the society for people with high IQs."

"I know what it is, Amy; I just can't believe you could be so Nazi! So you went to MENSA to try and bag some genius sperm? Freaking hell."

"It seemed like a good idea at the time. Well, how else are you supposed to meet intelligent people? I could hardly just stroll into All Bar One and hope to happen upon a reasonably bright bloke on a Friday night."

"Good God, you know for a clever girl from a council estate, you are such a bloody *snob*! How can you say that? How can you be so shameless about it? What do you want these sperm to do—read Salman Rushdie novels?"

"No, but—"

"Look, it's very simple, Amy. You go out, you find the first half-decent bloke, you do the dirty, you get pregnant. If Atomic Kitten can do it, so can you. Forget all this checklist bullshit."

"Yes, yes, OK, you're right, of course. Get back to Mr. Muscle or whoever he is."

"He's a six-foot hairy-arsed builder with dirty fingernails. Just my type," whispered Brendan with glee.

"Enjoy," said Amy, hitting the red button on her phone.

Lying on the bed, she took in Brendan's reprimand. It had been a pretty unpleasant mini-lecture, but she had to agree. The problem with not having a partner for this "experiment," this gamble with fate and nature, was that she was able to think coolly about what sort of man she wanted to father her child. Most would-be mums had that part of the deal sewn up—it was just a simple matter of whether or not they could conceive and carry a child to term. But Amy had the onerous luxury of handpicking her mate. Although this was the stuff of futuristic fertility fantasy—the genetic engineers of the world seemed hell-bent on a generation of designer babies—it was actually quite an unpleasant procedure to go through in person. Fine if you were flicking through a catalog of faceless donors in a sperm bank waiting room, but trickier if you had the task of tracking down your ideal donor and doing an on-the-spot appraisal of his genetic merits. She'd tried the intellectual first and where had it gotten her? Back in her own bed with a hangover and a wounded ego. She still couldn't work out what had gone wrong between her and Stephen. She looked at all the evidence once more. She remembered an article she'd read recently in a women's magazine at the hairdresser's. It was about three men who called themselves CBs—Committed Bachelors. All of them claimed to have given up on ever finding the right woman to settle down with and had instead carved themselves a life of domestic solitude. They had nothing but pity for the poor shackled men they drank with on the weekends, the ones who started to twitch at half past ten, wondering if they could squeeze another desperate pint out of the evening before the "Where are you?" phone calls began. Occasionally they indulged in a little affair with a woman, but it would always end in tears—always the woman's. The CBs had worked out that it was probably wiser to avoid the opposite sex pretty much altogether, as the fallout and e-mail character assassinations following a fling were too exhausting. *What did women want?* they wondered. They, along with most men, had been delighted that their generation of potential lovers had been so liberated. The women's movement had delivered a breed of sexually active girls whose first question was not "When do you want to settle down?" but "Your place or mine?" For a while they'd fallen for it, this veneer of free-floating promiscuity, but the CBs had worked out that beneath every ball-busting good-time girl beat the heart of a Doris Day wannabe. There was a very short slip between sex in the taxi home and weekends spent in Bride's World. Perhaps, thought Amy, Stephen was one of these men. He certainly seemed to be on red alert for any sign of potential intimacy. It made her furious that he could assume she had anything so mundane as marriage in mind. Such arrogance, assuming that every woman wanted to bag him for life. And all that tired talk of not "doing" relationships. He'd obviously seen all that crap about quirky-alones in the press and was delighted at the opportunity to jump on the bandwagon.

Never mind. He'd probably die laughing—but alone. Nothing to do but to forget the whole thing and move on. Pity she'd have to wait another month.

. 4 .

"Daaaad? Daaadddyyyy!"

Joe groaned. A twenty-hour shift was nothing compared to this.

"Where are you, Daddy?"

His peace interrupted, he decided to give himself up.

"On the toilet."

For most normal children, this would be enough information to ward them off for at least half an hour. Not his two. They knew that if Daddy was in the smallest room in the house, he was a captive audience. Sure enough, he heard the first of two sets of feet thundering up the stairs. *Shit.* He'd forgotten to lock the door. It was a new initiative now that the girls were eight, and he kept forgetting. They'd always been very open about nudity, but now it seemed a bit inappropriate, to use the social-worker jargon.

Francesca smashed the door open, thwacking the handle into the well-worn groove in the plaster from a thousand other such occasions.

"Daddy—urgh, it stinks in here."

"Cesca, I'm on the loo! Can I please just have a bit of privacy?"

He knew it was a rhetorical question, but like every parent, he lived in the hope that one day his children would suddenly say, "God, I'm sorry, Dad, you're absolutely right. You do such a good job bringing us up, and we feel mortified that we can be such a handful at times. We'll be in our rooms, reading quietly until such a time as you feel refreshed enough to see us again." *Dream on.*

"Daddy, I'm going to talk and I don't want you to say anything until I say 'End of sentence.' OK?"

"OK," sighed Joe.

She leaned precariously on the vanity sink and took a deep breath.

"There's this boy at school and I really love him I don't mean *love* love him but he really makes me laugh he does this really brilliant impression of the donkey from *Shrek* and he's got dead long hair longer than Laura's and even though he smells of mince he's really nice but he's not as bright as me 'cause he has to go with Mrs. O'Flynn and that's for people what struggle. End of sentence."

"Who."

"Charlie."

"No, *who* struggle."

"Sorry, *who* struggle. I always get them mixed up."

And with that, she turned abruptly and rattled back down the stairs, off to embrace some fresh mini-drama.

This was a new thing, this interest in boys, however grudging. Just a year ago, they'd both have made dramatic vomiting noises if anyone so much as suggested they'd been in the same room as a boy. They'd react with horror and revulsion at the suggestion that they even *liked* a boy, denying it as vehemently as any war criminal. He tried not to think about the inevitable day that they actually brought boyfriends home. Before he'd had his girls he could never understand his own father's silent fury when his sister Enza had brought her first beau back. He'd sat steaming as they all exchanged pleasantries over Limoncello in the good room at the front of the house, and his mother had hissed at him in Italian to be nice. And Enza had been twenty-six! But now all he had to do was think about some hairy, horny young guy discovering the little brown mole on the inside of Cesca's left bum cheek that she'd had since birth, and he knew he'd want to rip the boy's throat out. Though he hated to admit it, he was as much a doting father as his father had been. He sat anticipating the next onslaught— where one had been, the other also had to mark her scent. It was the way of twins. He counted quietly to himself.

"One, two, three, four . . ."

Thump thump thump up the stairs came the heavier tread of Laura, who'd inherited her mother's roundness.

"Dad . . ." she began as she faltered at the door, unsure of the rules if it was actually open, and not really knowing what she wanted to say anyway.

"Yeees?" said Joe, smiling gently at her obvious panic. What to say now that she was here?

"You know my sister?"

"Er, yes, I think I know who you mean."

"Well, she keeps on singing this song and it's really annoying me 'cause I'm trying to watch *The Bill*."

"Oh, dear. Do you want me to go and beat her?"

A giggle.

"No, but it's really annoying. It goes, 'I know a song that will get on your nerves, get on your nerves, get on your nerves, I know a song that will get on your nerves, all day long.' And she sings it over and over."

"Just ignore her."

"I can't! She just sings it louder if I ignore her!"

"Then try a bit of reverse psychology."

"What?"

Laura was so innocent, he wanted to eat her. It would never occur to her to be anything other than one hundred percent genuine. If something annoyed her, she shouted. If she hurt, she cried. If she was happy, she'd sing at the top of her voice.

"Next time she starts singing it, turn and face her and look really interested. When she gets to the end say, 'That's a great song, please sing it again! It's really relaxing!'"

Laura smiled slowly, understanding the ploy. She turned and thundered back down the stairs, ready to practice her new psychological management skill.

Joe sat and waited. Without missing a beat, Cesca started up again.

"I know a song that will get on your nerves, get on your nerves, get on your nerves, I know a song that will get on your nerves, all day long."

As she paused for breath, he heard Laura interject quickly.

"That's a great song, Cesca. Please sing it again!"

"I know a song that will get on your nerves, get on your nerves, get on your nerves—"

"Cesca, *shut up*! I'm trying to watch *The Bill*!"

Joe laughed out loud. Cesca would always win in a battle of wits.

"You shouldn't be watching *The Bill* anyway. And that's on at night."

"It's on video!" they shouted in chorus up the stairs.

"Since when did you start videoing soaps?"

"Trish taped it for us," shouted Laura, unconcerned by the implied parental censorship.

"And it's not a soap, it's a serial drama!" shouted Cesca.

Trish. He'd always hoped that the children would be playing chess with the nanny during those long nights he was on duty. Instead, they had developed a passion for trash TV. They would become rapt in awe upon hearing the theme tune to *Emmerdale Farm*. They would race from the garden, where he had been instructing them on the fascinating ins and outs of photosynthesis, as soon as they heard the opening bars of *EastEnders*, and they would scream with excitement at the very mention of *Coronation Street*. He would watch them as they stood slack-jawed in front of the telly, occasionally jostling each other for the best position. And although he'd gently suggested to Trish that perhaps the children watched a bit too much TV, she had made him feel that familiar sense of guilt.

"Yeah," she'd said, "you're probably right," but she had given the clear impression that nothing was going to change. And how could he insist? He couldn't enforce a regime of piano practice and private study if he was barely there, could he? He'd seen several of his friends struggle with the whole nanny vs. parent battle of wills, and the parents always came out the more bruised. It seemed to Joe that a whole generation of urban middle-class parents were slowly losing control over their offspring, no matter how hard they all tried to insist on organic lunch boxes and lessons in home baking; despite their best efforts at remote parenting, the nannies would always have the upper hand, *because they were actually there*.

"Daaaad?" came the cry again. Forget the *Guardian Weekend* magazine on the toilet, his weekly attempt at a moment's peace.

"Yeessss?" Laura was at the door again.

"You know Harrods?"

"Yeeessss." He knew what was coming.

"Can we go there? Pleeeaaasse, Daddy, pleeeaaasse, can we?"

Oh, Christ, thought Joe. He was so tired he could sleep for a year right there on the toilet.

But it was Saturday, and when he wasn't working, he always tried to take the girls out for the day. It didn't really matter where they went, so long as it wasn't educational. He'd long since given up on the museums—they'd fought, sighed, and groaned their way around the Natural History, the Science museum, and the V&A last year and he'd vowed to give it up as a bad job. They were far happier trawling round the Trocadero with a bag full of neon jelly sweets, gawping at foreign teenagers spraying each other's hair pink and snogging on the escalators.

Harrods was a new thing, too. Ever since Amber—the recent bane of his life—had gone into school with photos of her new baby brother, Laura had become gaga about all things baby. And whatever Amber had, the girls became passionate about—sparkly jeans, *Girl's World*, an electronic dance mat, a baby—it was all one and the same to the girls. Laura's bedroom had come to resemble a dwarf crèche. Miniature prams, plastic baby dolls in various states of undress, a pint-sized nappy-changing unit, and, bizarrely, a pregnant Barbie lay strewn all over the floor. Barbie's baby was detachable, and left its mother with a celebrity-flat tummy moments after birth. If only all births were as simple, perhaps he wouldn't be so drained and weary. As if that wasn't bad enough, both girls had begun nagging him about having another baby. Morning, noon, and night—and especially night—they would set up a relay of badgering. When one tired, the other would pick up the baby baton and run full-pelt at his wall of resistance. They weren't fussy about how he got hold of a baby—that was adult stuff they felt was his responsibility as a grown-up to sort out—just so long as he got one. As if babies just fall out of the sky! Laura had even begged him to steal one from work. He knew it had been a mistake to take them into the maternity ward one day, an error of judgment second only to telling them about that foundling a few weeks ago. (That had been a strange day. He'd never actually been through that procedure before, receiving an abandoned baby. He wondered what had become of the child. In good care, he hoped. And what of the woman? The guy she was with—husband or just boyfriend? She'd been pretty shaken, but he'd seen something very attractive in her attempted nonchalance. He loved girls who toughed it out but were secretly mushy inside. . . .) He'd gone home and told the girls all about it, and they were so moved (Laura even forgot to watch *Who Wants to Be a Millionaire?*) that they'd written maudlin poems for the anonymous child and stuck them on the fridge door. Francesca, perhaps embarrassed by a rare outburst of feeling, had distanced herself with a witty title ("Who Loves Ya, Baby?"), while Laura's had been called simply "Baby." They had not yet forgiven him for not bringing the baby home for the weekend—as though it were the school hamster or something. Ever since then, they'd demanded to be taken to all manner of baby-related retail outlets. His weekends had been spent in aircraft hangar–sized Mothercares, and the Babies "Я" Us section held a new fascination in their favorite toy shop. In an unfocused moment, he'd made the mistake of telling them about Harrods's nursery department, where you could buy a toddler-scale Bentley or a solid silver rattle. Needless to say, it had become their new Mecca, eclipsing even John Lewis's fourth floor in their minds' eyes. He knew it was pointless telling them that he was tired, that he'd been on his feet for twelve hours overseeing the delivery of babies—one breech, two emergency C-sections, and an overoptimistic water birth with complications—and the last thing he felt like doing was trekking into town to rub shoulders with overprivileged parents-to-be cooing over Louis XIV cot beds.

"OK. But put your coats on! No coats, no Harrods."

"Yes!" came the jubilant response, and for once they didn't even try to argue about the weather.

.5.

The front of Harrods always made Amy smile. It made every day like Christmas in Knightsbridge, regardless of rain or shine. Huge and glittery, it was like an ostentatious bauble plonked in the middle of an otherwise tasteful Christmas tree. Its portals promised much and, in Amy's experience, always delivered. She loved everything about the place, from its self-consciously themed window displays to the afternoon bagpipers employed by Al Fayed to roam the store. The first time she'd heard the unmistakable drone of the pipes, she'd been in the jewelry department and had asked the nonplussed assistant if it was Burns's Night.

"No," she'd replied. "Mr. Al Fayed just likes them." What a fabulously mad millionaire.

Entering the store now, she felt the familiar frisson of expectation. She didn't have anything to buy in particular, but that was the best time to go. She generally did Man Shopping (identify need, research market, go to specific shop, and purchase—do not pass go, do not collect two hundred sundry, useless items), but Harrods was a different story. She often came here and just wandered around, feeling fabrics, touching surfaces, and comparing designs with her own. Its baby department was second only to its pet section, where you could buy a chaise longue for your pussy, or a diamanté harness for your lapdog. Amy winced and fought off a tear as she remembered how she'd once spent more than a hundred quid on a rhinestone collar for Germaine. It was so nice she'd worn it herself a few times, and it had gotten more admiring remarks than her Theo Fennell crucifix.

Resisting the urge to go and see what puppies they had in stock today, she made her way up to the nursery, pushing her way past the tourists clutching their "cheapest thing in Harrods, but I had to get something in *that* bag" purchases. The place was mobbed. What was she doing here on a Saturday afternoon? Only out-of-towners and bored rich people went shopping in London on a Saturday. Amy convinced herself that it wasn't because she was feeling blue—she'd bounced back from worse things than a wasted egg and a knock-back from a weird, posh bloke—but because she needed to be thinking ahead. OK, she was taking a bit of time off from the shop, but that was no excuse to let her creative juices dry up. She should still make sure that she was keeping up with the competition, and besides, she suddenly had a bit of baby shopping to do. What a bizarre situation. Out of her close circle of friends, three were now pregnant. Ang, fair enough, that was her life's work, and Soph had always wanted a child, but Jules? That had really thrown her. And if she was honest, it had had some influence on her recent little plan. Damn them all for messing with her head. She would never have guessed that her conviction that she would remain childless could be so easily rocked. Except it hadn't felt like a bolt from the blue; it had felt as though the universe, whatever that was, was screaming out to her. The magpies, Germaine dying like that, the three sudden and simultaneous pregnancies of her closest female friends—surely not just coincidence? Surely some kind of sign that she too should enter the Pudding Club? She smiled quietly to herself. Who was she trying to kid? Maybe this was what she had wanted all along. How humiliating to be human after all. She brushed off the chagrin and turned to the matter at hand. She knew her friends had seen all her own baby stuff, and anyway, she couldn't give them her own *stock* for their little blobs of cells, so Harrods it was. It would give her a chance to have a look at their preschool toys—an area she was hoping to go into more. She took the lift, squeezing herself between a large American couple and an entire Japanese family dressed from head to toe in Burberry. The liveried lift attendants did their best to avoid the crushing so often found in the lifts of lesser stores—one shouldn't have to crush in Harrods—but Saturdays were a lost cause. This lift was packed, and on every floor more people got on. It was hot and sticky, she was sure someone had farted, and every time the lift lurched up a floor, her port-drenched stomach lurched with it. Everyone stood, eyes fixed firmly on the doors ahead, terrified that some unwanted intimacy such as a smile might occur between them and their neighbors.

"I know a song that will get on your nerves, get on your nerves, get on your nerves."

Stifled giggles erupted from the front of the lift. The American couple smiled indulgently.

Brats in the lift. That's all I need, thought Amy.

Why don't people teach their kids to keep quiet in confined spaces anymore? Their parents are probably frightened they'll stamp on their children's spontaneity or some such bollocks.

"I know a song that will get on your nerves, get on your nerves, get on your nerves."

Amy craned her neck, hoping to catch the eyes of the offending kids and give them her best terrifying strange-adult stare—it always worked on screaming toddlers, shocking them into silence. All she could see were the backs of two girls' heads bobbing backward and forward as they shoved each other from side to side, totally oblivious to the old lady next to them. Bad behavior made Amy so cross. Why didn't whoever they were with do something?

A loud fart noise broke the third-floor silence, and both girls screeched with laughter. Clearly one of them was the culprit, although it had sounded like an underarm faked fart to Amy.

"That's more than enough of that," said a quiet, defeated voice just behind the girls. A tall man in a good coat stood right in front of Amy. Was he their dad or just another irritated stranger?

Another fart noise and near-hysterical giggles. Clearly, he was their dad. Only a parent could fail so spectacularly to exercise control in a public place. *Poor bloke.* What was she thinking, letting herself in for this a few years down the line? Amy shot a glance at the woman who stood next to the man and wondered why, if she was their mum, she failed to take any disciplinary measures. Perhaps it was Dad's duty, or perhaps they'd had a domestic. He certainly had a defeated air about the set of his shoulders. Amy consoled herself with the fact that if she did eventually have a child, at least the nightmare of bringing it up would not be shared with the drudgery of a relationship gone silent and sour. In some respects, single parents had it easier. At the fourth floor, the man pushed forward and guided the girls out of the lift. Amy followed and noted that the woman had stayed behind. Either a very bad domestic or she wasn't the girls' mum. The man bent slightly to address the girls.

"Right, you two—you've got ten minutes and five pounds each, and no amount of begging, bargaining, or pleading is going to change those two facts, OK?"

Amy stopped and stared. She knew she had recognized the back of his head, but even now she struggled to place him. Her brain took a few seconds to catch up with her pulse, which for some reason had begun to race a little.

The doctor. From the hospital. The one who had been so nice to her. Seeing him out of context had thrown her momentarily, but now she couldn't believe she didn't recognize him straight away—he'd played such a huge role in such a formative event. Amy found herself blushing inexplicably. She felt oddly exposed—silly, even—as though she had just dropped her towel on a nudist beach. *What now?* What was the protocol for bumping into an attractive near-stranger who had helped you rescue an abandoned baby and who was now out shopping with his own children? Amy hated such chance meetings, even with people she knew very well. She had once actually crossed the street to avoid Greg because she always panicked if it wasn't planned. She always felt shy and unprepared. Best to avoid it altogether and pretend not to have seen them. Without thinking, Amy ducked behind a display of wooden toys. They'd be gone in a minute, and she could run to the nearest exit. From her vantage point, she could get a good look at him now. He was taller than she remembered, and even more handsome in his civvies. So it wasn't just the stethoscope and the white coat then. Pity about the brats. Not just married but fully sprogged, too. If she could just stick it out here for a few minutes, then a potentially excruciating encounter would be avoided.

"Dad! Look at this wooden school bus! It's, like, *so* adorable!"

Amy flinched as one of the girls, the plumper of the two, darted toward her hidey-hole. She watched, holding her breath, as a pair of sticky hands grabbed at a red bus just in front of her nose.

"Dad, look! How much is it? Can I get this?"

"I doubt it, sweetheart—it's probably about four hundred quid. Why don't you go and have a look at the plastic rattles over there?"

Yes, why don't you, thought Amy. Her knees were beginning to buckle under the strain of crouching, and the back of her neck throbbed.

"No, I want this, Daddy! It'll look really cool on my bedroom shelf, and it's got, like, little wooden children inside when you take off the top deck."

"Just piss off," muttered Amy, a bit too loudly.

"What?"

Amy was staring straight at a pair of round, blue eyes.

"Nothing," said Amy to the eyes.

The girl dipped out of view. *Shit.* Time to make a hasty retreat.

"Daddy! There's a lady hiding over there and guess what?"

Amy stopped stock-still. *Bugger.* Did she have time to put enough distance between herself and the scene of the crime?

"What?" asked the doctor wearily.

"She said P-off."

"I'm sure she didn't, Laura."

"She did! Look! Here."

Laura grabbed her dad's hand and dragged him across the floor. Amy found herself involuntarily doing a comedy creep toward the exit.

"Hello!"

Bugger. He'd spotted her.

Amy straightened up sharply. A shooting pain went from the base of her spine and down her right leg.

"Piss!" she screamed.

"She said it again!" Laura squealed with delight.

"Are you all right? Here, come and sit down," said Joe, pulling a chair from the wall next to the lift.

Amy hobbled to the chair. What a time for her back to go.

"Just ease down gently. There. Take your time."

He guided her slowly down onto the chair, and the pain began to subside. She kept her head down low until the last possible moment. When she could avoid it no longer, she lifted her eyes gingerly.

"OK now?"

Amy nodded. Could she pretend not to remember him? If she feigned surprise now, he would never suspect that he was the reason for her strange hunched demeanor.

"I'm the doctor—the baby? The baby you found?"

"Dad! Was it her? Did you find a baby?"

Joe ignored the question, his gaze fixed on Amy.

"Oh, yes," Amy began weakly. "Oh, yes, sorry, I didn't recognize you with your clothes on. I mean, with your normal clothes on. Oh, piss."

Joe raised his eyebrows in amusement and mock shock.

"Sorry. Shouldn't swear in front of your children."

"Or insinuate you've seen their dad naked."

"Has she, Dad? Urgh!" said Francesca.

So he was their dad. *Bummer.* She'd been half hoping he was an uncle, a godparent, anything but their dad. It was one thing hopelessly fancying a married man (not that she'd ever do that again—been there, got the lingerie), but a married man with kids? That was totally out-of-bounds.

Amy looked at the girls full-on now. One was taller and bigger than the other, about ten years old, although Amy was never very good at guessing ages. The other was willowy and about seven. Both had the most amazingly blond hair. Amy was reminded of that old black-and-white horror movie *The Midwitch Cuckoos*, where an entire village was rendered suddenly fecund and all the women, even the older and presumed barren ones, gave birth to spooky alien blond children with telekinetic powers. It seemed the only explanation for their total lack of resemblance to their father.

They stared unabashedly back at her. The bigger one looked curious and friendly, but the smaller one had a mean look in her eyes.

"Did you swear?"

"Yes, I'm sorry I did."

"Did you swear at my sister?"

"Er, no, I don't think so. I may have said something that sounded like swearing."

"You said P-off. You said P twice."

"Then you said S blank blank T."

"All right, girls, that's enough. Can't you see Amy's in pain?"

He remembered her name. Amy felt quietly thrilled.

"I'm all right now, thanks. I just get a bit of lower back pain now and again."

"What were you doing hiding behind those toys?" asked Francesca, who always had a nose for adult shame.

"I wasn't hiding, I was just . . . looking at something on the bottom shelf . . ."

Both girls turned slowly and looked at the bottom shelf. It was spectacularly empty. They turned back with as much triumph as their years would allow.

Joe smiled kindly.

"Perhaps it's gone now—the thing you were looking at."

"Oh, yes, so it has!"

The girls stared at her with renewed interest. Maybe this was one of those crazy ladies Daddy sometimes told them about.

"Thanks. I'm fine now, really," said Amy, trying to raise herself off the chair. She winced, and Joe held out his arm for support.

"I would get that seen to if I were you. Backs aren't my thing, but it looks like sciatica to me."

"Yes, yes, I will. Thank you, Joe."

Now it was Joe's turn to smile.

"She's fine, by the way."

"Sorry?"

"Precious."

"Is she? What happened?" Amy felt grateful to have a deflection topic, but more than that, she wanted to know how things had turned out for the baby. It had been hard not to call the hospital and find out. Brendan had dissuaded her, saying that Social Services would not give information out to strangers, regardless of the unusual circumstances of her involvement. Nevertheless, Amy was itching to find out.

"Yes. Her mother turned up at the police station three days later. Only fifteen. They've been reunited, and she's living in a special mother-and-baby unit. They're fine."

Amy was pleased. *Fifteen. So young.* When she was fifteen, she was still reading Cathy and Claire to find out how babies were made and to see if it was really true that sitting on a warm bus seat could make you pregnant.

"Oh, that's good. I think."

"They'll be looked after."

"Why didn't you keep it?" The Midwitch Cuckoos were at it again.

"Well, because she wasn't mine, and that would be like stealing, wouldn't it?"

"Finders keepers," said the smaller alien.

"Yeah, if the lady didn't want it, maybe she gave it to you."

"You should have kept it. Or given it to Daddy."

"Cesca, we've been through this. Sorry, Amy. Oh, this is Francesca, and this is Laura."

"Hello!" said Amy as brightly as she could manage.

Nothing. They stared glumly back at her from beneath their heavy, blond fringes.

"Which one is the elder?" ventured Amy. She was damned if she was going to be blanked by a couple of pint-sized freaks.

"We're twins," said Francesca.

"Double trouble!" said Amy with a hollow laugh.

Joe smiled and nodded his agreement.

"Come on, Dad, let's go now," said the bigger one, pulling on his coat sleeve. Francesca had another idea and got down on the floor. Wrapping herself around his ankle, she started to pull his foot away. Laura quickly cottoned on and began doing the same with the other foot.

"Girls, girls!" shouted Joe—but it was no use. It was clear who wore—or at least pulled—the trousers in his house. He raised his hands in a "Kids! What can you do?" gesture.

"Bye," said Amy, still sitting.

"Good to see you again," said Joe. "Such Precious Little Darlings!" And with that, he disappeared, dragging the two giggling girls along the floor with each step.

Amy laughed. He remembered the shop, too. He must have kept the bag. Such a good-looking guy. And he had definitely flirted a little. "Good to see you again," he'd said. Perhaps he was just one of those guys who twinkled at every woman he met. The eternal bedside manner. Amy pulled herself up short and remembered the wedding ring, the no-doubt-gorgeous Swedish blonde wife waiting at home for the return of her dishy husband and her two revolting Milky Bar kids. She also remembered a joke she'd heard last week. Why are men like public toilets? Because all the best ones are engaged and the only ones left are full of shit.

.6.

The sun never shines in Stockwell. There may be blue sky above Regents Park, the beams glancing off a thousand buses inching up Oxford Street may blind the passing pedestrians and the pavements may be sticky with molten gum as near as Brixton, but Stockwell would remain resolutely gloomy. At least that's the way it seemed to Stuart as he pulled the candlewick bedspread off the nail attaching it to the window frame. Another day, another dollar.

"Bollocks," he said out loud. His calves ached, and his back crunched as he stretched out, standing naked on the bed. A bored-looking young woman stared blankly back at him from her kitchen window in the opposite block. They'd built these flats so close to one another, you could virtually hear your neighbor's thoughts. Not that he was complaining—a council sublet was like gold dust in London these days. And sharing with Will hadn't turned out too badly, even if he hadn't seen the sink in a fortnight and they never seemed to have loo roll. Will had gotten it from a Serbian couple, Ivan and Lakka, who were now living in Leicester with relatives. They'd doubled the rent, but it was still half the price of a private let, and they hadn't had to fork out a huge deposit.

Stu idly scratched his ass, farted, and stepped down onto the floor. The worn carpet was covered in dirty clothes, CDs, books, and bicycle parts. He remembered the flat tire and groaned. What a drag having to fix that before work. A bloody flat tire on the Elephant roundabout at six o'clock last night. He'd promised himself he'd do it before bed, but then Rob had called and said that there was a promotion on vodka at The Crown, so he'd gone straight out. Happy hour in Stock-well. What a joke—three old gits and an alcoholic old lady propping up the bar while Sky Sports blared out from the opposite wall. Of course, they'd gotten smashed anyway—well, you have to make your own fun, don't you? Now the tire lay on the floor and his head felt like shit again. He began throwing bits and pieces from the floor onto the bed and set about mending the puncture. Why did he do it? Every night he swore he would stay in and start work on that book of short stories, but all it took was one call from Rob or Baz or Craig and he was out again, trying to forget the crap day—cycling round London delivering important documents to the proper people in their safe lit-tle jobs, being cut off by stupid truck drivers. It wasn't that he didn't enjoy these endless nights out—he loved his drink and his mates and the whole feeling of freedom London offered on a school night—but at thirty-seven he was beginning to feel as though he'd drifted a little too far, and for too long. He hated to concur with his *Daily Mail*–reading parents, but he was beginning to feel the urge to settle down. His sister had always done the right thing—university, then a great job, husband, and now Jake, born only last week—but Stu had always been the wild child. He'd been the one who'd done it all wrong, almost as though he'd set about being diametrically opposed to The Right Thing. The expulsion from school for drugs, the arrests at festivals, the endless string of pointless, no-hope jobs to finance his hedonistic lifestyle. His family had given up on him years ago and had long since ceased to ask about his "plans." But seeing his first nephew had set something small and insistent off in Stu's heart—a dull ache every time he saw a baby, and a twist of the stomach as he whizzed through a cloud of confetti at Marylebone registry office. Could it be that at last he was becoming normal? He shuddered at the thought. His dad had always told him one day he'd want to put down roots, find a nice girl, have children, and that he should be planning for that instead of tearing about on a one-man mission to drink London dry. Stu was beginning to think he might have been right. Glastonbury had been fun this year, but he'd had a bad acid trip and it had shaken him up. He'd dropped the tab and began to feel really, really old. Suddenly everyone around him looked youthful and full of hope, and their faces glowed with simple optimism, which only served to reinforce his sense of aging. It seemed to him as though each minute was a decade, and when he looked into the cocaine-dusted mirror, he saw the eyes of an ancient man staring back at him, the wrinkles submerging the eyeballs and the skin starting to fall off in rotten chunks. It was all he could do to stop himself from running screaming from the tent. But a nice goth girl had taken him under her batwing and looked after him until he came down, and he'd laughed about it the next day. But it had affected him deeply, and he wondered if he'd had his last trip. It wasn't so much giving up the drugs or the drink that depressed him, but the relinquishing of the creative lifestyle. If he "settled down"—got himself a proper job with prospects, out of London, with a mortgage and a car and a suit (a real one from Burtons, not some joky seventies retro flared number with huge lapels from a charity shop)—wasn't he then giving up on his writing? Not that he'd written much so far—a few stoned poems and half an idea (*Did they call it a treatment?*) for a screenplay—but the point was he had made the space in his life for the writing to happen *at some point*. You had to live a certain way in order to be creative. Those provincial types with their children and their Nissan Micras and their supermarket loyalty cards had effectively bricked off their brains so that their creative impulses wouldn't trickle through and unsettle the foundations of their pointless lives.

Stu didn't want to fall into that trap. He thought not for the first time that what he really needed was a sugar mummy, someone to earn the money so that he could stay at home and concentrate on his writing. He might even do a course. And if babies came along, then great, he'd take care of them while she was out at work. He pictured himself living the London baby lifestyle—the baby-massage class, the cinema club exclusively for mums and babies called Screamers, the one o'clock clubs in the park. It would dovetail nicely with his work. He might even get a short story out of it. Trouble was, how could he meet such a woman with his lifestyle? The only girls he met were either the grungy couriers he worked with—all dirty locks and pierced noses—or the dosy office girls in city pubs who had pram faces and low expectations. He never went to the sort of places a well-off single woman would go, and even if he did, why would she choose him? True, he had a good enough body—he cycled more than a hundred miles a week—but he knew he wasn't a head-turner, and he had nothing to offer materially. His bank balance was consistently in the red, and his household goods amounted to one pillow and no forks. He'd just have to get on with his Pulitzer Prize–winning novel and then he'd be loaded. That was the plan.

Out on the streets of London, the traffic was in a mean mood. Every road around Wardour Street was gridlocked, and it seemed to Stu that they were digging up the roads constantly. No sooner had one reopened than another was coned off. Two-way streets became one-way and thoroughfares became no-go areas day by day. London was like some weird maze designed by a vindictive bastard who kept changing the goalposts overnight. Not that it mattered to Stu. He went the way of all London cyclists, claiming the streets and the pavements as his own. It was pointless trying to cycle within the guidelines of the safe-cycling code—you'd never get anywhere. You had to jump red lights to avoid getting mashed by left-turners. You had to undertake as well as overtake or you'd be another dead-meat statistic within minutes. Car drivers hated cyclists, and cyclists hated the four-wheel road hogs who caused all the traffic chaos in the first place.

It had been a heavy day, but he had only one more thing left to deliver—a small package to an advertising agency in Kensington. He'd torn up the streets all day long. It was time to finish now. *Get back to Stockwell. Give Baz a ring—maybe go back to the scene of the crime, get a few games of pool in, maybe score some whiz for the weekend.* Stu chucked his knackered mountain bike in the direction of the railings outside his drop and took the steps three at a time. The reception blonde didn't even look up.

"Package for Josh Johnson." He smiled, always ready in the unlikely event that any of these sleek, flat-haired door bitches would yield to his sweaty charm.

"Not here," she intoned.

"Well can you give me your autograph instead then?"

"What?" she said crossly, looking up from her state-of-the-art game of computer solitaire.

"Can you sign for it?" said Stu, giving up on this one.

"Nah. Not allowed."

"What? What do you mean you're not allowed? It's not a bomb, you know."

"New company policy. The last girl here lost a contract worth two million last week 'cause she forgot to pass on a package that came to reception. You have to get the addressee to sign for it."

"But he's not here," Stu said incredulously.

"I know. I just told you that, didn't I?" said the girl hotly. Clearly, she was at a crucial point in her card game.

"Well . . . what shall I do with it, then?"

"Take it back, I s'pose. . . ." she replied, turning back to her screen.

"But that's ridiculous!" said Stu, not keen on the idea of having to go back to base in Soho.

"Surely he needs this today, or it wouldn't have been biked round to him?"

"Yeah. Probably. Oh, hang on. . . . Let me think. . . . He did say something about a parcel. . . . What was it?"

Stu rapped his filthy nails lightly on the counter.

"Oh, yeah. He said take it to The Wheelbarrow."

"What? What wheelbarrow?" Stu looked around for a farmyard installation. Nothing would surprise him about this place.

"It's the pub on the corner. He'll be in there."

"Bollocks," said Stu, turning to rescue his bike from outside. "Bollocking ridiculous."

At least the pub was just up the road. A quick half-pint would speed him on his way and oil his wheels all the way to Stockwell.

.7.

The ladies' loo at The Wheelbarrow was probably the tiniest cubicle on earth. Typical of British blokey boozers to give any woman brazen enough to enter its portals such a minute toilet, as if to say, "Come in, but don't think you're really welcome." Amy inched her way past the hot air dryer and squeezed past the vending machine—no tampons, just condoms. Also typical.

With any luck, I won't be needing either soon, thought Amy, clutching at the second ovulation test stick in as many months. She'd felt a strange twinge just after her first pint.

Perhaps this was what the Germans charmingly refer to as *Mittelschmerz*—a slight pain in the middle of the menstrual cycle associated with ovulation. She folded herself around the door, almost straddling the loo seat in order to avoid breaking her knees on it as it shut. Struggling with her tights, she attempted to wrestle her underwear to the floor. After a few attempts at getting her tights past her shins, she gave up and decided she would just have to aim properly. Weeing on target had never been her strong suit. How could she ever forget the time she'd been caught short on her way to the school disco and had managed to pee all over her new pink suede pixie boots? It had taken her six months of paper-round money to save up and buy them, and she'd gone home sobbing at her own urinary ineptitude, too ashamed to carry on in her now smelly, wee-splattered footwear.

She'd wanted to be the envy of year four, not the laughingstock.

She took the test stick from its plastic wrapper and nervously placed it between her legs.

Amy couldn't help but feel strangely excited. If two blue lines showed in a couple of minutes' time, it was all stations are go on the baby front. She would have to emerge from the loo like a lioness on the prowl and hunt down a suitable mate for the evening. All she needed was the green light—or the blue lines. But first she would have to wee on the stick, and try as she might, she just could not get started. She thought of waterfalls, dripping taps, hosepipes. Nothing.

"Bloody hell," she muttered out loud. Outside, the door to the washroom creaked open and Amy heard the quiet female cough alerting her to another visitor.

"Come on," she whispered. Still nothing. This was crazy. What a time for her pee phobia to rear its head again. Since the pixie-boot debacle, she'd often suffered aim anxiety when in strange urinating situations—backpacking through Europe had almost been ruined by her inability to squat in the bushes or on foreign train loo seats—but not usually on actual toilets. Her thighs were starting to tire under the strain of squatting, and the door outside creaked again. A small queue was beginning to form. Noise from the early-evening crowd began to leak in—obviously, the latest arrivals in the loo were having to prop the door open to stand in line.

Bloody marvelous, thought Amy. *But I will not give in. I need running water.* Pulling her skirt down around below her knees, she slid the bolt open and sidled out of the cubicle door. A line of about six office girls stood crossly from the hot air dryer to the hallway outside.

"Sorry!" said Amy, smiling sweetly at cross girl number one. "Having a few problems." Keeping one leg inside the cubicle, she reached over to the sink and attempted to turn on the tap. It wouldn't budge.

"Sorry!" she said again, as cross girl number two tutted and got out her hairbrush.

With a huge wrench, Amy released the stiff faucet. Water shot out, spraying her blouse and soaking cross girl number one.

"Shit!" she shrieked. "Thanks a lot!"

"Sorry, sorry, sorry!" said Amy, ducking back in and crouching over the toilet. Whether it was the gushing tap outside, the cold water all down her front, or the diversion of the utter humiliation she had just endured, Amy finally, blissfully, began to pee. She remembered just in time to push the stick under the stream, then placed it carefully on top of the toilet-roll holder. Pulling up her tights, she wriggled out of the cubicle and began to studiously wash her hands, skillfully avoiding eye contact with the cross girls as she switched on the hot air dryer. The noise drowned out any possibility of a verbal recrimination, and Amy rubbed her hands gratefully under the warm air. It wasn't until the dryer stopped that Amy heard the voice from inside the loo, which had the irritated tone of someone who had been calling for some time.

"*Excuse me!*"

"Yes?" Amy answered lamely.

"I think you left something in here?"

The test. Amy had forgotten to bring it out with her.

"Oh . . . yes sorry . . . do you just want to shove it under the door?"

"Not really. It's covered in wee."

"Oh, OK, I'll wait. Sorry."

There was a short pause.

"I can just tell you if you like," said the woman, clearly warming to the drama of the situation.

"Erm . . . OK," said Amy, keen to get out without having to face the woman.

"It's got a blue line in one window. . . ."

"Yes. That just means it's worked. Anything else?" asked Amy, by now flatly expecting a negative.

"And it's got another little window and . . . yes, wait a minute, it's a bit dark in here, I'll just put my glasses on. . . ."

Amy bit her lip in irritation as the woman rummaged in her bag, just visible under the door. After what seemed like about three hours, she spoke again.

"Yes . . . I think there's another blue line in the second window . . . yeah, definitely."

"Sure?" said Amy.

"Yep. Hundred and ten percent," said the woman.

"Thanks!" said Amy, adjusting her bra and dabbing on a fresh coat of lipgloss.

"Once more unto the breech, dear friends!" she announced to the slack-jawed toilet audience as she brushed past them and back into the smoke-filled bar.

. 8 .

"Bollocks! Bollocks, bollocks, bollocks!" shouted Stu, rubbing his bleeding elbow. He'd just pulled out onto the road again when a taxi shot out from nowhere and clipped his back wheel, sending Stu wobbling off to one side. Fortunately, it was the pavement side.

The taxi, of course, hadn't even bothered to stop, and although Stu made a cursory attempt to memorize the guy's license plate, he knew there would be no follow-up. What was the point? Cabbies did this kind of thing every day. Probably every minute of every day, someone was being hurled off their bike and into the street by some road-hogging, bleary-eyed, fat-arsed cabbie. He'd landed, bike still in his grasp, on the edge of a beer barrel being used as an impromptu table outside a pub. Blood was trickling from his forearm and his elbow, and he felt as though he were fourteen again, but not in that good way when he felt inexplicably hopeful or happy—just publicly humili-ated. A couple of guys about his age stopped their chatting about IT, or stocks, or whatever the hell those people talked about outside such pubs, and took the opportunity to resurrect their own inner fourteen-year-olds. They sniggered, pointed, then returned to their beers.

At least it was the right pub. Stu looked up at the inappropriately rural sign above the pub door—a smocked yokel pushing an ancient wheelbarrow full of corn through a wildflower meadow. A far cry from the cynical seven quid they were asking for a "ploughman's lunch" inside. He limped, bleeding, into the bar and looked around for a man who looked like a likely Josh. That hardly narrowed it down. Most of the occupants looked a bit poncy, a bit posh, and most of them were men in suits. Stu clocked the gaggle of women in one corner nursing their Bacardi Breezers, one of whom he noticed was now dabbing at her damp blouse. He could spot a wet bosom at a hundred paces. But even he was not in the mood right now. He had to locate this Josh bloke, deliver his parcel, and get back on the bike and back home before Baz and the others went out without him.

Clearing his throat, he addressed the whole room.

"Is there a Josh Johnson here?"

A few of the people close to him turned and looked dispassionately back at him before resuming their conversations. Stu tried again.

"Josh Johnson?" he shouted, waving the parcel hopefully in the air.

Still nothing. The girls had started to look at him now. One was pointing to his cycling shorts and making some comment, which her companions seemed to find highly amusing.

Stu was fed up now. The blood was dripping onto the booze-drenched carpet, and his elbow was beginning to sting like hell.

"Josh Johnson! Josh Johnson! A million quid for Josh Johnson right here in this envelope!"

The pub suddenly went quiet, and from the far corner of the bar, Stu saw a small group opening up.

"I am he!" boomed a large voice from within.

Stu made his way through the bar, finally ending up in front of the small group in the corner.

"Josh? Which one of you is Mr. Johnson?" he said, trying to mask his irritation.

"I am," said a voice from just behind him.

Stu turned to locate the joker. She was about his age, dark-haired, and casually dressed. She was the only woman in the group and didn't look like she fitted in at all in this environment. Her eyes met his as she broke into the cheekiest of smiles.

"At least, I am if you weren't joking about the million quid."

The men around her started to laugh.

"Watch her, mate, she bites," said one of the younger guys.

"Nice shorts!" said his mate.

"Gay!" shouted the first.

Stu ignored them and wrestled with his courier bag. Out of the corner of his eyes, he could feel the woman checking him out. Without thinking about it, he drew in his stomach and gently puffed out his chest. She was definitely up for it. Or was she just one of those women who were all headlights, no engine? Would she flirt and then leave, like so many of the thirtysomething women he wasted evenings on in bars? They acted like they were up for anything, but when it came to the crunch, they left with their mates, more interested in having a laugh for the evening than taking home some scruffy bloke. Gone were the days when women needed to bag a man to feel like they'd had a successful night out.

"Can't you find your package?" said a third guy with a northern accent.

"I can see it from here!" said the posh bloke, and the whole group erupted with laughter.

What a bunch of wankers, thought Stu as he finally located the brown padded envelope at the bottom of his bag. What was this good-looking, sexy woman doing with a crowd of plonkers like this? It never ceased to amaze him how guys like these managed to get really nice women to go out with them.

"Just sign there please," Stu said to the posh guy.

"You're bleeding!" the woman said suddenly.

"Oh, it's nothing—I just got knocked off my bike outside. Happens all the time. Nothing to worry about. Occupational hazard." He smiled, doing his best to look nonchalant but feeling slightly queasy at the amount of blood now oozing from his arm. The skin, he could see now, had come clean away and was hanging in an unsightly flap from his elbow.

"Ouch! You should get that seen to. Here, let me get you some tissue."

Before he could object, the woman ran off in the direction of the toilets, leaving him trapped in the circle of men who were finding so much sport in his presence. Which one was she with? Surely not this chinless git with the parcel? She didn't seem like that type. Not vacuous and "Chelsea" enough. What about the macho northern bloke, the one who'd made the crack about the content of Stu's cycling shorts? A lot of perfectly sane women were inexplicably attracted to such Neanderthals—he'd read it in an ex-girlfriend's *Marie Claire*. Something about an unreconstructed cave woman gene. Not her, though. She looked far too wry to fall for that chest-beating routine. Surely not these two idiots in their designer suits with their schoolboy banter? They only looked to be about twenty-five, and she did not look like a Mrs. Robinson. With the woman temporarily absent, the atmosphere took a sober turn. It was as if all the teasing, posturing, and competing had been solely for her benefit. So perhaps she wasn't with any of them? They started to chat among themselves, nudging Stu subtly out of the circle, returning him to his rightful social position—he was staff.

"Here you are," said the woman, appearing by his side with a large clump of sodden toilet paper.

"It's not very good, but it's all they had. No first-aid box. We should probably report them."

"Oh, thanks, it's fine, really."

"Let me see?"

"No!" said Stu, as she started to pull at his elbow.

She laughed and carried on.

"I don't even know you," cried Stu in mock-indignation. "And here you are, trying to get a look at my flesh wounds!"

"Urgh! The skin's coming off!"

"I know, now leave it! It'll be fine!" said Stu, playfully batting away her hand.

"No, it won't be fine. What is it with you men? You won't be helped, will you?" she said, clearly not a woman to be told no.

"And my name is Amy."

"Stu."

"Well, Stu, you really should get that seen to. Perhaps your girlfriend will be able to patch it up for you when you get home—if not, I'd go to Casualty if I were you and get it checked out."

"Smooth," said Stu, smiling.

"What?"

"Very smooth. 'Your girlfriend.' Like your style."

"What do you mean?" said Amy, coloring slightly. Had she been rumbled? Was her seduction technique that obvious? She hadn't even really meant to be fishing for information, but something inside her was propelling her on. Her biological clock needed no winding up.

"Yes, you're probably right. . . . I should get it seen to. And no, I don't have a girlfriend."

"I didn't—I mean, I wasn't—" stumbled Amy.

"Why don't you buy me a drink—for the shock, I mean—and we'll forget you ever said it," said Stu, sure now that she was within his grasp.

She hesitated for a second, then stuck out her chin and said, "Right. Large brandy coming up."

Stu watched as she wriggled through to the bar, a slow smile spreading over his face as he observed her round, velour-clad bottom disappearing behind a pillar. It bore the word "Juicy" in white letters over the curve of her lower back.

Hope so, thought Stu. In many ways this was the best part of pulling—the banter, the checking each other out, the anticipation of what lay beneath the surface layers of clothing, and conversational innuendo. He started to plan the evening. A few drinks here (he hoped she had some money, because he'd spent his last pound on a bottle of Lucozade at lunchtime, and it would be too much of a hiatus to nip out to the cashpoint and attempt to extend his overdraft again), then, his courage bolstered by the booze, he'd suggest they move on somewhere else. They couldn't stay in the midst of these blokes all evening; otherwise, she may mistake his interest for just general sociability. No, he would have to make his intimate intentions clear. No doubt she would "um" and "er" a bit, pretend to be in two minds, but she would eventually agree to meet him back at her place (he couldn't be sure that Will wasn't in the flat this evening, or that the pile of crusty washing up had been removed from the sink). Once back at her place, he could ask to have a shower—the hot water was dodgy at his flat so it had been a few days, and cycling around London all day did nothing for a boy's armpits, especially as he didn't believe in deodorant. Again, she might hesitate, wary of such an obvious ploy to get naked, but he would say that he needed to clean his wound and she would relent (you had to let chicks slowly realize that they want it just as much as you). From then on, when he had emerged from the shower with the towel around his waist (revealing his strong cyclist's upper body), it would be smooth sailing. Stu let out a sigh of satisfaction, his routine worked out. He wondered where she lived. He'd have to take his bike—couldn't risk leaving it chained to the railings overnight, or he'd come back to a one-wheeler in the morning. Presuming, of course, that it would be daylight by the time he returned. But surely, if he was careful and charming and didn't move too fast, he'd be able to snare this gorgeous and wholly unexpected treasure. It was at times like this that Stu loved his life. No one to answer to, no one to go home to, nowhere to be but wherever he wanted to be in that moment. And although this rootlessness had started to pall, every new liaison these days had an air of possibility. This could be the one. This chance meeting in a pub over a cut elbow could be the stuff of wedding day speeches, of "how we met" anecdotes in years to come. Life was great. Stu sighed again in anticipation of the evening ahead.

Just play your cards right. Not too keen. Not too predatory. Don't want to frighten the deer back into the forest, he reminded himself. The next half hour was crucial.

"Right. Drink up, then back to mine. Let's get that wound sorted," said Amy, thrusting a large brandy roughly into Stu's hands.

Blimey, she is keen, he thought, gulping back the liquid and trying not to cough. He hated brandy.

"OK, nurse. Whatever you say. But I'll have to bring my bike, so I'll meet you there."

"Oh," said Amy, "fine," scribbling her address down on a beer mat. "Don't be long."

"I'll be dripping blood on your doorstep before you're out of the West End," said Stu, memorizing the address.

"Oh, yeah? I've got a BMW," countered Amy, pulling on her leather jacket and ignoring the winks and jeers now coming from the blokes she was with.

"Race yer," said Stu, leaping to his feet and heading for the door. This would be fun. He'd heard all about female BMW drivers. By all accounts, this ought to be the night of his life.

. 9 .

It could be tonight, thought Amy as she sped along the Embank-ment. She made a conscious effort to take in the view she loved so much—it might be the last time she'd do this as an unpregnant woman. The London Eye, the South Bank, Waterloo Bridge—all her favorite bits of London crammed together along one stretch of stinky water. But she loved it. Her stomach lurched at the idea that tonight might be the last carefree night of her life. She remembered the good bottle of champagne she had kept for just such an occasion and worked out how long it would take to chill in the freezer. Stu looked as though he liked a drink. Better not get him too tiddly, though—intoxicated sperm were likely to miss their target and just hang around in her cervix, having a party. She didn't want to waste her second month, not when this guy looked like such a fit specimen. She had hardly been able to believe her eyes when she'd caught sight of his perfect Lycra-clad bottom. It had been a complete waste of time going for the intellectual last month. She should have guessed that anyone at a MENSA evening would be screwy. Much better to go for someone fit and physical, someone who let his body do the talking. She put her foot down on the accelerator and pressed her back into the leather seat. With a bit of luck, and with the traffic lights on her side, she'd have the champagne on ice and the candles lit before he got there. She might even have time to nip into the shower and attend to any bikini-line stragglers. As if to thwart her, the next set of lights switched to red, forcing Amy to hit the brakes hard. All along the Embankment for about a mile ahead Amy could see brake lights slamming on. *Great.* Now she was caught in a red-light chain. No chance of getting to Docklands before him. She'd seen the way those couriers slipped through traffic like freshwater salmon. Oh, well—at least he would be waiting eagerly on her doorstep. Amy swore she felt her womb lurch at the prospect.

.10.

R ob? Stu. Listen, mate, no can do tonight," shouted Stu into his mobile, one hand on the handlebars, the other fiddling with his hands-free kit.

"What a result, mate! Guess where I'm going?"

"Claudia Schiffer's penthouse suite," said Rob, clearly pissed off with the disruption to their dull drinking routine.

"Close, my friend, very close."

"What?"

"I have just picked up—no, correction, *been* picked up, outrageously picked up—by a gorgeous woman in a pub, and I'm on the way to meet her at her place. Mate, she drives a BMW!"

"Jesus."

"I know!"

"So I'm guessing you won't be joining us for a game of Winner Stays On at the pool club tonight?" said Rob, aware that it was a ridiculous question but hopeful anyhow. It was always a depressing

night for the remainder of the gang when one of them was out getting laid.

"Tough call, mate, tough call," laughed Stu. He'd tried that strat-
egy himself many a time when it was he who had been dumped by a
gang member in favor of some totty. He wasn't about to cave in under a bit of laddish pressure, and anyway, he knew that secretly they'd
all be willing him on, glad that at least one of them was getting his
end away. No doubt they'd want to know the details when he saw
them tomorrow night. Presuming, that was, she didn't keep him captive for weeks on end, addicted to his prowess. It had happened before. Well, once. Stu tried to suppress the little voice at the back of
his head, which was whispering nonsense about this girl possibly being "the one," about how this might be the first night of the rest of his
life. What would Rob think if he knew the girlish hopes that beat beneath his mate's muscular chest?

"But yeah—you guessed right. Listen, I'll see you tomorrow, mate—
where you going tomorrow night?"

The earpiece jiggled loose in Stu's ear. He tried to nudge it back in
with his shoulder.

"Fantastic night tomorrow, Stu—" started Rob, but now the earpiece fell clean out of his ear.

"Hang on, mate," Stu shouted as he lurched for the cord; it was
dangling down from the phone in his bag strap and threatening to get
tangled up in his back wheel.

If he'd not been temporarily distracted, if the earpiece had fit better, if he'd been prepared to let it drop and be crushed on the road and
pay out for a new one, if he'd not been on the phone in the first place,
if he'd just looked up a split-second before the ice cream van pulled
out into his lane, perhaps things would have been different. But life
makes no allowances for "if onlys," so things being as they were, that
evening Stu found himself not in the arms of a beautiful stranger but
thrown rudely onto the crossbar of his aluminum bike. It had happened, as all accidents do, in the blink of an eye. The pain didn't

come straight away. First there was indignation, then fear, then anger. But just as Stu opened his mouth to hurl abuse at the stupid van driver, a pain so intense, so compelling, so all-consuming, shot through his shorts and straight up into his testicles.

"Bollocks!" rasped Stu, and for once it was wholly appropriate.

.11.

J ules? Amy here."

"Hi, hon, what's new and different from the singleton frontline?"

"Very funny. I've been dumped. Again."

"What do you mean 'dumped'? I didn't know you were seeing anyone!"

"I wasn't. I was trying to, but he dumped me before it even began."

"Ah—wounded pride. Ouch. What happened? Tell mama all about it."

"It was a sure thing! I chatted up this courier in the pub and arranged to meet him back at my place and he just—never showed up! Three hours I waited! I ended up drinking a whole bottle of champagne on my own and shouting at *Question Time*!"

"That's bad, Amy, that's bad."

"Tell me about it! I was wearing my Agent Provocateur panties!"

"Ouch again. Doesn't sound like you, Amy. I've never known you to sit at home waiting for a man that wasn't going to show. Is the old radar failing? Are you losing your pulling power?" There was just a hint of pleasure, the tiniest touch of schadenfreude in Jules's tone. It was always Amy who got her man on their nights out together when Jules's relationship was on the rocks.

"I'm telling you he was gagging for it, and then nothing! That's twice in two months I've been rejected. Can I ask you something?"

"Of course."

"Do I look old?"

"Oh, Christ, that's not fair."

"Come on, you've had all that surgery, you're the expert. Do I look old?"

"Look, it's not your laughter lines that's putting them off, but it might just be the stench of desperation! Honestly, what's got into you? Why the sudden concern? So a couple of guys have blown you off—big deal! Welcome to my world! Not everyone is going to fall under your spell. Plenty more out there that will. Just get back out there and find them!"

"I know, you're right. But it's not normal. One rejection, OK, take that on the chin, character-building and all that, but two? Two's a pattern. A pattern I can't afford."

"Hello? Is that Amy? Sorry, for a minute there I thought I'd got a crossed line with Sad Bitches Anonymous. Why can't you afford two rejections? You've got your whole life ahead of you! I thought you weren't interested in settling down?"

Amy took a deep breath. It was the perfect opportunity to let her friend in on her guilty secret. So far only Brendan knew, and for once he'd kept his word and not spread it about, probably because he was so weirded out he couldn't bring himself to say it out loud. But she hadn't told anyone else, and it felt odd to be undergoing such a life-changing process without her female friends as sounding boards. She wasn't entirely sure why she hadn't told them. It was partly because they were all pregnant themselves and she didn't want them to pity her or keep asking her if she'd "had any joy" yet. It was also because she couldn't bear the idea of them laughing at her abrupt change of heart. She was sure they'd assume she was feeling left out of their club, and the idea appalled her so much that she was determined to keep her plans from them until the last possible moment, then perhaps present her pregnancy as a happy accident, a sort of "oops, oh well, this might be interesting" kind of thing. If she were honest, there was also an element of fear that they would disapprove of her methods. There was Ang, in her stable, traditional marriage with her "old woman who lived in a shoe" brood of kids, Greg and Soph with their conventional IVF response to "unexplained infertility," and Jules with her on/off long-term boyfriend of many years—all in their own ways coming at parenthood by acceptable routes. If she were to announce her wayward, scattershot, au naturel plans, they would probably be horrified and try to talk her out of them. In the back of her mind, Amy knew this was also part projection. She had started to feel as though the two rejections were nature's way of telling her to stop being such a trollop and find the right man first. She wasn't normally given to such paranoid assumptions, but these were extraordinary times. She needed her friends now, if only to stop her from freaking out. Nothing for it but to bite the bullet and tell Jules.

"Well, I'm trying to get pregnant," she blurted.

There was a pause—Amy noted how pregnant it was—before the inevitable mirth. Jules roared down the phone.

"All right all right! It's not that funny!"

"Sorry—I can't help it—I'm not laughing at you—did you say 'pregnant'?"

"Yes."

More laughter. Amy waited until it began to subside.

"Finished?"

"Yes. Sorry. What do you mean? You're seriously trying to get pregnant? How?"

"This is no time for the birds and the bees, Jules."

"No, I mean who with? Why? When? What for? So many questions! Answers needed right now!"

"Look, I don't know why, at least I don't right now, but I just am, and I've decided to try a different man each month for a year, and if it doesn't work then that's it, it wasn't meant to be, and we'll say no more about it. No fuss, no messy drawn-out relationships with sterile, needy men, no hospital intrusion, no petri dishes with frozen embryos, just me, my ovaries, and a one-shot chance per man. Got a problem with that?"

There was silence at the end of the line.

"Oh my God, she's serious," said Jules quietly.

"Please don't go all moral on me, Jules—not you, not now." Amy was suddenly terrified that she might be disapproved of. It was an unfamiliar and wholly unpleasant feeling.

"No, no I'm not. I actually think . . ."

"What? What? What do you think?"

"I actually think it's rather—wonderful," said Jules, before bursting into tears. "Fucking hormones," she wailed.

Whether it was relief or her own little burst of ovulation madness, Amy found her own eyes prickling with tears. What was happening to them?

"We'll have none of this! Come on, pull yourself together, fatty, 'cause I haven't done it yet, and who knows, I might not be able to! For all I know I could be shooting blanks!" said Amy, dabbing at her eyes with the cuff of her dressing gown.

"Not you," said Jules firmly. "You're from good Irish peasant stock. You'll just bang one out in the potato fields one day. No problem."

For once not rising to the casual joky racism of her friend's comment, Amy's face broke into a huge grin.

. 12 .

"I don't understand this at all," said Soph, sighing as she wriggled free of her Birkenstocks.

"Not six months ago you were virtually King Herod and now you're prepared to risk your sexual health to conceive a baby via a complete stranger."

Ah, the AIDS lecture—I wondered when that was coming, thought Amy. Soph had been one of those scare-mongers who'd gone around as if every vanilla, monogamous, non-drug-using, healthy person in the Western world was in mortal danger from HIV. She'd done all the ribbon-wearing, fund-raising, and benefit organizing, and every Sunday she'd volunteered for The Food Chain, a sort of Meals on Wheels service for people living with the disease—though quite what these innocent people had done to deserve Sophie's cooking was beyond Amy. Soph was big on AIDS and HIV awareness, to the point where one time, after a powwow with some lesbian friends who scared the living daylights out of her with tales of female-to-female transmission, she'd insisted on Greg using a dental dam for oral sex. Despite Sophie's hysteria—a word Amy had used unwisely one late night after too much Chianti—Amy knew that her friend had a point. It was something that she had thought about, but somehow she felt she was safe. She'd read Brendan's leaflets about how foolish such a fatalistic approach to the issue was, and about what other horrors there were lurking in every sexual encounter—chlamydia, herpes, crabs, and apparently gonorrhea and syphilis were making a comeback. Retromania had even hit diseases. But she'd always subscribed to the belief that you pays your money and you makes your choice in this life. No point skirting around the edges of life trying to avoid all danger— where was the fun in that? Grandiosity, perhaps, but she had decided to proceed with her plan. Besides, she'd read somewhere that, postprivatization, as a heterosexual woman living in the UK you had more chance of dying in a train crash than transmitting HIV.

"And don't give me that line about train crashes again," groaned Soph, who had heard it all before.

"OK, well let's call it quits then. No more lectures."

"Well, it's your immune system, you play Russian roulette with it."

"Thanks, Mum. And anyway, it's not as if it's been under threat recently. I haven't managed to get so much as a bottom squeeze so far. I don't know what's wrong with men today. I thought all this crisis in masculinity was just middle-class blether, but I've been knocked back twice, and frankly I'm worried! Me! Spurned! Can you believe it?"

"There must be a crisis," said Greg, who'd obviously been listening in the hall.

"Girl talk," said Soph, shooting him a "piss off" glance.

"Oh, let me play! It's just getting interesting. I'm a man, I can tell you where you're going wrong."

"Go on then," said Amy, sure that she wouldn't learn a thing from Greg's dated take on the sex war.

"Well, for a start, wow! I mean, *you*—trying to get pregnant!"

"Thank you, piss off, Greg."

"No, I mean, I think it's great. You can go to yoga with Soph and share breast-pump stories and everything!"

"Look, have you got anything of value to say or not?" said Soph, always protective of her friends.

"So you've been knocked back twice on this mission, have you? And how long have you been trying to get laid—I mean, pregnant?"

"Two months," said Amy glumly.

"And so far you've not even managed to do the necessary at all? Maybe, just maybe, men can hear the ticking of your clock."

"Rubbish," said Amy hotly.

"No, I read this thing in *Mother and Baby* magazine—men can tell when a woman is ovulating, and if they don't want children, they run a mile. It's the smell."

"Right, so not only am I losing my touch, but now I've got smelly hormones as well. Thanks a bunch, Greg."

"It's true! You've got to find men who are actively in the market for babies."

"That leaves a very small pool of first-date material, Greg. Most guys are willing to hop into bed with you quick as you like, but it's not babies they're after. I'm pretty sure most of them want to spill their seed on barren land, as it were."

"True. *Most* men. But not *all* men," said Greg, adopting his knowing smile.

"There are some men out there who are so broody, they'd be willing to sleep with anyone if they thought she could conceive their child. I mean *anyone*—even you!" said Greg, pleased with his tease.

"Yes, but you're missing the point, Greg. Amy doesn't want the man involved. That's why she wants it to be one-night stands. She's doing this on her own," said Soph, stroking her still-flat belly and placing Greg's hand lovingly on it.

Greg's mouth dropped open.

"Oh. I see. So after all those years of trying to get us where you want us—of basically making us into women with willies—we are now redundant, are we? Just milk us for our sperm, pat us on the head, and send us packing, is it? I see. Well, why don't you go the whole hog and just go on the Internet? Within thirty minutes of ovulating, you could get a jam jar full of hot spunk delivered to your door quicker than you can say 'Deep Pan Hawaiian with extra cheese'!" said Greg, only half joking.

"I know what it sounds like, but plenty of women bring up kids on their own these days. What am I going to do, spend the next year looking for Mr. Almost Right, then the next grooming him for parenthood? I haven't got the time. If I do it that way I'll be pregnant in my forties, and I'm sorry but I'm not Madonna," said Amy, who was ready for all of this.

"Hey, it's cool with me. Whatever. Don't get so defensive."

Amy always braced herself when Greg said this. What he actually meant was, "Here comes something to get your back up." She didn't have to wait long. He paused for a second then took a deep breath, warming to his theme.

"But don't you know that dads are the new mums? Look at that nutter who strapped himself to Waterloo Bridge dressed as Spiderman 'cause he couldn't see his kids—he made it on the news all over the world. Everyone knows dads are where it's at. Mums are so twentieth century," said Greg. Amy hated it when he got into one of these confrontational moods. Best to smile and nod and change the subject.

"Anyway, enough about me—how's the bump coming along? You must be about due for your second scan, Soph," she said, fixing a smile on her face.

"Yes, *we* are," said Greg. "In four weeks, actually. And don't change the subject. I can see you don't believe me, but just look around you the next time you go to the park or Pizza Express or the swimming pool—it's dads who are out and about with their kids. Mums are too busy having it all. Probably sitting at home writing columns for broadsheet newspapers on how hard it is being a working mum while the poor old dads are schlepping round city farms with nothing but a pocketful of organic rice cakes and futile dreams of copping off with the nanny for company. I don't see how you can contemplate going it alone. It's just not the done thing anymore."

"Oh, spare me," groaned Amy as Sophie grinned indulgently at Greg's game.

"I'm only saying this for your own good. It's not fair on the kids. 'What does your daddy do?' 'He's a one-night stand.' Wouldn't sound too good on the playground, would it? You can't just rub men out of the equation because you don't want to share your duvet with anyone."

"It's not like I haven't tried with men—but they're all so useless! I can't even get one to commit to a one-night stand, let alone years of sleepless nights and parenthood!" Amy was almost wailing now. This conversation had not gone as she had hoped.

"Go and look again. You'll find one. Just go to the right places and they'll come flocking. Look for the single guys hanging around the swings in the park."

"Sounds pretty creepy to me."

"Not those ones—the young guys. Not the ones in trench coats."

.13.

Men pushing three-wheel buggies, men carrying screaming toddlers into unisex baby-changing facilities, men wiping the noses of snotty infants, men blowing raspberries at their babies in supermarket trolleys, men carrying tiny newborns in fleece papooses, men wrestling wriggling children into too-tight coats, men asking for hot water to warm the baby's bottle in Starbucks. Greg was right. Everywhere Amy looked now there were men with children, and not just part-time, divorced, fair-weather dads—these dads had the careworn but devoted look of full-time parents. Now that she looked, they were everywhere. Problem was, they were already coupled up. Presumably. Most of the time, the men she saw with children were alone—no doubt allowing the mom to focus on her career—but she felt sure they were happily ensconced in units of two, and she drew the line at luring a married man to bed just to get pregnant, however obvious his fertility track record. And anyway, she had definitely decided that she was not going to hang around and go through the laborious preliminaries of a relationship before conceiving. So what was the point of trying to find a nice man? Any man would do, so long as he was healthy and not too hideous to look at. The last thing she wanted was some guy hanging around getting involved in her life. No, what she needed was a lucky date with a fit young guy who was either too horny to register her baby-making intentions or too broody himself to care. And much as she had poo-pooed Greg at the time, since their discussion she had found herself hanging out in all of the places he'd mentioned. She'd been to the local swimming pool for the first time in years; she'd loitered near playgrounds and even went to the kids' section of McDonald's to check out the single guys there. It had seemed logical, really—if you were looking for a potential father to your child, go to places full of children. These places were so revolting and chaotic that any single man there of his own choice must be good father potential, if only biologically. With twenty hours to go before her third ovulation window, Amy had come to her favorite London park, hoping to spot a likely candidate. Dumped on the top end of Hackney, nudging the borders of Tower Hamlets, Victoria Park had been a regular haunt of Amy's in her student days, home as it was to a rolling stock of political demonstrations from the Suffragettes to Gay Pride. The neat flower borders, the gated Old English Garden with its single lemon tree, and the toy boating lakes all looked pleasingly antiquated in the present-day grubby, crime-addled East End. It was dedicated to the great matriarch herself, Queen Victoria, so it felt like a good place to be trawling for a father. Firm once again in her resolve, Amy ordered her favorite park café treat— a hot chocolate with floating marshmallows. She'd not been here since Germaine had died, and it choked her a bit now to think how Germaine had always waited patiently for the piece of froth-coated marshmallow that signaled the end of the rest break. It was almost June, but the London sky refused to smile. Young girls shivered in their summer fashions and ice-cream vendors looked pathetically hopeful. The tulips were drooping and the daffodils were long gone, but still Amy detected the sap rising all around her. Boys whistled at girls in short skirts, builders shouted at women on the street, and middle-aged ladies serving in shops winked at male customers as they handed them their change. It seemed to Amy as though everyone was up for it. Or was that just projection? She felt sure that this month it would all be different. This month it was going to happen.

"Shall we sit here and feed the duckies, bubba?" said a warm male voice behind her.

"Da da da da da da!" squealed a little voice.

"What noise does the duckie make, Lola? Quack quack! Quack quack!"

"Da da da da da da!"

"No, quack quack quack quack! Let's go and feed the quack-quacks."

Amy glanced around to see the doting daddy behind her. He was about thirty, with cropped dark hair and the longest eyelashes she'd ever seen. He was wearing a tight white T-shirt and dark blue jeans, and his face was awash with love for his little daughter. She was about one, sitting up in her buggy with huge pink cheeks and a mass of blond curls. Two little podgy hands flailed around in excitement as she watched her daddy getting a plastic bag full of bread crusts from his rucksack.

"Da da da da da!" she squealed again. So it was true—little girls do love their daddies. Not for the first time, Amy started to doubt her plan. Could she really do this alone? Was it fair? But her child would have good male role models—Brendan, Greg, the guys in the pub . . .

"Da da da da da!"

Amy couldn't peel her eyes away from the twosome so engaged in each other's company. Suddenly, the man looked up and caught her eye. Amy was rewarded with a dazzling smile.

"No, not dada—*Andy*. Can you say Andy, bubba?" He turned and smiled again. Was it just her imagination or was there a hint of flirtation in the pointedness with which he corrected the little girl?

"Da da da da da!" she squealed again, oblivious to the facts.

"I don't think she's really listening," the man said to Amy.

"Doesn't look like it. I suppose one man is pretty much like any other at that age," said Amy.

"Oh, no! Babies can recognize their parents from about four weeks. It's just a blurry outline at first, but they definitely know who their parents are by this age," said the man as he idly ripped up slices of stale bread.

"Da da da da da!" said the baby emphatically, pointing a jammy finger straight at the man.

"Either she's very confused or you're in denial," said Amy, laughing. He couldn't possibly be lying in order to pick her up, could he?

The man's easy laugh put pay to any such possibility.

"I think she's confused. She doesn't see much of her dad."

"So are you Stepdaddy?"

"No. I'm her nanny," said the man, smiling in acknowledgment of the unusualness of his position.

"Blimey," said Amy. She'd never met a male nanny before.

"And here was me thinking all nannies looked like Julie Andrews."

"I know, it's a constant battle of altering perceptions. I just don't look good in the blue starched dress and the stiff white hat," he said. It was clear he'd had to go through the same routine many times. Amy felt conscious of not wanting to bore him with the same old questions, but at the same time, he fascinated her. Why did he decide to become a nanny? What sort of man would want to look after other people's children for a living? Was he gay? Did he get much work? Did people trust men to look after children? Was it harder for him? Did he not feel emasculated?

"And before you ask, I just like children and they've always liked me; I'm one hundred percent heterosexual; yes, it's sometimes hard work persuading potential employers that I'm not a weirdo, but generally I've not been out of work in six years." He smiled.

Amy blushed at the obviousness of her questions.

"Oh. Right. Er, thanks. Saved us both a lot of bother there," she stuttered.

"No problem. I'm Andy," he said, offering his hand.

"Amy. Pleased to meet you. And this is Lola, is it?"

"Yes, this is Lola. I've been looking after her since she was three months old. Her mum works in the city."

"And her dad?"

"Was a wild night under the stars in Namibia. The gamekeeper in a safari park. A bit of a shock, but she's managing well now that she's got me. She was a bit funny about the agency sending me at first, but I think she likes Lola having a man about the place now."

"So you're a father substitute, are you? How does that feel?"

Andy winced.

"Hmmm. Not sure yet. It's OK so far, but it's getting harder. She keeps calling me Dada. I think she's picked it up from the other babies at massage. It was funny at first, but now I'm thinking what happens if I leave? Or what if her mum changes her mind and wants a female nanny after all? As far as she's concerned, *I'm* her dad. What's it going to do to her if I'm suddenly not around?"

Amy noticed his forehead furrowed in genuine concern. It made him even more attractive. What was it about men who were good with children? Some of the men who'd come into her shop over the years had attested to the fact that having a baby in tow was the ultimate babe magnet. Forget flashy cars and full wallets—apparently, what the chicks really like is to see a man's nurturing side. She'd actually heard of men who'd borrow their friend's babies for the day in order to attract women. Apparently, it worked every time.

"Here, Lola—throw some bread for the duckies," said Andy, handing a fistful of bread to the baby.

The little fat hands lunged at the bread, then threw it all in one soggy heap into the edge of the water.

"No, little bits—little bits, Lola." He laughed gently, handing her some more bread.

"Care to join us?" he said, offering Amy a slice.

"Love to." Amy smiled, letting her hand brush against his fingers for a moment.

And for the next ten minutes they stood, the three of them quietly throwing scraps of bread to the squabbling ducks, to all onlookers the perfect little family. Amy suddenly felt calm and totally in the moment, absorbed in the simple pleasure of it. So this was the attraction of taking your children to the park. She'd never understood it before, but now it seemed so brilliantly Zen. Just her, him, the baby, and the rippling water. Only one thought niggled away at her. How was she going to get him into bed by tomorrow night? She knew only too well how hard urban nannies work—the long hours, the night duty, the expectation that they are on call twenty-four hours a day. Some of the au pairs she'd encountered at the shop were so exhausted they could hardly speak. Was he a good choice? Would he be a) available, b) interested, and c) energetic enough after caring for Lola? She needed more information. She cut through the contented silence.

"Do you get a day off at all?" She tried to keep focused on the ducks as her words hung heavily in the air. She might as well have said, "Shall we go into the bushes and have sex right now?" for all the subtlety she'd been able to manage.

Andy let out a hollow laugh.

"I do in theory, but I live in, so there's no knowing what will happen from one moment to the next. My boss is a bit chaotic to say the least. Why do you ask?"

He was really making her work for this.

"I just thought it might be nice to have dinner. There's a new Vietnamese restaurant over the road—great crispy duck."

"Shhh! Have you no tact, woman?" hissed Andy, indicating the duck pond.

"Oops. Not in front of the children."

"Well, I'm due an evening off tomorrow . . . but I expect that's too short notice for you."

"No! No, that's fine," blurted Amy, instantly aware of how over-keen she now looked. Had she blown it? There was an awkward pause. She fully expected to turn and see Andy sprinting off down the cycle track, pushing the three-wheel buggy as fast as he could in front of him, bread flying left, right, and center.

He was looking right at her.

"Great. Shall I meet you there at seven thirty?"

"Cool. See you then," said Amy, walking as casually as she could toward the park gates.

"And I promise not to order the duck!" she threw back as a witty afterthought, before crashing into a café table and sending a coffee cup flying.

.14.

This felt better. At least it was a proper date, more time to prepare, less chance of anything going wrong. She'd learned her les-
son the hard way—it was much wiser to try to net the man *before*
ovulation day. It meant she could relax and concentrate on the seduction rather than the entrapment. It had been a while since she'd
been on a proper date, and the novelty added a frisson that kept her
awake half the night. What to wear—a dress? Too formal. Jeans and
a sweater? Too casual. In the end, she'd settled on her good black
trousers and her low-cut Joseph T-shirt. It had never failed. It
wouldn't do to make too much of an effort—she'd obviously frightened Stephen off with her "fertilize me" shoes. Neither should she be
too complacent—imagine letting Stu make his own way to her flat!
She was asking to be stood up. This time she'd gotten it just right.
Nevertheless, her nerves were causing her stomach to clench involuntarily, and she wondered if she'd be able to eat her customary spicy
noodle soup. Was chili a good idea for a seduction night anyway? She
didn't want to repeat a nasty accident involving red-hot finger food,

unwashed hands, and clumsy foreplay. She'd finally worked out the purpose of bidets on that unhappy occasion.

She spent the day exfoliating and waxing her body into submission. By seven p.m. there wasn't an inch that wasn't hairless, skinless, or both. A twinge in her left side told her that she was indeed ovulating, as did the annoying smudge of discharge in her best skimpy knickers just before she was about to leave. Changing into the next best—less lace, more coverage—she headed out to the car. The young mum from two months ago was crossing the road, her baby now sitting upright in its buggy, grinning at some unspecified baby joke. The girl looked happy, even smiling at Amy, as she waited for them to cross. Amy smiled back.

"Might be me soon," she said with a nod to the girl. At that moment, as if part of the girl's party, a sleek black cat slunk across the road in the wake of the pram. Amy waited for it, too, remembering that along with magpies, black cats could be said to bring good luck.

Just as it reached the curb, it stopped short and fixed Amy with a serious stare, as if to say, "Yes. Yes, it will be."

She got to the restaurant first. She didn't mind. She'd often gone there alone and Su at reception waved her to her usual table—only this time it would remain set for two. She loved this place. It was a converted Victorian bathhouse that the local Vietnamese community had turned into a drop-in center and restaurant. Above the outside doors you could still see the entrances clearly marked "Women" and "Men." Paper tablecloths and rickety chairs gave the dining area a makeshift, temporary feel, but the food had been legendary for some years now and it looked as though it was set to stay. It was the perfect place to take a guy like Andy—not flashy, not too loaded, not too expectant.

Amy ordered a Hue beer and sucked on a prawn cracker, being careful not to smudge her newly purchased skin tone sheer matte lipstick (£23 for a natural finish). It was seven thirty-five. He was five minutes late. She liked that. It showed he wasn't hung up, that he didn't set any store by the old-fashioned idea that the man had to be waiting, cloak on ground, for the woman to step from her carriage. Besides, being first meant she could swig a quick nerve-stiffener down and choose the best seat—back to the wall, able to survey the whole room.

Seven forty-five. He was probably stuck in traffic. Did he have to come far? Of course not—Victoria Park was only half a mile away, and he looked as though they lived nearby. . . . In any case, he was bound to be here in less than five minutes. Twenty minutes late was on time in London. She waved her empty bottle at Su, who nodded her acknowledgment.

Seven fifty-eight. She'd drained her second beer, and it was only the slight feeling of dizzy wooziness that was cushioning her from the emerging reality of the situation. She'd been stood up. Again. If he wasn't here by five past eight, then she would leave, inventing some urgent business just in case Su raised an eyebrow. How humiliating. What galled her even more was the fact that they hadn't exchanged numbers, so she couldn't even send a jovial "Where the hell are you?" text. *Damn.* Why hadn't she got his number? Or given him hers? Perhaps he was lying in a gutter somewhere, having been mugged? Perhaps he'd been unexpectedly called upon to look after Lola on his night off? He did say that his employer was chaotic. . . .

No. She couldn't kid herself. If you want something, then you find a way. Look at what she was doing here, after all. Where there's a will, etc. He could have easily phoned the restaurant if he'd needed to cancel. Amy began to digest the unpalatable fact that he'd obviously backed out, thought better of it, and was either too spineless or too rude to let her know. *Great.* Now she was left with an empty evening, a bruised ego, and an egg going spare.

Eight oh seven.

"Right. That's it," said Amy out loud, gathering up her jacket and her bag. She felt more than a bit pissed now. She hadn't eaten all day, and the beer had gone to her head. The couple at the next table smiled pityingly up at her as she squeezed past them.

"Sorry, Su—got a call—have to be somewhere else—but I'm sure you can use the table tonight," she said, throwing a tenner down for the beers.

"Shit. Sorry, sorry, sorry!" said a voice behind her.

Turning unsteadily, she came face-to-face with a flushed, sweaty-looking Andy.

"I ran all the way here—Lola's got another tooth coming through and I just couldn't get her off to sleep, and Sasha's having a dinner party tonight, so I was on bed duty. God, I'm so sorry—were you about to go? I mean, can we get our table back? Is that—I mean, would that be all right? Do you want that?"

Whether it was the beer, the throbbing egg, or the ruffled suit and T-shirt combination Andy was sporting so well, Amy wasn't sure, but she did something uncharacteristically forward. She kissed him. Full on the lips, with just a hint of tongue. He responded after the briefest of stunned moments, and they stood locked in an embrace for a few moments. Su coughed gently and pushed the metal tray bearing Amy's change noisily across the counter.

"Right," said Andy as they pulled away. "It's a funny thing, but I'm suddenly not feeling that hungry."

"Me neither," said Amy, looking up at him. He was taller and even sexier than she'd remembered—so it wasn't just the daddy appeal, then.

"Want to see my etchings in Docklands?" she asked.

"Can't. Have to be on duty later tonight. Said I'd be back by eleven."

Amy did a rough calculation—half an hour there, half an hour back, which left about one and a half hours to do the deed. Long enough, technically, but was he the sort who needed to talk into the wee small hours to get warmed up? Were these New Men types comfortable enough with their feminine sides to care for children, these Metrosexuals with their gay hair, their pink shirts, and their gym-buffed bodies man enough to do wham, bam, thank you, ma'am?

"I've got a better idea—why don't you come back to mine?"

Amy frowned. Was that allowed? Could live-in nannies do one-night stands?

"I'm not sure Mary Poppins would approve," she said, testing the water.

"I've got my own room and my own bathroom up in the attic. The baby's room is next to mine. It's cool," he said, taking her hand in his. The touch sent electric shocks through her fingers. It had been a long time.

"OK," she said. "That's practically perfect in every way."

.15.

The house was brightly lit as they crept up the winding front path, ducking under the overgrown lilac tree and sending rain-scented rose petals flying. It had been years since she'd felt this daring. Here she was in the depths of Hackney, inexplicably creeping into a young man's room in order to get herself pregnant.

Someone should inform Social Services, she thought wryly.

"I'll just get my key," whispered Andy, fumbling in his trouser pocket.

From inside came the sound of middle-class people having fun—glasses were chinking, boorish comments were being over-laughed at, and the latest easy-listening compilation purred unobtrusively in the background.

"Bugger. Can't find it. Must have left it behind in the rush," hissed Andy again.

"Why are we whispering? I thought you said it's OK to bring people back," said Amy, starting to feel a little uncomfortable now.

"It is—it's fine, honestly. It's just that Sasha can be a bit, erm, a bit . . . territorial about me."

"Oh, great! So she's going to love me then!" said Amy loudly.

"Shhh! Look, it's not that bad—I'd just rather we didn't bump into her before—well, before—"

Amy raised a mock-quizzical eyebrow.

"Oh, you know. Let's just nip round the back," said Andy, tugging on her hand. Electricity again. This was going to be good.

The noise from within surged suddenly, and a corridor of light illuminated the pathway. Someone had opened the front door.

"Thought I heard someone outside!" shrieked a loud female voice.

Sasha was silhouetted in the doorway, her long, curly hair billowing around her bare, well-defined shoulders. She was about Amy's age, tall and strong-looking and effortlessly elegant in a mushroom-colored satin dress. She was barefoot, and the whole effect was Amazonian.

"Sorry," said Andy. It sounded like a reflex.

"You left your keys on the stairs. Again," said Sasha, every inch the niggling wife.

"Hello, I'm Amy," said Amy, offering her hand.

"Oh! Didn't see you there! Didn't realize you had someone with you. Oh, sorry, come in, come in!"

Andy waited for Amy to go in before mouthing something that looked like "Is this all right?" Amy heard whispered, "Yes, yes, of course," before turning to face them both.

"We're just about to have pudding—why don't you join us?" said Sasha, far too brightly.

Oh my God, she's in love with him, Amy realized.

"Er, no, no, you go ahead, we're just going to, erm, go upstairs and . . . listen to some music," said Andy, aware that he sounded like a fifteen-year-old on a dope-smoking mission. This was weird. He was a fully grown adult who was working for this woman, living in her house, and here he was acting like a guilty teenager. Or a cheating husband.

"Fine, great, see you later," chirruped Sasha, going back into the dining room.

"Just pop your shoes off if you're going upstairs, Amy, thanks," she added briskly. "Oh, and there's half a bottle of Bolly left in the kitchen—and some smoked salmon," she added.

Andy indicated for Amy to wait in the hall while he dipped into the kitchen. Amy stood uncomfortably for a few moments. She didn't want the scraps from this woman's table. It was odd to be in a house less expensive than her own whose owner instantly treated her like an inferior. Sasha clearly had a problem with other women, at least where Andy was concerned. Amy became aware of hushed voices at the dinner-party table—Sasha was obviously telling her guests that the staff had brought some totty home. There was a huge explosion of laughter. Amy couldn't help but feel it was at her expense. Why was she doing this? It had better be worth it.

The dining-room door opened again.

"Oh. He's not here," said Sasha, somewhat accusingly. The two women blinked at each other for a moment.

"He's in the kitchen," said Amy flatly.

"Right. Could you just ask him to check on Lola before you—he— go to bed? Thanks."

She ducked back into the dining room amid stifled giggles. This was silly. Was she some kind of jealous schoolgirl? Had Andy never had a woman back here before?

"Sure," said Amy, trying to sound as unfazed as possible.

Andy reappeared clutching the champagne and a foil-covered plate and ushered her upstairs.

"Oh—Madame says can you check on the baby," said Amy, as they got to the top floor.

"Right—take these," said Andy, thrusting the leftovers at her before tiptoeing into the child's room. Amy noted with some amusement that the wallpaper was one of her own designs—the Enid Blyton fairies from *The Magic Faraway Tree*. If only Sasha knew.

"All fine. Fast asleep. Want to see?" He held the door open to let her peek in. Lola was flat on her back, little fat fists clenched at either side of her curly head, her cheeks flushed and her eyelashes flickering gently as she breathed. She was the picture of contentment.

"Does she wake up much?" asked Amy, keen to find out if they were likely to be disturbed. The sight of the cherubic baby had reminded her to focus her attention on the task at hand.

"Nah. She'll stay like that until about six thirty—seven if we're lucky. . . ." He pulled Amy to him and began to kiss her hard on the lips. She responded, reveling now in the tension of the situation. Why did it feel so deliciously naughty? It wasn't as if he was in a relationship with Sasha—Lola wasn't his child, and Amy was single—but something about the fact that she was about to attempt to get pregnant via a male nanny in someone else's house thrilled her. It was a middle-class porn scenario for the working woman. Tucking the bottle under her arm, she reached round to grab Andy's ass, eager to move things on now—no point hanging around when with every minute her egg was becoming older and staler.

There was an almighty crash.

"Shit! The champagne!" The bottle had slipped and smashed all over the hardwood floor.

The glass lay glinting in puddles of bubbles.

Instinctively, they both turned to look at the baby. For a second there was silence, but just as Amy was about to breathe again, Lola let out a long wail that rose in pitch and volume like an air-raid warning.

"Waaaaaahhhhh!" she cried, a mixture of shock and indignation in her small, loud voice.

"Fuck," said Andy, hurriedly kicking the glass aside and rushing to soothe Lola.

"It's OK, it's OK, shh, shh, shh, go back to sleep, it's OK," he said, barely audible above the distressed sobbing that was now convulsing Lola's tiny frame.

But Lola was having none of it.

"Waaaahhhh!" she wailed, each new cry growing in intensity. Footsteps thundered up the stairs.

"What's the matter—is anything wrong?" asked Sasha, looking more pleased than anxious.

"We had a little accident with the bottle and it woke her up," said Andy, still in his baby-soothing voice.

"Oh dear, bubba—silly Andy! Silly Janey!" cooed Sasha.

"Amy," said Amy, a little too hotly.

"Did they wake you up, my bubba? Well, Mama's got her friends to play, so Andy will kiss it better and help you get back to sleep. Poor bubba," said Sasha. "The mop and dustpan are under the stairs—Amy. Would you mind?" It was clearly a rhetorical question, because Sasha wafted down the stairs very pleased with herself indeed.

"Sure. Great. Just what I wanted to be doing tonight," sighed Amy, trudging after her.

"Sorry." Andy grimaced, still frantically jiggling the screaming child. Lola was now turning an attractive shade of purple, her breath coming in jags between wails.

Returning with the mop, Amy set about cleaning up the mess. Lola was inconsolable, but Amy knew from having been around babies that it was sunshine and showers—one minute they would be beside themselves with grief, the next all giggles and smiles. All was not lost. If she could just get Lola's attention for a second, she could try to wrong-foot her. What was it that she always did to distract a crying child from its exaggerated display of suffering? Peekaboo! No child had ever been able to resist it. Amy put down the mop and picked up an elephant cushion—again, one of her own designs from the Noah's Ark collection. She got right within Lola's eyeline, then hid her face behind the cushion. The crying suddenly stopped. An expectant hush filled the nursery, and Amy knew she was onto a winner.

"Boo!" she exploded, pulling the cushion sharply away from her face.

Lola blinked. She blinked again. Then something very bad happened. Her bottom lip trembled, went in, came out again, and went in before finally wobbling miserably for a few moments. It was make-or-break time.

"Boo!" shouted Amy again.

Lola thought for a moment before breaking into a wail so much louder and insistent than it had been, as if she was redoubling her efforts to ruin their evening.

"What are you doing?" snapped Andy.

"I thought it would help—it usually works."

"Oh, dear, dear, dear sweetheart, don't worry—Amy was just playing a little joke. Ssh, ssh, shh," said Andy, jiggling away.

Lola wailed and wailed. She was a devoted wailer, a dedicated howler, a fundamentalist screamer, and in between wails, she peeped over Andy's shoulder just to remind herself who it was she was unhappy with.

Thump, thump, thump up the stairs and Sasha was at the doorway.

"What's happened now?" she accused, looking directly at Amy.

"I think she's teething, and Amy was just trying to cheer her up by playing peekaboo and she got a bit upset," Andy hollered over the din.

"Oh, bubba! Is there a strange lady in your room? Is she a bit frightening?" cooed Sasha.

"I think she's just overtired and teething. I'm sure it's not Amy's fault," said Andy, hugging the baby close to him. Lola, however, had other ideas, and kept popping up over his shoulder to get another look at the scary stranger.

"I think she's a bit freaked out, poor thing. She's not really used to seeing new faces in here—especially not so late at night," countered Sasha, clearly intent on blaming someone.

"It's only ten o'clock," said Amy gloomily.

"That's the middle of the night for a baby. How would you feel if you woke up to find a strange woman in your room in the middle of the night, smashing glasses and shouting 'boo' at you?"

"Delighted," said Amy. "I'd take her out for a pint." Why did she feel like she was back at school in front of the headmistress?

"Look, I don't mean to be rude, but I really think you ought to go. It's just that Andy needs to get her back to sleep, and I need to return to my guests. Sorry. Perhaps another time?"

Sasha had the stiff authoritarian tone of a parent rearranging her son's playdate.

Amy couldn't believe what she was hearing. Were they serious, the pair of them? One look at Andy and she knew all she needed to know—he smiled a thin apology, then carried on jiggling Lola.

"Right. No problem. I'll leave you to it," said Amy, brushing past Sasha and onto the landing. But at the top of the stairs, she stopped and remembered esprit de l'escalier—that moment when you think of the perfect exit line but you've already left the situation—so she gave herself a breath before turning and facing them again.

"And perhaps when you've settled Lola, Andy, Mummy will give you a nice bit of booby." Hardly Dorothy Parker, but it would do.

Behind the dining-room door, the chatter continued as Amy pushed her feet into her shoes and made her way out.

"Bloody, bloody, bloody hell," she muttered as she headed up the path. The overgrown roses now snagged at her clothes and soaked her in raindrops, and the scent of the lilac, so intoxicating just an hour before, was overpoweringly sickly.

What now? She stood on the street corner, furious and humiliated. *What a spineless jerk!* All he had to do was stand up to his employer— insist that Amy be taken downstairs and entertained while he settled the child, and all would now be well. As it was here she was, egg awaiting, stranded in a taxi-no-go area of Hackney. A hooded youth approached, idly pedaling a too-small bike up the street.

"Hey. You looking for company?" He laughed, toking on a large joint. He wasn't threatening, and Amy had lived in London long enough to know it's the ones who don't say anything that you have to worry about. For a split second she thought of asking him to go for a drink—weren't brown babies as fashionable as this season's kitten heels?—but even in her current situation, she couldn't stoop so low. Pick up some hapless black kid and make him a father? She drew the line at an evening that could end up on *The Jerry Springer Show*. The youth cycled a figure eight in the middle of the road before meandering off in the direction of the common for some other sport just as— miraculously—the yellow light of a taxi swung into view.

"Where to, love?"

"Anywhere."

"Like that, is it?" laughed the cabbie.

"Yep," said Amy, brushing the rain from her face. She suddenly felt exhausted.

"Take me to bed," said Amy, not caring about the ambiguity— if the cabbie were to misinterpret her, she could be in all sorts of trouble.

"Righto. All I need is your address, love, and you'll be up the wooden hill to the land of nod before you can count a dozen sheep."

Great. So even the cabbie was totally immune to her charm.

Three months down—nine to go.

. 16 .

Monday morning. Normally, the ache of self-pity felt by all wage slaves at the dawn of a new working week was anathema to Amy. Owning her own business meant that normal office hours were a thing of wonder. She ate, breathed, and slept the shop all week long, all year through. This Monday morning, the knot in the pit of her stomach had nothing in common with that of the thousands of commuters now pouring themselves into already packed tube trains. It wasn't grief at the loss of freedom the new week heralded, and it wasn't a sense of futility at a humdrum, repetitive existence. Amy felt sick to her stomach because for the third month running, she had not only failed to get pregnant (she could handle that, six months to a year was average) but had also spectacularly failed to even bed the required man. She lay in bed listening to the furious chattering of the magpies above. It was only too easy to interpret their row as hostile, mocking laughter. She put the thought out of her mind and tried to focus on what had gone wrong. It had all looked so good. She'd done what Greg had said—she'd deliberately found a baby-friendly man; she'd given him a day's notice; she'd not been too keen. He, for his part, had been as eager as her to do the dirty right up until the baby woke up. If it hadn't been for Sasha sticking her big nose in, she might now be the proud host of a blob of rapidly subdividing cells. It was clear that Andy and Sasha were in a codependent, fucked-up relationship. Sasha had been quite deliberate about her wedge-driving. Short of prostrating herself on the floor and screaming, "Don't sleep with her! Don't sleep with her!" she couldn't have made her feelings more clear. And Andy? Well, the only consoling thought Amy had was that when she got that all-important twelve-week scan picture in her hands, she wanted to be sure the child had inherited a backbone.

"Enough of this. Time to check on the troops," she said, jumping out of bed and throwing on the nearest clothes—a dirty sweatshirt and the oldest jeans in the world. It wouldn't matter that she wasn't smartly dressed; she was only going to pop in and make sure they weren't slacking in her absence. It had been a whole three weeks—unheard of for Amy. It was important that she go in and make sure the staff were not indulging their twee sides too much. Last time she'd popped in, she'd been appalled to discover the beginnings of a window display featuring a Tweenies picnic. *Yuk.* She'd stamped on that one pretty sharpish. Her style may be cozy, but it was a retro kind of cozy that *ironically* believed in fairies. The distinction was important, if only to Amy.

Traffic into town and out the other side was appalling. Crossing from East to West London was the absolute worst journey in the world at the best of times. Forget polar expeditions, forget desert trekking in arid conditions—Amy felt that if you hadn't been forced to inch along the Embankment nose to nose with fellow psychotic, dehydrated travelers, watching lights turn from red to green and back again before a single vehicle had moved, you did not know the meaning of the word "suffering." Attempting it on a Monday morning was tantamount to self-flagellation. In times of hardship, Amy always reverted to Catholic type by punishing herself like this.

One hour and fourteen minutes after setting out, Amy walked purple-faced through the doors of Precious Little Darlings. The "Teddy Bears' Picnic" shop bell sprang jauntily into life.

"Fucking London! I hate London! If one more bloody coach carrying fifty fucking pensioners pulls out in front of me and blocks two lanes off to let them take pictures of fucking Big Ben, I'm going to climb aboard and ram their fucking pathetic plastic cameras up their crumbly arses!"

"Morning, Amy," chimed Sarah. "Erm, you've got visitors. . . ."

Amy stopped mid-stomp and let out a dramatic sigh. *Visitors?* She hadn't told them she was coming, so what were they doing booking appointments? Or worse still, had she forgotten a meeting? No, that never happened, although perhaps with all this baby nonsense, she'd lost her head a bit and developed baby brain.

"Hello," said a vaguely familiar voice from behind her.

Turning slowly, Amy let it dawn on her that this was a not unwelcome visitor. There he was, the Good Doctor, standing just to one side of the till point, wearing a broad grin.

And there they were—the shining twins, giggling and poking each other and eyeing her with renewed interest as the best swearer in the world.

"Oh. Hello. Sorry about the—er, the language. . . ." said Amy, her head spinning with the possibilities. What was he doing here?

"What are you doing here?" she blurted, before her mouth had a chance to catch up with her brain.

"Half-term," said Joe apologetically. "They've been on at me for ages to come here. It's the baby thing. The obsession. There was a brief hiatus where I thought they'd moved on to dinosaurs after a trip to the Natural History Museum, but turns out it was just a temporary blip. Now we're back on track with added verve."

"Oh, right. Well, hello, Francesca and Laura. Welcome to the shop!" said Amy, both relieved and disappointed that it was these brats and not their striking but married dad who had prompted the visit. The girls stared back without bothering to reply.

"So—what do you think?" said Amy brightly, spreading her arms wide.

"S'all right," Cesca said testily.

"S'nice," said Laura with just the tiniest hint of enthusiasm.

"That's high praise from them," said Joe.

"Anyway, we've been here before," said Cesca. She stopped abruptly, aware that she'd just let a small cat out of a bag. Laura giggled, and Cesca smiled guiltily up at her dad. Both girls now stared at him expectantly—what was he going to do next? They weren't sure of the rules in this most adult of games.

Joe cleared his throat and tried to look nonchalant.

"Why don't you two go and have a look at that princess bed? It's got carriage wheels," said Joe, obviously trying to divert his audience.

The girls sloped off reluctantly but were soon involved in a pillow fight, instigated after a dispute over who should get to lie down first.

"So," said Amy, not really knowing what to say. This was most odd.

"OK, confession time. I brought them here last weekend."

"And the one before that," shouted Cesca, hardly missing a beat in her fight.

"Thank you, Cesca. And the week before that," said Joe, adding a flirtatious grin.

What was he playing at? A married man bringing his twin daughters to try and catch a glimpse of someone he vaguely knows three weeks running? Amy was flattered but more than a little annoyed. Did he think she was affair material? Did she look stupid? Maybe he was used to bedding any number of naïve nurses impressed by his "come to bedside" manner, but she was above such gauche enthusiasm for a stethoscope. Pretty much.

"Well, I'm flattered you like the shop so much," said Amy pointedly, refusing to be drawn into his web. She could see he was quite an operator—he wasn't in the slightest bit abashed.

"Oh, it's a lovely shop. One of the best—and believe me, I'm something of an expert in the field." Again that smile.

"Thank you," said Amy tightly.

"But it wasn't the shop I was coming to see."

"Oh."

"I was hoping to run into you again."

"Right." What to say now? He was totally brazen.

"Well," she started, not sure where she would end. "That's very nice of you, but I'm sure your wife must wonder where you are every Saturday afternoon," she continued, being sure to hit the word "wife" very hard.

"Not really," said Joe casually.

"Don't tell me—which is it? She 'doesn't understand you'? You have an 'arrangement'? Or you're virtually brother and sister these days?" Amy couldn't help the ironic edge in her voice just touching the wrong side of anger.

"None of the above," said Joe softly. Amy had obviously hit something on the head. "I just wondered if you'd like to have dinner with me."

"Hang on—let me get this straight—we meet in quite extraordinary circumstances, granted; we then run into each other in Harrods, where your children are rude to me; you then stalk me at my shop for several weeks; and when you finally track me down, you ask me out to dinner! Well, perhaps you ought to have a little chat with your wife first—make sure she's available to babysit!"

"She's dead," chorused the girls. They had stopped what they were doing and were standing on the bed, pillows in hand, ready to resume their own version of this adult fight.

The whole shop seemed to be staring at Amy now. Mrs. Cummings, newly arrived with a clutch of color swatches to return, stood aghast in the doorway. Sarah was slack-jawed at the counter, and a deliveryman had frozen in his tracks by the rear entrance.

"Fuck," said Amy. "Sorry. I had no idea."

"It's OK," said Joe, almost smiling at her uncomfortableness. "I didn't mean to tell you like that—bit of a conversation stopper. Difficult to know where to slip it in—you know, 'Hello, I'm Joe, my wife's dead.' It's been three years. I'm over the worst of it."

"God. Blimey. How?"

"The Big C. Breast. Bummer. Big bummer," said Joe calmly. "So. Now that you know that yes I am married but only to a memory, is it a yes or a no? I'm a big boy. You can tell it to me straight."

"Of course. I mean yes. That would be nice. Thank you."

"OK, great. Tonight?"

"Erm, yeah sure. Why not? Monday night—not a lot doing."

"I'll meet you at the trattoria on the corner at—what? Seven thirty?"

Amy did some quick math—home, shower, hair, makeup, shoe decision.

"Can we make it eight? I hate seven thirty—bad vibes."

"Fine. Eight o'clock then. Don't be late."

"I won't."

Joe shepherded the girls to the front door, his business done. Any pretence of the visit being for their benefit was now gone.

"And try not to bring any waifen strays along with you this time. . . ." he added as "The Teddy Bears' Picnic" sang him out of the shop. Strange, but it was no longer irritating when merely a musical accompaniment to one of the nicest asses in Christendom.

"Well!" gushed Sarah, who had been trying to busy herself with the stapler for the last part of the meeting. "Who's got an admirer? And here was muggins thinking it was me he was after! He's been in here every week for a month! Never buys anything, just loafs around a bit while the girls run riot, then leaves. He kept giving me these quizzical looks—I thought my luck was in! We were calling him the Italian stallion. Fancy!"

"Yes. Fancy . . ." said Amy, already calculating her next ovulation cycle. A July conception. An April baby. Taurus. Like Amy. *Neat.*

.17.

She had gotten him so wrong, cast him as Latin Lothario, the hot doc with an eye for any bit of skirt he could charm into bed. Although looking back now, it was easy to see that he was nothing of the sort. Was it hindsight or wishful thinking that made Amy now realize that they had had quite a striking attraction to each other from the outset, and that something about him had given off an air of wounded shyness? She had stereotyped him as a play-around, good-for-nothing European philanderer in order to protect herself from her attraction to him, when all the time it was clear she was capable of having him for breakfast. He was in actual fact a single parent, valiantly bringing up two girls and holding down a difficult job in a beleaguered NHS hospital. He was no shag-happy medic; he was a hero, and she had wasted three months of her precious fatalistic experiment on losers who either couldn't or wouldn't do the job. But why the wedding ring? It had been that, she now remembered, which had diverted her at the outset. OK, so he *was* married, but surely most people take off their wedding rings if they are widowed—especially at such a young age. Alarm bells started to ring. There was no question that he was telling the truth about his wife—the girls had told her, and he had displayed the matter-of-factness of the truly bereaved. But surely the fact that he still wore his ring, and the fact that he still referred to himself as "married to a memory," was a bit suspect?

Friends had warned Amy over the years about getting involved with anyone whose partner had died. Who was that printer she used to use—*Kath?*—who'd suffered horribly by comparison to a Dead Saintly Wife. There was always the danger, Kath said, that at any minute you would do something that the DSW would have done better, or want to go somewhere he'd been with the DSW. Whole continents had been forbidden territory to Kath and her man because he couldn't bear to revisit the joyous memories. In the end Kath had finished it, and the worst thing was that he'd seemed not heartbroken but relieved, as if he could now get back to the business of morbidly fixating on his dead wife's perfection. Amy didn't want to go through all that. She was not a natural second-fiddle player. She would be no one's sloppy seconds, no one's begrudging second best.

"Stop," she said out loud.

"This is not what this is about. You are not planning a wedding, Amy Stokes, you are planning a baby. Remember? A baby. You do not—repeat, *do not*—want to get emotionally involved with anyone right now. Especially while this project is on. There is no time for feelings. They get in the way. You *especially* do not want to get involved with a man who *already has* two horrible children of his own. You would not only be second-best woman but, *even worse*, you would be second-best mum. *No, no, no*, and, repeat, *no!* Got that? Good."

She felt better now. For a minute she had quite lost touch with reality. It was a dreadful habit, this daydreaming about the future, propelling into the distant future whatever embryonic situation she found herself in. It was a kind of misguided optimism. Her mum had always told her to be more "cute," more canny, less eager to see the good in every situation, for despite her outwardly cynical nature, she had always really been a disappointed romantic. If she wasn't on her guard, she was prone to the most ridiculously spew-making romantic fantasies, and this thing with the doctor was just another example. She could hardly blame herself, though. He was gorgeous, caring, and wore a uniform for a living—that wasn't playing fair. The hardest of women would melt. Amy quickly pulled herself together just in time to realize that the taxi had flashed past the restaurant.

"Stop! We've just passed it!"

"Sorry, love—I'll go round the block."

A minute to eight. Surely he wouldn't be bang on time?

The next sixty seconds seemed to take an age as they lurched round corners back to the restaurant, and just as they pulled up to the curb, she spotted him. He was taller than she remembered, his hair dark and longer at the back. Amy suppressed an excited grin as she stuffed twenty pounds into the cabbie's hand and leapt out.

"Hi! I made it!" she shouted. He was waiting outside.

"Hello." He smiled. He looked incredibly nervous. The relaxed, professional manner he had radiated was completely gone. Was it her imagination or had he just stubbed out a cigarette?

"Shall we?" she said, taking charge after a moment's pause.

"Yes, yes, sorry," said Joe, following her inside.

The restaurant was busy, filled with tourists and the less-well-heeled locals. Bottles of dusty Chianti hung from the ceiling, and waiters in tight black trousers sped back and forth past the dreadful mural of the Bay of Naples that claimed one end of the room.

"*Buona sera, signore, signora,*" said a portly man in a stained white shirt. "'ave you booked?"

"*Sì, Joe Nencini, per favore,*" said Joe.

The waiter launched into a long and furious-paced monologue in Italian as he led them to their table while Joe smiled, nodded, and added the occasional "*Sì.*"

"Impressive," said Amy once the waiter had handed them their laminated menus and left them to choose.

"Well, you know . . ." said Joe, burying his head in his menu.

"What was all that about?"

"To be honest, I haven't got the faintest idea. I only know how to order food these days."

"I would have thought you were bilingual."

"I was. Until I was about ten. But if you don't use it, you lose it," said Joe with a shrug. "Wine?"

"Ooh, yes, I think so, don't you? Chianti?"

"I could do with a stiff one first," said Joe, signaling the waiter. "*Mi da un whiskey, per favore. Grande.*"

"*Sì, certo, ma il vino?*" asked the waiter, confused. No one orders whiskey first.

"*Sì, ma prima . . . whiskey,*" fumbled Joe.

"*Subito. La signora?*"

"I'll have the same." Amy smiled. "When in Rome."

"I just want to say for the record that I wouldn't normally be knocking back hard liquor before dinner on a first date," said Joe.

"Right. Fine," said Amy. "I would."

"Oh, really? You do it all the time, do you?"

"Yes, I'm really quite racy." Amy laughed. "But I get the impression it's a big deal for you?"

"No, no, not at all. Well, yes, actually."

"What, is it a cultural thing, or have you got a thing about alcohol? Don't start giving me the units-per-week lecture—I know you doctors are always hitting the bottle."

"No, I'm not a booze fascist; I'll drink anything, even perfume. No, I meant the first-date thing. It's not something I do all the time."

"Oh, me neither!" said Amy.

"Really?" said Joe, visibly relaxing.

"Oh, no, I usually just cut straight to the first shag."

"Oh. Right," said Joe, beginning to study his menu overearnestly.

Amy laughed in delight.

"Your face!"

"What?"

"You looked terrified!"

"I was! I mean, I am!" Joe laughed, pleased to be able to admit it.

"Why? It was a joke! Mostly."

"Mostly? That just makes it worse! Now I feel like you're saying first dates are an inconvenience and that mostly you'd rather be shagging!"

"No, not at all!" Amy laughed.

"Oh, right, that's worse still! I'm so unappealing, am I?"

"No, I didn't mean that. Oh, God, this is going really well, isn't it?"

"Just shut up and order your food, then we can get out of here and you can go find some poor hapless man to devour," said Joe as the waiter hovered.

Amy had no idea what she wanted to eat. Food was the last thing on her mind. Her stomach lurched every time she looked at him, and she couldn't stop herself from imagining what their baby would look like. It was like a sickness she had developed—no man was safe. Every half-decent passerby had, in recent weeks, become subject to the same fantasy game whereby she transplanted the best of her features—hair, eyes, legs—with the best of his to create the perfect baby. This evening's baby, it had to be admitted, surpassed them all. Amy leaned on her hands dreamily as Joe ordered. He might even be worth a second try if it didn't happen the first time. It was her adventure, so she was free to rewrite the rules if need be. . . .

"*Signora?*"

Both the waiter and Joe were staring at her now.

"Oh, erm, I'll have the linguine," she stuttered.

"With *de vongole* or *de* ham?"

"Yes, please."

"Ham?"

"Yes, please."

The waiter scuttled off, tutting.

"So this is a first date, is it?" asked Amy, ready to turn up the heat.

"Well, yes, if that's what they still call it nowadays," said Joe, fiddling with a packet of bread sticks.

"So that implies it's the first of many."

"Or at least two. Technically. Mind if I smoke?"

"Go ahead, doctor. But what if we don't like each other and never see each other again—what will this be, then?"

"I see. Good point. Well, then this will become known as the slightly disastrous meal out with a glamorous but tricky arty type from Chelsea. You?"

"Oh, well, I'll probably refer to it as the night I nearly made my mother a happy woman by bagging myself a doctor."

"Jewish?"

"No. Worse. Irish Catholic."

"Ah. That's the naughty spark accounted for."

"You noticed. And a point of information. I'm not from Chelsea. I'm from Essex. And yes, it's all true what they say about Essex girls," she added, hoping he'd take the hint. OK, so she wasn't ovulating yet, but a practice run wouldn't hurt, would it? Not with such a great candidate. And two nights of passion didn't constitute "getting involved." She would be careful to stay aloof.

"And what exactly do they say about Essex girls? That must have passed me by," said Joe, stubbing out his cigarette and instantly reaching for another.

"Oh, you know, all those jokes . . ."

"Jokes?"

"Oh, come on, you must have heard them!"

"Nope. I'm kept rather busy at the hospital. No time for jokes. It's wall-to-wall vulvas for me. Dr. Nencini—at your cervix."

"That's very good. I bet you say that to all the girls."

"So the jokes, the ones that are true?"

"Well, like, how do you tell if an Essex girl's had an orgasm?"

Joe raised an eyebrow.

"She drops her kebab."

"I see."

"Or, what's the difference between an Essex girl and a Kit Kat?"

"Go on."

"You only get four fingers in a Kit Kat."

"Oh, God."

"Or, erm—"

"No, really, that's fine. I get the picture."

Joe had gone rather gray and was sucking furiously on his second cigarette. Amy felt instantly stupid. Why had she decided to go full-pelt for the up-for-it approach? That had worked in the past when she had wanted to pick up someone rough and ready in the pub, but this was a different affair altogether. It wouldn't do to be so up front that she risked scaring him away.

"Are you OK?" she asked, adopting a softer tone.

"Yes. Why?"

"You look a bit pasty and you're chain-smoking."

"Yes. Sorry. Actually, I think I'm going to be sick," said Joe, pushing his chair back and running for the toilet.

Well done, thought Amy. *That's him out of the frame. He's probably not sick at all—just horrified. He'll probably climb out of the toilet window. He's probably legging it down Walton Street right now, back to the girls and the nanny. Fuck.*

Amy sat gloomily, waiting for him not to return. The food arrived and her pasta started to congeal nastily on the plate while Joe's pizza turned hard and his salad wilted. Minutes went past and Amy stirred her meal, absentmindedly wondering what to do if he didn't come back. Surely he wouldn't do that? She'd had some rotten luck with men since this whole baby thing started, but surely he was a cut above cutting and running?

"Sorry about that."

He was back and looking better.

"Must have been the whiskey and the cigarettes. I don't normally smoke at all. Anymore. Truth be told, I'm a bit nervous. Well, actually, I'm fucking shitting myself. It's been a long time. Not since I first met Eve."

Amy gulped. So this was his first date since the DSW passed away? She didn't know whether that was a good sign (he must be keen on her) or a bad one (too much pressure, no possibility of ever living up to Eve). Either way, it was clear she had misjudged the importance of the evening as far as Joe was concerned. Time for some repair work before it was too late. Amy unconsciously pulled her cardigan over her cleavage.

"So I suppose me making repeated and brazen references to shagging and kebab-dropping hasn't been the gentle ease-in you were hoping for?"

Joe smiled.

"Not really. But it's no big deal. You didn't know."

"Sorry. I get a bit giddy sometimes. Shall we start again?"

"OK. No more shagging."

"And no more fagging," said Amy, screwing up the packet of cigarettes.

"Deal."

"We're just two normal people having a nice, unpressurized meal together on a normal Monday night in London."

"That's just it, though—this is not a normal Monday night. Normally, I'd either be on call or slumped in front of the TV with two screaming eight-year-olds jumping all over me. I'm not sure how to behave when I'm out alone after dark!"

"Has it really been that long?"

"Eighteen years."

"Eighteen years since you went out on a Monday night?"

"No, since I went on a first date."

"Jesus."

"Quite."

"How come?"

"Well, I met my wife when we were at university. She was my first girlfriend. My only girlfriend. Not deliberately—I wasn't waiting for The One or anything—it just happened like that. And since she died I just haven't felt like getting back on the horse, because I was never really on it in the first place."

"Eve. The first woman."

"And the last."

Now it was Amy's turn to feel uncomfortable. Here she was scheming her way into bed with a provenly fertile man in order to get herself pregnant and then disappear into the ether, and here he was on what had turned out to be only his second date *ever* after the death of his true love. Amy felt chastened. So far, it had never occurred to her that the men she had been chasing might have feelings and needs of their own. Everyone knew that men were out for all they could get. Hadn't Amy's mum told her as much in grave tones the day she found Amy's first packet of contraceptive pills? She had just assumed that the men she had targeted would be as noncommittal and easy as she herself felt, but in reality, she was finding it impossible to meet an uncomplicated bloke who would jump at the chance of a one-night stand. What was happening to men? Suddenly they had hang-ups, sensitivities, and emotional agendas. Men never had emotional agendas the last time she had looked. It had been the heartfelt cry of the more liberal feminists she had known at college: "Why can't men show their feelings?" Amy felt it was just her luck that the crisis in masculinity had struck the very year she decided she needed a man—for thirty-six hours, at least.

"Now you look ill," said Joe.

"No, I'm fine, I was just . . . thinking. So, well, I'm honored then! Here's to getting back on the horse!"

"*Salute*," said Joe, raising his glass.

"So . . . why me?"

"Well, I suppose because I had been thinking for a long time that I should try to meet someone, and then there you were, and I liked the way you came back to the hospital to check on the baby—yes, they told me you came back, I have my spies—because it reaffirmed my suspicion that beneath that flinty, joky exterior there beat a caring heart."

"Oh," said Amy, not expecting such a full answer.

"And why did you accept?" said Joe, much more assured now.

"Nice ass," said Amy, deflecting the intimacy of the moment.

Joe looked shocked, then visibly lightened up. He threw his head back and started to laugh. Amy joined him, and between them they made a tacit agreement to let go and just enjoy the evening. He had revealed his shameful dating inadequacy and she had inwardly re-solved that this was not going to be a potential inseminator. She couldn't do it—not now that he had chosen her earnestly as only his second date ever. Somehow it wouldn't feel right. They would just have a nice evening together and perhaps become friends. It was clear he wasn't ready for anything more, and she had her own plans for the rest of the year, so she was happy to be his stepping stone to some distant, wholesome lover who wanted a nice husband and a ready-made family. It wasn't for Amy.

Once the dreadful first hour was over, Amy found herself feeling more relaxed than she had since she started her pregnancy bid. It was nice to enjoy an evening out without constantly weighing what time of the month it was and whether there were any likely candidates in the near vicinity. Joe was easygoing and funny, despite his neurotic start. She was careful to keep the subjects light—she didn't want to provoke a bout of grief-stricken crying by bringing up anything rela-tionship related. If she was completely honest, her reasons for not mentioning Joe's late wife were not entirely altruistic; as the evening wore on, she found herself feeling inexplicably jealous of Eve. It was not a feeling she was happy about harboring, but try as she might, she could not shake it off.

This is what Kath meant, she thought to herself as Joe chatted on about work, the nurses, the inadequacies of the NHS, and how even they were overshadowed by the joy of working with babies.

He is absolutely gorgeous; he's bright, funny, and passionate about his fantastically worthy job; and yet he holds an invisible placard that states, "Don't think about getting close to me because I am a tragic, brokenhearted widower and I will not besmirch the memory of my dead perfect wife," thought Amy as they stirred their coffee.

"So," said Joe, helping her on with her coat outside. It was gone eleven. Three hours had passed in a blur, and Amy found herself hoping that, despite her resolution to remain on guard, they would meet again. It wouldn't do any harm, even though she already had enough male friends.

"So?" said Amy, wanting to put the ball firmly in his court. There was no way she was going to be accused of pushing him too fast too soon. If he wanted a friendship, he would have to continue to do the running. She liked things to be clear and simple, and she didn't want to give him the idea that she was pursuing him romantically.

"So what now?" he said, staring at the pavement. He suddenly looked sad and uncomfortable again.

"It's OK," said Amy softly, placing a hand on his arm.

"What is?"

"You don't have to do anything. It's been a lovely evening and I'm really glad we met properly, and I'm sorry about Eve, and I realize you must be feeling really mixed-up right now—but it's OK. You've made a start and that's good, but now you can go home and lie in bed and tell her all about it."

"But—"

"*Ssh.* You don't owe me anything, and I don't want anything from you. You're a lovely man and I'm sure you'll meet someone just as soon as you're ready," said Amy, sticking her arm out at an approaching taxi. She winced at her own stoicism, but it was for the best. The timing was not right, and to Amy, timing had become everything.

"Oh," said Joe, sounding suddenly winded.

Amy turned to plant a chaste kiss on his cheek but stopped short, taxi door ajar, when she caught sight of his face. He was the picture of abject disappointment. This was hard. How could she let such an important rite-of-passage evening end with such finality?

"Bye, Joe. Thanks for a lovely evening. And good luck," she said as she slammed the door shut and sped off into the night.

"So I suppose a shag's out of the question then?" Joe said to the car's taillights.

.18.

"Can you come over?"

Angela's voice was small and flat on the end of the line.

"Yes, sure. Is everything OK?"

"What time will you be here?"

"In an hour? Is that OK?"

Amy had never heard Ang like this. What on earth could be wrong? All the way there, she fantasized about what could be the matter. Dave? He couldn't have left her—they were devoted. Properly devoted. They were not at all showy or romantic in any stereotypical way, but it was clear to everyone how quietly besotted they were with each other, even after five kids and not enough money to go around. Was something wrong with one of the kids? It would have to be something deadly serious—Ang always took their bumps and bruises and childhood ailments in stride. She prided herself in being a coper. Knocking on the door, Amy felt a terrible sadness descend around her. Dave answered and let her into the hallway.

"Where is she?" Amy asked quietly.

"Upstairs. She's a bit upset," said Dave, whose own eyes looked red and watery.

Amy tiptoed up the toy-strewn stairs and knocked on the bedroom door.

"Come in," said the small voice.

Ang sat on the large bed surrounded by photos. Shoeboxes, albums, and envelopes covered every inch of the mock-satin bedspread, and strips of negatives lay scattered on the floor. Amy quickly noted that all of the photos were of their five children—family snapshots, crass photographer's studio portraits, family gatherings. A box of tissues lay empty on the bedside table.

"Ang—what's wrong?" said Amy, going to her friend's side. In all their years of friendship, it had always been Amy having the crisis, Amy needing a shoulder to cry on, Amy demanding instant sympathy.

"We've lost the baby," said Ang, before breaking into gut-wrenching sobs.

The baby. Of course. Ang must have been just over three months pregnant. Amy had almost forgotten. It was easy to forget—Ang had been pregnant or nursing an infant for pretty much the last fifteen years. It was her default state. Amy searched for something to say.

"Oh, God, Ang, I'm sorry," she said, rubbing her friend's back. "What happened?"

"I don't know. We went for the first scan today—we were really excited, we thought everything was OK, well, you just don't think anything's going to happen, do you? And they couldn't find the heartbeat at the antenatal clinic but they said not to worry, it's often hard to find this early but that the scan would show everything was all right, so we went up to the scan department and she put the jelly on me and switched on the machine but then she didn't say anything, she was just measuring things, white lines stretching across the screen and Dave was smiling but I could tell something was wrong—they usually say, "There's baby," or something, because it's hard to see where it is at this stage, but she didn't say anything for ages, then she just switched off the machine and said, "I'm sorry, but your baby has died. There's no heartbeat. I'll leave you alone for some private time," and Dave and me just looked at each other like it was a practical joke, then this doctor came in and asked me if I wanted a D and C or to let it come out naturally."

"Christ," whispered Amy. Her own eyes were full of water. The stomach-churning routine nature of tragedy in a hospital—so routine for them, so life-shattering for Angela.

"I'm so sorry, Ang. You poor things—it must have been a terrible shock."

"It is—we still can't believe it. It's never happened to me before. I just let them clean me out, couldn't stand the thought of the poor dead thing inside me. Oh, Amy!" Ang cried solidly for twenty minutes. Amy stared grimly at the digital clock and watched it click from twelve oh seven to twelve twenty-seven, hoping that each minute would help put some much-needed distance between Ang and the pain. While she stroked and comforted her friend, she felt terribly sad—it was never easy to see such a gentle, kind, and solid person such as Ang collapse so completely—but after a few minutes, Amy became aware of another, less comfortable feeling. A part of her wanted to pull back and get Ang to snap out of it, wanted to say, "Look, it's no big deal, it's not like it was your first—you've already got five children and you're no spring chicken. Can't you be happy with that? You could look at it as a blessing in disguise," but she knew it was neither the time nor the place for such brutal honesty. Instead, she sighed a long sigh, wiped her friend's eyes with her cuff, and said, "Well, thank goodness you've still got your five lovely babies to look after."

Ang stiffened and looked up for the first time in half an hour.

"I know that. But you don't understand. I used to think like that until I had my first—I could never get it, why people with kids got so screwed up about miscarriages. It's just a blob after all, pretty much until six months it's just a blob. And if you've already got one, or two, or even five, then you should count yourself lucky. I mean, look at Sophie and Greg—they've been trying for years, and here I am breaking my heart because I've lost my sixth. But what you don't realize, Amy, is that it makes it worse, not better—it's worse because you know what you're missing, that every day of that newborn's life is a miracle, and that every day they grow and blossom and become more and more themselves, and it just absolutely takes your breath away. So no, it's no compensation that I've got five already—it's not like too many little black dresses or too many pairs of shoes. I've lost a little person, a unique, once-in-a-lifetime possibility."

Ang was silent now, letting the full weight of her speech sink in. Amy sat and reflected on how, in the past, she would have bristled at the schmaltzy subtext to Ang's "sacred embryo" homily, but now she just didn't have the stomach to. Since her own private struggle with the baby demons, she had come to realize that the contents of her ovaries were not just an irritation to be flushed away every month but potential people. This had begun to sit uneasily with her glib disregard for the pro-life lobby—how could she feel so obsessed with fertilizing one of her own precious and by now dwindling eggs and at the same time support the idea of abortion? The answer, she saw now, was what she had believed all along. You had to respect every woman's choice—whether each individual pregnancy was wanted or not. It didn't matter what the personal circumstances of each woman was—frightened teenager, exhausted mum of three, ambitious career woman—if they chose to have the baby, then that was right for them, and if not, then that also must be respected. So of course she must support Angela, and let her grieve for this sixth but utterly wanted child. It was Angela's choice to have lots of babies, and it must be respected no matter what anyone else thought.

"I'm sorry," said Amy quietly. "You're absolutely right. I'm so sorry for your loss."

Ang blinked back her tears and looked at Amy for the second

time. Something in her eyes was questioning. It was as if she couldn't tell whether Amy was genuinely sympathetic or just mouthing easy platitudes. She detected some kind of shift in her old friend but as yet could not work out what it was. One look at Amy's solemn face reassured her of Amy's sincerity.

"Thanks," said Ang. "I know you find all this baby stuff hard to understand, but it means a lot that you've said that."

"I mean it. I know I've taken the piss in the past—there was an old woman who lived in a shoe and all that—but I suppose I've gone through a bit of an enlightenment, shall we say."

"Oh, Jesus, you've not gone back to the one true faith, have you?" said Ang with genuine horror.

"No. I'm past all that—there's no confessional big enough for my crimes. Let's just say I've gone a bit soft in my old age."

"Well, I know you went a bit gooey over that baby you found," said Ang, blowing her dripping nose.

"Yes," said Amy. *What to do now?* Should she tell Ang about her plans? And if she did, what would Ang say? This was a tough call. On the one hand she felt defensive—they had grown up together and Ang had always done the right thing. They had polarized into good girl/bad girl, and Ang had spent their teenage years and well into their twenties tutting and rolling her eyes in half-envious disapproval at every wrong turn Amy made. Surely she would disapprove of this latest madcap idea.

Amy cleared her throat.

"Well, yes, that was a bit of a watershed. In fact, ever since then I've been thinking that maybe I would quite like to have a go myself," she said, picking absentmindedly at the candlewick bedspread, a study in casualness.

"Have a go? At having a baby? You make it sound like skydiving!"

"Well, it is, isn't it? You take a running jump and hope that you get a soft landing."

"Blimey, Amy—are you sure about this? I mean, have you really thought it through? This is so out-of-the-blue. . . . I mean, how?"

There was nothing for it now. She was halfway in and the water was cool, but there was no getting back out—might as well take the plunge. Amy launched into her by now almost scripted monologue while Ang sat slack-jawed on the bed. At least it seemed to have distracted her from her own situation for a while, even if she did look horrified. When she had finished, Amy waited for the verdict.

"Well, well, well," said Ang slowly. "I think that's great, Amy. Really. It's just what you need."

"Oh, no, please don't tell me it'll be the making of me. I hate all that 'you're not a woman until you're a mother' bullshit, so spare me, please."

"OK," said Ang, smiling.

"If I do go through with it, if I find someone in time, if I do manage to get pregnant and I end up with a baby, I want you to know right now that it's not going to change me, you know. I'll still be the same chippy, difficult, borderline-alcoholic partygoing businesswoman I am now. I won't suddenly turn into some caftan-wearing earth mother with flip-flops and rusks in my hair. I'll stay completely the same."

"Of course you will," said Ang, patting her friend on the knee. "Of course you will."

.19.

Can someone please talk to the cleaners again about making sure there is toilet paper in the ward toilets? I had to go and fetch some myself for a woman who was bleeding heavily this morning. I've got more important things to be getting on with, like delivering babies and making sure no one dies. And nurse, put your mobile down when a patient is talking to you—there'll be plenty of time for texting your boyfriend at the end of your shift. And where's Aicha? Aicha—late again. We can't all wait for you before we decide someone needs an emergency C-section. Get it together."

Joe pretended not to notice Aicha sucking her teeth in defiance.

"Lord, doctor, I don't know who she is, but I hope she sweet to you soon—you is like a bear wid a sore head these days," said Patience as she brushed past with toilet supplies.

Much as he hated to admit it, her words stung. It was true. Ever since his date with Amy, he'd felt irritable and jumpy. It wasn't sexual frustration—after three years, he was used to that—but a sense of having let himself down and sold himself short. She had clearly been interested at the start of the evening—or else why would she have come along?—but something about the way he had conducted himself had put her off enough to send her speeding into the distance alone in a cab at the end of the night. He didn't have to think too hard about what it might have been. All that morbid, mawkish talk about Eve. Why couldn't he have just played it cool and not mentioned his nerves? He had clearly scared her off, come across as a depressive, neurotic, inexperienced nerd when what he really wanted was the chance to get to know her better. He wasn't sure why he felt this, but from the first time they had met, he had felt pulled toward her. It was what had compelled him to go along to her shop on several occasions on the off chance that she might be there. On his fourth visit, there she was, and it had seemed fated. If it hadn't been for the girls' compulsive need to tell virtual strangers their most intimate family business within seconds of meeting, he would have been able to tell her he was a widower in his own time. As it was she had found out in a very public way, which couldn't have helped. She was the first woman he had felt remotely interested in since Eve had died, and he had completely blown it. In the intervening week, he had tried to put it down to experience, tried to cast her from his mind. But Patience was right—she had set up shop in his heart and he could not rid himself of her. He had been grumpy and sullen all week. Even the girls, whose normal emotional antennae were only inwardly trained, had noticed, telling him he was turning into a "boring old git." On top of that, he had started smoking again. Off he sloped whenever he could snatch a minute to the roof of the hospital for a quiet fag. It didn't really help, but the image of himself standing alone on a rooftop blowing smoke into the wind was somehow soothing, making him feel more the macho Marlboro man than the mouselike medic he had become. It was to the roof he found himself going now for what would be his fifteenth cigarette of the day, and it was only two o'clock.

Sod it, he thought, pulling the packet from his trouser pocket. It felt smooth and reassuring in his hand, as if it were saying, "Don't worry, whatever happens, whatever shit life throws at you, I'll always be here for you." Joe felt the familiar sense of soothing expectation as he flipped the packet open. It was empty.

"Shit!" he shouted, throwing it down. *What now?* "This is ridiculous. Enough. That's it."

Joe took his mobile from his shirt pocket and dialed, only moderately ashamed that he knew the number by heart. No matter that she probably wouldn't be there—it had been pure luck (or serendipity?) that he had managed to see her there at all—that irritating woman behind the counter who always smirked whenever he went in would just have to give him Amy's home number. He could make up some excuse about having lost it, or left it at home or something. Never mind the fact that she hadn't ever actually given it to him in the first place. His hand shook slightly as he heard the ringing tone—was he sure about his? What if she didn't want to know?

"Hello?" said a cross voice at the end of the line.

"Oh," said Joe, thrown by the abrupt manner and lack of corporate identification. He had expected the girl to announce "Precious Little Darlings" in her usual sickly baby voice. She'd done it often enough whenever he'd been there.

"Can I help you?" said the voice again.

"Is that Precious Little Darlings?" he asked, feeling silly. Of course he must have the wrong number, and how humiliating to have to say the name of the shop to a wrong number.

"Yes, sorry, yes, Precious Little Darlings," said the voice, sounding flustered and distracted.

It was her. Joe froze. *What to do now?* It had been easy to prepare for asking a third party for her number—he'd have spent the next twenty-four hours working out his next move—but here she was at the end of the phone, and he had no idea what to do next. He panicked.

"Sorry, I think I must have the wrong number," he muttered before hitting the off button on his phone.

"Jesus, that was close," he said, simultaneously thrilled and appalled at his odd teenage behavior. He breathed deeply and started to let himself relax.

His phone vibrated. Someone was ringing him. *What now?* "Number withheld" showed on the screen.

"Hello?" said Joe, glad of the distraction.

"If you knew it was Precious Little Darlings, why did you say you'd got the wrong number?" said Amy, sounding a little rattled.

"What?" said Joe, stalling for time. Damn women and their command of caller ID.

"You just rang and you asked me if this was Precious Little Darlings, and when I said yes, you said you'd got the wrong number."

"Yes. Yes, I did. I meant to ring someone else," said Joe lamely.

"Oh."

"Sorry."

"That's OK—it was just a bit odd. And I can't help thinking I know you from somewhere."

"Really?" said Joe, totally out of his depth now. Should he confess and risk looking an absolute fool, or ring off again and look like a mad stalker?

"Is that . . . is that Joe?" said Amy, sounding suddenly nervous.

Shit. He'd blown it. Nothing for it now but to appeal to her sense of pity.

"Yes, yes it is, Amy."

"Oh, hi. I thought I recognized the voice—so, why did you ring and then say you'd got the wrong number?"

"Because I didn't think you'd be there."

"You rang because you didn't think I'd be here? So, do you want to speak to Sarah? Are you planning on working your way through my staff?"

She was teasing him now. That was a good sign. At least she didn't think he was a weirdo.

"No, it's you I wanted to speak to, but I thought I'd have to get your home number. You didn't give me it when you rushed off like that the other night." Time to put the ball in her court.

"No, no I didn't, did I. But here I am. So what can I do for you, Joe?" her tone was friendly but businesslike. Too late for demurring now.

"I just wanted to say that I'm sorry if I was a bit of a crap date, and I wanted to know if you'd like to do it again—go out, I mean, for dinner, or a drink, or maybe we could do something else like go the pictures or . . . I don't know, what do people do on dates? Go bowling? We could go bowling."

"Bowling?" said Amy, laughing.

"Is that crap? Sorry. Dinner then?"

"Dinner would be lovely. Why don't you come to my flat tomorrow night and we can decide from there?"

"Great," said Joe. This had gone much better than he could have hoped. He scribbled her Docklands address down on the back of his hand and they chatted for a few minutes before ringing off. What a result! He felt elated, but at the back of his mind was the niggling thought that she seemed to have changed her tune a bit. One minute she was all "Good-bye, it's been nice meeting you," and the next "Come on over to my place." He had expected to work much harder for his second chance. What could have accounted for her change of heart? Perhaps in the last few days she'd realized that she'd had a nice time, or perhaps she'd been persuaded by friends to let her defenses down a bit? Maybe she was one of those Rules women who insisted on men doing all the chasing. In any case, Joe walked back to the ward with a spring in his step. For whatever reason, she'd accepted a second date and he was more excited than was befitting for a man of his age.

Back in the shop, Amy opened her diary and smiled as she penciled in the name "Joe" alongside a little picture of an egg surrounded by exclamation marks.

.20.

The candles were lit, the bed linens fresh, and a variety of tasty tidbits were in the fridge just in case she got lucky and he opted out of dinner. Amy flitted about the flat making last-minute man-visit checks—removal of self-help books bought in moments of girlish weakness, careful placement of "I've got a life" ticket stubs and laughing photos with friends. Popping into the bathroom, she paused over the depilatory cream before stuffing it down to the bottom of the toiletries basket—everyone had unwanted body hair, but there was no need to advertise the fact. All the while she laughed at herself for her fastidiousness—it was only a potential shag, and here she was acting like one of those retarded desperate singletons who see every chance encounter with a man as a bridal audition. Why was she making such a special effort for this one? She told herself over and over that this was just man number four.

The fourth month. July already and still not even one attempt at fertilization. Amy felt sure this was not what the statistics meant when they said it took the average woman twelve cycles to get pregnant. Those stats were based on women in relationships—what chance did a poor single girl with itching ovaries have? Despite the fact that each month so far she'd been let down at the last minute by one hapless bloke after another, Amy couldn't help but let herself feel excited again. This, she felt sure, was it. At first she'd written him off as a potential donor-on-tap—he was far too needy, clearly still in love with his dead wife and . . . well, she really liked him. She'd chided herself for falling for the Good Doctor routine, but it was more than that. He was gentle but not wimpy, strong but not hard.

"Bloody hell, you make him sound like a toilet roll—soft, strong, and incredibly long!" Brendan had laughed when she'd told him about her feelings. He'd rung that morning to ask if he could come over—the latest unsuitable man had just let him down again, and Amy was always his safety net. Not tonight.

"Sorry—I'm busy tonight."

"You slag—who is he?"

Amy paused for effect. "The doctor."

"The baby doctor? Ooh! Can we share?"

"Nope. If there's any emissions this evening, they will be gainfully employed, my friend."

"You're not doing what I think you're doing, are you? With the doctor?"

"I don't know what you mean. . . ."

"Amy, are you ovulating?"

"Did you ever in all our years of knowing each other think that you'd be seriously asking me that question?"

"Stop avoiding the answer—are you planning on getting pregnant by that nice doctor? Oh my God, you are!"

"Enough! No comments, I made you promise right from the start!"

"I know but it's been three months—"

"Four."

"Four months—I thought you'd have got bored with the whole thing by now. I mean, three failures to even do the dirty—that should tell you something!"

"Shut up, Brendan. Have a lovely evening on Gaydar, try not to get killed, and good-bye."

Amy had felt mildly guilty all day—not for letting Brendan down, but because of what he had said: "that nice doctor." It was more than just an observation, it was an accusation.

Yes, Joe was "nice" in a way that Amy was not. She got the impression he had lived a life of moral correctness: married his first girlfriend, trained long and hard to become a doctor, been a great father to his (horrible) twin daughters, and seen them through the untimely death of their mother. He had done nothing to deserve being trapped into unwitting fatherhood by an inexplicably hormone-crazed serial commitment–phobic, thong-wearing, would-be baby machine. He'd talked about their evening as a "date," showing that he was expecting some kind of emotional development in their relationship.

How could Amy string him along like this when she knew that all she wanted from this evening was the content of his testes? And she was certain that that was all she wanted. There was no way she was going to get involved with a widower and father of two precocious children. No way.

The buzzer went and Amy rushed to the intercom, trying to ignore the lurch in her stomach—surely it was just the charade that she felt nervous about? It would be difficult to pretend that this was going to be the first of many such evenings when all the time for her it was a one-way ticket to motherhood, no returns, no second chances.

"Hi, it's Joe," said Joe unnecessarily.

"Come on up."

Amy waited at the door as he ascended, carefully wetting her lips and flicking her freshly blow-dried hair over her bare shoulders. It was hot, and she felt flushed with anticipation. The lift doors slid open and there he was—white shirt open at the neck, faded jeans, and brown loafers. Amy grinned in appreciation. He looked like the sort of man they cast in car adverts—smoldering but unthreatening sexuality, racy but family-oriented. He was carrying two blue plastic bags and he thrust them at her as he stepped out of the lift.

"What's this?"

"Dinner. I thought I'd cook for you. If that's OK," said Joe, pausing briefly before planting a small kiss on her cheek. Her nose bumped into his ear as she misjudged the gesture as a hug.

"Great! I wasn't feeling in the mood for going out anyway, and I hate cooking!"

Amy peered inside the bags—fresh pasta, a jar of white truffles, various tubs of olive oil–soaked Mediterranean vegetables, some floury ciabatta, and a huge chunk of fresh Parmesan cheese, all wrapped in Carluccios's distinctive quality paper.

"Italian, then," said Amy, going to the fridge for the champagne she'd been chilling since midday.

"Yes—I'm afraid it's all I know how to do. Mama, you know . . ." said Joe, casting a glance around Amy's flat.

"Very nice, very . . . urban. Is that what they call it—urban living?"

"I prefer *urbane* living—urban is so nineties," said Amy, handing Joe a glass.

"And champagne—how nice. Cheers. Here's to urbane living."

"Cheers."

They sipped their champagne in silence until a familiar sound broke the tension.

"Ak ak ak ak ak!"

"What the hell's that?" said Joe, peering up.

"Oh, just the resident lunatics in the attic."

Joe stared at her in horror. There was something blissfully naïve about him.

"Magpies. Three of them. They've installed themselves on my roof terrace—been driving me mad for months now."

"Three for a girl," said Joe.

Amy smiled. He knew the rhyme, too. It had been partly her Catholic superstition that had set her on her present course of action—the three magpies had seemed to nag her into it. But in truth, she hadn't heard them for a week or so. She hadn't even noticed that they'd stopped their incessant squawking. Was it just synchronicity that they had chosen to pipe up now?

"So what are you going to cook for us tonight?" said Amy, trying to deflect her attention away from Joe's admiring glances. He seemed different tonight—more assertive, more present than he had the last time they had met. She was keenly aware of his physical presence close by. His body seemed to occupy its space with vitality, electricity almost.

"Well, that depends," he said, moving closer. If she wasn't mistaken, he was moving in on her.

"Carluccios—I'm guessing pasta?" said Amy unnecessarily while her stomach turned somersaults.

"Are you hungry?" asked Joe, slipping an arm around her waist. Amy noted that he had almost stopped breathing.

"Erm, well, not really, but I don't want to eat late and then you bugger off and leave me with all the washing up."

"Bugger off? It's you that buggers off."

"What I mean is, just so that I know how much time we've got, I mean, that sounds awful, I mean just in terms of the basic shape of the evening—Christ, that sounds crap—look, what time do you have to get home? Just so that I know."

Joe's mouth flickered into a grin as he put his other arm around her waist. They were face-to-face now. Amy cursed her knees for submitting to the cliché of the moment by almost buckling.

"I don't," said Joe quietly.

There was a long pause, which Amy silently noted would be, if this were a movie, where they kissed for the first time. So this was it then. Full steam ahead.

"If that's OK with you," said Joe eventually, nuzzling into her neck.

Amy rested her chin on his shoulder and caught sight of the ovulation test stick jutting out of the bin, its window slashed through with a thick blue line. She bit her lip hard.

"That's more than OK. That's excellent."

.21.

Amy woke early. By the light trickling in through the gaps in the blinds, she guessed it must be about five a.m., although it could have been earlier. It was difficult to tell in high summer. She resisted looking at the clock. She didn't want to break the spell with harsh reality. What a night. For a slow starter, Joe had proven himself to be a passionate and enthusiastic lover. Maybe he was making up for lost time, and maybe it had felt so good for her because it had been a while since she had shared a bed with anyone, but she couldn't remember a better first time. *First time?* Amy checked herself. *One-night stand.* Although there would be no harm in doing it again in the morning, just to be on the safe side. Turning her head slowly so as not to wake him, Amy ventured a peep at her bedfellow. She jumped. He wasn't there. *Where the hell had he gone? And when?* Amy sat up and grabbed the clock. Five twenty-three. Where the hell could he have gone to in such a hurry at five in the bloody morning? Surely it wasn't the girls? He must have had the nanny staying overnight, and surely she could hold the fort until a reasonable hour on a Sunday morning?

Amy felt hot tears prick at her eyes. *Shit. What was this?* She'd done the same thing herself often enough—woken in a strange bed and tiptoed out before dawn. Why were her eyes wet? Was it indignation? Here she was, secretly trying to get impregnated, and the man of her choice has upped and left before the cells had even had a chance to divide. *Typical.* That's why she'd decided to go this alone—men could not be expected to stay around long enough to be of any real use, so why not do it all yourself and literally cut out the middleman? Amy reminded herself of this as she wiped her eyes with a corner of the duvet, leaving a trail of black mascara in her wake. At least the deed was done. Amy tried to rouse herself. There would be no getting back to sleep now. The dull ache of disappointment in her chest was weighing her down too much to sleep.

"Stop it," she said out loud. "You're doing it again—acting like some lovelorn loser. It was a shag. Hopefully, a baby-making shag. Job done, no hard feelings, cancel and continue."

Amy pulled on her robe and got out of bed with exaggerated care—she didn't want to risk dislodging anything that might be attempting to subdivide deep within her.

Treading softly into the open space of her living room, she noticed glumly that the roof hatch was open. She must have forgotten to close it in her haste to get him into her bedroom. Better get up there and close it before it decided to piss down. Amy climbed the ladder delicately, taking care not to trip on the cord of her gown. Sticking her head out of the hatch at the top, she was greeted by a pair of hairy legs.

"Morning," said Joe. "Did I wake you?"

A huge and stupid surge of relief ran through her.

"No, no, I just thought you'd gone," she mumbled.

"Gone?" Joe looked genuinely shocked. "Why would I have gone?"

"No reason. People do. They stay and then they go."

"How extraordinary. Well, I didn't go. I'm still here," said Joe, helping her out and pulling her to him.

"What are you doing up here at this ungodly hour?" asked Amy, resisting the urge to grab him and start a repeat performance.

"Couldn't sleep."

"Was I snoring? Sorry."

"No, you weren't snoring, you were being lovely. That's why I couldn't sleep. You kept curling up behind me and wrapping your arm around me. It was nice."

"Did I? How extraordinary." Amy blushed. How treacherous her body could be. How dare it show neediness in her sleep.

"Is it? Well, I liked it. And I had a great time last night. And I'm excited. So I got up," said Joe, planting a soft kiss on her lips.

"Oh," said Amy, disarmed by his forthright, unabashed enthusiasm. There was no getting away from it—Joe was really, really nice. This was going to be tough.

"And I'm slightly ashamed that in the heat of the moment, I didn't use any protection. Me being a doctor and all."

"I know. I didn't have anything. But it's OK. I'm fine, and you're practically a virgin, so . . . ."

"Well, thank you very much, Miss Sleeparound. You sure know how to make a man feel better." Joe's eyes sparkled despite his obvious concern. He wasn't used to doing this, or to having this kind of conversation. Amy put her hands under his shirt and gave him a squeeze. He was ludicrously attractive. She almost wanted to punch him for it. She would have to have another go before sending him off into a liberated future while she waited the two weeks until her period was due to see if their liaison had yielded any results.

"Easy, tiger," said Joe as she squeezed his bottom.

"You know you want it," she teased.

"Of course I do—how could I not? You're a sex goddess. But we should probably use something."

"Too late for that, big boy, a definite case of shutting the stable door after the horse has bolted. I mean, we're both healthy, very low risk of HIV . . . what's the worst thing that could happen? I get pregnant!" said Amy, smoke-screening the issue with lightheartedness.

"So you're not even on the pill?" Joe laughed, responding to her touch now. His hands stroked the back of her neck in an expert mixture of massage and caress.

"Nope. Bad for you."

"Well get you!" said Joe, laughing at her devil-may-care attitude. It was curiously attractive.

"I know, I'm such a free spirit, such a maverick, I'll get my comeuppance one day, I'm sure."

"Well, you've got no worries with me."

"Oh?" Amy tried not to wriggle as he gently kissed the length of her neck. For someone so woefully inexperienced, he was good at this. "You seem to be firing on all cylinders to me. . . ."

"I may be firing, lady, but they're all blanks."

Amy froze.

"What do you mean?" She tried to keep the panic out of her voice.

"The good news for you is . . . I had the snip. Just before Eve's diagnosis. Bastard timing, but I don't want any more anyway, so I don't mind. I'm free to come and go as I please. As it were."

Amy pulled away and let his words sink in.

"What's the matter?" said Joe, stepping back and letting go of her arms.

"Nothing. Nothing."

Her head was spinning. This was a totally unexpected blow. How could she have been so stupid as to not anticipate this one? Here she was on the fourth month of her baby quest, in danger of falling for a man whose sperm were rattling around in his body with just a cul-desac to swim into. Amy's mind flooded with images of dead ends, brick walls, and stagnant ponds. This was not part of the plan. She suddenly felt dizzy and sick.

"You look like you've seen a ghost. Sit down. Keep your head down. Let me get you a glass of water."

Amy sat reeling as Joe slipped down the stairs to the kitchen. She had finally managed to bag herself a really nice man at the perfect time to conceive and he turned out to be a dud. She felt deeply disturbed—more so because she suddenly realized that she had been harboring a secret "and they all lived happily ever after" fantasy from the first moment she'd met Joe. It was crushing to come face-to-face with her own denial. If she gave in to her feelings and pursued a relationship with Joe, there would be no baby. That possibility suddenly cut her to the quick. She was shocked by how deep the idea of becoming a mother had rooted itself within her heart. If she was serious about having a child, then there was no way she should take this any further with Joe—she would be wasting her time, and his. He was too vulnerable to be messed around with. He didn't deserve it. Amy knew that the next few minutes were vital. If she didn't make her decision either way, she would get sucked into a relationship that would leave her forever childless. Momentarily she clutched straws, reminding herself that vasectomies can be reversed—but he'd said himself he didn't want any more children, and in any case it would be a complete nightmare having a new baby with the twins. She didn't want to be the wicked stepmother. Amy held her head in her hands and let out a moan.

"Drink this," said Joe, offering her a glass of iced water. "You look like you might faint. I didn't realize I could have this effect on women. All those wasted years!"

"I'm fine. Really. Must have got up too quick or something." Amy was aware that her voice had a new coldness. What was she doing? The words fell like odd-shaped pebbles from her lips.

"I think I need to go to bed," she said flatly.

"OK, let's go and have a lie down."

"No," Amy heard herself saying. "On my own."

There was a long and awkward silence. Amy resisted the urge to look at him—it would be giving away too much to show her face. She could scarcely believe what she was doing, but she told herself over and over that it was for the best. His bombshell had put things into sharp focus. She wanted a baby. Very badly. The realization overwhelmed her, and there was no room for anything else.

"Right," said Joe. "Well, at least let me help you down."

"I'll be fine, honestly."

"OK, if you're sure . . ." said Joe, sounding confused and more than a little shocked himself.

She heard him slip past her and down the stairs. She sat and listened to him dressing, collecting his things and, no doubt, his thoughts. She estimated the amount of time it would take him to get to the front door and leave so that she could time her good-bye when he was at the point of no return. Finally, she ordered her legs to move and went down to see him out.

She had gotten it just right. He was standing at the door, checking his pockets.

"Bye," said Amy, trying her best to sound as though she did this all the time.

"Is that it?" said Joe, almost hotly.

"What do you mean?"

"I mean, I don't get it, one minute we're getting along really well, and the next you're packing me off home. Was it something I said?"

"No, I'm just tired," said Amy lamely.

"Bullshit! Look, I think we've established that I'm no expert in this field, but I'd say this is fairly odd. Or maybe it's not. Maybe this is the way it goes—is it? You meet a guy, go to bed, and then act like strangers in the morning? I suppose that's what you were trying to tell me on our first date, was it?"

He really didn't know. Of course he didn't—it would be the last thing in the world he would think. Why would a thirty-nine-year-old self-confessed child dodger be at all upset that he was sterile, especially so early on in what he was probably hoping was their "relationship."

Amy steeled herself. Despite the fact that a large part of her wanted to rush to him and reassure him that he was fabulous, perfect, and ideal, and that she could imagine herself curled up in front of the TV with him for many years to come, she stuck out her chin and dealt her final blow.

"You're a really sweet guy, Joe, but I'm just not looking for a relationship right now."

Amy held her breath and wondered if it sounded as unconvincing to Joe as it did to her. She didn't know which was stronger—the desire for him to just leave or the desire to have him fight back, argue, beg, and persuade.

"Christ, in my day, that was the man's line. How things change. Well, good luck, Amy, with finding whatever it is you *are*, as you say, 'looking for.' And whatever it is you're not looking for, I hope you never find it." Joe shut the door quietly behind him and was gone.

Amy sat on the floor and let herself breathe. With each breath came a single tear, and within a minute she was sobbing. She cried for Joe—for his wounded face and his confusion; she cried for Ang's lost baby and Brendan's loneliness, for Mrs. Cummings's empty nursery. But mostly she cried for herself. She knew what she wanted more than anything now, and it had taken a huge sacrifice to find out. She promised herself it would be worth it.

Third
Trimester

.1.

It had been years since Amy had been lost in Hackney. When she'd first moved to London, it had been her stomping ground of choice—the late eighties were Hackney's heyday, albeit in an alternative kind of a way. She'd gravitated there naturally along with all her politico friends, Brendan having declared it the gay capital of Europe. It was true—you had to walk only ten paces and you'd be passed by a couple of Jimmy Somerville look-alikes, all shaven heads and tight jeans, holding hands defiantly. Another ten paces and you'd be bound to happen upon a pair of Hackney dykes, cropped and quiffed and full of reproach as they bull-dagger-swaggered along in their matching leather biker jackets. Hackney was where it was at. There was a good stock of roomy, dilapidated Victorian terraces ripe for squatting, the local council was lefty, and the cultural mix—West Indians, Bengalis, Pakistanis, and Africans living alongside old East End pensioners—made for a vibrant and interesting community. Walking down Ridley Road market on a hot Saturday afternoon you felt as though you could have been on several different continents at once as the fat, sweaty fruit traders yelled out their bargains—"Pound of mush, fifty, fifty yer pound o' mush"—next to Jamaican Yardies selling knockoff electrical goods with bass-loaded reggae blasting from what they jokingly called a "Brixton Briefcase," and persuasive Asian men pushing rolls of cheap sari material under your nose. She'd spent many long nights drinking Special Brew at the Hackney Empire while socialist comedians made achingly right-on wisecracks about Thatcher. If it hadn't been for her early business success, Amy felt sure she would still be there now, cycling to sign on and spending her dole money on hash and vegan co-op groceries. She had loved it, and had known every backstreet and rat run in from the Kingsland Road to Hackney Wick. It had been only fifteen or so years since she left the borough for a loftier postcode, so why was she now so utterly lost? She'd bullishly left her map at home, confident that she would find her way easily. Up and down the Richmond Road she went, the website printout crumpled on the passenger seat next to her. The meeting was due to start at eight, and it was already ten past. She would be late. As if it weren't embarrassing enough to be doing this without being stared at by a group of strangers, no doubt on beanbags. The streets were empty—didn't anyone walk in Hackney anymore?—and all of Amy's old orientation landmarks seemed to have disappeared. Gone were the sixties tower blocks and depressing concrete estates. Now on every corner there seemed to be loft-style development with a swanky show home on display, or a trendy gastro pub selling sausage and mash for twenty quid a go. Amy ignored the inner voice telling her that this was a sign that she should turn around and go home, despite the fact that it had been her inner voice that had insisted on the significance of signs at the start of this venture. She would get to this meeting if it killed her.

Finally she recognized a grocer's shop that had so far resisted the urge to sell up and become something more glamorous, and she swung onto the road, craning her neck for the right house number. She knew what she was looking for—it would be the one with the ethnic planters full of giant poppies or sunflowers growing out of old bread bins. There would be a wind chime hanging over the window, where tasteful unbleached linen curtains would partially obscure the view into the natural-wood-floor sitting room.

Amy crawled along the curb, squinting at the doors, none of which seemed to be displaying numbers. How anyone got their post in the morning was a mystery. Out of the corner of her eye, she noticed a thin woman walking nervously along the pavement next to her. The woman was dressed in the kind of loose, murky clothes Amy instantly associated with this evening's purpose, so she pulled over and leaned out the window.

"Excuse me—do you know where number seventy-two is?"

The woman smiled in recognition.

"It's that one there," said the woman, extending a bony finger in the direction of a bay-fronted house with a lavender door.

"Thanks. Are you—"

"Yes," hissed the woman edgily.

"See you there!" said Amy, pulling on the handbrake and grabbing her bag.

The woman scuttled across the road in front of Amy without looking back. Anyone would think she was heading into a Gamblers Anonymous meeting by the way she was behaving.

The front door was open, and Amy tiptoed into the hallway. A variety of worthy footwear was laid out in two neat rows along the length of the hall, and Amy paused momentarily, trying to decide if she should take her own shoes off.

"We should start," said a female voice from inside the front room.

"There's someone else coming," said the nervous woman.

"We should start," reiterated the first woman. "She can catch up. Well, welcome to the first meeting of MO—Man Optional. I hope you like the name—I think it just about sums us up!"

There were a few nervous titters from within. Amy held her breath and listened on, teetering on the verge of tiptoeing out again.

"I'm Pam, but then you all know that from my advert. We are all here because—for various reasons, some by choice, some by necessity—we want to conceive a child outside of a quote/unquote normal heterosexual relationship. Some of you, I know, have already tried to conceive in the old-fashioned way some time ago, some of you are conception virgins, so to speak, some are single women, some are in lesbian relationships. But what we all have in common—am I right?—is the fact that we want to have a baby via so-called quote/unquote artificial insemination by donor."

There were various sounds of assent. Amy stood stock-still, wondering whether to enter or not. This was a curious portal to be teetering on, and part of her was compelled forward by nosiness alone. Another part of her wanted to put her sneakers back on and slip out before anyone spotted her. Without consciously making a decision, she began forcing her foot into her left sneaker. The laces were still done up, and she had to shove her foot in while pulling at the heel. She was panicking and wanted to run for the hills. What had she been thinking? Without warning, she lost her balance and crashed straight onto the living-room door, which the nervous woman had thoughtfully left ajar.

"So let's start by—"

"Hello," said Amy, facedown on the ethnic rug, as a room full of thirty- and fortysomething women peered down at her.

"Ah, you must be our latecomer," said the leader, a large, assertive-looking woman with aggressively hennaed hair and dangly earrings.

"Yes. Sorry. Amy."

"Shoes, please, Amy," said the woman, who appeared to have taken an instant dislike to Amy. "We leave shoes in the hall."

"Yes, I was just trying to get them off—"

"OK," said the woman, pressing on. "Where was I?"

"You were saying that we all want to find alternative ways to get pregnant," offered the nervous woman.

"Yes, yes. Now there has been a lot of press lately about certain groups who use the desperation of women to conceive as a way of making money. I have set up this group to counteract that kind of cynical exploitation of a woman's need to have a baby. You all responded to my website, and here we are. What I would like to do is set up a network of donors who are willing to contribute their sperm as a philanthropic gesture."

"Envelope provided—please give generously!" quipped Amy. Nobody laughed. Pam frowned and plowed on.

"But before we get stuck in, I should say that although I have set this group up—devoting a considerable amount of time to research, collecting a database of likely donors, looking into the legal aspects, and publicizing the service for no financial remuneration at all—I should in no way be considered the leader. This group is for all of us, and I want this to be a quote/unquote safe space for us all to share the ups and downs of the process. So please feel free to chip in whenever you want and let me know how you want things to be organized. OK?"

Several of the women nodded.

"Great. But I should perhaps mention that on the skills front, I do have a City and Guilds basic counseling certificate, and I did my project on effective group dynamic management. So we'll begin with a round-robin. Everyone give your name, your quote/unquote marital status, and say why you are here. Starting with you," said Pam, picking on the nervous woman.

"Oh. OK. Erm, phew, well, I'm Sara. I'm divorced from my husband. Just quite recently actually, erm, so still a bit raw," tittered Sara.

"You're doing really well," said Pam, resting a bangled hand on Sara's shoulder. "Go on."

"Right, yes, so we split up a year ago because he was very unsupportive of the whole IVF process, actually. We tried for three years, and then he wouldn't pay for any more. I don't think he really wanted children anyway. In fact, I think he was quite relieved every time it didn't happen. He denied it, but I caught him almost smiling once when the consultant said it hadn't worked."

The group murmured their support and a few clucked their disapproval of the man.

"What I'm hearing you say," said Pam portentously, "is that you feel your husband was pleased that you didn't conceive." Pam fixed Sara with a piercing, insightful stare.

"Yes. That's right," said Sara, confused by the repetition.

"Good. OK. You?" said Pam, moving on to the next woman in the circle, a very centered-looking woman in her early thirties who was sitting next to a gray-haired woman in her late forties. Amy noticed that they were wearing matching pink socks with double women's symbols printed all around the elastic.

"I'm Lyn, and this is my partner, Cheryl."

"We want to have a baby, but for obvious reasons we can't have one between us, so we are looking for a donor."

"We feel quite strongly that we don't want any involvement on the part of the man."

"Apart from the obvious."

"So we can't ask anyone we know."

"Because we feel that they would want some control over the child."

"And we don't think that would work."

"Because we both have quite strong views on how children should be brought up."

"And in our experience, men try to take over."

"OK," said Pam, trying to reclaim the floor. "You?"

"I'm Louisa. I'm forty-five and I'm single. I never thought I wanted children until a year ago, and although I think it's probably too late—unless you're Madonna—I would like to try for a child before the menopause kicks in."

"Hey, never say never," said Pam.

It was Amy's turn. She hated this kind of thing, and Louisa's story had sent a shiver down her spine—forty-five? Thank God she hadn't left it until that late.

"I'm Amy, I'm thirty-nine—big four-oh next, how did that happen?—and a bit like you, Louisa, I'm single and I'd like to try for a baby."

The group smiled thinly at her. There was a lot of sadness in the room, and it was all Amy could do to stop herself from getting up and fleeing. She felt as though she were at some kind of grief clinic. It wasn't what she had expected at all, although she wasn't quite sure what she had expected. Women with their legs in stirrups, holding turkey basters while queues of men snaked around the block guiltily clutching porn mags?

"Great. So. Let's talk a bit about what brought you here. Who has already tried to conceive? Sara, you mentioned IVF. Anyone else?" said Pam, who had produced a flip chart from behind the sofa and was now brandishing a marker pen. She scrawled "IVF" in the top left-hand corner of the chart.

"We tried self-insemination."

"We had a gay friend who said he would donate with no strings."

"We used a syringe and a pillow."

"To prop her bottom up for twenty minutes afterwards."

"It was horrible. Sticky."

"It didn't work."

"And then the next month, he said he didn't want us to call it Lola if it was a girl."

"So we stopped with him. He wanted control."

The group nodded again. Pam wrote "Self Insem" alongside "IVF."

"Louisa?"

"I've not been trying. I had two abortions, though. One when I was seventeen, and one when I was thirty-two. They'd be twenty-eight and thirteen now. If I'd had them," said Louisa brightly. Nodding seemed inappropriate, but nobody could think of anything else to say or do. It was as if Louisa had plonked the fetuses down in the middle of the room like a cat delivering a dead sparrow.

"Am I right in thinking you feel some sense of regret now over your past decisions? You mustn't beat yourself up about it—that was then and this is now. You shouldn't put yourself through this hell," said Pam passionately.

"I'm not. I'm fine," said Louisa.

"Grief has a funny way of surfacing, Lou," said Pam darkly. "Amy?"

What to say? Nothing for it but the truth—it was the Catholic in her. She always felt the pull of the confessional.

"I found a baby on the street and handed it in and then all my friends suddenly got pregnant and there were these three magpies on my roof and then I ran over my dog and it just seemed like someone was trying to tell me something so I started trying to sleep around to see if I could fall pregnant but it didn't work, mostly because I had real trouble finding men to sleep with—not that I couldn't get the dates, I got the dates, but none of them would do the deed, I mean, the first one, he was what you'd call a habitual shag-dodger, all come-ons but no follow-through, what you'd call a clit tease, I suppose, and the second one just didn't show up and the third was a nanny and had to babysit—hah! The irony! Then I finally got to go for it but turns out, wouldn't you know, he's had a vasectomy!"

The room was silent. Pam stood, pen poised over the flip chart, not knowing what to write. There was no column for this method.

"And to top it all, I think I've fallen in love with him," blurted Amy.

Now it was her turn to be gob-smacked.

.2.

It had been two weeks of hell. Ever since that night with Joe, Amy had hardly slept a wink, and she had mostly got by on Diet Coke and fun-sized Bounty bars. At first she thought she must be sickening for something—the ache in her stomach and the fist in her throat could easily have been the onset of a nasty bout of gastric flu. Amy had had it before, although never with the accompanying tearful episodes during soaps. Love scenes were especially problematic at the moment. She put it down to her hormones. Brendan had another theory.

"You're in love, you silly bitch," he had scolded the night before the MO meeting, as they sat picking at a pizza. It had gone cold and rubbery. Neither of them seemed to have any appetite tonight.

"Who with?" asked Amy, wide-eyed.

"The man you've been on about for months now. The one you had a passionate sperm-free night with the other week. The man you should really be—"

"*Stop!* Don't say it! Don't do that thing you always do, telling me what I feel, what I should do!"

"Ooh, excuse me. Touched a nerve, have I?" said Brendan, smirking.

"No. You haven't. And I have so not been going on about Joe for months. I've only seen him twice."

"Three times if you count Harrods."

"I don't. And I am, as we have established over the past twenty years, incapable of falling in love."

"Not incapable, just massively resistant to. Hence your current inability to realize what's happening to you right now. But I see it."

"What makes you the expert all of a sudden? Had a rush on Diamonique pavé eternity rings at QVC, have we?"

"Now don't get nasty, lady, just because you're in denial."

"De Nile is a river in Egypt. And anyway, people over thirty don't fall in love. It's unseemly."

"Oh, don't we? What do we do, then?"

"We make lifestyle decisions. And mine is to have a baby."

"Oh, right, yes. Sorry, I forgot. The fantasy baby. You know, you used to be fun. Now you're just Ally McBeal with cellulite."

"Thanks for that, Brendan—I know I can always rely on you to cheer me up."

"I'm just feeling smug."

"Why? Did you manage to bag that pasty teenage barista in Starbucks? Spare me the details. People are going to start wondering how you've got all these nephews when you're an only child."

"You mean Skinny Latte? No, not him, I've given up on him."

"Blimey. Did he get the police onto you? Did you lose control and grab him by the muffins?"

"Ha, ha. No, I've . . . met someone." Brendan looked down at his beer glass shyly. Amy hadn't seen him do shy since 1986 when he bumped into Boy George on Old Compton Street.

"Who? When? Where?" said Amy, glad of the diversion away from her own angst.

"You don't know him," said Brendan, stalling.

"So where did you meet him?"

"At a charity dinner. For Stonewall. We had a QVC table because we donated some tatty baubles for the auction. He was on the next table." Brendan was actually looking quite coquettish.

"Oh my God! Who is he?"

"His name's Oscar. Oscar Wodehouse." At this, Brendan glanced up to get her reaction.

"Not *the* Oscar Wodehouse—that weird gay Tory foxhunting city bloke who's always on the telly, banging on about gay mortgages?" Amy laughed at the very idea. There was no way Brendan would fall for anyone remotely right wing—not with his impeccable gay credentials.

"Yes. *That* Oscar Wodehouse. We just really hit it off and he wants me to move in with him—he's got this fantastic flat in Soho, but he wants us to move to the country soon, Somerset, and he's so, *so* not what you would expect."

Amy blinked in astonishment.

"Are you taking the piss?" He must be. There was no other explanation.

"I'm deadly serious. We spent the whole night talking, and he's really a Libertarian, but more than that, he's really sweet and funny and clever, and I've never met anyone like him. He took me on—we argued politics for three hours when we got back to his place, and although I didn't change my mind about anything—I never would—he just did something to me, I don't know, stood up to me, challenged me. And I fucking loved it. I am completely, deliriously in love with a toffee-nosed conservative bastard!" Brendan let out a whoop of joy so alien that Amy could only assume he was channeling Graham Norton.

It had been a shocking evening. Through all her trials and tribulations in life, Brendan had always been a reliable touchstone—always ready with a world-weary aphorism to keep Amy down with him in

the depths of cynicism. Why get too involved with anyone or anything when it always ends in tears had been Brendan's take on life
ever since he realized that his best friend at school didn't love him in
quite the same way. Heartbroken at nine years of age, he'd resolved to
keep his heart to himself forevermore. Until now. It was deeply un-
settling to see him like this. How could he leave Amy all alone on
Sneerer's Island? But here was the rub. Although she hadn't quite
hopped over to the Loved-up Mainland, she was definitely offshore
and all at sea. Perhaps Brendan had unsettled her mostly because she
too was feeling an unfamiliar loss of control over her heartstrings?
Damn him for seeing it, as if having his veil of cynicism removed had
enabled him to see everyone else's love aura or something. But worse
than that new age flimflam—what if he was right? The thought had
been pushed violently over a cliff in her mind and she had gone to
the MO meeting with renewed baby focus. She would not let this diversion get in the way of her greater purpose. Despite her resolve,
however, there was one thing she just could not, for some reason, let
herself do: start the whole dating process again. The idea of going to
bed with anyone now seemed absurd. It had nothing to do with Joe,
she told herself, and everything to do with getting real and not behaving like a tramp. Surely she'd be better off at least trying some
other avenues?

She'd heard about these websites where you pick a donor from an
online catalog—you could choose hair color, personality, even the
blood group of the father without ever having to meet him. Within
minutes of ordering, a motorcycle courier would pitch up at your door
carrying a fresh vial of the selected sperm and the rest was up to you.
It cost a fair bit, and although money was not an issue for Amy, she
could not bring herself to do it. It had somehow seemed so Nazi, ordering a bespoke baby from an Internet site and waiting for a leather-
clad storm trooper to deliver the ingredients to your door. And also so
comical. How could she order sperm just like she had ordered pizza?
Amy wondered if, like the pizza business, you got your money back if

they didn't get it to you within thirty minutes of ordering. Perhaps they did special offers on multiple purchases—a free side of sleepless nights and bitter regret with every tub of salty gloop delivered.

MO had seemed different—the chance to find a donor, but by referral rather than by catalog. She hated the idea of blokes wanking into a yogurt pot for a few quid and then some maverick dot-com millionaire making a mint out of it by selling it to desperate women like Mrs. Cummings. She did not want to be bracketed with Mrs. C, nor did she want to line the pockets of some faceless middleman—or woman—while she lined her womb. But it had been awful—not just the sad little group led by the boorish Pam, but the outpouring of truth to which she had fallen prey. It wasn't until she said it out loud—"I think I've fallen in love with him"—that she knew it to be true. So just as she felt incapable of playing the dating game again, she also found it almost impossible to entertain the idea of getting intimate with any other man's excretions. It just felt wrong, even if it was via a syringe. She'd left pretty soon after that—MO was obviously not for her at the best of times, and this was not the best of times. Amy wondered how it was possible to want two mutually exclusive things so badly at the same time. Not for the first time, she questioned her own motives—was she falling prey to the old "wanting what you can't have" syndrome yet again? Here she was, pushing forty, single and childless, trying her hardest to find someone to inseminate her and at the same time falling in love with a neutered but wonderful man. Maybe, she thought to herself now, she was just being contrary. She'd been accused of it so often in her life that the label had ceased to have any currency for her, but perhaps they'd been right all along, and perhaps all her hard-nosed political years, her cutting-edge artwork, her maverick business acumen all boiled down to this one single personality tic—Amy always wanted to be on the outside of things, looking in. She'd backed herself into a corner. If only she hadn't accepted that second date! She could be out there now, free and at liberty to sleep with whomever she liked. She could even be pregnant by now! The thought fired her up. She would get over this. She would stop this silly mooning about over Joe—he hadn't exactly fought her, and he hadn't been in touch since, so it could hardly be described as the love affair of the century. It was obviously all one-way, so she should just do what she'd always done— get over it and get on with it.

So why did the resolution ring so hollow?

.3.

Amy woke grumpy and hot on a sultry Saturday morning in mid-August. She staggered to the bathroom and stared gloomily at herself in the mirror as she peed. "Didn't you used to be Amy Stokes?" she inquired politely. It was an old line she remembered hearing in a chat show anecdote. It felt too resonant now. She hadn't been herself at all, and it felt as though it was time to get the glad rags on and emerge from the flames. Even if she didn't feel like it, perhaps the act of going out and having a good time would work its way inside her soul. If you fake it well, you end up believing you're having fun.

"Bollocks to this. I am not this mopey, sad bitch with no life and no interests beyond babies and cot trimmings. I am Amy Stokes—hear me roar." She let out a feeble growl. Maybe the girls would be free for a bit of partying tonight? If she rang Soph, Ang, and Jules now, they might be able to hook up later. Except that of course they would all be on bloody mineral water. Or maybe not. Maybe Ang would be back on the odd bottle of Bacardi Breezer now that she was no longer . . . Amy felt a pang of guilt at the realization that she might have a drinking partner after all. Well, at least she could help Ang drown her sorrows. She'd go wherever they wanted, which, if it was up to Ang, would probably be some kind of awful McPub with doubles for two quid and dreadful young men in cheap aftershave. But it would at least be fun. They could get kebabs on the way home and it would be like old times. Except not.

Sod it, though, she needed a good old-fashioned night out. Anything to take her mind off the baby issue—and Joe.

"Bollocks to it all!" she cried, and leapt up to get the phone.

"Ang—can Dave babysit tonight?" she said, full of purpose.

"Erm, oh, hello, Amy, sorry, we were just—" Ang sounded flustered and embarrassed.

"Oh my God, you weren't doing it, were you?" Amy felt sick. Not her best friend!

"Sorry," Ang giggled.

"Well, right now I bet you could get him to agree to anything. Get your glad rags on and meet me in town at seven," ordered Amy.

"What for? Where?"

"For a *laugh*. Remember that? We used to have one occasionally in another lifetime."

"OK, fine. Can we go to that pub in Leicester Square?" Ang always liked it there because she felt it was "real London" (i.e., touristy and overpriced), but the chain pub was at least huge enough to offer seats, and cheap drinks were its specialty—always a consideration for Ang.

"God, I suppose so," sighed Amy. "See you there at seven."

One down, two to go.

"Jules? Amy. Moon Over Water. Tonight. Seven p.m."

"Christ, what are we now, World War Two spies? The Fox flees by dusk under a heavy sky."

"What?"

"Code. Forget it. What's the deal?"

"I just want to have some fun. Can you manage that?"

"As long as they've got seats and I can be near a toilet."

"Rock on, baby," sighed Amy. "See you there."

This last one would be the hardest. Soph would probably be doing antenatal yoga round the clock and would have to be pried kicking and screaming from her battered mat.

"Soph? Fancy a night out tonight?" she ventured, full-on now.

"Erm, well . . ."

"Don't tell me—you've got to rub vitamin E cream in all night."

"No! Honestly, I'm not that bad! I'm just a bit tired. Oh, hang on, Greg's saying something. . . . He's got a gig tonight."

"Wonders will never cease."

"Stop it. He's doing really well. Got loads of new material on babies, going down a storm apparently. So he says why don't I go out and have some fun rather than stay in alone again."

"Well? What do you say? There's a whole world out there!"

"OK. But I'm not dressing up."

"Come in a bin bag if you want. Just be at The Moon in Leicester Square at seven."

"Great!"

"And Soph?"

"Yeah?"

"The bin bag thing—I wasn't being literal."

"Piss off."

So that was it. The girls' night out was planned. Amy spent the day in retro heaven, doing all the things she used to do in her twenties when a big night was in the offing. She had a long bath, slathered herself in twenty different back-of-the-bathroom-cabinet lotions and potions, waxed her legs, plucked her eyebrows (and one or two stray top-lip horrors—the joy of aging), and even used the toe separators to paint her toenails. Her soundtrack was from her corny "Girls Just Wanna Have Fun" CDs—the crass collections of pseudo-empowering "women's songs" she could never resist at service stations, and she treated herself to a constant picnic of whatever was in the fridge. Sushi, rice pudding straight from the tin, artichoke hearts in olive oil, and strawberry Pop-Tarts. It felt good. It had been ages since she'd been this indulgent. By five she was ready to go, dressed in a slash-neck eighties black top and tight jeans topped off with her killer "Don't Fuck with Me" ankle boots. Looking in the mirror now was like meeting an old friend.

"Damn, girl, you look good—and where you been all this time?" said Amy out loud to her reflection. It had been too long since she had done this—got togged up for a night out that had nothing to do with men, babies, or peeing on plastic sticks. She noted with a little irony that in fact she was right in the middle of an ovulation window. But bugger that tonight. Tonight was about her, Amy, trying to re-capture a bit of the old.

"I'm back!" she shouted. "Time for a little celebratory drinkie."

If a girl couldn't open herself a bottle of bubbly now and again, what could she do? Amy necked the first glass pretty much down in one. Was it just excitement that was making her stomach churn? Not quite. It was like excitement, but when she stopped to examine the feeling, she realized with a little shock that she felt nervous. "Maybe I've lost it," she thought, suddenly deflated. "Maybe I've turned into a middle-aged woman with all this baby stuff and all this bloody falling in love with Mr. Wrong." Pouring her second glass of champagne in as many minutes, she wondered just whose sorrows she was planning on drowning tonight. But enough. She had to shake herself out of this mood. She was going out to have a good time, and that was what was going to happen, come what may. It was a point of principle now.

The pub was packed. Only seven p.m., and it was bursting at the seams. A fog of smoke hung above the crowd, and it took Amy a few moments to register that something was odd. It was packed, but there was no loud male braying or joshing, and when she gently pushed her way through to the bar, the crowd just as gently yielded and let her pass. It was packed—with *women*. Shrieks of near-hysterical laughter filled the air, and groups of women stood around dressed in their best going-out gear. Fat women, skinny women, young girls in their late teens, middle-aged mums of three with chubby arms and ill-advised hairdos, women near retirement age who looked as though they hadn't been out in a decade and were intent on making up for it in one night. Several groups seemed to be on hen nights, judging by the L plates, mock-bridal-veils, and devil's horns on display, as well as the border-line pornographic phallic objects adorning a few deely-bopper Alice bands. What on earth was going on?

"Yes, love?" said the barman.

"A bottle of your bubbly and four glasses, please."

"Celebrating, are we? Wedding anniversary?" he said with a wink. Was he flirting?

"God no, not married."

"So what's the big occasion then?"

"Just being here, I guess," said Amy, flashing him a grin. He was very cute, but there was no way she was going to let a boy get in the way of her good time tonight.

"That's nice. Well, you have fun, love," said the barman, pressing her change into her palm with another wink.

"Thanks. I'll try. Oh, what's all this about tonight? What are all these women doing here? Is it ladies' night or something?"

"Ladies' night? That ages you! We don't do that anymore!" laughed the barman. "No, it's the show across the road—disgusting, I call it!" said the barman with a laugh, before dashing off to throw the same charm at the next gaggle of girlies. He was clearly in his element.

Amy headed for the ladies' toilet. She was sure she'd find her gang as near to the lavs as humanly possible, what with their latter-day propensity for vomiting and urinating.

"Amy!" shouted Ang, already flushed and overexcited. "Over here!"

"Hiya, girls!" said Amy, plonking the champagne down in front of them. "Who's ready to rumble?"

Soph and Jules allowed themselves a weak smile and sipped at their orange juice wanly.

"Oh, come on! You can do better than that!"

"Amy, darling, much as this bloody pregnancy sobriety is starting to pall, I'm afraid I'm too vain to allow myself to have a child with fetal alcohol syndrome, so if you don't mind, I'm staying off the grog 'til it's born," said Jules.

"Don't forget there's breast-feeding, too—about five percent of the alcohol crosses the breast milk," added Soph.

"Breast-feeding? You don't think for one minute I'll be doing *that*, do you?"

"Yeah, wise up, Soph, Jules thinks 'breast is best' is something to do with a Sunday roast," said Amy, pouring for herself and Ang. "Well, cheers anyway, you miserable bitches. Here's to us!"

"Chinky cheers!" said Ang, necking her bubbly fast.

"So what's happening tonight? What's the plan, ladies? A few here and then on to a club? Are you allowed dancing? Good for the pelvic-floor muscles!" said Amy. She could tell that this evening was going to be an uphill struggle.

"Oh, Amy, guess what? That show's on over the road—you know, it was on *The Big Breakfast*—*Puppetry of the*—you know . . . !" said Ang, giddy with possibility.

"*Puppetry of the Penis*? How horrible," shuddered Soph.

"It's meant to be great—a right laugh," said Ang, trying not to show her hurt.

"I wouldn't mind seeing that, as it happens," said Jules. "I could do with a good cackle at a cock. Haven't seen Justin's since last month."

"What do they actually *do*?" asked Amy. "Do they have puppets, or is it really their penises?"

"There's no strings and no puppets, it's just two Ozzie blokes kicking off their pants and doing dick tricks," said Jules, who prided herself on having her finger on the pulse of every cultural event be it low- or high-brow.

"Shall we go? Oh, go on—it'll be a laugh!" said Ang, jumping up and down in her seat. She was wearing a puff-sleeved gypsy blouse and her old charm bracelet. She clearly hadn't been out in ages, either, and was as up for anything as Amy.

"Oh, God, do we have to?" moaned Soph. "My feet are killing me just from walking from the tube."

"They've got seats, comfy plush theater seats," cooed Amy, quite interested in the show herself now. Why not follow the crowd of good-time girls and hope to become one of them, laughing in unison at male genitalia? She could think of worse Saturday nights.

"Tell me more," said Jules, wanting to be persuaded.

"We can sit in the dark near some toilets and eat ice cream. . . ." added Ang.

"Sold to the woman with the puffy ankles," said Soph. "Anything to get out of this smoke."

"Really? Are we going?" Ang clapped.

"Why not? Drink up, ladies, let's go and find us some dick," said Amy, topping up her glass.

The foyer was mobbed. The atmosphere was thick with female energy, and there was a distinctive whiff of progesterone in the air. After some careful manipulation of the box-office assistant, Jules managed to get four seats together on an aisle five rows from the front—perfectly situated for the toilets and the exit, should the spectacle bring on any vapors. The girls nestled in their seats with laps full of pick 'n' mix, any reluctance now gone. The sense of expectation was immense. It was like a massive netball rally, or school prize day at an all-girl comprehensive. Dotted around the auditorium were a few sheepish-looking men, who clearly had no idea why they had thought it would be a good idea to come. One or two clutched raincoats to their knees. The crowd was beginning to grow impatient now, and Amy, in a fit of teenage rebellion, started a slow handclap. Pretty soon nearly everyone in the theater was clapping along, until some other joker decided a chorus of "Why are we waiting?" would be a good idea. Then, as if in response to the growing restlessness, the lights slowly dimmed and a drumroll reverberated around the auditorium. A great wave of overexcited *ooohs* accompanied the buildup.

"Ladies and gentlemen, welcome to *Puppetry of the Penis!*" boomed a disembodied voice from behind the curtain.

More ridiculously infectious screaming. Amy was already crying with laughter, and Ang looked as though she was about to faint with anticipation. Even Soph and Jules were smiling.

"But before we start, there are a couple of rules. . . . There should be no photography of any kind during the show."

A chorus of pantomime cries of disappointment from the crowd.

"You came to see our penises, not take them home with you! And secondly, now would be a very good time to switch all pagers and mobile phones . . . to *vibrate!*"

Whoops of joy.

"Now, would you please go wild, go crazy for . . . *Puppetry of the Penis!*"

To screams of The Bay City Rollers circa 1974 proportions, two cloaked Australian men swaggered onto the stage oozing charm. A souped-up version of Rolf Harris's "Two Little Boys" blasted out in surround sound.

"They'd better not have two *little* toys," shouted Jules.

"G'day!" shouted the two Aussies in unison.

"Now before we get started, ladies and gents, we just want to make sure that you've all got the right show," said the taller and more muscular of the two.

"That's right, we had a couple of pensioners in last night who'd come to see *Little Orphan Annie*," said the one with the long hair.

"You should all be expecting *full-frontal male nudity!*"

A huge scream of affirmation filled the room. This was already more fun than Amy had had in ages. She hurriedly pushed a random image of a naked Joe out of her mind.

Within seconds the cloaks were off and eight hundred women shrieked their appreciation.

"We're going to start with a few warm-ups, then get down to the serious art of genital origami."

And with that, the two men launched into an hour of pulling, tugging, stretching, and yanking, the likes of which Amy had never seen. The Eiffel Tower, the Hamburger, the Roller Skate—Amy felt sure that if she were a man, her eyes would be watering. The tricks were projected onto a huge screen, so that every last testicular detail was writ large. It was oddly and intoxicatingly liberating to be in such close, blown-up proximity to not one but two penises without any hint of sexual expectation, but it had to be said that the magnification of the scrotum, the testes, and the penis did nothing to improve their aesthetic appeal. Amy wondered how babies ever got made, given the hideousness of the equipment. On and on the chirpy Aussies went—the Slow Emerging Mollusk, the Wrist Watch, the Windsurfer. In an hour of good-natured banter, the guys never once stopped fiddling with their bits, but after ten minutes the crowd became blasé with the nudity, so much so that when a volunteer was requested for the finale a sea of hands shot up—among them Ang's. By this point, Ang had consumed the four alcopops she had concealed in her handbag and was obviously pretty merry. Before the other women had a chance, she was out of her seat and skipping up to the stage.

"Hello there, sister—you're pretty keen! Give her a big hand, ladies!"

The guys went to shake Ang by the hand and she comically recoiled.

"I'm not touching them—I know where they've been!" she screamed into the mic. Amy roared her approval.

"Go Ang!"

Soph and Jules grinned behind their hands.

"My friend Friendy here is going to help you out—you're going to help us with a little installation called the Fruit Bat! Ready?"

"Ready, Horse," said Friendy, positioning Ang center stage and standing behind her. Ang grinned idiotically and made a grab for Friendy's lovely bottom.

"Hey, lady, don't touch what you can't afford," he mock-chided. They were clearly used to drunken women groping them. On any other night, Amy would be mortified by implication, but not tonight. This was fun.

Horse took a running jump and ended up in a handstand facing out, his legs gripped firmly at the ankle by a surprised Ang, whose head was now positioned between his upturned legs. The view must have been astonishing.

"Don't look down!" ordered Friendy, supporting Ang from behind. The girl on the video link in the front row shot up and took a Polaroid, handing it to Ang as she was escorted off the stage. Her face was aglow with pleasure as she ran back to her seat, self-consciously holding on to her bosoms all the way up the aisle.

"Well done," managed Sophie.

"How was it? Did you see his chocolate starfish?" asked Jules.

"Urgh—stop it!" said Soph.

"It was great! Sandwiched between two lovely naked men—heaven!" Ang laughed as the guys waved their good-byes.

As the lights came up, there was a rush for the bar and the foyer—the guys had announced that they would be signing their book after the show, and scores of women were already crowding round the merchandise desk with tenners clutched in their hands.

"Make way, ladies!" shouted Horse from behind the crowd. "Hah—you didn't recognize me with my clothes on, did you?"

Despite the fact that he was a blatant Australian crass exhibitionist, there was something deeply attractive about Horse. He had a kind of "fuck you" attitude but without a hint of aggression. He looked like the kind of man who could start a party in a mortuary. He twinkled and flirted just a little with each woman who gingerly requested a special message on the inside cover of the book, all the while swigging from a half-empty bottle of Wild Turkey. Amy found herself pushing forward to get a closer look, telling herself that Brendan would probably love a copy of the graphically illustrated companion to the show. Ang was right behind her, waiting to get her ticket signed.

"Getting a book?" She giggled.

"Yeah, well, I thought Brendan might like it, you know. . . ."

"Get in there, girl—I saw the way you were looking at him!"

"Rubbish." Amy smiled. *Well, why not?* Maybe it would be fun to get off with one of the penis boys? She was ovulating after all, and surely now that she didn't care whether or not she got pregnant—well, nearly—it might be the perfect time. They always say it happens when you've given up. . . . And imagine conceiving a child by a penis puppeteer? It'd make a great anecdote. In many ways, it would be perfect—he'd be off on the next leg of the world tour before she'd even finish peeing on the stick.

"Hello, ma'am—you were our Fruit Bat, weren't you? How'd you like the show?"

"Oh, it was great!" gushed Ang. "Haven't had such a laugh in ages!"

"Terrific stuff—do you want me to sign your book?" said Horse, catching sight of Amy and brightening his smile.

"Oh—I, erm, I haven't got enough money for a book, but would you sign my ticket for me?"

"I can do better than that, young lady—have a book on me," said Horse, signing his name with a flourish, keeping eye contact with Amy all the while.

"Thanks—that's really sweet of you!" said Ang, hesitating before planting a kiss on Horse's cheek.

"Easy, lady! And how about you, beautiful? Do you want a book? It'll give you something to try out on the old man when you get home." Horse smiled.

"Oh, she's single—there's no one expecting her home!" blurted Ang.

"Thanks for that. Nothing like making a girl look sad in front of a star," said Amy. "Yes, I'll have a book please, and could you sign it 'To Brendan'?"

"Lucky Brendan," said Horse, signing the book.

"Oh, he's gay," said Ang, still giddy from all the attention.

"Well, what's the matter with these British men, leaving a gorgeous girl like yourself on the shelf?"

"Tell me about it," said Amy.

"Oh, she's not short of offers, she's just very choosy," said Ang.

"Is that so?" asked Horse, a smile creeping across his face. He was definitely rising to Ang's bait.

"Yeah, well, you know, there's a lot of morons out there," said Amy.

"You're not wrong there, sweet cheeks. Well, how about you meet me at the stage door in fifteen minutes and I'll try and restore your faith in mankind?"

Ang giggled nervously. What to do now? He probably did this every night. The stage door keeper probably felt like a pimp. And this was supposed to be a noncomplicated girls' night out. *No*. She should definitely turn him down and go home with the girls.

"OK," she heard herself saying.

Ang pulled her away sharply and collapsed into a fit of giggles.

"Wow! You're going to cop off with a penis man!"

"Maybe," said Amy. "If he plays his cards right."

"What's this?" said Jules, who'd just emerged from the toilet.

"Amy's got a date—with Horse!" Ang clapped.

"Christ—are we going to hear the pitter-patter of tiny hooves?" asked Jules. She was joking, but one glance told Amy her friend could spot her intentions a mile off.

"If he can still do anything with it after that display," tutted Soph.

"Oh, come on—you enjoyed it!" said Ang, not willing to let anyone piss on her fire.

"It was interesting in its phallic iconoclasm, I suppose."

"What? I just thought it was a good laugh!" said Ang. "What we gonna do now?"

"Go home to bed," chorused Jules and Soph.

"Boring! And I can hardly hang round with you, Ms. Love Goddess, can I? Suppose I'll just have to go back with Tweedle Dee and Tweedle Dum here."

"Sorry, Ang." Amy grimaced. "I didn't think this would happen."

"Oh, go on and enjoy yourself—you've been a right miserable cow since—"

"Uh-oh—don't mention the J-word, Ang—she was just starting to enjoy herself," warned Jules.

"Oh, get lost all of you," said Amy, stinging a little from the Joe reminder.

"Sure you'll be OK? Text me when—if—you get home," said Soph.

"I'll be fine. I'm a big girl."

"Yeah, well you just think about it before you rush into anything you might regret. . . ." warned Jules darkly.

"Bye—have fun!" shouted Ang as they dragged her off.

"I will!" shouted Amy, not so sure now. Damn Jules for knowing her so well.

Over at the signing table, Horse looked up and mugged his impatience. She smiled shyly and felt suddenly stupid, waiting for a stranger's attention in a public place. What was she doing? Despite the thrill of the pickup, a hollow feeling tugged at her unwilling consciousness, and she battled to suppress it. Horse signaled that he'd be five minutes, so she headed out of the building in search of the stage door. It was usually round the back somewhere. She'd often seen sad provincial types hanging around clutching theater programs. She had never thought she'd become one.

On her way around the building, Amy watched gaggles of women tottering off into the night, no doubt off home to various husbands, boyfriends, children. And here she was—pushing forty and still relentlessly unattached. It was an odd feeling—she wasn't sure in this moment whether she felt free and in charge of her own minute-by-minute destiny in a way that those women could only dream of, or if the sense of weightlessness was now disturbing. She suddenly felt ghostlike, as if she were hovering, blurry-edged, two feet above the mortal world and all its blissful failings. She slumped against the stage door and pulled out her cigarettes. Five minutes passed, and several girls clattered into the side street in search of autographs. They were in their twenties and full of it all. Amy glanced at her watch and began to feel so deflated that she felt it must be visible. Her mouth drooped, her shoulders dropped, and her whole body seemed to be about to hiss out all its air. It wasn't that she felt disappointed or stood up. She felt sure that Horse would appear at any moment—and that was the problem. She couldn't go through with it. Try as she might, it was just too soon to be dating anyone else.

"Bugger," she said out loud, stamping out her cigarette.

The stage door flung open and Amy heard Horse's voice on the stairs. What if she did sleep with him tonight, and what if she did get pregnant? What then? That would definitely be the end for her and Joe. How treacherous her heart had been—here she was, pretending to be a carefree perhaps soon-to-be mum, and all along she'd been harboring the secret hope that things might yet work out between them. *Bugger.*

"Hello, ladies—what can I do for you?" he boomed. "I've got about one minute 'cause I've got myself a hot date!"

"No you haven't," Amy heard herself saying as her legs suddenly carried her running up the street. "No, you haven't."

Maybe it was just the excess alcohol, or the strong breeze up the alley blowing grit into her eye, but Amy's cheeks were streaked with tears all the way to the tube.

.4.

September. Amy always hated September. She could never escape the feeling that she was about to return to school or college. The end of August would find her tossing and turning at night, trying to shake off nightmares about being made to re-sit through exams, or being forced to go back and start again at the age of thirty-nine. It didn't help that these days, the shops were full of "Back to Skool" signs by the end of July, and no sooner had they announced the onset of the summer holidays—"Skool's out 4 Summer!"—than they were desperately peddling new uniforms and brightly colored stationery packs. This September it was even worse. Amy felt the familiar sinking feeling in the pit of her stomach every time she caught sight of a Woolworth's shop front, but there was an extra layer of dread. This time she was returning to school without having completed her project. In fact, she hadn't even begun, due to three false starts and a couple of wrong turns. How could it be September already? Almost five months since the beginning of her pregnancy mission, and so far any conception would have to have been immaculate. And Amy was not feeling remotely like The Chosen One.

Tuesday morning saw her slumped in front of her computer, idly surfing fertility pages. Most of them were American and full of dire health threats and guilt trips just for would-be moms, along the lines of, "The Surgeon General says that, when you are pregnant, if you stand next to someone drinking a small sherry, you are *evil* and are *actively maiming* your unborn child. *You need help*, you sick, diseased, selfish alcoholic witch." Despite the popular perception that pregnant women are automatically deified, it seemed to Amy as though they became less important. Yes, they may be offered seats on buses and helped with their groceries, but really the concern was for the growing angel inside them. The woman just became a husk, a host organism whose needs were at best secondary, at worst derided as irrelevant. Pregnant women weren't allowed to take any drugs, barring the occasional Tylenol (and that only if a leg were hanging off), and as far as Amy could tell, this was largely because no one had bothered to test anything. It wasn't that they actually knew nasal sprays or migraine pills or sleeping tablets were harmful to the baby—it was just that everyone thought pregnant women should just put up with all the irritating little ailments gestation can bring. If she was to believe all the women she read about online who were suffering with ear problems, wind, heartburn, congestion, thrush, cystitis, piles, varicose veins, morning sickness, constipation, and cramps, it didn't exactly look like a heap of fun being pregnant. And yet the desire grew and grew. She had thought that she was over it, but lately she'd taken to watching the Discovery Health Channel from midday until three—they were showing a series of programs from America and the UK called things like *From Here to Maternity* and *Birth Stories*. She had become obsessed. Every day, the same ritual. Get up, check e-mails, search a few baby-related sites to kill time, then straight on to the TV to sit blubbering as woman after woman was shown cursing and yowling her way through birth. Amy found herself weeping at these programs with alarming regularity. She no longer knew whether it was just the sheer miracle of it—and it never ceased to inspire awe to see that little head pop out in a gush of fluid and shouting—or because of the emptiness of her own belly.

The American stories were the worst. The way Americans were so unabashed about their feelings would, under normal circumstances, make her cringe to her toes, but these days if Todd and Rachel or Randy and Charlene planted a tree for their newborn baby girl, wearing matching autumnal sweaters out in the backyard, she would sit nodding her head in empathy and dabbing furiously at her eyes. It was hideous.

"Get a grip, woman!" she said to herself, hitting the off button.

It was time to get back out in the world and start again. Amy reminded herself that there was no school to return to, no homework to be handed in. She was a mature woman, her own boss, in charge of her feelings and single-minded in her purpose, beholden to no one. She got dressed quickly and silently gave thanks that Jules had asked her to go shopping today. It was just too tempting to sit gawping at cervixes all day long. No wonder Joe loved his job. . . . She stopped mid-thought and checked herself.

What was it that therapist told you to say? "I will not accept anything less than what I absolutely want." At the time, Amy had laughed—she'd been cornered by some intense shrink at a party and they'd argued about how therapy can make people selfish and unrealistic until Amy had been able to use his affirmation against him during a clumsy lunge. But now it seemed to offer some kind of direction. Why should she compromise now? She'd got this far more or less alone; she could carry on now.

"I will not accept anything less than what I absolutely want," she repeated in the mirror, before sticking her tongue out and heading out the door. If only it were that easy.

.5.

'Ow many months are we?" oozed the smartly dressed twig with the French accent.

"I'm not any months, but my fat friend here is almost five," said Amy, fixing Le Twig with a stare. Jules had insisted on the French shop Formes for maternitywear, claiming that she was too old to wear High Street fashion.

"I don't want to look like some pram-faced Atomic Kitten reject," she'd said when Amy had held up a pair of low-slung jeans and a tight flared T-shirt inscribed "Big Hot Mama." Le Twig was unruffled.

"We 'ave some beautiful things for you—for work or for ze lezure?"

"I didn't know there was a choice."

"Oh, yes, madam, we 'ave a selection of smart clothes for ze office, casualwear, and somesing more glamorous for ze evenings," purred Le Twig, looking at Jules as if she were some kind of simpleton.

"Urgh—glamour wear—I won't be needing that, I'm not going anywhere looking like this. Just bring me some stuff. I'll be sitting on the floor in the communal changing room, crying."

Le Twig skulked off to select some outfits while Jules and Amy en-sconced themselves in the fitting room.

"I don't know why I'm bothering—I look like Placido Domingo whatever I wear at the moment," sighed Jules, lowering her bottom onto a wicker chair.

"Rubbish. You look . . . blooming," said Amy.

"Oh, please. Not from you. I'm so insomniac at the moment, I've got more rings than Tiffany's, my ankles are so swollen I look like I've put my legs on upside down, my nails are chipped and weak, and my skin resembles a pepperoni pizza with extra cheese. I look like shit. So don't give me that crap about blooming."

"Sorry. Yes, you don't look the best I've ever seen you. Just remember that your body is doing amazing things right now! But that's no reason to wear crap clothes. I have *never* seen you in leggings before, and quite frankly, I don't wish to repeat the experience, so get trying on, Miss. Here, have a go of this skirt and wrap-over blouse. If you can work out where all the straps go . . ." said Amy, flinging a few items at Jules. Le Twig winced.

"Ze straps are designed to allow ze garment to grow wiz you," she muttered before disappearing back into the shop.

"Look at this dress—it's like a five-year-old's painting smock," said Jules, flinging it to the floor.

"Come on—you've got to get some new clothes. My treat."

"Ooh, get you. Feeling generous today?"

"Well one of us might as well be treated."

"Oh, dolly, don't despair. Is it the baby thing?"

"Sort of."

"And here's me moaning on and on, and all the time you're proba-bly thinking you'd give your right arm to be in my position. Sorry."

"Left arm, maybe. Come on, try this suit—it's nice."

"No news from Joe?" Jules wouldn't drop it now.

"News? Like what? 'Hello, let's have dinner sometime, and by the way, I've had my tubes re-tied?' No. No news from Joe."

"Bugger. Ain't life a bitch."

"Yep."

"And you're absolutely sure that he's worth giving up for this baby thing?"

"No, I'm not, but I've made my bed and I'm not going to lie in it, not with him anyway, so let's not say another word about it, OK?"

"OK. OK. God, you're like a rottweiler when you get an idea in your head. I pity the poor little bastard already if you do manage to have a baby. So what are you going to do now then? Go back on the prowl?"

"I suppose so. But I can't quite get it up for all the elaborate court-ing, all the chat, the dates, the stupid game playing you have to do. It's bloody hard work at the best of times," sighed Amy, idly slipping a stretchy dress over her head and pulling it out at the stomach. "It all just takes so bloody long! And I've only got another seven months."

"Well, you just need to act fast."

"Don't tell me—tell them! All the hopeless eunuchs, castratos, and sexually complex men out there! Why is it that the shelves are full of men's mags, lads' mags, and porn mags, but it's nigh-on impos-sible to find a man who will actually sleep with a real woman?"

"Speed dating."

"What?"

"That's it—that's your answer. Cut the crap, straight to the point, three minutes, suss them out and move on," said Jules triumphantly.

"But you did it one time when you'd split up, and you said it was full of sleazy desperados just out for all they could get!"

"Exactly! Bingo!"

It took a moment for the realization to happen. Jules was right—it was still a knee-jerk reaction to trash anything as shallow and mer-cenary as speed dating, but in actual fact it was exactly what she needed. Why waste precious time trawling the bars and clubs, track-ing down vaguely interested boys, when she could go to one room and come face-to-face with about thirty up-for-it men all in the same night? If she timed it right, she could even get pregnant the same night! Speed mating! It was so perfect, she kicked herself for not thinking of it herself.

"What do you think?" said Jules, spinning around in a smart black suit with a hideous elasticized pouch where the fly should have been.

"Perfect," said Amy, not looking at all.

.6.

D ad! Cesca's nose is bleeding!"
        It was the second time that day.

"Well, just get some tissue and hold it until I can stop," said Joe, trying to find a place to pull over. It wasn't easy in Soho. The girls insisted on Leicester Square for every movie trip—they liked the crowds, the big screens, and the obscene buckets of popcorn, and didn't care one bit that it cost Joe an arm and a leg to park. And to top it all, Francesca's bloody nose had started again. Joe spotted a loading bay and swung into the curb. Cesca sat triumphantly in the back cupping a large pool of blood in both hands, watching with rapt attention as it splash, splash, splashed onto the newly cleaned upholstery.

"Oh, Cesca! Why didn't you say earlier!" shouted Joe, scrabbling around for a tissue.

There were never any when he needed them.

"I thought it was going to stop," said Cesca unconvincingly. The truth was she was absolutely fascinated by bodily fluids, especially her own.

"I haven't got any tissues—quick, just pull your T-shirt up and hold it there."

"Urgh, gross, Dad—it's my new Busted T-shirt—I don't want to get blood on it."

"You don't mind getting blood all over the car!"

"'Course not—the car's yours," said Cesca with childish logic.

"There's a bar there, Daddy—get some from the toilets!" shouted Laura, delighted by the sudden drama.

Joe jumped out of the car and ran into the bar. It was just after midday, and the Australian barman was setting up for the day.

"Sorry, mate, we're not open yet." He scowled.

"I know—I just need some tissue."

"Sorry, mate, the toilets are for customers' use only."

"Oh, come on!"

"Sorry, mate—rules."

"Well, OK, I'll have an espresso then," said Joe, rummaging for some coins.

"Sorry, mate—we're not open yet."

"Oh, for Christ's sake—it's after twelve!"

"Is it?" asked the barman without a flicker of interest.

"Oh, forget it!" said Joe, turning on his heel and grabbing a fistful of linen napkins he'd spied on the bar.

"Oi!" shouted the barman after him.

"Thank you!" shouted Joe, reaching the door and trying to work out if he should push or pull. A large, hand-written poster was obscuring the handle. Joe took in its content: "Speed dating with QuickMatch—here, 7:30, Monday." The words burned into his eyes.

"I'll bring them back on Monday!" shouted Joe over his shoulder.

Well, why the hell not? he thought. *Things couldn't get any worse.*

. 7 .

From her vantage point across the street, Amy could see everyone who went in and out of Bar Soho in Frith Street. She was playing a great guessing game of "Who's going downstairs for speed dating and who's just out for a drink?" with herself, usually getting it very wrong. All the young, attractive men were stopping short of the stairs to the lower level and ordering drinks at the bar after joining large groups. All the balding, paunchy, sartorially challenged men were making a beeline for the room downstairs. Conversely, every woman who entered the bar looked glamorous and capable—and they all headed straight for the speed dating. It wasn't at all what Amy had been led to believe the clientele would be like. The company's website, QuickMatch.com, had claimed that the age range was strictly twenty-eight to forty, and that only the very best applicants were selected for the evening's fun. This ragbag of men was hardly select. Most of them looked as though they hadn't even made any effort for the evening. About seventy-five percent were in suits—obviously, they'd come straight from the office—and the rest were dressed in what looked like Marks and Spencer chinos and sports casuals. Amy shuddered. How could she sleep with a man in a polo shirt? Why was it always like this—the available women in the world were mostly highly evolved and at least averagely attractive, while the flotsam men were dull, hairy-eared dorks? In fact, a couple of the women had been downright gorgeous. She couldn't believe it when she saw the tops of their shiny blond heads bobbing downstairs. She thought about going home, not even bothering to go in. If any decent men did turn up, the leggy blondes would nab them straightaway. What was the point? She finished her espresso and played with the fifty pence piece change. Heads she'd go in, tails home. *Heads*. Best of three. *Tails*. This last one was the decider. *Heads again. Shit*. She'd have to go in now.

Once inside the bar, Amy toyed with the idea of stopping upstairs. There were about twenty or so guys who she could imagine creating beautiful babies with; the only problem was that most of them looked young enough to be her son. She didn't fancy her chances against the lithe young things that were now shimmying in through the door, and it would just seem wrong somehow. She had always imagined herself to be young and coquettish, and had never had any problems picking up younger men. But these days it had started to feel a bit sordid. Fine when you're thirty-five, but almost forty? Wasn't that a bit sad really? A bit "there's life in the old girl yet?" No. Amy would do just as she had planned and go downstairs. She comforted herself with the fact that at the very least, she would come away with some great anecdotes. She took a deep breath and headed down. Things were just about to start. Small, numbered interview tables lined three of the four walls. A sweaty-looking woman who looked about twenty had a microphone in one hand and a school bell in the other.

"Right good evening, ladies and gents, I'm Susan, and welcome to

QuickMatch! So you probably know how it goes—I see a few familiar faces here tonight, a few regulars!—but for the QuickMatch virgins amongst you, here's how it works. Girls stay put tonight—find a numbered table, girls, and sit there waiting for each Prince Charming to make his way to you. You, if you could start there," said the woman, pointing Amy in the direction of the first table, "and the rest pop yourselves at a table each. Boys, pop on your number badge, then you'll go round all the tables clockwise until you get back to the number you started at. You get three minutes, and you'll know when it's up 'cause I'll do this—"

The sweaty woman rang the school bell with gusto. Amy's ears rang for minutes afterward, and the crowd tittered with nervous excitement.

"When you hear that sound, you move on. I don't care if the woman you are sitting in front of is just about to tell you the secret of multiple orgasms, I don't care if she's getting out photos of her victory parade after winning Miss Nude Pole Dancer 2004, when you hear the bell, guys, you move on. OK? And a quick word about questions—try not to go for the obvious: 'Where do you live? What do you do for a living? What are your hobbies?' *Boring!*"

Amy mentally noted the amount of crestfallen male faces around the room. Clearly, they would now be dumbstruck.

"Now, when you like someone, you tick their number—just try to do it discreetly!—and if you both tick each other, we'll send you e-mail addresses and then it's up to you. That's the official line, anyway. Most people just hang out in the bar after and hook up that way. And I can assure you this does work—we've just heard of our first QuickMatch engagement!"

A cheer went up. There was no denying it—the atmosphere was as exciting as the Friday-night school disco Amy used to frequent, despite the fact that most of the men seemed to have crept under the QuickMatch age radar—they were mostly at least forty.

"OK, so guys, get yourself a starting point; ladies, reapply the lippy;

here we go!" She rang the bell to signal the first three-minute "date," and Amy sat down at the corner table she'd been allocated.

"Unlucky for some!" said an eager-looking man in his early forties as he plonked himself down in front of her, clutching his date card.

"Sorry?" said Amy.

"Thirteen—my badge number—unlucky for some! And you are?" he asked, grinning.

"Amy. Hello," she said with as little enthusiasm as possible without being blatantly rude.

"Gary."

"Pleased to meet you, Gary," she lied. He had only three teeth on the bottom row, and she could smell his sour breath from four feet away.

"Very important question—do you like motorbikes?"

"Motorbikes? They're OK. I've never had one, but I've been on one a couple of times."

"Excellent!" said Gary, ostentatiously ticking her box on his card. It seemed to be more than enough information upon which to make his perfect-match decision.

"Right," said Amy, not really having any desire to find out anything about Gary. The halitosis and the fact that he was dentally challenged were enough to be going on with. There was no way he would make a suitable inseminator.

"Do you want to ask me anything? Go on—you can ask me anything at all!" said Gary, clearly having the best time of his life. It was obvious that most of the men here, far from being limited by the three-minute format, were reveling in the undivided attention of some lovely women.

"Well, let's see . . . no, no, I think you're a pretty simple kind of guy. I mean, in a good way! I think I can see what kind of man you are. I hate asking questions," she lied.

"OK, well, let me tell you a bit about myself," said Gary, undaunted.

He proceeded to embark on a pitiful attempt at self-promotion that included such cringe-making information as his bank balance ("Let's just say you wouldn't go short of anything with me!"), the number of long train journeys he'd taken (and their collective mileage), not forgetting his school sports day achievements circa 1972. In some men, this sort of quasi-autism was charming. Not in Gary. After what seemed like an eternity, the bell rang mercifully.

"Well, I'd love to chat some more, but I have to move on now, Amy. Hope to see you soon!" he said chirpily, blissfully unaware of his personality bypass.

"Yes, bye," said Amy, placing a dark cross next to Gary's number.

"Hello," said the next man to sit down in front of Amy. He was about thirty, wearing a baseball cap and skater-boy clothes. Something about him made Amy immediately uncomfortable.

"Hello. I'm Amy," she said, offering her hand.

"Tony," said the man, shaking her hand so limply it felt sarcastic.

"Do you come here often?" said Amy, attempting a joky cliché to get things started.

"Yeah. I've been every month. Bit crap tonight," mumbled Tony.

Charming. This was going from bad to worse.

"Really? Why's that?" asked Amy, determined to at least give him enough rope to hang himself.

"All a bit old."

Ouch. Lucky for Amy, she wasn't the slightest bit interested in him.

"Still, you must have met some nice girls over the months? How does it work out for you—what's your average?"

"None."

"None? Oh, I can't believe that, Tony—a virile young man like yourself getting no matches?"

"Oh, they tick me but I don't tick them."

"Oh, so the ones you like don't tick you?"

Tony looked at Amy as if she were simple.

"No—I haven't ticked anyone yet."

"Blimey—you must be either very picky or very shy."

"Picky. I've got standards. Very high standards." Tony jiggled one leg constantly. He lit a cigarette and cast a bored glance around the room.

"Well, I won't waste any more of your time, Tony—I'm obviously too old and unattractive to meet your 'very high standards,' so why don't you just pop off to the bar for a couple of minutes?" said Amy. She wasn't cross—he was clearly a moron—but she was damned if she was going to babysit him until the bell rang.

"Can't. Have to wait until the bell goes before you move. Looks bad on you if I go early. Might put other blokes off," said Tony, pulling hard on his fag.

"Oh, don't worry about me—I can look after myself."

But Tony stayed put. Whether it was the pressure of the evening, the strain of the past few months, or ovulation hormones she didn't know, but something inside Amy snapped. Who did this idiot think he was? What was he expecting, with his slumped attitude, his dandruff, and his complete lack of charm? Beyonce wiggling her bottom at him provocatively? Britney puckering up for a big kiss? Kylie grinding her hot pants in his face? No, Kylie was probably too old.

"No, really, why don't you go and have a drink. I think I'd rather suck my own vomit through a straw than spend another moment in your presence." Amy's cheeks burned with indignation, but still Tony sat, gazing dispassionately at her from beneath his baseball cap.

So they sat in silence for the next two minutes while all around them the hubbub of couples talking, laughing, flirting filled the air. Amy noticed that even Gary—now sitting opposite a rock chick with a Harley Davidson tattoo up one arm—seemed to have struck lucky. She let her eyes wander around the room. Over in the far corner near the door, a woman sat alone. Obviously, they were one man short tonight—that would explain the oddball men they'd "selected." She was blonde, pretty, and looked sparky enough. She sat chewing the edge of her card, waiting for the bell to ring. Amy wished she could swap places and have the luxury of a moment's solitude. The woman looked so serene among all the hustle and noise. Then the woman's face changed suddenly—her mouth shot into a practiced rictus grin, and she flicked her hair flirtatiously out of her eyes. A man was now standing at her table, jacket over one arm, obviously making a big, humorous apology for being late.

It was Joe.

Amy let out an audible gasp that caught even Tony's attention. "Shit."

"What?" said Tony, almost interested.

"Nothing," said Amy, not wanting to share anything so dramatic with this retard. Amy watched in horror as Joe sat down and started chatting to the girl. He leaned forward and the girl helped him pin his number badge on, giggling. What the hell was he doing here?

She felt betrayed, stunned. It was as if she had just caught her husband in bed with another woman. It took a conscious act of will to remind herself that if anyone was responsible for the breakdown in their relationship, it was she. But what was a man like Joe doing in a place like this? She couldn't believe it. Surely he was above this? With a chill, Amy realized that she was damning herself, too. He could also ask what she was doing here, she who did not want to "get involved." Her mind racing, Amy tried to calculate how quickly she could get up and get to the door without being noticed. But what if he saw her? He would be sure to get up and speak to her, try to stop her leaving, and have it out with her. She had seen the wounded look in his eyes when he left that morning two months ago, and although she had regathered her strength in the meantime, seeing him now only served to reiterate how dangerously close she was to loving him. This would not do.

The bell clattered, and there was a screeching of chairs being pushed back on the wooden floor. Tony jumped up and moved on. With a start, Amy realized that although Joe was on the other side of the room, he was due at her table next. There was no escape. He would have to cross the width of the room to get to her, and he was right by the exit. All around her, new couplings had begun. Joe stood and nodded a warm good-bye to the blonde (who was obviously smitten with him) before consulting with Susan. He was clearly confused by the layout. Despite the awfulness of the situation, Amy was transfixed. It was like watching your own car crash—in slo-mo and on a big screen. She watched, frozen in terror, as she saw Susan consult her clipboard, then point to Amy's table. Joe's eyes registered the general direction, but he did not seem to register who was awaiting him. He crossed the floor quickly, head down, feeling as out of place as she did. It was only when he had his hand on the back of the chair that he looked at her. The smile he had prepared froze on his face and everything in the room seemed to stop.

"Hello," said Amy quietly.

"Amy," was all he could think of to say.

"Yes. Sorry. Had no idea, obviously, that you would be here."

"No, me neither, I mean, I wouldn't have—" Joe faltered, then straightened his back. A new resolution seemed to fill him, and he sat down stiffly.

"Don't feel you have to spend these three minutes with me—I mean, I'd understand if you just want to skip to the next—" stumbled Amy, her mouth going inexplicably dry.

"That would suit you down to the ground, wouldn't it? Don't face things, stick your head down, and move on. God forbid there should be any exchange of feelings. Well, I'm sorry—hang on, am I sorry? No, I'm not sorry, I'm not going to make it that easy for you."

"Oh." Amy felt a scolding coming on. Much as she hated to be told off she found herself aching to hear what he had to say. He looked hot and angry, but something softer illuminated his eyes. Amy realized with a pang that it was hurt.

"Three minutes. Right. Here goes," said Joe.

Amy took a deep breath and held it.

"At the risk of sounding like a mad, stalking, no-life, I chased you for weeks because when we first met, I felt something akin to what they describe in the movies as an instant and profound attraction to you. And it wasn't just because you are clearly gorgeous. I thought I saw something in you that I really want in my life. I thought I saw a woman with spirit and charm and energy, but who also wanted to love and be loved. Then, when we finally did get together, I knew I was right, but you rushed off in a cab without leaving so much as your phone number. Then when I tracked you down again, we had a fantastic night together—at least, that's how it seemed to me— but early the next morning, you sent me packing as if I was some stranger you'd just picked up for a one-night stand. Now maybe that's all it was to you, and maybe I'm just a stupid, romantic one-woman neo-virgin, but somehow I don't think so. You know there's something here between us, which makes your brutal and frankly rude treatment of me even more bizarre. I can only think that you're scared. And if that's the case, you're not half the woman I thought you were."

Amy's eyes stung.

"If only you knew . . ." she began, self-pity bubbling to the surface.

"Knew what? How hard it is to let someone in? How risky it is giving yourself to someone in case you get hurt? How frightening it is to imagine losing that person? Well, I do know, actually, probably more than you ever will. I'd like to say no hard feelings, but I can't, so the best I can say is good luck with whatever you're after tonight— another quick shag, is it?—and I suppose I owe you a thank-you for at least getting me back in this bloody dating minefield. Quite what I'm doing here I don't know—as you probably said to yourself as I left that morning, 'It seemed like a good idea at the time.'"

And at that, the bell rang. It was as if Susan had been primed.

"Bye, Amy," said Joe, putting on his jacket. Amy sat stunned as Joe got up and walked out of the room. She watched his feet disappear up the stairs. Her heart was racing, her face was red, and her ears were rushing, and every particle in her body was urging her to get up and run after him, to tell him he was right and that she was scared and that yes, there was something very special between them that she felt terrified of. But her feet would not move. Try as she might, her feet remained resolutely stuck to the floor.

"Cheer up, treacle, it might never 'appen!"

"It just did," said Amy. Her next date had arrived; a big, friendly-looking bearlike man sat down in front of her. He was about fifty if he was a day, bald, and wearing an England football shirt.

"Roy," he said, his eyes twinkling warmly as he held out his big paw.

"Amy," she replied, grateful for his firm handshake. The room was spinning, and her mind was thick with fog. She felt much in need of something stable.

"You look like you've seen a ghost," he said, concern in his voice.

"The ghost of Christmas future," said Amy, staring straight ahead.

"Seriously, love, are you all right? Do you want me to get you some water?" Amy looked at him and saw a sweet, caring man. It was all she could do to stop herself from flinging herself at him and sobbing on his shoulder.

"Better than that," she replied. "You can get me out of here."

Roy look confused but delighted, like someone who never wins a thing bagging the jackpot without even buying a ticket.

"As it 'appens, I've got me cab outside—I'm a cabbie—but don't worry, I won't stick the meter on!" said Roy, leaping up and helping Amy out from behind the table.

On the way out, Amy noticed with a jolt that the blonde had also left—had she followed Joe? A pang of jealousy shot through her. They quickly swept past Susan, who tried to grab their cards and ask them why they were leaving, but Roy expertly shielded Amy and rushed her up the stairs. Below them, the dull hum of woeful self-projection continued into the night.

.8.

Outside, the streets were clogged with Monday-night revelers—the sort of hardcore party people who preferred to do their serious drinking and clubbing on a school night, when all the amateurs were tucked in bed. Amy took a deep breath and tried to relax her shoulders. She would not let the unexpected encounter with Joe sway her. Roy was as good a candidate as any—a bit older than she would have liked, but he seemed keen and uncomplicated, two attributes that all the younger men so far had failed to show. If she could just bring herself to blank Joe out again (as successfully as she had been able to over the past few days), she could be pregnant tomorrow. She might as well go for it. She was in her peak ovulation window, and Joe's words had affirmed her own fears about herself. He was right. She was too afraid to get involved. Far better to stick to her original plans than to let go and fall for someone who could never provide a child. What if the relationship failed, like all the others, after a year or so? She'd be left childless and old, her fertility in terminal decline and her chances of conceiving even slimmer than they already were. It was too high a price to risk paying. And despite the fact that she felt sick every time she saw Joe—a sure sign that she was in love—there was no guarantee that the feeling would last beyond the honeymoon period. History bore testimony to her crapness in the long haul. In the relationship Olympics, she would always be a sprinter. Better just get used to it.

"Where to, guv?" said Roy, sliding the glass partition over and smiling back at Amy. He was enjoying this.

"I don't know. Anywhere."

"Okeydoke," said Roy, lurching out onto the road.

For a few minutes, there was silence. Amy tore herself from her own thoughts and tried to concentrate on Roy. What on earth did he think was going on? He must think she was pretty weird, asking to be taken out, then not caring where she went. Plus, there was the fact that she was clearly in some sort of demented state. He was either too tactful or too emotionally retarded to comment.

"So tell me all about it then," he said eventually, eyeing her in the rearview mirror.

"What?"

"Come on. I know women. There's something up. What—or who—are you trying to forget? You can tell me, I'm a cabbie. I've heard it all."

"Oh, something and nothing."

"No such thing in the female world. Who was he? Come on, treat this cab like a confessional. Most people do. If it helps, I won't look at you!"

"Don't tell me you're a left-footer!" said Amy, trying to deflect the attention.

"Yep. Irish parents. I can spot a fellow Catholic a mile off. So come on. Let's be 'aving you."

Amy thought for a moment. Should she be candid? It was true that the cab felt conducive to spilling the beans—something about the in-timate yet impersonal setup. It was always easier to confess to the side of the priest's head—no off-putting facial reactions, no eye contact.

"OK. Forgive me, Father, for I have sinned."

Roy let out a laugh of recognition.

"And how long is it since your last confession?"

"It's been . . . about twenty-two years, Father."

"Tut-tut, my child."

"I've been busy."

"Busy sinning?"

"Yes, Father. And no, Father. You see, it all started when I decided I wanted to have a baby."

"And you're not married, my child?"

"No, Father. But that's not the bad bit. The bad bit is I decided I'd try to get pregnant on my own, as it were, by sleeping with a succes-sion of men until I hit the jackpot."

"Oh," said Roy, sounding slightly out of his depth. "Go on."

"But it's not as bad as it sounds, Father—I didn't actually go to bed with any of them, although I must confess that was largely because they let me down at the last minute, not because I repented in time. But then I met this one guy."

"I think I know where this is going."

"And we just sort of clicked. And we spent the night together. But then he told me he had had a vasectomy, so I pushed him away."

"And then you tried to carry on—hence QuickMatch tonight—but you found your heart wasn't in it?"

"Something like that. He was there tonight, and I know he likes me a lot. But I pushed him away again. And now here I am with you. Hoping that you can help me out . . . ." Amy sat forward and looked at Roy in the mirror. "You see, I have a feeling if I don't do it tonight—and I could get pregnant tonight—I won't carry on. I can feel my resolve weakening. And it feels important. Don't say anything yet—

just hear me out, Father, sorry, Roy—you wouldn't have to do anything else, you wouldn't ever hear from me again, and I wouldn't want any money or anything. It would just be one night."

There was a long pause.

"See. I told you I was a sinner."

"Well," said Roy after what seemed like an hour. They were cruising along an eerily deserted Euston Road. "I said I'd heard it all, but that just about takes the biscuit, my darlin'."

"I know it's weird, but I just thought I'd be honest. I mean, I could have just done it without telling you and you'd be none the wiser, but you did ask me what was wrong. . . ."

"I know, I know I did."

"And you can't lie in confession. So what do you think?"

Roy chewed his thumbnail. They were at a set of traffic lights near Regent's Park. Amy watched the sequence of lights ahead all switch to red. *Stop.* If only she had her one red light. She needed something to halt this ludicrous situation. Her ovaries had taken over and were about to set her on a one-way journey to single parenthood. What was she doing? Amy gazed out the window, waiting for his reply. It had become a game of chance. If he said yes, then she would go ahead. If he said no, then she would probably end up abandoning the whole thing. Another taxi pulled up alongside them with a couple in the back. The woman had her back to the side window and was talking animatedly to the outline of a man. Amy hated them, for no other reason than that they were doing something very ordinary—going home as a couple, probably after a lovely night out, to go to bed and curl up in each other's arms. Why had her life turned out so weird? She stared at them for a few moments. Suddenly, the woman flicked her blond hair back and laughed. As she threw her head back, she revealed more of the man, and Amy's heart stopped. It was Joe and the blonde from the bar. In a taxi. Together.

"All right," said Roy. "I'll do it."

"What?" Amy couldn't take her eyes off the pair in the next cab.

What was he doing with that woman after the big speech he had laid on her about love, fear, and fickleness?

"I'll do it. No questions, no demands on either side. If I can be of assistance, I'll do it. I hate the idea of women not being able to have a baby if they want one. I've thought about donating my sperm as it goes, and now I can—as a direct deposit!" Roy laughed heartily.

The lights turned green and the cab next door sped in front while Roy recovered himself.

"No. Look. Sorry. I've changed my mind. Follow that cab!" said Amy, clear now.

"What?" said Roy dumbly. "Why?"

"It's him. The one. The man I was telling you about. Sorry, but I have to stop him. He's with a girl. Follow them!"

Roy rolled his eyes. "All right, where's the bleeding camera? This has got to be a setup."

But Roy did what he was told, and Amy moved forward to the fold-down seat nearer to the front of the cab.

"I'm not being funny, love, but I'll have to put the meter on."

"Fine, fine, whatever, just don't lose them."

Roy sped off in pursuit of Joe's taxi. They followed Joe and the woman all the way along the Marylebone Road, out onto the flyover, along to Uxbridge, and out toward the M40, Amy biting her nails and cursing herself for her stupidity. The words of Joni Mitchell always seemed to fly out at her in times like these: "Don't it always seem to go that you don't know what you've got 'til it's gone?" It occurred to her that she didn't even know where Joe lived. Were they on the way to his house? She knew he was based in West London. Or maybe they were on the way to the woman's flat? The thought sickened her.

"Catch them up—you're losing them!" Amy shouted. "Sorry, but this is really important—this is the most important taxi ride of my life!"

"All right, all right, keep your knickers on—I won't lose him, don't worry!"

They turned left, then right, then along a long road full of speed bumps. Roy was good at this—he made sure he kept enough distance so as not to arouse suspicion, but he never lost sight of their taillights. Finally, somewhere around Acton, the cab in front pulled in along-side a terraced house with a beaten-up old Triumph Herald in the drive. Amy knew this was Joe's house. It just had to be.

"What now?" said Roy, whose crossness had subsided.

"I don't know!"

"Well, go out and talk to him!"

"No! I can't! What would I say?"

"Tell him the truth! Tell him you love him and that it doesn't mat-ter about the baby thing."

"He doesn't even know about that!"

"Oh, Jesus. Well leave that bit out—but tell him you've been a fool and you want him back. Men love all that."

"They do?"

"Yeah!"

"Oh, fuck, they're going inside! What am I going to do now?"

"You muffed it. Missed your moment. Too late. That's it now. All done and dusted. They'll go in, have a drink, have a chat, he'll be feeling sore 'cause you dumped him, and he'll find consolation in the arms of another. Classic."

"Thank you very much! I could go and ring on the bell. . . ."

"And what? Pretend to be an Avon lady?"

"Let's just wait."

"What for? You're on a hiding to nothing, love, trust me. I know men."

Amy slumped back in the seat. This was very bad indeed. She had no idea what to do but wait. Surely Joe wouldn't be so predictable? He was made of stronger stuff than that. If he had really meant what he said an hour ago, there was no way he would be keen to jump into bed with anyone else now. *Was there?* The thought ate away at her, and she contemplated decisive action—either she could just get Roy to take her home right now or she could get out of the cab and walk the plank to Joe's front door. But in her heart she knew she would do what she always did in such circumstances. Nothing. And even if she had to sit and wait all night to see the blonde woman emerge tussle-haired and smiling at dawn, kissing Joe a fond good-bye on the doorstep as he stooped in his dressing gown to pick up the milk, at least then she would know that Joe was not all he seemed, and she could go home then to her cold bed, safe in the knowledge that he turned out to be like all the rest—full of bullshit.

"I'm gonna sit this one out," said Amy finally.

"Fair enough. I'll turn the engine off," said Roy, now enjoying the drama of it all again.

Amy watched grimly as the front room light came on and then was dimmed—no doubt to enhance the romantic atmosphere. She shuddered, but still her feet would not move. Roy folded his arms and sighed dramatically. Minutes passed, and neither of them said a thing. Roy started to fiddle with the radio, and settled on a London radio talk show.

"Just a quick reminder we're taking your calls on relationships this evening—so give us a call 020 7224 2000—we've got Doctor Gillian Liechtenstein here with advice on how to deal with infidelity, what to do if you're with someone who just won't commit—I think we all know a few of those!—and, for the desperado singletons out there, how to bag your man!" twittered the husky-voiced presenter.

"Oh, turn it off!" snapped Amy.

"Ooh—too close to home, is it?" teased Roy.

Amy said nothing and hunkered down for a long wait. Roy closed his eyes and attempted to sleep. An hour passed. Amy watched people come and go in the street. A man returned to the house next door to Joe's and was greeted by a young child at the door. He was just an ordinary man—so unfair that he should get to live so close to Joe that his child probably played with Joe's kids, and he didn't even appreciate how lucky he was. Such were the workings of Amy's love-addled mind. Suddenly, even Joe's tired-looking potted plants took on an almost sacred aspect. A woman arrived at a house a few doors up on a large bicycle, carrying a bottle of wine in a carrier bag. A casual Monday-night dinner party with a few close friends. Amy ached when she thought about how little she had seen of her own friends these past few baby-obsessed months. A young Asian man delivered takeaway menus to every door on the street. If only she had such unfettered access to Joe's letterbox—what would she post there? She watched and waited, one eye on Joe's door at all times. Watched the evening turn dark, the post-summer trees black against the dark blue sky. The light from Joe's front room glowed with a taunting warmth as Roy started to snore gently in the front seat.

What am I going to do now? Amy asked herself. *What if we're here all night? Am I really prepared to let this slip by?*

Another hour passed. Roy stirred and wiped the dribble from his chin.

"It's clocking up now," he said, indicating the still-ticking meter. "174.60 pounds so far," he chirped, stretching. Getting no reply, he turned to find Amy slumped in one corner of the cab, fast asleep. As quietly as he could, he got out of the cab to fetch the tartan rug he kept in the boot and gently placed it over his sleeping oddball passenger. It was good to be here, really, in the service of true love—if not in receipt of it. He looked up at the stars and smiled the wan smile of a man used to romantic rejection. The night was still and the first hint of chilly autumn was in the air.

From across the street came the sound of voices now. Roy turned in time to see a tall, blonde, disgruntled-looking woman stepping out of a house and talking to a dark-haired, handsome man. She said something curt and marched off up the road as the man in the doorway hung his head. Roy found himself smiling. He recognized the woman as the one in the bar (she had been so abrupt with Roy in their three minutes that he had almost laughed out loud, and when he joked that he thought he could pass for thirty, she had snootily suggested that that would only be possible during an eclipse)—and he also knew the mask of a woman scorned.

"Taxi!" she shouted when she saw Roy next to the cab. Why did people always do that even when they could see that your light wasn't on and you were therefore not available?

"Yes, love," said Roy, enjoying every minute.

"Can you take me to Chelsea, please?" she said, not even recognizing him. Hardly surprising, seeing as she had looked at him only once during their "date."

"Sorry, love—I'm booked."

The woman stared at him crossly for a moment—obviously, she was used to getting what she wanted out of life, and two rebuttals in one night was startling—before continuing her march up the street.

"Nice night for a walk, though," shouted Roy after her. "They say there might be a lunar eclipse, love!" The woman turned, momentarily confused, then flicked her hair over one shoulder and disappeared around the corner.

Roy clapped his hands with glee, then turned back to the matter at hand.

"Amy! Amy!" he hissed as he opened the cab door.

Amy shot up from under the blanket. "What? What time is it?"

"She's gone. Quick! He's on the doorstep now!" Roy tugged at her arm.

Before she could gather herself, she found herself half flung out onto the road.

Disoriented for a moment, she looked around to get her bearings before her eyes finally settled on Joe's house up ahead. He was standing there. Alone. And for once in her life, Amy stopped thinking about anything. Her feet, once again with no permission from her head, began moving quickly toward Joe. He spotted her almost straightaway, his jaw dropping open but a smile spreading across his lips.

"What are you doing here? I mean, how did you find me?" he spluttered.

"How did you find me?" said Amy, breathless now that she was in front of him.

"You found a baby—" started Joe, before stopping himself. There was little point in going over old ground now. "Look, about that girl—I just wanted to get out of there, and she followed me, and we got chatting, and I thought you really had lost interest, so I thought I'd do what you said and just try and get on with things—"

"And did you—'get on with things'?" said Amy, trembling now.

Joe sunk his head again.

"No. I couldn't. All I could think about was you."

It was Amy's turn to look at the floor. He even had perfect toes. Should she jump or should she run?

"OK, then."

"OK, then what?" said Joe, leaning against the doorframe like a grounded teenager.

"OK, then let's see what happens," said Amy, kicking at a stone on the ground.

"What do you mean? A couple of hours ago, you didn't want to know. I thought you'd chucked me."

"Well, things have changed. And for your information, no one says 'chucked' anymore. I haven't 'chucked' anyone since I was fifteen."

"It's been a long time. I'm a bit rusty. So. Will you . . . go out with me?" said Joe, smiling now and enjoying the regression.

"Yeah. All right," said Amy, joining in the game. "You can take me to the school disco."

"Cor," said Joe, reaching for her now. "Wait 'til I tell my mates."

"But I'd rather stay in with you."

"Result," said Joe.

And there on the doorstep they kissed. They kissed like desperate kids with nowhere else to go. If they'd had half an ear on the outside world, they would have heard the jubilant sound of a taxi horn honking in celebration. They'd have heard the rattle of an upstairs window and two young girls mock-retching.

"Urgh! Dad's kissing that lady! Yuk!"

"I preferred that blonde one—where did she go?"

But as it was, they had ears—and eyes, and hands—only for each other.

.9.

She'll be here in under an hour and the icing isn't set on the cake yet. I told you, Brendan, you should have done it earlier. Oh, Jesus, Mary, and Joseph, and all the saints, look at the cut of it." Amy's mum was in a prize flap. It had seemed like such a good idea to organize a surprise fortieth birthday party. Amy had been saying since Christmas that she didn't want any fuss, that no one was to do anything special or go to any trouble. But if a mother couldn't throw a party for her only daughter's birthday, what could she do? Bad enough she had no grandchildren to dandle on her knee without Amy denying her this small pleasure. She sighed and brushed her hands on her apron for the hundredth time that day. Amy's place looked nice, despite Brendan's attempts to sabotage things by trying to erect a "Look who's fifty!" banner across the front door, and despite the fact that trying to make an old tobacco warehouse look festive would try the patience of a saint. That anyone would want to live in an old shed was beyond belief.

"Calm down, biddy, and have a shot of the hard stuff, for God's sake. It'll all be fine. Anyway, no one's here yet."

"I'm here!" said Ang cheerily, tying a poorly inflated bunch of balloons to a retro arc lamp.

"That's what I said—no one's here yet," said Brendan.

"Now, now, darling," chided Oscar from behind the *Telegraph*. "What did we say about being nice to people?"

"Ang isn't people—she's just Ang," said Brendan, ruffling Oscar's hair. "But OK—I promise to be nice to people today. Just for you."

"Not just for me, darling—they'll never let you join the small-town cake-baking circle if you can't curb that nasty tongue of yours."

"Ooh, you know how to strike fear into a girl's heart!" Brendan shrieked. No one had ever been able to tell him off with such authority and charm, and he marveled again at the turn of events that had led him to be living in a beautiful converted farmhouse in Somerset with a Tory MP, two spaniels, and a Range Rover, for God's sake. They even had a houseboy! In time he was planning to do some volunteer work—they'd talked about fostering a gay teenager, and Oscar was already heavily involved with various equal-rights lobbying groups. Life was, he almost admitted to himself now, great. It wouldn't harm him to be nice to baggy old Ang for once.

"Hey, chubs, have you lost weight?"

"No, Brendan, I haven't, you cheeky bastard. And stop picking on me."

"No, I mean it, you look really . . . well."

"As a matter of fact, I'm putting on weight."

"Ooh, tubs, you can't really afford that, can you? But then I suppose your catwalk days are over. . . ."

"Brendan!" warned Oscar.

"Sorry. No, really, you look almost—glowing!"

Ang beamed.

"Oh, Christ, you're not, are you?"

Ang nodded her answer.

"Four months! I haven't told anyone 'cause of last time, but yes, it's true. I'm having a baby!" cried Ang.

"Oh, God love you, Angela, congratulations!" said Mrs. Stokes, rushing over and hugging her tightly. "I'll say a prayer to the Blessed Virgin that everything goes to plan this time—she'll protect you."

"Well done, Angela—many congrats," said Oscar, getting up and patting her on the shoulder. "I think this calls for champagne. The Widow all right with everyone?"

Oscar cracked open the Veuve Clicquot.

"Where is everyone? I told them all to be here by quarter past, the useless bastards," said Brendan, picking up the video entrance monitor and peering into the screen. Nobody there.

"Calm down, darling, they'll be here soon. It's not as if they don't have good excuses these days."

Brendan humphed.

"Soph and Greg have got the little twins to get ready, then they've got to pick up those awful big twins, then get round here," reasoned Oscar. "And you know what Greg's like with the babies in the car—drives like an old woman."

"I suppose that is quite a lot for a man who needs a month's workup to scratch his arse. How they're going to cope I don't know." Brendan sighed, accepting a glass and downing it in one. Oscar refilled it wordlessly.

"And Jules has got to get herself *and* Harry ready—and we know how long that takes," laughed Ang.

"Yes, ten minutes to bathe, change, and feed the baby, three hours to replaster and grout her craggy old face and heave her saggy body into something in a Lycra/concrete mix."

"Not so saggy. She got them to do a tummy tuck at the same time as the C-section," said Ang, conspiratorially.

"The Portland? Marvelous. Too posh to push," said Oscar.

"Too much information," said Brendan, sticking a finger into the cake to see if it was any nearer to setting.

"Leave! Don't be putting your dirty fingers all over the icing, Brendan, God bless us and save us!" said Mrs. Stokes without turning round. Where cake was concerned, she had eyes in the back of her head.

The buzzer sounded.

"You're late!" barked Brendan into the intercom, before buzzing them in.

"Hiya!" shouted Ang as Soph and Greg appeared dark-eyed at the door, each carrying an identical baby car seat.

"Sssssh!" they chorused.

"They've just got to sleep as we got here. We've been driving around for half an hour trying to get them down," said Soph, sinking onto the sofa and lying down.

"Yeah, it was, well, boring," said Cesca, emerging from the hallway and slouching against the wall.

"I thought it was cool," said Laura. "I got to hold their binkies in."

"I thought you weren't having binkies?" asked Ang.

"Ah, that was in the dim and distant delusional past when we believed we'd have babies we could rock gently to sleep before going out for a meal, or having a proper conversation, you know, with sentences and everything, or just having an uninterrupted poo," said Greg, grabbing a glass and filling it with champagne.

"I'd shove a French stick in their mouths if I thought it'd give me a moment's peace," yawned Soph.

"You love it, though, don't you?" cooed Ang, peeking at the sleeping babies.

"Not yet. But I'm sure we will."

"Eventually," added Greg.

"Yeah, we love it," said Soph. "A bit."

The buzzer sounded again.

"Here they are!" shouted Laura. "Quick, hide!"

"Dur brain. It's not them. That other woman with the baby's not here yet. The scary one." Cesca sneered.

"Jules," mouthed Soph to Ang's quizzical look. Brendan stifled a giggle and opened the door in readiness.

"Get me an effing drink!" shouted Jules from the hall. "And who's got a fag? I'm gasping!"

"Breast-feeding going well then?" asked Brendan, shoving a large glass of champagne at her.

"You know you really shouldn't be drinking if you're breast-feeding," said Soph, unable to hold in her disapproval any longer. She'd read all the books and did everything by them.

"Oh, spare me—I know you're doing everything right, drinking herbal tea, eating your greens and organic compost, but I'm over it already. My nipples have had it. He's on the evil baby formula."

"Oh," said Soph. "What a shame."

"Not really," said Jules, refusing to be guilt-tripped. "Means I can go out and get lashed once in a while, which can only be good for Harry in the long run."

"I meant it's a shame for him," said Soph, adjusting her nursing bra. Two dark discs of leakage had started to spread their way across her pale shirt.

"I think it's for the best," said Brendan.

"Thank you, darling," said Jules, handing him the baby and plonking herself down on the sofa.

"I mean, your boobs are hardly Mother Nature's doing anyway—the poor little sod was probably only getting saline solution, weren't you little man?"

"Piss off," said Jules, laughing despite herself.

"Hey," shouted Laura. "Don't swear in front of us—it's naughty."

"Shut it, small fry," snarled Jules. "Go and play with those Tamagotchi things I gave you—where are they?"

"Dead," chorused the girls.

"Fine. Then go and play with the traffic."

"They'll be here soon will everyone have a quick tidy up and get that cake hidden, Brendan, or she'll see it the minute she comes in should I make the sandwiches now or after?" muttered Mrs. Stokes, flitting around the kitchen island nervously.

"Calm down, missus, she's bound to be late."

"There's Daddy's car! Quick, everyone, hide!" shouted Laura, who had been keeping watch from the window ever since she arrived.

The children disappeared professionally, leaving the adults scrabbling around for halfhearted hiding places, Brendan and Oscar behind the sofa, Jules and Mrs. Stokes beneath the island, and Ang not quite tucked away under a hanging coat. A couple of minutes passed. Someone farted, and everyone giggled. Another minute passed.

"Where are they? This is boring," tutted Cesca, before Laura's hand clamped over her sister's mouth.

Finally, they heard muffled voices on the stairwell, then the turn of a key on the lock. It occurred to Brendan then that they hadn't agreed on a signal. No one knew when to burst out, shouting "Surprise!" or "Happy birthday" or whatever. They hadn't even agreed on that.

There was an awkward pause, everyone clearly waiting for someone else to instigate the reveal. Amy spoke.

"Oh, look! Someone's left us three babies, Joe! This is getting to be a habit with you and me."

"Surprise!" shouted Laura, unable to bear the tension any longer. The adults followed lamely, and only at the last minute did Brendan remember the party popper he'd stowed in his pocket.

"Well, well, well. Thank you," said Amy, having dreaded something like this all day. Now she was here, though, she felt suddenly touched by the shambolic and unsophisticated party they'd thrown together for her. Her mum's customary buffet was laid out on the trestle table—shop-bought quiche going curly round the edges, a joint of cold gammon and some boiled potatoes in a Pyrex dish, a large trifle whose "Hundreds and Thousands" topping was already leaking color all over the whipped cream.

"Did you know about this?" Amy asked Joe. He'd been a bit preoccupied all day.

"No, I swear," said Joe, unconvincingly. "Well, maybe just a bit. You're not cross, are you?" Amy shook her head, wondering how anyone could be mad with such a gorgeous, kind, and gentle man.

"Happy birthday, darling," said Jules, kissing Amy on both cheeks.

"Yeah—we did this for you," said Laura, struggling to gain control of a large brown envelope that Cesca was hanging on to.

"Let me do it!"

"No! It was my idea!"

"Dad! Tell her!"

"Why don't you both give it to Amy?" said Joe in a vain attempt to once again promote The Middle Way.

There was a scuffle and then the sound of paper ripping.

"Happy now?" said Cesca, throwing her half down on the ground. Laura started to cry and ran back to the window to strike a dramatic pose.

"It's OK, I'll stick it back together," said Joe, handing Amy the two parts of the homemade card.

"It doesn't matter—it's just a stupid card," said Cesca moodily.

"Let's have a look at it, then," said Amy, trying her best to be nice to the brat. Laura wasn't so bad if you got her on her own, but together they were horrendous. How Joe could have sired such tiresome, spoiled kids was unfathomable.

Amy put the two halves of the card together. It was a painting. Two little girls stood, each holding on to their daddy's hand. A big yellow sun shone in the sky, and an oversized flower sprung from the spiky grass. A typical child's idealized view of the world. But another figure had been added. On the very edge of the paper, in a slightly rougher and less careful hand, Amy recognized a portrait of herself. Her mouth was slightly turned down, and she noted that they had put some wrinkles around her eyes. They'd even included her newly rounded belly. "Happy birthday," read the simple misspelled inscription, although the subtext was a lot more eloquent. "You are not our mum. You are not part of our family. Keep off our dad." Or was she being paranoid? Hardly. They'd made it clear on many occasions in the last six months that Amy was at best an unwelcome interloper, at worst their arch enemy. They'd left vicious diary entries tantalizingly open for her to happen upon. They'd played up when she tried to take Joe away for a weekend, Cesca somehow managing to bring on chronic laryngitis and Laura claiming a brain tumor. It wasn't in Amy's imagination. But she knew it was early days, and if they didn't like having her around, then the feeling was entirely mutual. She wasn't going to get sucked into some kind of "love me" competition with two eight-year-olds. In time, they would just all have to learn to tolerate one another. Until then, she wasn't going to show her hand.

"Thank you, girls, that's lovely," said Amy, putting the card carefully away in her handbag. She caught Cesca's look of disappointment at the nonreaction. Ten points to Amy.

"Happy birthday, you old bag—have a pie," said Brendan, shoving a pork pie at her.

"Although, by the looks of you, you've already had quite a few." It was Brendan's favorite new subject—Amy's gently expanding girth.

"Oh, bless and save us, you're not, are you?" said Amy's mum, clutching at Brendan's arm. Amy hadn't had the heart to kill her mother's newfound enthusiasm for a grandchild.

"No, Mammy, it's not a baby—it's just contentment," said Amy, squeezing Joe's hand.

"Well, plenty of time yet, Amy, you never know your luck," said Mrs. Stokes, smiling madly.

"Yes, plenty of time yet," agreed Amy, trying to mask the newly forming horror for the idea. "Although it's more likely Mrs. Cummings is going to have a baby first."

"Oh, she's got one! I forgot to tell you—she came in the shop with a picture of this gorgeous fat Chinese baby—a little girl. She's getting her next Thursday," said Jules.

"Bloody hell. Well, good for her," said Amy. Even Mrs. Cummings had ended up with a baby. "And they say money can't buy you love. Now, what about all these babies? How come they're all asleep? Have you given them a drop of gin, Mammy?"

Bang on cue, Jonty and Milo struck up their catlike wailing. There was no warning, no apparent cause, no initiator—they did everything in unison.

"Uh-oh—you woke them up," said Cesca, dipping her finger into the trifle.

Soph and Greg sprang into action, grabbing a twin each and jiggling like mad. The next two minutes would be key—if they could get the twins back to sleep now, they might just get an hour's peace. Oscar tried to busy himself by filling everyone's glass for a toast, which he insisted had to be done right away, and inadvertently nudged Harry's car seat. So as not to miss out on any of the fun, Harry decided to wake up and wail, too. Laura and Cesca started maniacally jumping around, singing the *Tweenies* theme tune in what appeared to be an altruistic helping gesture—shut the babies up by distraction—but was in fact just an excuse to join in the noise-making.

"Don't pick him up right away, Jules, let him cry for a bit, you're making a rod for your own back!" warned Amy's mum as Jules stubbed out her fag and got up.

"He's too young for controlled crying, Mrs. S, I think he needs burping," sighed Jules.

Amy and Joe surveyed the bedlam for a moment.

"What the bloody hell was I thinking, Joe?" Amy laughed. "I mean, can you imagine what I'd be like with a baby? I think I must have been having some kind of an early menopause or something."

"I think you'd be a great mum," said Joe, somewhat too broodily for Amy's liking.

"Hey, don't even go there. Your two monsters are more than enough for me, even part-time. And besides, your tubes are tied, or had you forgotten, Mr. Medical Man?"

"It's reversible. Although the procedure is only about ten percent successful."

"Exactly. I'm not having anyone messing around with your gonads now I've got my evil hands on them! Now do me a massive favor, will you? I love my friends very much, but I have a feeling if I stay here one moment longer, I will start rocking and moaning in a corner before spreading my own poo all over the walls. Get me out of here!"

"We can't!" said Joe, delighted by the idea. "Can we?"

"They won't notice—they're busy, and Mum's got the kids tonight."

"True."

"I know a place where they do the best champagne cocktails in London."

"Sounds interesting . . ."

"The Oxo Tower."

"Oooh."

"Exactly. And they have a 'no kids' policy."

"Sounds ideal."

"On one condition. That you promise to get me drunk, shag me senseless, and let me be foul to your children all day tomorrow."

"I do."

And with that, she dragged him gently out of the front door and into the lift. Inside the flat the chaos raged on, and Amy's stomach lurched as they began their descent. Was it the motion or the by now familiar feeling of excitement Joe promoted in her? He was great at going along with her need for spontaneity. Amy smiled up at him. This morning there had been not three but four magpies on her roof garden. Those bastards had started all this. Four for a boy. She silently thanked God she'd found hers.

It was so much better having a life than creating one.